The Exhibitionist

BINGO

Challenge

By Allison Eden

—

Words Are Swords Publishing

The Exhibitionist Bingo Challenge

Written by Allison Eden

Published by Words Are Swords Publishing

2nd Edition

Disclaimer

This book is intended for mature readers (18+) only. It contains graphic sexual content and intimate situations between two or more consenting adults, explicit language, and the occasional dash of violence. While some readers may find the explicit content in this book distressing, distasteful, or disgusting -- I call it a good time. Still, reader discretion is advised.

If you're under the age of 18, this is where your journey ends. Go show this book to your parental figure(s) and confess to all of the perverted stuff that you've been doing.

Then tell your mom that she needs to do a better job of hiding her "mommy time" books. (That's what my mom called them, anyway. She was also bad at hiding them. Shrug.)

Also, tell your dad to call me back.

XOXO

~ *Allison Eden*

This book was heavily influenced by the Los Angeles fetish and kink community. From the Ontario hotel gangbangs to the San Fernando Valley play parties, you're all amazing people and I'm honored by the amount of respect and courtesy with which I was treated while I pretended I was just there to "research a book".

Thank you to the fine folks at Words Are Swords for mistaking my hyper-sexual dirty mind for an ability to write novels.

Lastly, I want to thank all of the men and women in my life who have ever made me cum. Thank you for giving me something sexy to think about while I'm in the shower.

To capture the true feeling of being an exhibitionist, I wrote most of this book while sitting naked in front of the large bay window in my house that overlooks the street. Also, thank you to my mailman, who always had something sweet to say when I answered the door nude.

Now, if I could only find my own real-life version of Josh, I'd be happy as a clam...

-   Allison

Message From the Author

This book was a long time coming, but at last, it's here - and I have 8 more books in the series following Jess and Josh that I've already finished writing at the time this book was published. They are currently in the long process of editing, but I hope to release them as quickly as possible.

There is a good chance if you're reading this that my other books in the "A Very Poly.." series are already available. When you read the full titles, the series name makes sense, since they all involve polyamory on some level and all explore different kinks. They can be read in any order, though this is the order I would recommend.

Books in the *A Very Polyamory* erotic romance series:

Prank War

The Exhibitionist Bingo Challenge

A Very Polyamory Music Festival

A Very Polyamory Throuple

A Very Polyamory Submissive Unicorn

A Very Polyamory Toxic Breakup

A Very Polyamory Murder Mystery

The Rave Tapes

Beachside Brothel

<u>Non-fiction by Allison Eden</u>

Love Forever Sex Position a Day Calendar

Sexy Games for Couples

Sexy Games & More (10th anniversary edition)

Downright Dirty: A Raunchtastic BDSM Adult Coloring Book

*The Kinky Stuff Handbook: A Guide to F*cking Awesome Sex*

Table of Contents

Message From the Author..6

Day 1 - Library... 10

Day 1- Restaurant... 19

Day 1 – Home.. 31

Day 2 – Jess's Work.. 35

Day 2 – Home 38

Day 2 – Parking Lot 42

Day 2 – Movie Theater...50

Day 3 - Home 66

Day 3 - Balcony 74

Day 3 - Office..87

Day 3 – Josh's Work 93

Day 3 – Park..101

Day 4 – Café 124

Day 4 - Office... 148

Day 4 – Restaurant 157

Day 4 - Gym 160

Day 4 - Sauna 177

Day 4 - Home 199

Day 4 - Bar 203

Day 4 - Nightclub 224

Day 4 – Rooftop 249

Day 4 – Back Alley 264

Day 5 - Train 289

Day 5 – Beach 295

Day 5 – Fitting Room 308

Day 5 - Bodega 321

Day 6 - Church 337

Day 6 - Carnival 355

Day 6 – Home 374

Day 7 - Home 379

Day 7 – Drive Thru 387

Day 7 – Hot Tub 405

Day 7 - Museum 431

Day 7 - Home 446

Epilogue - The Gentleman's Wager 450

Exhibitionist Bingo Card 456

About the Author 457

CHAPTER 1

Day 1 - Library

Jess walked briskly through the reference section of the library, dragging her fingertips along the dusty spines of ancient encyclopedias neatly stacked on the shelves. As light-footed as she tried to be, her yellow Gucci heels clomped with her every step down the aisle, making stealth just a suggestion.

Her sunny yellow summer dress stood out vividly among the old pine wood bookshelves. Every step made her dress flutter behind her, her heels sending a clomping sound reverberating down the library Halls.

Maybe this was not the most congenial outfit for the library, Jess thought to herself.

Her lemonade-yellow summer dress with white lace trim stopped mid-thigh and covered more of her shoulders than it did her cleavage. Jess was particularly fond of it because of the way the dress flowed and fluttered behind her as she walked.

Hip's swaying, taking long steps with soft, tanned legs, she clip-clomped behind Josh while he sat behind a large faux-oak table with his head down in a book. She shuffled behind him and placed a hand between his shoulder and neck. Josh gently clasped his hand over hers without looking up.

"How is the book search going?" Jess purred, her voice dripping with velvet sweetness.

"I haven't found it yet. But I could have sworn it was in one of the books in this pile." Josh answered in a casual baritone that matched his height as he turned the page on yet another book of colorful patterns. "It's only a matter of time until I find it," he added in a confident library whisper.

Josh flipped the page, then pored over the Persian rug patterns on the next page.

Josh's job as a graphic designer required him to reproduce elaborate of often elusive patterns that clients specifically requested, and over the last few days he had been obsessing over a specific image that he swore he seen in a bork about Persian read at The Last Store in Downtown Los Angeles a few years back.

His client, an independent movie producer, had offered him a sizable sum to produce a movie poster, and Josh had been obsessed with finding the pattern he had once seen, claiming it would be perfect for the poster.

He had been in a flurry over finding it ever since.

"I'm bored," Jess whined.

Josh didn't seem to be paying attention, but when she leaned in and whispered her hot breath in his ear, "Let's take a break," Josh immediately slammed the book shut and jumped up from his chair.

Jess took his big hands in hers and led him through the city library aisles, which on mornings like today were completely deserted - other than the middle-aged librarian and a handful of transients using the computers.

Jess led him back across the dust-covered reference section and over to a very small collection of books on the same aisle with the words "Sexual Education" on a label glued to the shelf. In total, there were barely more than two dozen books in that section. Certainly under three dozen.

Jess poked her head over into the aisle of books next to them. When she saw that there was no one around them in the Sexual Education section, she pulled Josh close, hooked her hand around his neck, and whispered low into his ear, "I want you to educate me, baby."

Jess pushed him back, then turned to the bookshelf and spread her legs to shoulder-width apart. Bending at the waist, Jess hunched her back forward so her booty popped out ever so slightly.

Reaching back, she grabbed the bottom of her dress and tugged the fabric over her bare bottom so it clung to her back. Then she placed both hands on the bookshelf in front of her at the same width as her feet.

She felt the prickling chill of Josh's fingernails on the back of her thigh, lightly tickling her skin as he ran his fingers up to her bubbly butt cheeks. The way he grasped just one of her cheeks, taking the entire mound of flesh into his lustful claws and squeezing, Jess could tell that her boyfriend was aching to give it a good, hard slap.

Because the couple was only two people out of less than a dozen in the small library, Josh naturally refrained from doing so. Still, she could feel his burning desire to bring hand to flesh and a seething ire that he was forced to withhold.

Instead of the loud slapping sound of flesh on flesh, Jess heard the unmistakable zip of pants being undone.

Jess closed her eyes and focused all her attention on her tactile sensations. The feeling of Josh's chest pressed lightly against her back, his hot breath on the back of her neck, and his lips on the side of her neck sent chills all down her spine.

Parting her lips, all the air was forced out of Jess's lungs in a breathy sigh. At the same moment she felt the tip of his hard cock lightly rub against her wet undercarriage. As soon as she sensed his member gently kissing her pussy, a visitor knocking at the front door, Jess was suddenly filled with an urgent need for him.

Josh bit her earlobe as he eased himself into her. Having her earlobe nibbled drove Jess absolutely wild and as soon as she felt her boyfriend's thick dick slide into her, Jess couldn't help but gasp loudly, then let out a soft moan.

Josh immediately let his grip on Jess's ass go and her cheek fell into place, on either side of his cock. Although Josh enjoyed the feel of her ass partially wrapped around him while he drove his dick into his girlfriend's pussy, her big booty impeded his ability to fuck her even deeper from this angle rather than if her were to pull her ass cheeks apart. As it was, he couldn't give her the full length of his cock because the sound of his hips clapping against Jess supple ass cheeks would surely bring them unwanted attention,

Josh that was forced to release his grasp on Jess ass that he could cover up her mouth. Josh was working his half-thrusts into a fast and steady rhythm, and Jess couldn't stop herself from making throaty little moans punctuated with gasps that had the ability to take Josh's breath away.

"Ah, oh my *God*!"

At least Jess had the decency to whisper in the library.

But Josh wasn't taking any chances.

He covered up Jess's mouth with one hand, which she seemed to take as an invitation to moan even louder since she knew they would be muffled. With Josh's other hand, he was holding Jess waist steady to make sure that he didn't accidently give her too much dick and clap his abs against her booty.

But just like how Jess couldn't prevent herself from moaning, Josh couldn't stop his hand from wandering up her back, across her flat stomach, and to the front of her dress where the yellow and white scoop design revealed plenty of cleavage, though still not enough for Josh's liking.

The cute summer dress was the only thing that Jess had thrown on that morning in her hurry to follow Josh to the library. She was wearing no panties and no bra, so one stiff tug to the front of the dress sent Jess's ample breasts spilling out and bouncing in front of her to the rhythm of Josh fucking her from behind.

Josh took one of her D-cup breasts in his hand and gave it a firm squeeze. Her small nipple stiffened when he pinched it with his thumb and index finger. Jess mumbled something inaudible from underneath Josh's hand, then she took her arms off of the Sexual Education bookshelf in front of her and bent her back down at the waist even further and her right hand reached back as she pulled tight ass cheeks as far apart as she was able.

Josh seized the opportunity and started fucking Jess's pussy even deeper. From this angle, he had enough room to rub his cock up against her G-spot with every thrust. The added length he was able to soundlessly penetrate her with did not go unnoticed.

Although she did her best to control it, Jess was never very good at restraining herself. The ferocity and frequency of her moans increased dramatically. Josh was remiss to let go of Jess's breast, but did anyway so he could give the back of her hair a rough tug in hopes that it would send her a message that said, "Shhh! We're a library!"

It did not.

As soon as he pulled her hair, three things happened.

First, Jess's head suddenly jerked back, which caused Josh's hand to come off her mouth for a fraction of a second. In that instant, she let out a loud moan of pleasure that rang throughout the library, but before he could clasp his hand back over her mouth, the damage was done.

Second, pulling her hair sent Jess falling back a few inches, which drove the full length of his cock deep into Jess's tight little pussy. Embracing the added length of his dick inside her not only caused her to moan loudly, but it breeched the distance between her ass and Josh's hips, creating a loud clapping of flesh on flesh that echoed throughout the empty library, sending her tits bouncing out in front of her.

Third, the librarian, who up until that moment was very much engaged in replacing a cart full of children's books back on shelves in the kids section on the other side of the library, craned her heck at both of the unmistakable sounds, which she had heard plenty of times before in her long career working in the library and expected to hear plenty more times between now and her retirement.

Although everyone heard them in the library, she was the only one who went to investigate.

As soon as it happened, Jess and Josh knew they fucked up. Because the couple was always so in sync, they also both knew that there was only one solution.

Finish. And finish fast.

Throwing caution into the wind, Josh started giving Jess the full force of his thrusts, each time his hard cock slid into her pussy, hitting her G-spot, his hips slapped Jess's ass cheeks loudly. While he was still pulling her hair so that he could penetrate her deeper and with much more force, speed, and power than ever before.

As soon as Josh and Jess entered, "Fuck It Mode", he removed his hand from her mouth so he could get a film grip on Jess's full tits, which bounced even more vigorously now that he was fucking her with the determination of someone who needed to finish as soon as possible.

Jess no longer held back her moans of pleasure.

Keeping one hand dutifully spreading her ass cheek she quickly moved the other one down between her legs to her wet pussy, where she wasted no time at all fingering her clit.

As she heard footsteps approaching, Jess could feel Josh increase his pace, fucking her even harder than ever. She was right on the cusp with the finish line in sight, she squeezed her eyes shut, her fingers moving even faster than before.

Fuck, it feels so good, she thought to herself.

But the approaching footsteps were distracting.

"Oh, fuck. Oh, fuck, OH!" She cried as she felt the warm tingling orgasm flood through her body.

The next sound she heard when she opened her eyes was neither from her nor the man inside of her.

"Oh my God!"

It was the prudently dressed, middle-aged librarian woman who took them both by surprise.

Jess was able to cum in that same moment she heard the scream as a wave of euphoria took her.

The librarian started screaming as soon as she saw couple fucking right in front of her.

And as soon as Josh realized that both Jess and the librarian were screaming, Josh missed his next thrust and instead of penetrating Jess's vagina. His dick slid upward between Jess butt cheeks, sending his dick stabbing into Jess's firm, muscled ass cheek painfully.

Josh yelled out from the pain of his hard cock stabbing Jess's butt cheek at full speed, throwing him off balance and sending the two reeling back when he lost his footing.

Josh accidentally fell forward onto Jess, who pushed off the bookcase in front of her. Jess tried to grab the bookcase to prevent them from falling, but instead, the couple tumbled backwards.

Josh, who still hadn't cum yet, fell back on his ass still holding Jess at the waist. She fell back on top of him, still clinging to the bookshelf in front of her.

As the two fell to the ground, the bookshelf came tumbling down on top of them, raining a barrage of sexual education books on top of the naked couple, showering them in a rain of pages featuring reproductive anatomy and sexual position suggestions.

To this day, visitors to the L.A. County library can find a sign posted that reads, "Warning: No Sex in the Library."

CHAPTER 2

Day 1- Restaurant

Later that day, the couple stopped for food at Taco Bell on the way home. They were joking and laughing about what happened in the library.

"Did you see her face? I mean, she looked terrified. Like a deer in headlights," Josh joked in between bites of his Doritos hard taco.

"I think I saw a twinkle of jealousy in her eye there at the very end. That poor, old lady probably has never been fucked like that in her life," Jess added before pressing a cinnamon twist into her mouth.

"That poor lady? I'm the one who stubbed my dick on your ass!"

"Oh, don't be such a baby. I'm the one who got stabbed in the ass. I'm going to have a bruise on my butt for, like, three weeks."

Josh laughed. "I'll make it up to you. That is, if my dick doesn't need to be set in a cast first," he said through a mouth full of food. "Are you going to kiss it and make it better?"

Jess got that lascivious look in her eye. Then gave Josh the smile that she only gave him.

"That reminds me," Jess said, then stuck a hand deep into the cleavage of her dress and, after fondling her breasts for a few seconds, pulled out a small, crumbled piece of paper. They set it on the Taco Bell table and flattened it as best she could.

"What is it?" Josh asked, staring at the rumpled paper quizzically.

"I think it fell out of one of those books. I thought it looked interesting, so I grabbed it as we were making our getaway. I figured, at least we should come out of this with a souvenir, right?"

"That's my baby," Josh smiled, unable to take his eyes off the page torn from a book. "You would make an awesome burglar."

Jess gave him a look of incredulity. "What do you mean? I *AM* an awesome burglar."

The paper was handwritten but done so very professionally with lines that made up a five-by-five grid. A location was written inside each square. The title at the top of the page read "Exhibitionist Bingo." The middle-most space read "FREE". Only one box was crossed off with a red pen. It said "Library".

"Bingo." Josh mouthed, then looked up at Jess. "This is a handmade Bingo card."

She nodded, a lascivious smile creeping onto her soft, pink lips. "Looks like we're not the first couple ever to hook up in a library."

"This fell out of a sex ed book?" He asked.

Again, Jess nodded.

Josh mouthed a few of the locations written inside the boxes made on the Bingo card. "Movie Theater, Library, Balcony, Park, Gym... Are you seeing what I'm seeing?"

The couple locked eyes, a glint of recognition in each other's faces.

"Restaurant!" They said in unison.

Together, they abandoned their meal and made for the Taco Bell bathroom. Jess doubled back to their table to grab the Bingo card and stuff it down her dress.

Josh was already waiting for her, a beaming smile on his face, holding the door to the women's bathroom open. She returned the smile as she passed into the restroom.

"Ooh, what a gentleman," she whispered and shut the door behind them. It had no lock and could be pushed open by anyone at any moment.

The very thought caused Jess's smile to widen a degree.

She chose the first of the three bathroom stalls, although she really wanted to get fucked leaning on the sink – or better yet, hand drier – she did not relish the thought of getting caught twice in one day.

When Josh entered the bathroom stall behind her, she leaned over him and locked the door, then pulled a toilet seat cover to protect her bare ass from germs and God knows what

with her whatever he will, hoping he would ravage her right there in the Taco Bell bathroom stall.

She was not disappointed.

Still, she wanted to make him earn that Bingo square. Josh pulled the bottom of her skirt up to her mid back, exposing Jess's glorious ass. The moment he let go of her skirt, it fell back down, covering her bottom like a theater curtain blocking his line of sight to the main event. Josh silently cursed gravity. He would have to hold it up the entire time.

"Stand back up." He said, his hand delicately on her elbow and shoulder, guiding her.

Jess complied, still facing away from him in the tiny bathroom stall. She let him move her body like the world's horniest Barbie doll.

Josh crouched down as best he could and grabbed the bottom of Jess's dress at either end.

"Hands up." He whispered.

Jess threw her hands straight up in the air, anticipating her boyfriend to try some kinky new sexual position. Instead, she felt him lift her dress up and over her head. Jess shook her long jet-black hair across her back as she stood completely naked in front of Josh. She glanced over her shoulder and bit her lower lip hungrily as she watched Josh drop his pants to the restroom floor.

When his hard cock brushed up against her soft cheeks, she backed up into him. His dick slid between her thighs, right underneath her eager pussy.

"Holy fuck, you're so wet," Josh whispered in surprise.

"Duh," Jess replied. "Stop fucking around. I am so fucking horny right now."

Josh coughed a laugh.

Not the ideal response, Jess thought.

She reached back with both hands, grabbing two palms full of ass and spread her cheeks for him, revealing the glistening cleft between her thighs.

"Damn." He whispered.

Josh effortlessly slid into her wet ass pussy.

There it is.

Jess did not hold back. She started making noises not unlike the soft grunt she made while working out at the gym. Josh grabbed hold of her forearms and pulled her back, causing his hips to slap against her ass loudly. With every thrust he used more force, getting better leverage so he could fuck her harder and harder, working up to a consistent, fast rhythm.

As Jess leaned over the porcelain toilet, her tits bounced wildly against her chest. She got the feeling that Josh wanted desperately to grab and play with her breasts, as he was often fond of doing during sex, yet they continued to bounce teasingly just out of his grasp.

Although this position was pretty much just a repeat of what they had done in the library just a few hours ago, the small amount of privacy afforded to them by the thin plastic public restroom stall walls made a significant difference. When they allowed themselves to fuck without restraint, without censoring themselves, they were able to fully indulge in the pleasure of each other's bodies while enjoying the kink of getting it on inside a Taco Bell bathroom.

As Josh worked up his pace, he was able to feed Jess's pussy the full length of his cock with no recourse from his hard abs, hips, and the palms of his hands slapping roughly against Jess's firm, supple, and quickly reddening ass.

The subtle sound of the restroom door creaking open brought all of that to a screeching half.

Josh froze mid-thrust. Jess's voice caught in her throat. She mentally cursed him for stopping because now they had to start all over.

But first, they had to wait until whoever was entering the restroom to leave. But what if they took forever to pee? Or started to take a shit? Oh my God! Jess couldn't wait. She wouldn't wait. She could feel Josh's hard cock still inside of her as she bent over the toilet, legs spread.

Jess released the grip on her ass cheeks and they fell into place around the base of Josh's dick. She grabbed the top of the toilet and, slowly and stealthily, she began pushing her ass back and forth, taking his dick as deep inside her as it would go, savoring every throbbing inch of him.

She felt Josh's hot breath on the back of her neck as he exhaled deeply, moaning slightly. Slowly, she grind her ass flush against his hips, then moved forward until the tip of his cock just barely kissed her outermost pussy lips.

Then she *squeezed*, causing him to inhale in a sharp gasp. Josh covered his mouth with his hand but otherwise didn't budge. Jess's heart was racing. Slowly, she pushed back against Josh, hiding a mischievous smile on her face.

Although grinding her ass up against him made barely any noise at all, in a bathroom that was otherwise dead quiet, the slippery, squishy, sounds of Josh's throbbing cock sliding in and out of Jess's sopping wet pussy turned their otherwise clandestine sex into a fireworks show.

"Hello?" a timid female voice asked from the next stall over.

Suddenly, Jess realized her bright yellow sundress was draped over the top of the bathroom stall divider, half of it hanging down on the side with the other women in the bathroom.

A spike of adrenaline hit Jess. It was the same feeling she got when Josh had her bent over in the library. The feeling was even more intoxicating than the already incredible sex she and Josh had on the regular.

Jess braced her hands firmly against the edge of the toilet. Throwing caution into the wind, she threw it back at him harder and faster. Jess wiggled her bottom down Josh's shaft as her eyes rolled to the back of her head in ecstasy.

"Oh, FUCK." She whimpered.

"Are you okay over there?" asked the voice on the other side of the stall.

Jess didn't hear her peeing. She didn't hear her washing her hands. Was she just nosy? What was wrong with this lady? Why couldn't she just leave them alone?

One thing was clear to her: she wasn't going to cum anytime soon with this slow-motion sex. Turtles fucked faster than this. And they didn't have to worry about getting caught fucking by other turtles.

She wanted to laugh. She wanted to tell her to mind her own fucking business. Instead, she clenched her pussy around the base of Josh's hard cock and began to twerk up against him.

Then her hands slipped, and she accidentally flushed the toilet.

"Oh, fuck yeah," Jess said in a breath voice, ignoring the interloper in the next stall over.

In response, she heard footsteps pattering quickly out the door.

"I think she's gone," Josh whispered a moment after they heard the door swing shut.

Jess looked back at him over his shoulder. She reached back and brushed her fingertips up and down against his chiseled abs. Even with half his clothes on, he still had a way of turning her on like no one else ever could. Granted, his cock was currently still inside of her in that moment.

Jess bit her pink bottom lip and drank him in as the two locked eyes meaningfully.

God, even his eyes make me horny.

"What is it?" He asked.

"I want you to fuck me until I cum on every inch of this Taco Bell bathroom." She told him in a husky voice.

That comment lit up Josh's face like a Christmas tree. He brought one hand down hard, slapping her ass, while his other hard pulled her hair, sending her entire body backwards up against him. Jess squealed in delight.

Strap in, she thought, *it's going to be a bumpy ride.*

A moment later, it somehow felt as if Josh's dick got even harder, penetrated even deeper inside of her. He started fucking her with renewed vigor and raw energy. Once more, the two became unrestrained in doing what they did best. Their primal, animalistic bathroom sex caused her to work up a sweat as Jess started to close in on an orgasm, but it was barely out of her reach.

"I'm close! Fuck me harder!" she yelled between loud moans.

Possibly too loud, because a moment later, they heard the bathroom door swing open once more. This time, Josh didn't stop. He wouldn't dare stop.

He doubled down and began pulling her hips back, grinding hard up against him as he fucked the shit out of Jess. Her own panting and moaning was even louder than the sound of skin slapping against skin. They both knew there was someone else in the bathroom with them, but the bathroom stall was enough of a curtain of privacy for them to ignore everything and everyone around them.

Until someone started banging on the bathroom stall door like they were the police.

"Hey! You two need to stop what you're doing and leave!" It was a man's voice. "This is the Taco Bell manager, and I'll call the cops!"

To his credit, Josh did not stop or even slow down. He started fucking Jess even harder and faster than ever before.

"A-almost done in here!" Jess called back to him, barely able to make her voice steady while her boyfriend's cock pumped inside of her. "Be out in a minute!"

The manager continued banging on the door as Josh continued to bang Jess. She started screaming exaggerated porn star moans to try and drown him out, louder than anything Josh had ever heard from her before.

"I said fuck me harder! FUCK! ME! HARDERRRR!"

Happy chemicals exploded in her brain while adrenaline pumped through her veins. At the same time, she felt a warm sensation flood her pussy. *God, I love it when we cum at the exact same time.*

Josh began to slow, then stop, and then pulled out. Jess sighed a sigh of utter satisfaction and relief.

Then, more banging.

Oh, yeah.

Josh had Jess's sundress in both arms, like a gentleman, ready to dress her.

Oh, yeah. Clothes.

She giggled as she turned to face Josh, completely nude. Sometimes she became a giggly mess after a really great orgasm. She gave her boyfriend a quick kiss on the lips as she took her dress from him, then pushed passed him to the restroom stall door.

"I'll call the cop!" a man shouted from the other side of the thin plastic door.

"Hold your horses!"

Jess unlocked the door and pushed it all the way open. She stepped out into the Taco Bell bathroom completely naked, striding past the manager, who couldn't have been older than 20, and a small, timid-looking Hispanic woman standing beside him. They both stood frozen, eyes wide and locked on Jess, taking in her every curve. She smiled mischievously, savoring their horrified looks.

"We were just leaving." She said as she slipped the sundress over her head and pulled it down to her thighs.

Josh had just finished clasping his belt when Jess took her hand in his. She blew the Taco Bell manager a kiss before running out of the bathroom with her boyfriend in tow, narrowly missing the arrival of the cops and getting arrested.

Or whatever they do when two consenting adults have a good time.

CHAPTER 3

Day 1 – Home

Jess didn't pull out the Bingo card again until the two were safely home. She laid it down in the middle of the dining room table and flattened out the wrinkles on the page. The two of them stared at it in silence for a few minutes before she finally broke the silence.

"Does the library count if only one of us had an orgasm?"

Josh looked at her, incredulous. "Either way, I am *not* going back to that library. Besides, it's going to have to count since we got a lifetime ban from all L.A. County libraries."

"And all Taco Bells." She reminded him.

"And all Taco Bells!" he threw up his arms. "But I have no intention of doing any more of these ridiculous exhibitions."

He gave her a smile and squeezed her hand.

"Does that mean you're in?"

Josh gave the sheet of paper in front of them a good, hard stare.

Exhibitionist Bingo.

Jess watched as he silently mouthed the words, seeing how they felt on his tongue. Who in their right mind would create such a thing?

But Jess and Josh were not in their right mind. Jess knew that. Josh was still in denial about the couple's eccentric proclivities.

"Oh, I'm definitely in." He said at last.

Yesss.

"I'm just trying to envision how we're going to get away with some of these." He went on. "I mean, so far, we're two for two in getting caught." Josh put his hand on her shoulder. "Sweetie, I think we're really bad at this."

"That's only because we need the practice!" She pleaded.

Josh read the look of anticipation on her face and gave a long sigh. "If we're going to go through with more of these, you'll need to be quieter. Baby, I *love* the noises you make, but this is a stealth mission."

Jess smiled and tapped her index finger against her temple. "I actually have some thoughts on that."

"Good." Josh's gaze returned to the Bingo card on the table. Jess was relieved he didn't ask her any follow-up questions. She followed his line of sight to the Bingo card.

"Home," she pointed at the square in the middle of the page. "We can use that one as practice."

Josh's eyes never left the card, his handsome face deep in thought. "So, it seems like if we already did library – and if we can count banging in the Taco Bell bathroom as the restaurant square –"

"I mean, barely." Jess interrupted.

"– Then we only need these three here to get a Bingo."

Josh tapped the squares on the Bingo card that read Movie Theater, Grocery Store, and Sauna.

Jess put her hand on Josh's broad shoulder. He turned to face her, looking down, as he was at least a foot taller than her.

"Or – crazy idea, but here me out, babe – what would you say if I told you I wanted to do all of them?" She rocked on the balls of her feet nervously as she bit her lower lip, anxiously awaiting her boyfriend's answer.

Slowly, Josh turned his gaze back to the Bingo card and whistled low. The ensuing silence only served to make Jess even more nervous as to how he would answer. She studied his face as he studied the Bingo card like he was solving a complex mathematical problem. He looked especially cute when he was thinking hard.

The silence dragged. Jess started to second-guess herself. Just as she opened her mouth to tell him *never mind, it was a silly idea. Your hyper-sexed girlfriend can find other ways to entertain herself,* Josh replied, "I've got to be honest with you, Jess. The thought did cross my mind..."

Her face lit up like a sunrise. "Yes! You see? This is why we are *so* synced up!" She took his hands in hers and gave them a little squeeze.

"But..." Josh started, and Jess's smile wilted. "But we can't just jump into them like we did today. We need to approach each one of these with a plan. Because today was kind of a fucking nightmare."

Jess couldn't help but laugh as she pictured the Taco Bell manager's face when she walked out of the bathroom stall butt ass naked.

"Okay. I one hundred percent agree with you, babe." She leaned forward and planted a kiss on his lips. "We can do this." She kissed him again. "I know we can."

Josh wore his cute "problem-solving" face to bed shortly thereafter. Both of their minds were on the Bingo card. For the first time in a very long time, the couple went to bed without having sex beforehand.

Instead, both of them excitedly fantasized about all of the different places they could fuck in the coming days.

CHAPTER 4

Day 2 – Jess's Work

Both Jess and Josh worked the following day. The first thing Jess did when she jumped out of bed in the morning with an uncharacteristic amount of energy was to take a picture of the Bingo card on her phone. That way, the physical Bingo card could remain safely at home while the two of them could essentially bring it to work with them.

Jess knew that it would be the only thing on both their minds that day, and as a result, neither would get very much work done.

Around lunchtime, Jess pulled out her vibrating phone to see a text message from Josh. *Been thinking about this all day. Some of these locations we've already done.*

The same thought had crossed Jess's mind as well. *Really? Which ones?*

Remember the music festival? And the Ferris Wheel at the music festival? And the parking lot at the music festival?

Jess knew exactly what he was referring to, but if she was lucky, she could turn this conversation into an afternoon work sexting session.

What if we just do it in the bathroom at each location on the card? She sent her reply. Had being in an exclusive relationship made her this bad at flirting via text?

She waited nearly an hour before she got a reply from Josh. Every minute that passed made her second guess the message she sent even more.

At last, when her phone vibrated at her desk, she pulled up Josh's message with lightning reflexes. *Sounds like cheating.*

She rolled her eyes. Of course he would think that, given his proclivity for following the rules. Although if there was one thing that Josh liked more than sex, it was a good challenge, and Jess could use that.

At home, she would routinely Tom Sawyer him into doing household chores like dishes and laundry by making it a timed challenge between the two of them.

Just as Jess went to set down her phone, it buzzed again in her hand. Josh's message read: *There are 24 boxes on the Bingo card. Think we can do them all in a month?*

Jess laughed out loud, drawing the attention of her co-workers at neighboring desks.

"Mind your own god damned business, Laura!" She snapped.

Laura, the middle-aged woman sitting at the desk next to Jess, gave her a *humph* and returned to the papers on her desk.

Jess typed her message to Josh: *22 left? Too easy. Let's do them all in a week.*

Send.

And then, an instant reply.

OK. Bet.

Jess felt a mischievous smile spread across her face.

CHATPER 5

Day 2 – Home

Jess wanted to look good for a night out at the movies. She spent upwards towards an hour curling an intricate series of ringlets. By the time she was done, her shiny black locks were entirely made up of springy curls.

Josh walked in and became entranced by her hair. He received an endless amount of entertainment pulling the bottom-most curls and watching them spring back into place. He continued pawing at her hair like a playful kitten as she changed.

She chose a form fitting red dress with shimmering sequins that ended just above her knees. The zipper-backed dress wrapped around her collar and had a heart-shaped cut-out in the center of the chest that revealed ample cleavage. The dress hugged her every curve, but did not show very much skin aside from the cut-out over her chest.

Josh was taken aback when he saw her. He looked like someone just hit him in the head with a baseball bat, causing his jaw to slacken. The scene caused Jess to giggle as she sauntered over and shut it for him.

"I... I thought we were going to the movies, not a movie premier." He stammered when he at last regained his wits.

Jess gave him an annoyed look.

"I mean, you make that dress look beautiful, babe." He added.

She beamed. "Well put. Now, put on the clothes that I picked out for you."

She waved her hand to the button up dress shirt and pair of black slacks laid out on the bed. Josh started towards the bed, stopping as he passed his girlfriend to deliver a quick kiss.

"God, you're beautiful." He whispered as he leaned in close.

Jess stood on her tippy toes so she could press her pink lips right next to Josh's ear and whispered in a low, erotic voice, "Brush your fucking teeth."

Josh smiled as he changed and finished getting ready for a night out at the movies. When he was done, he resembled something closer to a proper gentleman.

As Josh fixed his sandy blond hair in the mirror, Jess stood behind him and wrapped her arms around his waist, hugging him tight. Josh pulled her in front of him so he could stand tall behind her, his strong arms encircling her small waist.

"I am so grateful to be in love with a woman of such refined class and exceeding beauty." He said, then kissed her bare neck above her dress.

Jess tilted her head so she could give him a kiss on the lips. As Josh squeezed her close to him, the coupled swayed gently from side to side. "You're not so bad looking yourself, you know, mister. Though I suppose you are exceedingly lucky to have me."

Josh coughed a laugh. Jess turned around towards him and took his face in her hands, pulling him down so she could give him a real kiss.

He hungrily kissed her back for several minutes.

When Jess realized she was moaning through their kiss, she forced herself back away from him. "Down, boy. Save it for the movies."

Jess went to go grab her purse and coat before Josh swept by, escalating things with another deep kiss.

"About that..." he said between breathes while making out. "Have you given any thought about what movie we're going to see?"

"Hmm." Jess barely got out the words in the brief moments their lips were apart. "Doesn't." Kiss. "Matter" Kiss.

"Hmm." Josh tried pulling away, but Jess's lips followed him. "Have you thought about." Kiss. "How we're." Kiss. "Going to." Kiss. "Not." Kiss. "Get." Kiss. "Caught?" Kiss.

Jess pulled back, looked him in the eyes and gave him a little nod. "'Course I have."

"And?"

"And you know I can't think when you get me all horned up like this." She pounded her tiny balled fist against Josh's broad chest. "So, stop it!"

Josh smirked. "Seriously, we need a plan."

"Wait! I wrote it down in the notes app on my phone." Jess hurriedly pulled her phone out from her little red clutch.

"What's it say?"

Jess scrolled through her phone. "It says, 'Don't get caught.'" She said, then dropped her phone back in her purse.

Josh slapped his palm to his forehead. Jess disappeared into the night outside with Josh at her heels, frowning.

CHAPTER 6

Day 2 – Parking Lot

Josh drove an Audi. He didn't buy the Audi because it was particularly fast or flashy or even because he liked Audi's – which he didn't.

He bought it because he got a great deal on his Audi A3. Josh bought the car from a close friend who had to sell it after getting arrested for drug trafficking. He had to sell it quickly before the car was taken by the government as part of his case, so buying the vehicle was able to help his friend and his family with their overwhelming legal fees by paying for the car in cash.

It was a win-win – at least from Josh's perspective. Not so much for his friend, who was currently residing in a federal prison. from the incident, Josh came out with the Audi A3, barely used and only 2 years old, with roughly the same number of miles as dollars he paid for it, a deal which was enough to make any dealership weep openly.

It was the fastest car that Josh had ever owned. The only problem was that once Josh got behind the wheel, he liked to push it to its limits. While Jess considered herself a thrill seeker, Josh's driving almost always terrified her.

"Slow. Down!" She screamed from the passenger seat, both hands firms gripping the Oh Shit Bars.

Josh just laughed and slammed on the gas, doing 120 on the uncharacteristically empty freeway. Fortunately for Jess, the traffic when approaching the movie theater exit forced Josh to drive like a normal person.

"I'm just trying to get your heart rate up before tonight. Think of it as foreplay." Josh said as he slowed to meet the pace of traffic.

"This is NOT foreplay!" Jess screamed as her chest heaved.

Josh couldn't help but laugh. "Tell you what, I'll let you pick the movie."

"I'm going to pick the worst movie available so that there are as few people in the theater as possible," Jess said as she smoothed out her dress.

"That's no fun. I want to at least watch a decent movie as I bone you."

The parking lot was packed with cars and people going to and leaving the theater. They had to drive around a bit before finding the only free parking spot available, dead in the middle of the lot.

Once the car was parked and off, Josh looked over at Jess sitting in the passenger seat. He looked her up and down with those hungry shark eyes of his, taking in every inch of her body.

"What? I didn't pee on myself this time, if that's what you're thinking."

He shook his head.

"Not what I was thinking."

"Then wha- Oh... OH!"

"Parking Lot?" Josh said, referencing one of the squares on the Bingo card.

Jess nodded, biting on her lower lip. "Mm-hmm. Parking Lot."

Jess looked around the car. In every direction of the parking lot there were people walking to and from their cars. Almost as soon as they parked, an old couple got into the Nissan parked next to them and drove off.

Suddenly, Jess had a very worried look on her face.

"I didn't think there would be this many people." She said with a sense of awe, her head on a swivel.

Josh chuckled. "Babe, it's called Exhibitionist Bingo for a reason. What did you expect?"

Now Jess could see why Josh was so apprehensive about this in the first place. Jess had envisioned the two of them being alone, with the slight chance of being caught, like in the Taco Bell restroom. That sort of exhibitionism got her heart racing and blood pumping. But with all of these people walking around, some casually glancing into their car windows with a clear view of them, her heart was racing out of panic.

Josh leaned over Jess and tapped the button next to the passenger seat to slowly move her seat back as far as it could go. Jess scooted back up, body rigid with terror.

"Jess, look at me. Look into my eyes." Josh said, doing his best to calm her.

She locked eyes with him, muscles tense.

"It's only you and me here, okay? There is no one else."

"But–"

He took her chin in his hand and tilted her face towards him, then kissed her big, beautiful, pink lips. "Just you and me."

Jess's face softened considerably as all her worry melted away. Well, most of it. The two started making out in the car as strangers continued to walk by their car, paying them no mind.

Now that there was more room over the passenger seat, Josh very clumsily jumped from the driver's seat across the center console over to the passenger seat and directly on top of Jess. It was very difficult to keep the sexy passion going with Josh's huge, muscular body nearly crushing her petite frame. Josh pulled on the lever beside the seat so that it slid all the way back, forcing Jess to lie down flat. That made all the difference.

The Audi's windows were not tinted by any means, so although people could see the two lying on top of each other and making out, not many gave them a double-take. Now Josh could lie atop Jess while putting his weight on his knees, which dug into the seat on either side of her.

As they continued their passionate kiss in the reclined seat, their hands explored each other's bodies. Josh fit his knee between Jess's legs and lifted her dress up to her hips. She moaned into Josh's mouth as his knee grazed her moist slit.

"Hmm, no panties?" Josh whispered as he pulled the bottom of her dress up above her hips.

"Babe, you know I hate underwear."

Josh smirked devilishly, pulling her dress up further.

"But what if someone sees?" Jess said softly.

"It's just you and me." He said as he gently kissed her neck. "Nothing else matters. It's just us. Here. Right now."

She gave a slight nod, then ran her fingers through Josh's hair, caressing his neck and pulling his head to hers as their lips met.

With help from Jess, Josh managed to get his slacks off. His hard cock presses against Jess's stomach teasingly. She took him in her hands, stroking him gently while she guided him between her legs. He bit Jess's earlobe as he entered her, and she threw her head back in ecstasy. Jess lost her breath as she felt Josh fill her completely.

When they locked eyes, Jess realized he was right. It was just him and her. Nothing else mattered. Josh held himself up with one arm on the passenger seat, careful not the crush his petite girlfriend under his muscular frame. His other hand grasped Jess's shoulder and neck, pulling her toward him as he penetrated her deeply. Jess unconsciously wrapped her legs around his waist. Her mouth hung open wide, gasping and moaning wildly as she pulled him closer.

Josh thrust himself slowly between her legs, setting the delicate pace that Jess most often associated with lovemaking rather than fucking. She had thought they were going to have a quick fuck in the car before the movie, instead he was taking his time making love to her as if they were in the comfort and privacy of their big bed at home.

What a fucking gentleman, she thought. *Is it the dress? It must be the dress. Are we attracting too much attention? What will happen if someone sees us? What type of snacks will they have in the theater? How much will they cost?*

All these thoughts, along with her stressors and anxiety throughout the day, vanished as the next wave of pleasure swept through her. There was only him and her, here, in this moment.

Only his love.

Only our love.

Only us.

It's crazy how a really good orgasm will make you forget about all of your problems.

Her red, sequined dress was bunched up to her stomach. Her bare ass wiggling against the passenger seat. His weight on top of her, pressing down gently like a warm security blanket. A blanket with its dick inside of her.

Jess's hands were all over him, pulling him closer, deeper into her. She wrapped her legs around Josh as he made love to her in the passenger seat of his car. He made her feel like a teenager again.

As he thrust deep inside of her, Josh whispered lovingly into her ear, "I fucking love you, Jess."

"I fucking love you." She heard herself mirror his words.

"You feel so good."

"You feel so good." She echoed.

"You drive me wild."

"You drive me wild." She repeated.

"It's just you and me, baby. Only you and me."

"Yes." She gasped and he drove his cock deep inside of her, brushing up against her G-spot. "You... and me."

Caught between breathy moans, Jess arched her back, heaving her breasts upward. "Oh fuck, I'm going to cum!"

"Then cum with me, my love." He whispered gently, moving his hips faster still.

Jess moaned louder. Her heart beat faster. She breathed harder. As Josh's mouth pressed firmly against her soft, pink lips, she felt his wet tongue dance up against hers. She tasted his delicious salty sweetness, a taste distinct to him alone.

Jess opened her vivid green eyes and met Josh's brilliant blue, icy gaze. She swam in his eyes like oceans. When she moaned in ecstasy, it was like she was breathing him.

In one gloriously amorous moment, the two orgasmed together at exactly the same time.

During the post-coital afterglow of their lovemaking in the movie theater parking lot, Josh held Jess in his arms. She lay underneath him, grinning and basking in his warmth. Josh continued to slowly slide his still-hard cock in and out of Jess after having just filled her with cum.

Jess couldn't decide which she liked better: when her and her boyfriend cum at the same time, or laying here with her boyfriend after they both cum at the same time.

Jess exhaled deeply. It was a sigh of relief.

"I know that sound," Josh said as he continued fucking her. "You only make that sound when you're *really* satisfied."

She stifled a giggle. Jess wanted to scowl at him, but she couldn't stop grinning.

"I love you, Joshua Jacobs." She pulled him close and lay her head against his chest.

"Full names? Now I know you're satisfied."

"Mmm." She agreed without verbally agreeing. "Pull you dick out of me and let's go see a movie?" she asked.

"My pleasure." Josh kissed her once on the lips, then rolled over to the driver's seat and pulled up his pants.

Jess pulled her dress back down her thighs, then smoothed it out, check it for cum stains and grateful she found none.

"Are you ready?" Josh asked her, hand on the car door.

Jess pushed her tits up in her dress.

"Psh, I shot out my momma's pussy ready."

CHAPTER 7

Day 2 – Movie Theater

They both hopped out of the car at the same time and walked together through the parking lot and into the movie theater, holding hands. Jess had a bit of a spring in her step the whole way now that her anxiety of having sex in public had vanished.

"I still say that doing it at a drive-in theater would have been way easier." Jess teased.

"Who says we can't still bang at a drive-in theater?" Josh replied with a smirk. "You know, just to be thorough and to meet the Bingo card requirements in full."

Jess laughed a throaty laugh. After a moment, "Thank you for doing that, by the way." She said sweetly, wrapping herself around Josh's thick, muscled forearm and laying her cheek on his shoulder as they walked.

"Uh, you're very welcome… but just so we're clear, what exactly are you thanking me for?"

"For being so gentle." She said in a soft voice. "For taking it slow when you knew I was nervous."

"Oh, that? I thought you were thanking me for giving you such an awesome orgasm."

"That, too!" She leaned in close so she could whisper in his ear. "And… thank you for cumming inside of me."

He slipped his arm around her, pulling her close. "Baby, we're just getting started."

Jess sighed. She could still feel the warmth between her legs. "You know, sometimes I think that my life is so good, I wonder if this is really real or if it's all just a dream."

Without missing a beat, Josh said, "You know what would be a dream? If that dress popped off at the top so I could play with those unbelievable tits of yours."

Jess punched him hard in the shoulder. "And as soon as I start to think you've got a little bit of gentleman in you, I wake up and realize I'm dating a total perv."

Josh shrugged. "There was a compliment in there somewhere."

As soon as they reached the box office, the argument over which movie they were going to see was put to rest. Because of the time they arrived, plus the time spent in the parking lot, there was only one movie which started at a reasonable time — one which neither of them wanted to see. It was a compromise, but if everything went according to plan, they wouldn't be paying very much attention to the movie anyway.

After buying two tickets from an overly judgmental woman working the box office, Josh and Jess headed straight to the bathroom to clean up. In the short time that Jess spent in the woman's restroom, six different women complimented her on her dress and one that Jess was pretty sure thought she was a celebrity stopped to take a picture with her.

The plan was to meet up in the theater independently of one another, entering at different times. After washing up, Jess entered the designated, dimly lit movie theater. Instantly, she realized that entering separately was a terrible idea.

The theater was pitch black and more crowded with people than she thought the movie they were seeing deserved. It had already started and Josh was nowhere to be found. Jess walked up the theater steps until she reached the very back, then...

"Jess! Pst, Jess!" came a loud stage whisper from the unmistakable voice of the man she loved.

She recognized his tall silhouette and shuffled past a couple of people already in their seats to get to him, apologizing as she went. Jess sat in the only unoccupied seat on Josh's left.

"Where were you?" he whispered, taking her hand in his.

"Some woman stopped me to take a picture. I think she thought I was someone famous." Jess whispered back, then kissed the back of his hand.

"See? It's the dress!"

The two simultaneously got shushed by everyone in the back row.

After a moment, Jess whispered softly, "That is *not* a good omen."

Josh put his lips to her ear. "We can do this. Just be quiet and do your best to stifle those sexy little moans you make."

"What moans?" she replied in a normal voice.

"You know, the ones that really fucking turn me on."

"Ah, yeah!" Jess moaned loudly in her best porn star impression, drawing the attention of everyone who just shushed them.

Josh slapped her bare thigh. "Knock it off!"

"I'm just having fun." She whispered in his ear, then licked his cheek.

"Being famous sure has changed you."

"Oh, shut up!"

Shhhh!

Jess rolled her eyes, a wasted gesture considering the theater was too dark for anyone to notice.

"If you start getting anxious, just remember it's only you and me and no one else is paying attention." Josh whispered softly, then squeezed her hand sweetly. He was someone managing to make this whole Exhibitionist Bingo thing romantic in a way that only he could.

Jess leaned over and pressed her lips right next to Josh's ear. In the sexiest, most seductive siren voice, she whispered "I want to eat Raisinets while I fuck your brains out." She planted a wet kiss on his neck. "Give me ten bucks. I left my purse in the car."

He did. In the next five minutes, Jess ran to the concession stand and back, returning with a small box of chocolate covered raisins. That she paid ten dollars for.

"Okay. Now I'm ready to fuck." Jess whispered with a mouth full of Raisinets.

When she looked over, she saw in the dark that Josh had a hand covering his face and was trying his hardest not to laugh. Three times he leaned over to whisper something back to his girlfriend, only to sit back and start laughing uncontrollably at how ridiculous his girlfriend really was.

"When I say so, pull up your skirt and come sit on my lap, okay?" He said after finally regaining his composure.

Jess nodded in agreement.

The movie was not sexy. Or funny. Or, in Jess's opinion, very entertaining or good in general. Ane whenever Jess got bored, her absolute favorite thing to do was vex her boyfriend to no end. So while Jess was waiting for Josh to give her the green light, she made a show of playing with herself in a way that only he would know about or see. Probably.

The closest people sitting next to Jess were separated by one empty seat, but when she looked down the isle she could see them all perfectly. So she assumed that they could all see her perfectly as well. Fortunately, they were in the back row with no one sitting behind them.

Jess spread her legs enough to scrunch the bottom of her red dress up to her hips, giving her fingers easy access. Looked at Josh as she stuck her middle finger all the way in her mouth, sucking it playfully, but Josh was focused on whatever was happening on the screen. Without turning away from her boyfriend, she began flicking her clit discretely. When she realized no one was paying any attention to her, Jess started to rub her pussy in wide, dramatic circles, moving her entire arm to get the job done.

She spread her legs further, bumping Josh's knee in the process. He did a double take when he finally looked in her direction.

"Knock that off, Jess. Come on!"

"What?! You want me to cum on you?!" She asked loudly.

She got shushed by the row of people sitting in front of them.

After that, Jess wanted to see just how far she could pull the form-fitting dress all the way up her body without anyone noticing.

After a bit of shimmying, she was surprised to find that she could hike the tight dress which normally fell to her knees over her ass and all the way up to her rib cage.

If she really tried, she could might be able to pull it up and over her tits, but not without risking damaging the dress. Plus, she didn't like the idea of her bare ass touching the disgusting movie theater seat, which had probably never been washed and seen a million farts. So instead, she went to work trying to get the dress back down to cover her bottom, a task which was proving more difficult than she had imagined.

Jess had to stand up to pull the dress back down over her big, round butt cheeks. Although she stood only 5' 2", the red heels she wore gave her an extra few inches. Standing in the dark movie theater fully exposed her ass and pussy as she swayed her hips from side to side, struggling to pull her dress back down.

Josh face-palmed upon seeing his girlfriend half-naked standing next to him. Knowing full well the type of havoc that Jess would cause when bored and left to her own devices, he promptly pulled out his dick, drawing her attention.

The only problem was that Josh's meaty cock was only half-hard when he whipped it out. But to Jess, that one problem had a very simple solution.

Jess brushed all of her hair over to one side. She forgot about her dress and exposed bottom half as she crouched down in front of Josh.

Taking the base of his dick in her hand, she immediately brought her mouth down over his cock, taking all of him into her mouth. She created a vacuum in her mouth, taking his dick to the back of her throat while massaging it with her hand. As he stiffened and grew in her mouth, it because more challenging to bring her lips all the way to the base of his cock.

Now fully hard, Jess pulled his cock out from the back of her throat and began licking the full length of it. She didn't even realize her free hand had wandered in between her own legs as she subconsciously rubbed her clit at the same time.

Both of them found out just how difficult it was to refrain from making the animalistic noises of pleasure they typically associated with sex.

Jess felt in that moment that there were eyes on her. That strangers were staring at her, silently judging her as a little slut.

That's fine, she thought. *Let them stare. There is nothing wrong with being a slut. It's just him and me.*

She did not look around to see if anyone was watching. She thought about how far she wanted to take this blowjob. She really wanted him to cum in her mouth so she could taste his deliciously salty, sweet semen. She wanted to feel his hot load dripping down her lips and in the back of her throat after swallowing his cum.

God, that sounds so good right now.

But if he went soft, she would have to start this whole process over. Besides, it would defeat the whole purpose of her getting him rock hard so he could fuck her brains out in the middle of a crowded movie theater.

She had to stay focused. The Bingo card. This was all for a game of Bingo.

Josh's big dick was at maximum hardness. Jess slid her hand up and down his saliva-soaked cock a few more times, chagrined to let it go. She ran her fingers over the tight hole between her legs and felt just how wet she was. A few drops of her womanly fluids dribbled onto the movie theater floor.

"It's now or never." She whispered, more for her benefit than for Josh's.

He gave her a silent nod. Jess quickly stood and turned to face the screen, then sat back on Josh's lap. She slowly worked his massive cock into her little wet hole. Despite having fucked in the car just moments ago, Jess's vagina had already snapped back to it's original size – a power possessed by all of the women in her family.

Thankfully, having licked and sucked on his dick to nearly the point of orgasm made it slick and slippery. Playing with his dick in her mouth had also gotten her unbelievably wet once again.

Within moments, Jess was able to squeeze the entirety of Josh's cock inside of her to the point where it just looked like she was sitting on his lap. Although she managed to do it all soundlessly, the expression on her face said otherwise. Jess's eyes were as wide as saucers and her jaw might as well have hit the floor, where her pussy juice pooled in a little puddle.

Although she couldn't see Josh's face, she imagined it the same way. He placed his big hands over her dress on either side of her tiny waist and physically lifted her entire person up a few inches, then pulled her back down.

Jess loved being thrown around like this and wanted more. She wanted badly to start bouncing up and down on his dick. She wanted him to be rougher with her, but of course she couldn't tell him that in an otherwise quiet movie theater. That would quickly blow their cover. Public sex wasn't always about having great sex, it was about being discrete.

Focus on the mission. She told herself.

Jess gripped either side of the arm rests and pushed herself up and down in rhythm with Josh.

Maybe public sex can be great and *discrete?*

She started grinding her ass on his dick in circles as he lifted her up and down. It felt good, but it wouldn't get either of them to cum anytime soon.

She felt one of Josh's hands slide up her dress, over her breasts. Jess rolled her eyes. *Why does he love my boobs so damn much?*

"Lean forward." She heard him whisper from behind her.

Jess looked back at him and realized that Josh couldn't see the movie screen with her sitting on his lap like this. Of course. That's why he wanted her to lean forward.

Jess grabbed her little box of Raisinets sitting in the cup holder, dumped all of them into her mouth, then hunched forward so her boyfriend could watch the stupid movie as he fucked her.

Behind her, Josh sighed loudly. *Great, what did I do wrong now*, she wondered as she was still bounce her ass up and down on his dick.

"Grab the seat in front of you." He whispered loud enough for them to get a dirty look from their neighbors in the next seat over. Jess had a dirty look ready for them in return.

"Mind your own fucking business." She hissed.

In order to place both hands on the seat in front of them, Jess had to bend at her hips and lean forward until her back was level flat. At last she understood what Josh was trying to get her to do.

To any onlooker, the couple looked innocent enough. Jess sweetly sat on her boyfriend's lap while leaning forward enough for him to see the screen. But from this position, she was able to twerk her ass up and down on his dick discretely while smashing her G-spot each time as she drove her pussy down on top of him.

The movements were so subtle that they might as well have been imperceptible in a dark movie theater, yet they gave Jess the freedom to bounce her bubbly booty up and down on Josh's cock as much or as little as she pleased, giving her full control. And she was quite pleased to bounce on his dick all throughout the movie.

Jess was content that she could make good on her threat that she would fuck Josh's brains out throughout the entire movie.

After a while of riding Josh's cock, she straightened up, pressing her back against Josh's chest and wiggling her bottom, grinding him in circles as if she were a stripper giving a lap dance. Josh played along, kissing her on the neck and palming her tits over her dress. Nearly an hour later and he was still as hard as ever.

Jess looked back to see Josh's grinning face. The darkness of the theater made it feel even more stripper-esque.

"I could do this all night long." She whispered in his ear. "So just tap my left should when you're ready to cum, okay, baby?"

Josh nodded dopily.

The two were no strangers to tantric, marathon sex sessions. They both understood that the longer the investment, the bigger the payout. And their long-term investments were always well worth it whenever they could find the time to invest in such feats of athleticism. *There is nothing wrong with a quickie, but delayed gratification is the best gratification.* Jess thought to herself while she pushed up against Josh's armrests.

She pushed one hand between her legs to find her clit once more, rubbing and playing with herself as she twerked on his dick. This was it. This was how she would cum. She felt an imminent orgasm growing ever closer, but lingered on the cusp of cumming. She wanted to wait until the credits started rolling until she claimed her prize.

But, God, if this doesn't feel so fucking good.

Of course, if they were to somehow get caught and chased out of the movie theater before then, it would all be for nothing and they would have to return another day to restart the process. Assuming they didn't get a lifetime ban from the movie theater.

So with great expectations and a little more anxiety building in the back of her brain, Jess leaned forward discretely once again. She began bouncing her booty on Josh's lap with even more enthusiasm than before as she pleasured herself, fingers moving faster than ever.

It took all of her mental fortitude to not cum right then and there. Somehow, she kept bouncing her ass on Josh's big hard dick, up and down, side to side. She tightened her pussy as she rode his pole. It was all she could do to not let herself cum from one moment to the next. *But soon... it has to be soon.*

The movie seemed to stretch, but focusing on something so completely un-sexy helped her stave off her own orgasm a little bit longer.

He has to be close, though... right? Wait. How am I going to hide an orgasm this fucking big?

Just as Jess began to ponder than question, she felt a light tap on her left should. It made her jump as she pictured a theater employee behind her waiting to throw them out. Then she remembered what she told Josh.

He was ready to cum. And so was she.

Jess threw caution into the wind. She firmly gripped the top of the seat in front of her, arched her back, and began shaking her hips, gyrating on her boyfriend's dick as fast and aggressively as she was physically able. To her own surprise,

Jess was able to remain mostly silent while fucking the shit out of Josh in the theater.

But even in the dark and crowded movie theater, the wet sounds of skin on skin do not go unnoticed. Josh had unfortunately decided to cum during a stretch of the movie that involved a long, dramatic, and silent pause.

Although they didn't make a sound, Jess thought she might as well have been screaming like a porn star the way that people were all looking at them. Yet, with all of the attention they were getting, Jess realized that their window was closing soon.

Jess shut her eyes to concentrate. She felt Josh's big cock throb inside of her and knew that in moments he would begin to fill her little pussy full of hot cum. Then, as his semen dripped out of the cunt and onto the theater floor, even Josh would start to go soft for a short time. This was their only shot. And she was still nowhere near orgasm.

Josh and her were typically so in sync, but that was when they didn't have to censor themselves, when they had incredible sex in the privacy of their bed. And their couch. And the kitchen table. And countertops. Or the floor. So pretty much every inch of their house.

With her eyes shut tight, Jess just continued to bounce her ass on Josh's dick, grinding him while she furiously rubbed her clit.

It's only us, Jess thought. *Just me and him. No one else matters. It's just us. Holy fuck, his big cock feels so fucking good inside of me. Oh my God, he's cumming inside of me right now. So warm and... ah, oh my God, I'm going to cum!*

As Josh started to cum hard inside of Jess's pussy, and while she began to cum hard all over his dick, everyone in the movie theater turned to watch them.

Waves of ecstasy shot through her. She froze. The muscles in her legs started twitching. Jess gasped for air. She opened her eyes, only to see dozens of eyes staring back at her. That cut her orgasm short.

Jess couldn't help but feel like she was cheated out on what could have been one of the best orgasms of her life up to that point.

The only thing she could think was *fuck, if they were all going to watch me anyway, I shouldn't have held back. We could have given them a real show.*

Their joint orgasm lasted nearly 30 seconds, but with a room full of eyes on them it seemed like 30 shameful, excruciating minutes – after which, every person in the theater started to cheer.

Josh quickly tucked his dick back into his pants, then stood up and gave a bow. Jess's face lit up in a shade of bright red, though no one in the dark theater could see her blush.

She pulled her dress down to cover her pussy and pushed past Josh towards the exit. As she did, she could feel his cum between her thighs. Jess used to love the feeling of walking around in public with her boyfriend's fresh cum dripping from her pussy. Now it just made her embarrassed.

It's only you and me. No one else matters.

She wanted to run out of there, but she was a lady and would not give them the satisfaction. So she pushed past the people sitting in the same row as her and Josh as they clapped and whispered about them.

"What a show."

"God, she's hot."

"Hey. You're so fucking awesome."

Jess looked up as she shimmied past the three people on the way to the theater exit. They were all women.

"E-excuse me?" Jess said softly when she made it to the aisle.

"I wish my boyfriend had the balls to do what you guys did. Maybe he would, if I were a pretty as you."

She was younger than Jess, but not by much. A gorgeous young blonde woman with short, curly hair. She could have been a model.

"What? But you're, like, so beautiful!" the words were simply Jess's reaction.

"You really think so?" the blond replied.

Another gorgeous blond woman who could have been related to the one she sat next to approached Jess.

"That was *so* hot! Are you, like, a famous porn star?"

"Excuse me!?"

"Time to go, babe!" Josh quickly caught up Jess and rescued her by leading her by the hand over to the theater emergency exit.

This was definitely one of those things that could be filed under "laugh about it later". And they did laugh about it on the entire drive home.

The first thing they did upon arriving back at the house – even before Jess got a chance to wash all of the cum out of her pussy – was to put a big, red "X" through "Parking Lot" and "Movie Theater" on the Exhibitionist Bingo card.

CHAPTER 8

Day 3 - Home

It wasn't until the following morning that Jess and Josh were getting in the shower that the Bingo card came up. Typically, the first one to get up in the morning was always Jess. She was already in the shower and trying to achieve the perfect water temperature equilibrium when Josh entered large master bathroom adjoined to their bedroom.

"Morning, baby." Jess said as sunny and bright as the morning sunrise.

She twisted the hot water dial up a fraction and put her hands underneath the water, waiting for it to adjust.

"Morning." It was more of a mumble than a greeting.

Josh's eyes were still half closed when we stumbled over to the toilet, lifted the seat and let loose a powerful stream.

Josh never considered himself a morning person. It took him a while to build up steam so he could get his day going. He enjoyed sleeping late, and although Jess would let him on days that they could afford the luxury of sitting in bed all day, she often had to physically drag him out of bed.

Jess fell on the complete opposite side of the spectrum. She identified as a morning person her entire life and would often greet the day by literally catapulting out of bed. Her chronotype and circadian rhythm couldn't have been more different than Josh's.

Jess was a lioness, rising with the morning sun and preparing to hunt her prey while at her peak in the a.m. hours. Josh was a wolf, who enjoyed hunting by night and got some of his best work done after the sun went down and the moon was out.

And yet, they not only co-existed. They were so perfectly in sync in virtually every other aspect of life that they effortlessly achieved their domestic bliss – a loving relationship that would make any therapist green with envy.

Josh and Jess enjoyed and celebrated their quirky differences in each other's personalities. Instead of merely tolerating their differences like most couples they knew, lovingly embracing them was how they deepened their love for one another.

Having incredible sex regularly also helped.

Jess gave him a devilish smile as she finished adjusting the temperature of the water until it was perfect. Josh returned a sleepy smile as he finished pissing, gave it a shake or two, then placed the toilet seat down and flushed the toilet.

Because the couple always went to sleep completely naked, jumping in the shower together first thing in the morning was part of their routine.

Josh slid open the glass shower door and stepped inside straight away. It was just the thing he needed to help wake him up, and though the thought of turning the cold water all the way up did cross Jess's mischievous mind, she didn't want to ruin her perfect water temperature equilibrium. Instead, she stepped in beside him and began to lather her body with soap and a pink body scrubber.

Their limestone shower was spacious and enough for more than two people to occupy at once, although they had yet to test this feature. Jess stood in the back to make room for Josh, who basked underneath the downpour of warm water. Josh closed his eyes as water trickled off of his corded muscled and down his sculped abs.

"Ahhh," he let out a relaxed sigh as steam rose in the shower.

Every inch of Jess's body was covered in soapy white suds save for her face. She thoughtfully brought the pink scrubber up her inner thigh, toned stomach, and circled around her large natural breasts until her tiny pink nipples hardened. Her wet skin prickled with thoughts of last night as she tried to remember the feeling of Josh's cum inside of her after fucking him in a public movie theater for hours.

She palmed her breast with her free hand while soaping the other with the scrubber. Josh's back was turned away from her. Her free hand slid down the front of her lean stomach, gliding over the lathered soap and down between her legs. She couldn't resist touching herself with fingers slick with soapy. Her skin warmed at the thought of last night.

God, why am I always so horny in the morning?

She needed a distraction.

"I've been thinking about some of those BINGO locations." She said at last.

Josh's head perked up from underneath the shower. He spun around to face her. "Really? I've been fantasizing a lot about them, too."

"No, not like that. I mean, yes, I have been doing a lot of that, too. But I mean how we can get away with some of these. Get my back?"

Jess handed him her pink body scrubber and turned around. He started lathering her backside the same way she did. He started with her calves and quickly worked up to her thighs before focusing on her big, bubbly butt. Jess gathered her wet, black hair together and pulled it over her shoulder and out of Josh's way so he could get her back. But Josh had other plans.

"Get my back."

"Hold on, let me rub this in really good." He said, ditching the body scrub and lathering her ass with both hands.

Jess giggled. "Josh! Really, now, get my back."

"I am. What's the plan?"

"The plan is you wash my back."

"What's in it for me?"

"You get to feel what it's like to be a thoughtful boyfriend."

"Been there, done than."

"Josh! You can play with my ass later."

"Bet. So, what's the plan?" He picked up the pink body scrubber and began lathering Jess's back. "I mean, we go to each location, we hump, we dip. I'd say the strategy is working pretty well so far."

Josh reached underneath Jess's arms to grab a fist full of her breasts, but she quickly spun around and slapped his hand.

"Move. I need to rinse."

The two switched places. Jess stood underneath the steamy shower, thoughtfully rinsing until every part of her naked body glistened from the water covering every curve of her wet skin.

Josh was in the back of the shower. He grabbed a bar of Irish Spring soap and started scrubbing his washboard abs, his bulky biceps, tree trunk legs, and barrel chest.

Jess looked her naked boyfriend up and down. As good as he looked without clothes on, he typically looked just like a normal, everyday 6' 2" guy off the street. Jess's friends often referred to Josh as her "secretly super hot" boyfriend. But Jess knew in her heart that she would love him even without all of his statuesque muscles. Or his chiseled handsome face. Or his ridiculous donkey dick. She would be in love with this man no matter what.

As long as his dick worked and he still choked her during sex, she would love him no matter what.

"I have to admit, this is actually a lot harder than I thought."

Josh looked down, then looked at Jess and frowned.

"No, I'm talking about the Bingo locations, sweetie. I want to do all of the hardest ones last." Jess was trying to angle her body so the shower water rinsed the soap from her breasts.

"We can do them in any order you want, babe." Josh was still scrubbing his thighs, butt, and penis. *Very* thoroughly.

"Okay. Good. Also, it seems to me that we can conquer most of these places just by fucking in the bathroom." Jess said while pushing her tits up underneath the water, doing her best to get a rise out of her boyfriend.

"You're kidding." Josh said while he continued "washing" his dick.

"Hear me out. Bars, gyms, nightclubs, even beaches all have bathrooms. If we just fuck in a bunch of bathrooms, we can bang out everything in, like, a week or two."

Josh folded his arms and sighed deeply. "That's not exactly the point, though, is it?"

"What do you mean?"

"I told you, that's cheating, babe. The whole point of Exhibitionist Bingo and being able to confidently cross out each square is finding a way to creatively get down in and every location on the Bingo card. It's not enough to technically fulfill the requirements enough to cross out a square. Babe, it's about the *stories*. The *memories*. The excitement that we might actually get caught.

Besides, do you *really* want to have sex in all of those filthy bathrooms? Wasn't Taco Bell enough? Hey, I need to rinse."

Jess stepped to the side as Josh took her place underneath the shower, letting the warm water rinse the soap off his body.

"I guess you're right. And to think I had to convince you to do this with me."

Josh laughed. "Trust me, it didn't take much convincing."

"But that was my plan big for a lot of these places." Jess said, crestfallen.

"Tell you what," Josh said, washing the last of the soap off his chest, shoulders, and biceps. "If it makes you feel better, we can practice having sex in the bathroom right now."

Her face brightened. Jess knew he was just teasing, but she considered his offer for a moment.

When a playful smile appeared on her face, Josh knew he was in trouble.

"I want you to fuck me on the balcony." She said with a brilliant grin.

Josh was letting the water fall over his face. "The balcony? *Our* balcony?"

She nodded, though Josh's eyes were closed and facing the shower. "It's the easiest one on the Bingo card! Honestly, I'm surprised we've waited this long to do it there."

"We've had sex on our balcony countless times. We had sex on that balcony last week!"

"Not since we got the card!"

"You want to have sex on the balcony right now? In broad daylight? While people are out going to work?" He asked, incredulous.

She folded her arms underneath her breasts, putting her weight on one foot. This time, Josh saw her reaction and knew he was in even more trouble.

"I think that was clear. And weren't you just talking about making memories?"

"Going to jail is not a memory I want to make!"

Jess sniffed around the shower like she just smelt something bad. "I think you need another shower, babe, because I smell a pussy." She jabbed a finger into his chest.

Josh put his hands up in surrender. "Alright, alright. I'm into it. I just hope you realize that there are going to be a lot of people out there right now."

Jess pushed passed Josh so she could step out of the shower. Dripping wet, she grabbed a fluffy white towel and wrapped it around her naked body.

"I'm counting on it!" She gave Josh a wink, turned on her heel and ran out of the bathroom with an excited spring in her step.

Josh chuckled to himself, turned off the water, and got out of the shower.

"This should be interesting."

He didn't bother drying off and followed Jess out the door stark naked and wet.

CHAPTER 9

Day 3 – Balcony

It was a windy Wednesday morning and the city of Los Angeles was still waking up. Cars zipped by the busy street their balcony overlooked. Neighbors were out walking their dogs. Gardeners were already up and out and hard at work.

Jess threw open the sliding glass door to their balcony overlooking their front yard and filled her lungs with crisp, cool morning air. Or, as it's known in Los Angeles, smog.

Wearing only a white towel that stretched from her chest to her upper thighs, she flipped her dripping wet hair to one side and took a seat on one of the wicker chairs on their balcony. She kicked her feet up on the wicker ottoman while she waited for Josh.

The sun felt amazing on her freshly scrubbed skin. Droplets of water from her wet hair rolled her cheeks, glistening in the sunlight. The wiggled her feet, feeling the cool air on her toes. *Why aren't I always out here after a shower in the morning?*

When Josh finally stepped out onto the balcony, Jess was a little surprised to see him wearing clothes.

"Josh, did you forget how to have sex, baby? It's easier without clothes on, you know."

He was wearing blue jeans and a simple white cotton tee that clung to his still-wet chest. Like jess, his hair was still wet with water droplets falling on his face and shirt.

"I can still fuck you silly with my jeans on." He said and took a seat on the wicker chair next to Jess. He leaned back, putting his hands behind his head and kicked his feet up on the same ottoman as Jess, then smiled a cocky smile.

Jess looked him up and down.

"Promises, promises."

She returned the smile, then they both laughed playfully.

"Well?" Jess raised an eyebrow.

Josh gave her a puzzled look. Frustrating man.

"I didn't come out here to work on my tan, babe. Whip it out."

"I..."

Jess lowered her head and looked up at him menacingly. "Are you going to make good on your promise to fuck me silly or what?"

Josh unzipped his jeans and pulled them down just enough to reveal his flaccid penis.

Jess heaved a sigh. "Do I have to do everything around here?"

"Yes. Yes, you do." He put his hands back behind his head and leaned back. *This frustrating man.* She thought, but she knew he had her pinned.

Jess motioned for him to take his feet off the ottoman. Her first thought was to suck his cock until it was hard enough to ride, then she thought better of it. *That's exactly what he wants.*

"Hold on, I have an idea."

"Should I be scared?" He said facetiously.

"More like you should feel lucky that your girlfriend is as hot as all this."

Jess pulled off her towel and hung it on the arm of the wicker chair, then sat down on Josh's lap facing him. She reasoned that all she would need to do to get him hard was press her wet, naked body up against him.

And she was right.

The look in Josh's face was one of genuine surprise. She could tell he wanted to say something the way his jaw just dangled mid-air, but she had rendered him speechless.

She was sure that he was about to call her crazy or tell her to cover up or remind her of all the people out there who could see them right now, like their neighbor from across the street who right at that very moment happened to be walking his Yorkshire terrier right in front of their house who made eye contact with Josh.

He wanted to remind her of the dangers of exhibitionism and of having sex in public, not only to their reputation in the community and with their neighbors but the larger risk of having someone call the cops on them and going to jail. Josh considered the worst case scenario of flaunting their most intimate experiences in public and the very real possibility that they could both end up on a sex offender registry, and how having to register as a sex offender would bring ruinous disaster and despair to their happy, love-filled lives, the likes of which they could not fathom.

He thought about all of these things and how they were all very good reasons why he would not recommend anyone having sex in public without first considering all of the serious risks. He was not an ignorant person by any means. Both Josh and Jess knew about and accepted the risks.

Along with the risks and the danger came a certain thrill. A rush of adrenaline that hinged on the fact that they might actually get caught. That strangers could be watching them have sex. And that other people were turned on by watching them have sex only added to the twisted eroticism. The possibility that other people might be see them in their most intimate, vulnerable of moments was a turn on.

Josh didn't understand why it was such a turn on, but he did understand the release of adrenaline and dopamine and serotonin and oxytocin and all of the other feel-good chemicals involved.

And the release of semen. That, he understood very well.

Instantly, Josh understood the appeal of exhibitionism. And Josh wanted to tell Jess all of this. He wanted to tell her about the entire epiphany he just had, but he never got the chance.

Before he could even get the first word out, Jess pushed her big tits in his mouth.

Josh rolled with it, taking her cue and started sucking on her perfect little nipples. He felt them stiffen in his mouth as he rolled his tongue off of them, nibbling playfully.

Josh's mouth on her felt tantalizingly good. Like little sparks of electricity through her body. Jess threw her head back, making sure her wet hair slung behind her. She stabled herself by bracing her hands on Josh's broad shoulder, then started grinding her hips up and down his lap. As Jess dragged her wet slit over his cock and balls, she could feel him getting harder underneath her.

Jess did her best impression of a stripper giving a lap dance. Although she had never been to a strip club in her life, she had seen Hustlers enough times to get the general idea.

The fact that there was no music didn't stop her. Jess figured she was doing a pretty good job so far. Her boyfriend's massive erection was proof of that. So she continued to grind her hip across Josh's abdomen, tracing his hard cock with her slit.

The feeling of Josh's tongue aggressively licking and sucking her nipples was getting her so wet that she might as well have been washing his dick with the outside of her pussy. Jess paused when her clit stroked the engorged tip of his cock.

"Ooh." Jess said in surprise. "I think I just found something new I like."

She repeated the action again and again, brushing her clit up against the head of Josh's dick rhythmically.

"Hmm." Josh replied with a mouth full of titty.

"What was that, babe?" Jess arched her back and pulled her nipple out of Josh's mouth with an audible *pop*, like pulling a pacifier from a baby's mouth.

"I th–"

Jess shoved her tongue in his mouth, kissing him deeply. The way she felt his cock throb and flex beneath her, she reckoned he didn't mind being interrupted like that. Jess didn't think it was possible, but she could feel his dick grow bigger still.

"Mmm." Jess moaned into Josh's mouth as she ran her fingers through the back of his hair.

She tilted her hips so that her clit rubbed up along his hardness. When she could stand it no longer, she leaned forward to slip the tip of his cock inside of her. She was so wet that it effortlessly found its target.

"Oh, yeah." She sighed, looking back over her shoulder to admire her ass and the long length of dick left untaken. "Oh my God. Did I ever tell you that your dick might be *too* big?"

Jess rocked back and forth on his hard cock, sliding down just a little bit more each time. *Fuck, I can feel every inch inside of me.*

"You said th–"

Jess shoved her boobs back in Josh's mouth.

"Sh, sh, sh. No talking. Lick mama's titties."

He started aggressively sucking, licking, and playfully nibbling on her breasts, going back and forth between one and the other. Just before one started getting sore, she grabbed her other boob and attacked it with his mouth.

Jess loved it when her boyfriend played with her tits, and this was the most pleasure she could have expected from him. It was the perfect amount of roughness that she enjoyed – and she didn't even have to tell him what to do. Josh just knew. She loved that.

"Ho-ooh my *God!* Ooh, I like that." Jess's eyes rolled to the back of her head. "Okay, now fuck me."

She had time to run her fingers through his thick sandy blond hair before he raised his hips, plunging the full length of his cock inside of her. Jess froze, breathless, with her mouth wide open.

Jess was such a petite young woman, and Josh had a monstrously big by comparison, which was the way she liked it. Though it was always a shock to the system when she took every inch of his dick all at once. Plus, it always seemed like her pussy was at its smallest when she first woke up. Painful, sometimes, but *never* in a bad way.

Besides, Jess thought, *the hard part is getting my mouth around that thing.*

Josh mouthed her tits, holding them in place so they didn't bounce while he fucked her hard and fast from underneath her. Jess recovered her senses and began to move in sync with Josh's movements.

"Fuck," Josh looked up at his girlfriend as her tits bounced in his face. "You feel so g–"

Jess pulled his head back by his hair and pushed her tongue past his lips in a rough kiss. She bit his lip as she pulled back.

"Ow!"

"No talking. Now lay still, baby. I want to ride your dick."

Josh stopped thrusting his hips upward long enough for Jess to straighten her back and adjust her footing on either side of his legs. She rested her hands atop Josh shoulders for balance once more as he leaned forward in his chair so he could suck on Jess's tits.

Suddenly she felt chills shake her entire body.

"Ooh, God, I love it when you do that. Mmm, babe, you're going to make me cum just sucking on my titties." She said jokingly.

"Mm-hmm." Josh said as he flicked the tip of his tongue back and forth over the tip of her small, hard nipples.

Honestly, she wasn't sure if he could *actually* make her cum with just his mouth on her breasts. But Jess had *very* sensitive nipples, and she was happy that Josh took full advantage of that knowledge.

She sat there for a few seconds just basking in the moment of bliss.

Then she remembered she had a dick inside her.

Jess started shaking her ass up and down wildly on Josh's cock, riding his pole from base to tip. She looked over her shoulder to watch her booty clap while she twerked faster and faster, making the full length of his cock disappear inside of her like a magician. *Well, I've been told my pussy is magic.*

The real magic was that she managed to ride his dick this long and not cum immediately.

Their flesh clapped loudly in the morning breeze. Josh grabbed her by the waist, lifting her up and slamming her back down onto his dick. Each time he forced Jess's ass down to his thighs, he drove his massive cock deep in her pussy. The impact felt so fucking good that each smack of flesh on flesh brought her more pleasure and closer to orgasm.

She let go and gave him full control over her body. The way that Josh was able to effortless lift her up made her feel weightless, like a tiny fuck toy made for his pleasure. The way that Josh made her feel turned her on without fail.

His powerful hands lifted her up to the heavens, where her pussy straddled the very tip of his cock, nearly popping out of her pussy each time – but not quite. Then he forcefully pulled her back down to the earth, using all of his strength to pull her close to him while his big dick pounded her pussy.

Each time was harder than the last.

Every thrust went deeper.

He started fucking her faster and faster.

Jess felt herself lose all of her inhibitions as she heard herself panting and moaning breathlessly. Now Josh was the one doing all of the work, but here she was, completely breathless.

Oh. My. God. It. Feels. So. Good.

She felt the compulsion to kiss Josh, but Jess's brain shut down. She couldn't breathe. She couldn't speak. She couldn't think. All she could do was focus on the feeling of Josh's tongue playing with her nipples and his dick fucking her silly.

Pop.

Josh pulled her boob out of his mouth and leaned all the way back in the wicker chair. She felt a powerful arm cuff around her back and pull her chest flush against him. Jess was confused at first, but with her brain sex-scrambled, she was content to let him use her as his little fuck toy and go with the flow.

He held her down tight and started thrusting his hips up, fucking her quick as a rabbit, jackhammering her from below. Her breasts were squished up against Josh's solid chest. She could still feel a pleasant tingling from her hard nipples.

Her head was beside his, mouth hanging open, making incomprehensible sex noises she had never heard herself make before. Her lips formed the beginnings of words, but they all ended in a deep inhalation of air midway through.

"Oh fuh! Oh mah! Guh! Ooh fuh! Gah! Hah! Shiii!"

Jess was pretty sure she was drooling, but didn't care.

Josh had fucked her brains all the way out of service.

Josh tilted his head to her ear. "I want to cum inside of you while you cum on my dick at the same time." And then nibbled on her earlobe.

Sometimes, all you need is a little dirty talk to push you over the edge. And sometimes, a little nibble on the earlobe will have the same effect. Jess felt a climax steadily building, like filling a bathtub full of water, and now it was about ready to completely submerge her.

Josh never relented, fucking her harder and faster still. He bit her earlobe once more.

"I'm going to fuck your brains out and then fill your tight little pussy so full of my fucking cum that you'll taste it in the back of your throat for days. Then I'm going to fill your throat so full of cum until it replaces the brain that I fucked out of you and starts leaking out your ears. And I won't stop until every inch of you in covered in my cum from the inside out.

But first, be a good girl and let Daddy feel your cum all over his dick. And don't stop until you can feel your own cum dripping down your thighs."

Holy shit.

She felt a wave of release throughout her entire body as her pussy began to convulse and twitch around Josh's dick. She could feel it throb inside of her, and then a warm, wet sensation. Josh squeezed her ass as he continued to drive his cock inside of her, each thrust delivering more of his hot load.

"ohgodohgodohgodohgod." Jess screamed.

The powerful orgasm was almost too intense for her.

Jess kissed Josh as he slowed down but kept going. Josh's grinding from below just felt too good and she was too sensitive. She slapped his hands away so she could slide up and down his dick at her own pace, surprised that she was still cumming and Josh was still hard.

Everything felt warm and wet and squishy now. She felt dopey and warm with a wide grin plastered on her face. This was similar to how she felt after smoking a ton of weed.

Jess hooked her hands around his neck while she slowly bounced up and down on his dick at the same pace as their heart rates.

Two hearts, beating in sync.

Jess's legs continued to spasm long after it was over, making it impossible to stand up or even move. Still, she didn't want to get up off of his still-hard dick just yet. She didn't want this moment of post-coital bliss to end. It was moments like this when she felt that all was right in the world.

I could sit out here and ride his dick forever.

If only.

A car in front of their house started blasting its horn long and loud, sending Jess crashing back into reality. It was so sudden and scared Jess so much that she jumped up off of her boyfriend and on her feet.

It literally scared the dick out of her.

As soon as the driver saw that Jess had noticed him, he sped away. But not before the naked, cum-soaked woman on the balcony offered him two middle fingers as a parting gift.

When Jess stood up, a trail of cum still connected her pussy to Josh, like thick, white spider webs. She felt a warm, wet sensation on her inner thighs, so she spread her legs to get a better inspection.

"Hoooly fuck. Babe, you actually made me cum so much it's literally all dripping out of my pussy." She spread her glistening pussy lips so he could get a better look. "See?"

Indeed, a glob of white goo was running down her thigh.

"I think most of that is mine, sweetie."

"Are you sure? You made me cum, like, *really* hard!" Her eyes rolled to the back of her head. "Like, I can't remember the last time I came that hard."

"Trust me. I know what my own cum looks like on your body."

She wiped up the cum running down her thighs with two fingers, then stuck them in her mouth. "Mm. No. You're right. It's yours." She scooped up another dallop of Josh's semen on her leg and licked it off her fingers.

Josh handed her the white towel draped on the arm of the wicker chair. Jess took it from him and made a pouty face.

"Does this mean I need to shower again?"

"Yes. I don't want you known as a load hugger at work."

Before she went back inside the house, Jess took one long last look over their balcony. It was such a beautiful morning in L.A. though the city was buzzing with activity, the only one staring at her named body was their neighbor across the street who was pretending to water his lawn.

Jess smiled and waved at him. He pretended not to see her, looking down at the grass he had watered so much it could have been classified as a marshland. When he looked up again to see if Jess was still looking at him, she blew him a kiss before going back inside the house.

She had just enough time for a business-only shower before work.

CHAPTER 10

Day 3 - Office

"Jess. Jess. Jess. Jessica. JESS!"

Jess looked up from her desk at her co-worker, Ashley, standing above her clutching a stack of papers to her breast.

"Huh? Ashley? Did you call me?" Jess looked up and blinked with a blank expression on her face.

"Only about a million times. Jess, are you okay?"

"Me? I'm great. Tired, but great... Greatly tired?"

"You've been sitting there starring at the Festival Drip logo for almost an hour now."

Jess looked down at her desk and the company letterhead on the piece of paper in front of her. Then she looked back up at Ashley.

"Have I?"

"Yes!" Ashley laughed.

She pulled an empty rolling chair from the desk behind Jess's and sat down, setting her stack of papers on the corner of Jess's desk.

Ashley was a few years older than Jess, though she looked much younger. She was skinny as a rail, her tiny frame contributing to her youthful look. Ashley's subtle curves were the only thing that denoted objective maturity about the girl.

She wore a checkered skater-style skirt that fell just below her knees and a fitted V-neck long-sleeve top that looked like it was made out of the softest material known to man. Ashley had tiny, circular-rimmed metal glasses that sat on her little nub of a nose. She typically wore her plain brown hair pulled back in a ponytail.

Jess couldn't tell if Ashley always wore a lot of blush on her unnaturally high cheekbones or if she was blessed with rosy cheeks and a fair complexion, though she suspected it was the latter.

"What's up with you, girl? All this week, you've been walking around with your head in the clouds. Yet you're walking around the office, glowing and grinning like you just finished playing with a pile of puppies. Wait, did Josh finally pop the question?" she asked excitedly.

"What? No! Josh and I have no interest in getting married."

"Then what has you walking around in such a daze?"

Ashley's words were slow to register with Jess. She was still thinking about last night.

Is it that obvious?

Jess looked around the office to make sure that no one else was around to unexpectedly walk into their conversation. She really wanted to tell someone about her recent exploits. Although what was on her mind was almost certainly not office appropriate conversation, she felt like she just had to tell someone.

Jess picked up her phone, unlocked it, and cycled through her images. Ashley edged in next to her to get a good look.

"Oh, my goodness! Whose dick is that? I'd be walking around here giddy as a schoolgirl too if I had that in my life." Ashley said softly as a deep crimson blush spread across her face.

"Not what I wanted to show you. Sorry, I should have organized that into my 'Not Safe for Work' album."

"You have a whole Not Safe for Work *album?*" Ashley giggled nervously.

Jess ignored her as she continued searching on her phone. Ashley leaned in so that she could get a look at every single photo Jess thumbed through.

"Here." she said at last, holding her phone so that only Ashley could see.

Ashley stared at the photo on her phone long enough for her to start to worry that showing her co-worker was a big mistake. Though only a few seconds had passed, it seemed like an eternity of torture to Jess.

"Exhibitionist Bingo?" Ashley read from the photo on Jess's phone. "Jess, what on earth?" she started giggling nervously once again. "Why is library crossed out?"

Jess could feel her face match the red blush of Ashley's.

Ashley let out a little gasp and covered her mouth with her hand. "Wait, Jess, you didn't."

I knew this was a bad idea.

"Jess, this is... It's... This is..."

Disgusting. Perverted. Slutty. A fireable offense. Clean out your desk and leave at once, you vile whore. This is why I don't open up to co-workers.

"This is exactly what I've been looking for!"

A wave of relief visibly washed over Jess. But also, confusion.

"Freddie and I love doing games like this. You know, the ones you can buy at gift stores? We get them all online now, but after a while they're pretty much all the same. But I've never even heard of anything like this before! And... not to sound like a slut, but I've played all of the sex games out there... Jess, where did you find this?"

Jess told her the truth about the incident at the library, about how the Bingo card fell out of a book and she stuffed it in her dress. Ashley leaned in and hung on her every word, smiling lasciviously.

"Wow, so someone made this Bingo card and just stuck it in a book, like a bookmark?"

Jess shrugged. "I don't know. I thought that since it fell out of a book in the sex education section, it was part of one of the books."

Ashley shook her head. "It doesn't have bindings or tears on the sides, so it couldn't have been a part of the actual book."

Ashley double-tapped on the photo on Jess's phone to zoom in on the photo of the Bingo card.

"And look here. This wasn't printed. This was done entirely in pen. Jess, someone went through a lot of trouble making this by hand."

"Really? You can tell all of that just by looking at a picture?"

Ashley gave her a look. "Jess, what do you think I do here? I basically stare at documents all day long. And when I get home, I read all night. Unless Freddie and I are playing one of our games, which we haven't in quite a long time." Ashley looked around the office conspiratorially, switching to a low whisper. "Hey, do you think you can, like, send that to me?"

Ashley bit her bottom lip nervously while awaiting an answer.

"Of course, Ashley."

The two co-workers exchanged numbers and Jess sent her a picture of the Bingo card.

Jess liked Ashley well enough to form a rapport built on small talk over the last year or so that she had been working as a clothing designer at Festival Drip. But this was by far the longest and most intimate conversation that the two women had ever shared.

So, I guess now we're friends? That, or she is going to use this as evidence to file a sexual harassment complaint and get me fired. Definitely one or the other.

Ashley grinned at Jess, squinting her eyes as she smiled warmly.

"Let me know how it goes with Fredie," Jess said after she sent the photo.

"Oh, we'll have a Bingo before the end of the week," Ashley replied as she stared at the photo on her own phone.

That makes two of us, Jess thought.

CHAPTER 11

Day 3 – Josh's Work

"And the final action item for this month's meeting is our new romance author client. She needs four new book covers by the end of next month. She has specifically requested Josh be her cover designer for this project, and all projects going forward, so that will be your top priority, Josh.

"... Josh?"

Josh sat in the chair furthest in the back and to the left during their monthly meeting at the downtown L.A. creative talent agency. He stared at the lime green walls, mentally miles away, replaying the recent events between him and Jess on the balcony that morning.

Sitting in the chair next to him, Jon elbowed him. "Dude!"

Josh shot upright in his chair. "Yep. Yes, romance. Uh-huh."

Tasha, Josh's boss sitting at the head of the table, sighed. She put her fists on the table and pushed out of her chair, visibly frustrated.

"Josh, is this going to be a problem? We really need this author as a client and God knows why she keeps requesting you, but she does, so we need-"

"Four book covers this month. Yeah, Tasha, I got it. Thanks."

Her eyes narrowed at him. Josh was only half-present.

"Adjourned." She growled.

All of the chairs around the table shot backwards. Josh started on a hasty stride, trying to get out of the office before he had to interact with anyone.

"You, Josh! Hold up!" Jon chased him down, grabbing his elbow to get his attention. "What was that back there?"

"What? With the book covers?"

"I mean, that's not what I was talking about, but let's start there, yeah."

Josh sighed and shook his head, "That's a long story, buddy. Walk with me to my car. I don't want to get cornered into a conversation with Tasha."

Instead of taking the elevator to the parking garage like everyone else, Josh ducked into a stairwell with Jon closely in tow behind him.

"So, why would that romance author specifically request you by name at a talent agency that employees nameless freelancers?"

"You mean, Madeline? Yeah, she knows I work here."

Jon caught his shoulder as Josh was going down the next flight of stairs. Josh turned to face Jon.

"*Medeline*?" Jon repeated with a raised eyebrow, pronouncing every syllable. "Is there some sort of history between the two of you?"

Josh rolled his eyes. "It was a long time ago. She wasn't even an author back when we were dating."

Jon was taken aback. "*Dating*? Josh, I've known you since college. I've seen all of the women you brought back. I was your roommate in case you forgot. But in all of that time, I've never seen you with this *Madeline*."

"This was... after college."

"But still, you were banging a romance author and never told me?"

"I didn't know! She certainly didn't strike me as the author type. Beside, our encounter was very... brief."

"Brief? You mean, you were her booty call?"

Josh didn't say anything, but shook his head slightly.

"She was *your* booty call?" Jon said incredulously.

"I mean... sometimes."

"What?! Josh, you dirty dog! Did you take her on long walks on the beach? Romantic dinners? Be honest, how many times did you take her horseback riding?"

"It wasn't like that!"

"It must have been something like that, because whatever you did to her, now she's writing romance books about the two of you."

"This is why I didn't want to tell you."

"So, how does it feel to be the mean squeeze in some chic's boner book?"

"I'm not the... What? Stop that. Her books aren't about me. Just, like, some of the things that we did during the *very brief* time we were together."

"I knew it!"

"Somehow she found out that I'm a graphic designer and she just so happens to hire the talent agency I work at to specifically requests me to do her book covers? I don't know if she is trying to throw her fame in my face or if she hopes we're going to somehow get back together, but either way, I don't care."

"Right. In a relationship with a romance author. That sounds like... a lot. Well, what was the last conversation you had with her?"

"In person? I forget what was said, but I remember it ended with her spitting my cum into my face."

"Yikes. Why do women always do that? Wait, why did you say 'in person' like that?"

"She contacted me... recently."

"Not over Instagram."

Josh nodded sullenly. "I told her I was in a happy, committed relationship."

"And?"

Jon had known Josh for years and knew when he wasn't telling the whole story.

"And I think she may be internet stalking Jess."

"There is no way. She is a well-known author. She has better things to do with her time. And so what if she is? Isn't Jess into girls, too? Haven't the two of you had a threeway with another girl before?"

"I mean, a few times, but Jess always gets to pick the girls."

"So, introduce her to *Madeline*." He said her name in a sort of sing-song way.

"I *really* don't think that is a good idea."

"Yeah. Having a threesome with two insanely hot women is *always* a terrible idea, Josh. What was I thinking?" Jon said, dripping with sarcasm.

"Dude, why do you think I had to stop seeing her? She's a Stage 5 Clinger. Plus, now she's technically my boss."

"Na-uh. We're *freelancers*, remember?"

"Okay, well, she's paying the agency that is paying me to design four of her stupid book covers. Four!"

"Dude, chill. I can do two of them for you, no problemo."

"Really? You would do that for me?"

"Come on, bro, how long have you known me?" Jon seemed offended that he would even ask. "Besides, I'm pretty sure I have at least one book cover mockup that will fit the bill perfectly."

"Okay, cool, because I swear to God if I end up doing all four covers I would put, like, so many subliminal messages in them that it would get her canceled."

Jon laughed. "Yeah, it's no prob, bro. And all you have to do is introduce me to *Madeline*."

"I *knew* there would be a catch!"

"Would it kill you to throw your old friend a bone every now and again?"

"You married!"

"So? Just introduce me over IG and I'll slide into her DM's so smoothly that her next book is going to be all about *me*."

"Oh my God, you need therapy. Wait. No. Are you still banging your therapist? You need Jesus."

"Okay, now that we have that settled, are you going to tell me why you were spacing out during the meeting?"

Something flashed in Josh's eyes as they changed subjects. He was no longer thinking about all of the weird, kinky stuff that Madeline made him do. Now he was thinking about all of the weird, kinky stuff that Jess made him do.

"That's right. I didn't tell you, did I?"

"You don't tell me much of anything nowadays, it seems." Jon stood with his hands on his hips, tapping his foot impatiently.

Josh told Jon about the Bingo card that Jess found, about their exploits thus far and about how they were trying to complete every square on the Bingo card in just one week.

None of that seemed to make any sense to him until Josh pulled up the image of the Bingo card that Jess had sent him on his phone.

"Becha I can finish all of them before you."

The was about the reaction that Josh was expecting from his friend. As long as Josh had known Jon, he had been hyper-competitive. Especially when it came to women.

"You really think your wife would go for something like this?"

Jon laughed. "Oh, please. If I can talk her into getting breast implants, I can talk her into having sex at... what does that say? A church? Are you fucking kidding me?"

"I mean, if you don't think you can do it, that's okay. You two can just go for the straight BINGO. You only need to have sex five times! You can do five, can't you, buddy? But Jess and me? We're going to do *all* of the spaces on this card." Josh mercilessly taunted his friend.

"You're on! Whoever can complete *all* of the spaces on this Bingo card first wins." He extended his hand. "A gentleman's wager."

Josh took his hand and gave it a firm shake.

"A gentleman's wage."

"If you and your girlfriend think you can do all of these in seven days, my wife and I will do them in five."

"Yeah, yeah. Try not to sprang your dick too hard."

"And *when* I win, not only do you have to take all of my work load for the next month, you have to introduce me to Madeline. In person."

"No. Anything but that."

"Listen, my wife reads those trashy romance novels. I'm sure she knows who Madeline is. It would score me big points with her. Besides, if you're so confident that you'll win, what does it matter?"

"Fine. I'll do it for Isabel. And *when* I win, you and your wife have to come camping with Jess and I at the next big music festival. Jess has been bugging me to bring a friend along and she's dying to meet the two of you."

"Alright. Deal."

"A gentleman's wager." They said in unison.

CHAPTER 12

Day 3 - Park

Jess had only one thing on her mind that day, and it dominated every corner of her mind while at work.

How fucking hot was that morning balcony sex?

Even for Jess and Josh, who had pretty great sex on the regular, what they did on the balcony that morning was some of the best sex that Jess had ever had up to that point.

But there were still many spaces left to go on the Bingo card.

Could we really do all of them in just a week? Jess thought to herself. *That means we only have five more days, not counting today, which is almost over.*

When Jess got home from work that day, Josh was nowhere to be found.

"Hello? Babe? I'm home."

She set down her car keys then walked down the hallway and into his office.

"Josh? Are you here?"

Josh's office was unusually clean and uncharacteristically empty. She checked the bedroom next.

Nothing. Where could he be?

She walked over to the kitchen.

"Joshy?

No answer. Now she was concerned. Josh worked from their home office every weekday and was always there to greet Jess when she got back from work.

Except today, apparently.

She walked to the kitchen table where the Exhibitionist Bingo card sat. Next to it was a folded blue piece of construction paper. Jess took a step closer and say that her name was written on it. In Josh's handwriting.

Her heart started racing. Had Josh been kidnapped? Was this the ransom note? Jess scrambled to pick it up and started reading.

Jess,

I've prepared a surprise for you. Meet me at the park across the street as soon as you get home.

Love, your awesome boyfriend, Josh.

P.S. – Don't change beforehand. I'm sure you look beautiful.

She placed the note back down on the table. A smile curled her lips. He could have texted her, sure, but he left her a note. Jess found that irresistibly thoughtful and charming. *He really gets me.*

Without hesitation, she started walking towards the small park a short two block walk from their house. The city took relatively good care of the park. It sported basketball court, gazebo seating, rolling grassy hills encircled by a sidewalk skirt and a cookie cutter, standard fare playground set in a pool of sand. The latter Jess avoided at all costs.

As fond as she was of swing sets and slides, the thought of cleaning sand out of her heels made her cringe. She was still finding the occasional grain of sand in her Chuck Taylors from the time she wore them at the beach. Three years ago.

Jess was there in less than three minutes. The only problem was that Josh's note didn't say where in the park he would meet her. it was still about an hour until sundown and there were a few families lingering at the playground along with what looked like a fiercely competitive pickup basketball game.

Josh could be anywhere. She surveyed her options. If he was working on some sort of surprise then he would more than likely be waiting for her at the gazebo. *Josh is a lowkey romantic at heart and gazebos are the height of romance, after all.*

She walked up a steep hill punctuated with cypress trees on either side of the sidewalk. As Jess crest the hilltop she could see into the gazebo. The cement picnic benches underneath it were completely empty. Still, she continued upwards. Maybe once she got to higher ground she would be able to find him.

Jess reached the gazebo and climbed on top the concrete table to get a lay of the land. When she looked down at the entire park she saw that the families were starting to all leave now that it was getting dark out, though the basketball game was still raging on.

Josh was nowhere in sight. She was enjoying this game of hide-and-seek, but now she was getting a little frustrated. *Should I just call him?*

"You'll break your neck standing up there. Get down this instant!" Someone yelled from behind her, startling Jess so much that she jumped and lost her footing in the process.

The ball of Jess's foot landed on the edge of the table and she teetered, then screamed as she fell and shut her eyes tight.

She expected to land hard on the concrete ground underneath the gazebo. Instead, she felt two bulky arms catch her. Jess opened one eye and saw a familiar, handsome face smiling back at her.

She punched him square in the nose.

"Jerk!"

"Ow! My nose!" Josh cried.

"You scare me half to death! Literally, I was halfway to falling to my death."

"I mean, I don't think fall from a 4-foot table would have *killed* you."

"You just said I'd break my neck! Put me down!" Jess squirmed in his arms.

"Okay, okay, chill."

"Wait. Is your big surprise close by? Will you carry me?"

Josh laughed, hefting her in his arms and pulling her close to his chest. "That's probably for the best."

He was wearing a fresh button-up shirt, black slacks, and a matching coat that made him look dashing.

"Why did you tell me not to change when you dressed up? Babe, you look so good!" She said, pawing at his coat.

"Thanks. I thought that for once, maybe I could be the good-looking one in the relationship."

"Hey!"

He chuckled. "You know I'm kidding. Baby, you always look ridiculously beautiful."

"These are my work clothes!"

"You can make any outfit look sexy."

"Aww. No cap?"

He nodded. "No cap."

She gave him a quick kiss on the lips. Josh carried his girlfriend up a grassy hill away from the sidewalk path. Jess was content to just be held by her boyfriend, kicking her feet contently in his arms.

She couldn't stop smiling. It really was a beautiful day. Funny how she only noticed that when she was with Josh.

"I have a surprise for you, my love." He said, walking with her up the steep hill.

Duh, she wanted to say but stayed her tongue. *I got your stupid, cute note.*

"I've been thinking." He started.

Uh oh.

"This morning was so hot, and I wanted to follow that up with a very romantic evening. So, I prepared us a picnic in the park."

As they reached the top of the hill, Jess saw a large blanket laid out, held down by four rocks on each corner so the wind wouldn't blow it away. In the center of the blanket was a bottle of red wine and wicker picnic basket that Jess had never seen before. *Did he run out and buy all this?*

The view from the spot Josh had picked out was quite remarkable and easily one of the best views the park offered. From their spot atop the hill, Jess could see the entire downtown L.A. skyline of high rises and skyscrapers. Vibrant green rolling hills blanketed the area all around them at the small, quiet park where the couple sat.

Jess gasped audibly at the rare sight of lush greenery in L.A., where the heat from intense summers typically kills all vegetation. There was only about one month out of the year in early Spring where plants and trees thrived before inevitably succumbing to the heat and wildfires Southern California was known for and turning a lifeless shade of brown.

Jess clutched one hand to her breast as she took it all in. It certainly was a picturesque sight to behold. The rolling green hillsides always reminded Jess of the castle in Super Wario World.

"Oh, wow, Josh. This is beautiful." She clasped her hand to the side of his face and gave him a gentle kiss. "And very romantic."

Josh grinned at her handsomely. Josh carried Jess over to where the picnic blanket was laid out and carefully set her down in the middle, next to the basket and wine. Then he sat down beside her and began removing items from the basket.

Jess took in the gorgeous view once more. Although it was a beautifully sunny day out, sitting on top of the hillside left them vulnerable to the wind. Powerful gales bombarded their picnic, threatening to uproot the blanket Josh had weighed down with rocks.

When she turned back to face Josh, she saw the incredible spread he had pulled from the picnic basket. Laid out across the blanket on paper plates was a loaf of French bread that looked fresh from the oven, a small block of sharp cheddar (her favorite), pre-cut fresh fruit including watermelon, pineapple, and red grapes (also her favorite), and to Jess's delight, a jar of peanut butter and strawberry jelly.

After laying out the platter of food, Josh uncorked a bottle of wine. Jess caught a glimpse of the label out of the corner of his eye. It was an old-ish vintage of shiraz – her favorite wine.

She spotted two plastic wine glasses peaking out of the picnic basket and grabbed them just as Josh finished opening the bottle of wine with a satisfying *pop*. She smiled at him amorously, holding out the glasses as Josh filled them both halfway, then took one out of her hands.

Josh held his glass high into the air. The sun shined brightly through the crimson spirit, illuminating their glasses. Jess joined him, raising her glass to his. The plastic cups did not make *clink* as they toasted, but rather a dull *thunk*.

"To the smartest, most beautiful, funniest woman that I have ever had the pleasure of laying my eyes upon. Not a day goes by that I don't think about how lucky I am to have your love in this journey through life, and every day, my love for you grows impossibly deeper.

I know that no matter what adventures await us in the future, our love will protect us. Always."

"Cheers." Jess's voice cracked as she began to tear up. She downed her wine in one big gulp, trying to force down the lump in her throat.

Her boyfriend's sweet, honest, and deeply romantic words moved her to tears. What he said echoed precisely the way that she felt about him, although she would never be able to put it into such eloquent words the way that he did. Josh had always been good at that sort of thing – words and talking and all that bullshit – and she felt lucky to have him because of it.

Still, she felt like she should say *something*.

Josh refilled her glass with the sweet-tasting shiraz. She gulped down her second glass and he refilled her third without a word. She could chug the entire bottle by herself if she wanted to and he wouldn't judge her for it. *Hell, he's probably stashed a second bottle around here somewhere. Stupid perfect boyfriend.*

"Cheers."

There was a silence between them while they just sipped their wine and listen to the wind.

"Babe, you're awfully quiet. And it's making me nervous." Josh said at last.

Jess swallowed the rest of her wine trying to get the lump in her throat down. She didn't know if her words would fail her or not.

"I'm sorry." As hard as she tried to fight them, the tears came anyway.

"All of this is just so beautiful, Josh. It's thoughtful and romantic and just so... So beautiful." She wiped her years on the back of her hand. "You did good." She cooked back another soon. "You did really good."

He smiled a sort of sad smile, happy that she liked it, obviously not so much that she was crying. He pulled a cloth napkin from the picnic basket and handed it to her.

"Thank you." Jess dabbed her eyes and did her best to regain her composure.

"Would a peanut butter and jelly sandwich dry those tears?"

She chuckled. "Yeah, actually, I think it might."

As Josh removed the cutlery from the basket and went to work on the sandwiches, Jess took in more of the scenery. From their vantage point on the hill, they couldn't see much of the rest of the park. This is probably one of the reasons Josh chose the location, aside from the sprawling green hillside and distant cityscape, the spot looked very secluded.

Josh looked up from putting the finishing touches on the sandwiches when he heard Jess gasp.

"What if it?" Josh brandished the butter knife he used to spread the jelly like a weapon to fend off any would be attackers who might dare to spoil an otherwise perfect picnic.

"Look!" Jess pointed to the downtown L.A. skyline on the horizon.

The sun was setting behind the city, illuminating all of the buildings and skyscrapers in a gorgeous explosion of yellow, orange, and pink. The scattered clouds that hung just over the city and foothills below lit up like the heavens themselves were opening up. The entire horizon looked like a picturesque painting that belonged in the Getty Museum.

"Josh, this is incredible." She gushed. Jess held her hand gently against his cheek. "You're incredible."

"The sunset is boring compared to your smile."

She knew it was cheesy. She knew it was something she expected to see in a greeting card. But after everything that just happened - the perfect picnic and one romantic gesture after another - his words made her melt.

Jess whispered in his ear, "Come over here and kiss me before I tackle you."

He held up the jelly-covered knife. "What about sandwiches?" He said with one raised eyebrow.

"They can wait." Hey voice was husky with desire.

She took the knife from his hand and threw it down the hill into the grass, then grabbed a fistful of his shirt and pulled him on top of her.

She wanted him more than she had ever wanted anything in her entire life. She wanted to taste his mouth on hers. She wanted to feel his powerful body pressed up against her. She wanted to be filled with his love as they watched the sun set over the city.

Jess wanted romance fulfilled.

Josh may have had time to dress up like a dapper gentleman ready to woo a young lady, but Jess looked quite the opposite. Having just come from work, she still wore her basic black stretchy pants that cling to her every curve, along with a dark green tank top. Anyone who sat her enter the park earlier would have guessed her for a jogger.

She had her hair tied in a tight pony tail, but undid it so she could feel the wind in her hair from atop the hill. Despite her long dark hair sometimes whipping her in the face.

Jess typically only wore makeup for special occasions, however, she wished she was wearing some now.

She did not feel sexy.

That was another reason that Josh's romantic gesture had hit her so hard. He always had a way of making her feel beautiful, even when she doubted it herself.

When Jess pulled Joshed on top of her, he quickly removed his sports coat so it wouldn't rip and delicately cast it aside. Their hands were all over one another, pawing at each other lovingly. They traded delicious little moans of excitement in each other's mouths as their tongues allow danced at sunset, biting, sucking, teasing, tasting.

Jess ran one hand down Josh's built bicep while the other she held to his heart. She could feel his heart rate quickening with each kiss.

His lips caressed her neck with little sucking kisses that made her shudder. Jess pushed back against his chest, then slipped her hand underneath his shirt and ran her fingers up and down his stomach, feeling each individual muscle on his chest and abs.

Then she began unbuttoning his shirt, over by one, revealing more of his statuesque flesh as each button came undone, until finally she could take her fingernails across his back as she pulled the shirt off of him.

Jess leaned forward so she could plant delicate little kisses all over his muscled chest, stopping only to flick her tongue over his nipples. When they hardened under Jess's wet lips, he chuckled and pulled away.

"That tickles."

With her hand on his strong arms and chest and with him holding her back and cupping her face, the two lovers stared into each other's eyes as the wind whipped their hair wildly around them.

"I love you more than words can say, Josh." She said, then laid her head against his chest.

"I love you more than love itself, Jess." He said, then pushed back a strand of hair out of her face.

They spent a moment in that warm embrace, a moment that Jess never wanted to end.

Without moving from the safety and comfort of his arms, she asked him, "Will you make love to me as we watch the sunset over the city?"

Josh smirked handsomely. "I was beginning to think you'd never ask."

He held her head close to his chest like a precious treasure he could bare to part with. Jess could never remember feeling so safe and comfortable in her entire life. So loved.

With his free hand, Josh ran the back of his fingers up the side of Jess's thigh, all the way to the top of her curvy black pants. She felt the four fingers slip inside her pants just below the small of her back and slowly pull them down. Jes felt her big, bubbly butt bounce out of her pants and into the cool evening air. He pulled her pants down as far as he could using one arm, down past her thighs where they hung at knee level.

But when Jess felt a gust of cold air against her smooth pussy, she felt a spike of anxiety.

"Wait! What if someone comes up the hill from the park and sees us?" She pulled her head from his chest and looked around frantically.

Josh caught her eye. "It's just you and me, baby. Remember? It's just you and me. Always."

She nodded. She knew she was being silly. In essence, this was no different than what they had done on the balcony early that morning.

"You're right."

She gave him a fearless smile and sweet kiss, then peeled her tight pants off the rest of the way.

Memories of the balcony came flooding back to her. Jess eagerly pulled her boyfriend on top of her, laying flat on the blanket as she began removing his slacks. Josh kicked off his dress pants while Jess impatiently tried to pull off his boxer briefs.

She didn't get far before a massive erection sprang out of his underwear.

"Wow. How long has that been there?" She could not take her eyes off it.

Josh smiled cooly. "Pretty much my whole life."

She wanted to punch him but didn't want to ruin the mood. Instead, she helped him get naked.

"Wait, don't take them all the way off."

Jess raised an eyebrow. "If I have to be naked, you have to be naked." She yanked the last shred of clothing off of him. "Besides, it's just you and me, remember?"

Using his words against him left Josh speechless. And now she had him nude in the middle of a public park at sunset. *Delightful.*

Jess took his hard shaft in her hands and began stroking him while they continued making out. Josh always said that he felt huge in Jess's tiny hands.

It feels even bigger than it looks.

It was times like these that she was shocked - Intimidated even - that she could for that entire thing inside of her.

When she was ready, Jess lay flat on her side, facing the sunset. Josh lay down behind her, his chest pressing flush against her back. As he kissed the back of her neck, Josh threaded his fingers through Jess's, draping his arm over her, then placing it over her breast. He ran his other hand softly up and down her creamy white thighs, tickling her lightly with his fingertips.

Josh's skin looked bronze compared to Jess's milky white complexion. Her midnight black hair hung to one side, fluttering gently with the breeze like leaves on a tree.

Jess could feel his throbbing cock behind her aching for attention. She finally lifted one leg, bending at the knee to let him in. with one hand planted on her hip, Josh slowly easing his hard cock into her tight, wet pussy. He started thrusting his hip from behind her, penetrating deeper with every movement.

Jess did not hold back when it came to letting the pleasure she derived from him be known. Every thrust from Josh brought a new cry of ecstasy from Jess.

"Oh, yeah. Ooh, fuck. Ahh, yes. Mmm, God. Oh, fuck yeah."

Josh lifted up the front of her tank top, pulling it up and over her head, but Jess caught his arm.

"No. I *don't* want to *be* completely *naked* out – *Oh my God!*"

Every time Josh filled her up, bringing his hips flush against her ass, she emphasized every other word.

"If I have to be buck-ass naked out here, you do, too." Josh said without slowing his pace.

"No-*oh!* The double standard doesn't apply that way – Oh *FUCK!*"

Josh brought his head next to her and whispered in his ear. "Come on, baby. This is no different than what we do in bed every night. And look at that sunset! See how beautiful it is?" Josh said as he pulled off Jess's top, tossing it neatly in the pile with their other clothes. "The only thing more beautiful than this sunset are you amazing tits."

He unhooked Jess's bra, but she stopped him.

"Come on, baby. It'll be *so* romantic." Josh said and kissed the back of her hand. She let him peel her bra away, freeing Jess's boobs from their prison.

"How did you get so good at talking women into taking off their clothes?" She asked while Josh palmed her breasts as he fucked her.

"A lifetime of hard work and practice." He whispered in her ear, then kissed the spot on the back of her neck that made her shudder.

Strangely, she *did* feel better now that she was completely nude. The warm California sun felt incredible on her skin, even at sunset. Plus, she had to admit that being fully naked in a public park was turning her on just a little bit.

Jess had always been very comfortable with her nudity. She walked around completely naked in front of strangers at music festivals on more than one occasion. She didn't think twice about walking out onto their balcony completely nude just this morning.

But she felt *comfortable* in those situations. Plus, there was just something about this place that made her want to cover up.

It's just us. Only Josh and me. No one else is here. No one else matters. She repeated the mantra in her head at first, then aloud.

"Just us. It's just us. Nothing else matters," She whispered under her breath.

"That's right, baby. It's just us here. And I love you more than anything."

"Oh. That's right. I love you, too, baby." She didn't realize he heard her talking to herself.

Jess tilted her head back as far as she could so that their lips just barely touched. She extended her tongue to lick his lips and the stubble on his face playfully. Josh continued to pound her from behind, hips clapping loudly against her ass.

Josh was over a foot taller than Jess. When they were laying horizontally making love, he seemed even taller still.

When he cupped her right breast, it reminded her of the way they slept every night, spooning in an identical position. Every night, Jess fell asleep in the safety of Josh's big arms wrapped around her, one supporting her head and the other cupping her breast. That way Josh could pull her closer to him all night long in his sleep. It made Jess feel like a big, cuddly teddy bear getting snuggled all night. And getting fucked every night.

That was the one rule they had agreed upon in their relationship. Sex is mandatory every day, at least once a day. Naturally, it always ended up being much more than once, but on days where they were both busy at their jobs they could always stop whatever they were doing to fulfill this agreement.

The two were wildly attracted to one another and in their sexual prime. Some days, it was difficult to keep their hands off of each other. Some days, they didn't leave the bed at all except to hydrate. For this reason and more, Josh and Jess were always in sync.

And now they were both laying completely naked in a public park, making love on a picnic blanket and watching a one-of-a-kind sunset over the city.

In a public park, where literally anyone could walk up the hillside and see them. Jess couldn't decide – was this incredibly romantic or downright crazy. She wasn't sure. And she wasn't sure if she cared.

It felt good. Not just to be making love and watching the sunset, not just because of the thrill of getting caught, but being with the man she loved more than anything else in the world.

And the sex wasn't half bad either.

Josh pawed, pushed, and played with his girlfriend's perfect round, supple tits while at the same time pulled her body closer to his chest. His biceps, corded with muscle, wrapped around her abdomen. Forearms pressed tightly against her rib cage, he gave her breasts a loving squeeze at the rhythm with which he penetrated her.

This entire sensual experience was a world apart from the lust-driven primal need and animalistic sex that they shared on the balcony that morning. This was a celebration of their love on a emotional level that reinforced their bond to one another. It furthered their relationship. Made them grow as a couple. Their sex that morning, by comparison, was nothing more than a good fuck.

But this – this was spiritual. Transcendent. Jess felt full on an emotional level. Physically, mentally, emotionally, she felt complete.

This was a familiar ritual that she was used to doing in the privacy of their own bedroom each night. But she had to admit – it felt pretty good to make love under the twilight sky for all the world to see. Jess felt like it was a romantic declaration to the universe. An act that professed their love and further solidified their bond.

After the initial shock of bringing their most intimate moment out into the open, after she got over the cold sensation of the wind blowing against her bare skin and naked body, Jess no longer worried about getting caught in the act.

A part of her *wanted* someone to see her and her boyfriend naked, making love over a blanket on the grassy hillside. Yes, it was the kinky side of her, but she felt like someone should bear witness to their love making. It was only right that someone else appreciated this as much as she did.

Because she no longer exercised any level of restraint, the sounds from the couple grew progressively louder, echoing off the surrounding foothills.

"Ah! Yes! Oh, Josh! Yes, Josh, yes!"

Screaming his name only served to turn Josh on even more. Though Jess wouldn't have guessed it possible, she felt his thick cock throb and grow even larger inside her. He gripped her thigh and lifted her leg as he pounded her harder from behind.

Jess moaned and screamed louder and with even more passion. It was as if she was daring some stranger to come up the hill and watch them.

With Josh's hard body pressed up firmly against her back, she could feel his hot breath and the smell of red wine on the back of her neck. She could feel his heart racing in his chest. She listened to his masculine grunts co-mingled with moans of her own as he threw all of his passion into making love to her.

Each time he reeled back for another powerful thrust deep inside her, she felt his abs slam flat against her back as his hips smacked up against the flesh of her ample bottom. With a sharp inhale, Jess took one final look at the sunset over the downtown Los Angeles skyline, savoring its beauty.

When she squeezed her eyes shut tight, she still saw the incredible pink, orange, and yellow glow on the horizon as an explosion of rapture erupted through her body. Tingling fireworks were going off inside of her, paralyzing her with a wave of sudden ecstasy. Warmth filled her, flooding her naked body.

"Oh my fucking God." She said a few moments later, once she was again able to speak. "I love it when you cum inside of me."

She looked over her shoulder so she could kiss him on the lips.

"What a coincidence. I love filling your perfect little pussy with cum." He said, stealing another kiss as he continued to fuck her. "I'd make a full time living from it if I could."

She laughed loud and deep. "You *do* make a full time living of it!"

"Does that mean you're going to start paying me?"

"I don't know," she said coyly. "I'm going to expect something pretty *extraordinary* if you want me to start paying you."

He grabbed her by the throat and pulled her head back so he could whisper in her ear, "Baby, I could twist you into a pretzel and we could do *all* of the positions tonight. If we had enough time."

He nibbled on her earlobe until Jess shuddered like electricity shook her whole body.

"*Careful* talking like that. You know how much it turns me on." She reached back and grabbed Josh's ass, feeling him flex his glutes. "Don't pull out just yet. Let's just lay here."

Josh continued to slowly slide his still hard cock into her slippery, cum-soaked pussy.

"I know, baby. I know."

Jess always asked him not to pull out immediately after he shot his load inside of her. And he always complied. It didn't matter if it was vaginal or anal, Jess reveled in their post-coital aftercare so long as there was a dick inside of her.

"It is starting to get cold, though." Josh said as he wrapped his tree-trunk arm around her like a warm blanket.

The sun had already completely set, and it was starting to get dark out.

"Okay, okay, you pussy." Jess teased with a sigh. "Let's at least finish this wonderful picnic spread."

She reached behind her and pulled Josh's dick out of her, then began putting her clothes back on. Josh did the same.

The wind picked up now that the sun was down, so they ate the remaining picnic spread with haste. Neither of them had time to savor their meal before the darkness of night completely descended all around them. Jess had trouble seeing anything more than a foot in front of her nose, so she harried Josh into packing everything up so they could go.

"This really was a nice surprise, babe. Thanks for making this such a perfect day." Jess said before she popped the last bite of her peanut butter and jelly sandwich in her mouth.

"It was nothing. Besides, now we can cross 'Public Park' off the Bingo card, right?"

Jess blanched. "That was why you did this?" She smacked the palm of her hand to her forehead. "Of course. I'm such an idiot."

"I mean, I did it mainly because I love you." He recovered. "It being on the Bingo card was just a happy bonus."

Jess laughed a musical laugh.

"You're a sly as a fox, Josh Jacobs, and slippery as an eel."

Everything was packed away into the picnic basket. Jess helped Josh fold the blanket with one hand as she snacked on grapes with the other.

"Remember, seven days. And I can't wait to see how you follow up this, Mister Romance."

Jess wrapped her pink lips around the last grape on the vine and sucked it into her mouth with a *pop*. Josh watched her as he carried the blanket and the picnic basket down the hill.

The walk down the hill proved considerably more difficult in total darkness. But even in the dark of night, Jess could see the outline of his erection bulging in Josh's pants.

Wow, I really hope he got a boner just from thinking about what he has planned for us this weekend and not from watching me eat grapes.

"Well, if the weather is as nice as it was today I was thinking about a trip to the beach."

"You know I'll never turn down an excuse to go to the beach."

"Okay. And Sunday that church down the street is doing a fundraiser carnival in the parking lot."

Jess gasped with excitement. "Will there be rides?!"

"Wouldn't be much of a carnival if there weren't."

She pushed him on the shoulder. "You little pervert. All of these are on the Bingo card!"

He nearly tripped over his feet in the dark, but recovered as they neared the bottom of the hill.

"So you *do* remember!"

Jess threw her hands up in surrender. "Guilty as charged."

"Psh, who's the pervert now?"

"Still you! Talking about bending me into a pretzel and whatnot."

"And? Are you saying that you *don't* want to be pretzeled?"

"Well... I didn't say *that*."

"Good. Then my offer still stands."

He smiled and held her hand as they walked the rest of the way home.

"...Josh? The weekend is still a few days off... What are we going to do until then?"

Josh put his arm around Jess and pulled her close. She rested her head on his shoulder.

"I'm sure we'll find some trouble to get into."

CHAPTER 13

Day 4 – Café

Jess awakened about 90 minutes before her alarm went off the following morning. It was one of those times when she woke up full of energy. She knew instantly that there was no chance of falling back asleep.

She felt something hard poking her in the kidneys and immediately realized what woke her up. Since Josh and her fell asleep spooning every night, his chest pressed flush with her back, she was not surprised to find that he was stabbing her in the back with an enormous erection while still asleep.

Knowing she wouldn't be able to fall back asleep and with 90 minutes to kill before she had to get out of bed and get ready for work, Jess saw that there was only one thing for her to do.

She punched Josh hard in the stomach.

"Babe. Wake up. I want morning sex."

Jess sat up in bed and shook Josh until he began to stir. He yawned lazily with eyes open just a crack.

"Mm? Just pick something off the Bingo card and I'll fuck you there." He said sleepily, then rolled over on the bed out of Jess's reach and shut his eyes.

Jess heaved a sigh. She peeled back the comforter and hopped out of bed. Still naked from head to toe, Jess walked into the kitchen where the Exhibitionist Bingo card still sat in the middle of the table.

She leaned over the table so she could get a better view of the Bingo card, studying it for something suitable that Josh and her could do in the next 90 minutes.

Only one location seemed doable. And it was a perfect spot for morning sex.

A devilish smile grew on her face as she fantasized about what was to come. Grinning mischievously, Jess walked her bare feet across the hardwood floor back into the bedroom.

Josh was fast asleep.

Well, there is only one way to deal with this...

Jess grabbed the comforter with both hands and yanked it off of Josh's naked body. She kept pulling on the sheets until all of the bedding was on the floor in a tangled mess.

Josh's bare body lay exposed on one side of the bed.

"What? Why?" Josh half-mumbled, half-groaned while half-asleep.

"Your dick started this and now your dick is going to finish it. Now put some clothes on, and for God's sake, sheath that thing before you put someone's eye out."

Ten minutes of constant prodding later, they were both in the car and fully clothed.

Although Josh was almost always the one behind the wheel whenever the couple went anywhere, Jess sat in the driver's seat that morning, fastidiously adjusting everything to her height. Jess preferred that her boyfriend drive, but considering Josh could hardly remain conscious in the passenger seat, that wasn't an option.

It was still dark out as she pulled out of the driveway. The streets of L.A. were all but deserted this early in the morning.

"I said *what?!*" Josh said between yawns.

"You mean you really don't remember telling me to pick a place off the Bingo card for us to have morning sex at?"

"I say lots of things in my sleep! All I remember is I was having a dream where you punched me in the stomach, and the next thing I know, you're ripping all of the sheets off the bed like a lunatic."

"Wow, that sounds like a crazy dream. But if you don't remember saying it, then I'll take credit for it, and we can call this my idea."

"You still haven't told me what we're doing or where we're going."

"I told you. We're going someplace to have morning sex. It's a surprise."

"Wait, wait. So, we were both in our warm, comfy bed."

"Yes."

"We were both naked."

"Uh-huh."

"Then I woke you up with my morning wood."

"You did."

"And you had us put on clothes so we could drive away from our nice, comfy, warm bed… so we can have sex?"

"That's the gist of it, yes."

Josh had a confused look on his face like his brain broke.

"Babe… That's like… The reverse order of how this is supposed to go."

"Oh, hush. You're the one who said I should pick a place for us to have morning sex."

"I thought you wanted this to be your idea!"

"Only if it works out. If we get arrested, it was definitely all your idea."

Jess beamed a very self-satisfied smile.

As she pulled the car around the corner, a sky-blue building came into view. There was outdoor seating, and even in the early morning hours the sparse tables and chairs were already populated. It was still dark out, but the little coffee shop was a hub of activity.

"Intelligista Café? You can't be serious!"

Jess gave him a look that said *this is my serious face. Grr!*

Intelligista was Jess and Josh's favorite coffee shop in Los Angeles. With a variety of delicious and unique drinks in addition to well-made classics, friendly baristas, and an ambiance that was both calming and energizing, Intelligista had a lot to offer that couldn't be found at retail coffee shops in the area. The fact that the cafe was also an epicenter of community activity and gossip only added to its rustic, hipster charm.

"Babe, this place looks packed. Plus, I'm still half asleep."

"I know, that's why a coffee shop is the perfect spot for morning sex. *Duh.*" She didn't want to admit it, but the place *was* a lot busier than she had expected.

"No, a *bed* is the perfect spot for morning sex."

"Oh, you're just grouchy because you haven't had any coffee yet." She parked on the street between two cars. "Let's go fix that." She gave him a wink as she got out of the car.

Josh groaned as he followed close behind her.

"Come on." Jess said in a sweet, sing-song voice as she took Josh by the hand and led him inside.

Maybe the coffee shop being so busy could work to their advantage. Maybe people would pay less attention to Jess and Josh with more customers about.

Or maybe it meant that there was absolutely no way they could get away with this. Maybe any one of these people would call the cops the moment they suspected what the couple were up to.

Maybe this was a *terrible* idea after all.

But Jess had it all planned out from the moment she saw "Café" on the Bingo card. There was one booth-like bench facing the corner, opposite the counter where drinks were made. It was made to fit two people sitting side by side, but one person could sit on the other's lap without drawing a second glance. It was perfect – whether there were a lot of people there or not.

Her only concern was that it was about 8 feet away from the front counter. And that she almost always had a hard time keeping quiet right before she was about to cum. She hadn't worked that last part out just yet.

Part of her was hoping that it would be like the movie theater where everyone gave them a round of applause after Josh and her came. *Or were they all cheering because we were leaving the theater?*

As soon as Jess set foot inside the café, she realized her mistake. Not only was the place booming with activity, they had changed the seating arrangements since Jess had been there last.

The spot she had in mind no longer existed. Instead, the tables were all arranged in a uniform pattern, with an equal amount of seating available on either side of the café. Four on one side. Four on the other side. All facing one another.

Her little booth nook was gone.

Worse still, over half of the seats were already filled with people getting their morning caffeine fix with more people arriving still. The sun wasn't even up yet.

Damn it. Why did I have to choose the most popular coffee shop in L.A.?

As Jess and Josh got in line, she started to spiral. This was the couple's favorite café. If someone discovered what they were up to, they might never be able to show their faces here again. Jess didn't think she could handle a lifetime ban from Intelligista.

What was I thinking?

She wasn't thinking. It was still early and she was horny. What seemed like a good idea in theory turned out to be a nightmare in practice.

And now she was in another situation that was giving her anxiety. Ever since the Bingo card fell into her lap – or more accurately, her blouse – she realized that anxiety was the total opposite of horny. The two were like oil and water. And it would be impossible to reach orgasm while dealing with this level of stress.

Coffee will help, she told herself. *Coffee is historically excellent for dealing with anxiety.*

Jess let out a big sigh. She was fucked, and not in the way that she wanted.

She stepped up to the counter to order.

"I'll have an espresso for him and an Americana for me."

She looked at Josh standing next to her. He bobbed his head up and down like he was nodding out on fentanyl.

"Make that a triple espresso, please."

The young barista gave them a look of silent judgement before taking her money. *Whatever. She is caffeine drug dealer.*

They took a seat at the nearest empty table while Jess surveyed the layout of the room like she worked for the FBI. Josh, meanwhile, slumped down in the chair beside her, snoozing.

Jess had very strategically picked out her wardrobe that morning with special consideration that she might also have to wear the same outfit if she had to drive straight to work from the coffee shop. She wore a scarlet blouse with a scoop neck that showed just enough cleavage. She paired that with a risqué maroon mini skirt that stopped just below her ass, barely covering her cheeks when she sat down. No underwear, for obvious reasons.

Jess felt liberated any time she could go out in public without the burden of a bra or panties. She found both very restrictive and downright uncomfortable to move around in. True, she would occasionally wear a thong, but that was usually because it was part of a nice lingerie set. And you just don't break up an elegantly paired lingerie set.

Although Jess conceded to wearing undergarments for strictly formal occasions and events (such as work), she was one of the many women in the fashion world who argued that their clothes looked and fit better without the hinderance of things like underwear or modesty.

Unless a stranger was intensively starring at her tits – which happened more frequently than she wished – no one would be able to tell she wasn't wearing a bra or see her hard nipples poking through her top.

Part of her didn't mind it when perverts starred at her while she wasn't looking. Jess appreciated the fact that she had the boobs of a woman ten years younger than her. Year after year, her tits continued to look the same in a bra as they did without one. At some point she decided to stop wearing a bra entirely.

When she could get away with it, at least.

Why she was blessed with such big, resilient breasts, she could not say. Good genetics, maybe. She didn't make a big deal about it. All she knew was that they were the object of envy for most of her friends and the object of lust of most men she encountered.

But at the coffee shop first thing in the morning, no one seemed to notice the fact that she wasn't wearing a bra or panties.

At least, not yet anyway.

On the way out the door that morning, dressing her near-sleeping boyfriend was like dressing a cadaver. She chose a simple long sleeve gray cotton shirt for comfort and a pair of pajama bottoms with a sublimated design printed on them that made them look just like denim jeans. They were Josh's favorite for lounging around the house which, presumably, he did plenty of while working from his home office.

But the reason Jess chose to dress Josh in pajama pants wasn't for his comfort – it was for hers. Most notably, they did not have a fly or zipper. And the less sharp, jagged metal rubbing up against her genitals during intercourse, the better.

Josh was traumatized after watching *There's Something About Mary*. He would never admit to anyone but her that getting his dick caught in the zipper of his pants was his personal nightmare phobia.

Plus, the thought of Jess slicing her clit on a jean zipper made her shudder.

But their wardrobe was the easy part. It was the logistics that were proving a little tricky. But as Jess saw the judgmental barista setting their drinks on the countertop, she decided to go for the Hail Mary.

"Hi! Thanks so much for preparing our coffee! Looks yummy. Say, when did you guys rearrange all of the tables here?

You know, it looked so much better the way it was before. Do you remember? So cute! I miss that old booth by the down there in the corner. That was actually where I first met my fiancé here. Do you think we could put it back for old times sake? We would love to get a few pictures for our wedding invitations. Really? Oh my God, thank you so much! No, *you* have a great day!"

Did that actually just work? Sometimes I am so good that I even surprise myself. I should get bonus points for shoveling that pile of horseshit pre-coffee!

Next, Jess directed Josh as he pushed the booth to the spot she indicated. The seat looked like a normal booth at a restaurant, only it was made entirely out of wood and looked as if it had just been chopped from a tree.

Their seat now faced opposite the counter, looking straight at the back wall of the coffee shop with a floor to ceiling glass window to their right.

Even though Jess had their seat exactly how she imagined it, she only now realized a fundamental flaw. Every single person who walked up to the counter to get their order would be looking straight at them. Or at least, facing in their general direction. Plus, there was the window overlooking the street to cope with.

Well, nothing in life is perfect.

She mentally shrugged as Josh and her took their seats on the bench. This was the best she could do given the circumstance, and she thought she did a damned good job, all things considered.

Now for the fun part.

"Love, real love, is something you earn for who you are. It's not a prize to be won in bed."

She couldn't help but overhear two women talking at the table behind them. She casually glanced over her shoulder. One was a customer, about her age. The other was the judgmental barista she just duped into letter her rearrange the furniture.

Jess wasn't sure if the two were flirting or if it was a lover's quarrel. Either way, getting into a deeply emotional conversation about the very nature of love seemed like a very Intelligista thing to do.

Jess wanted so very badly to butt in. Instead, she exercised an uncharacteristic amount of self-control and sipped her coffee.

"Fiancé, huh? Did we get engaged when I was asleep?" Josh asked after finishing his second espresso.

Jess smiled back warmly. "Babe, you know I can't stop the things that come out of my mouth when I'm horny."

"You have a hard time stopping the things coming *in* your mouth, too."

She kissed him on the cheek.

"Make your jokes, but I can be pretty motivated when I want dick."

Josh laughed, "Is that how you lured me back to your bed when we first met?"

"As I recall, it was *you* who lured *me* into your bed on our first date."

"Be that as it may, didn't you lure me down to this coffee shop first thing in the morning for a reason? I mean, I could still be sleeping."

She scooted down the bench until the two were pressed up against each other shoulder to shoulder. Jess held up Josh's hand and, without breaking eye contact, she very slowly and seductively licked his palm up to his fingertip. Then she proceeded to insert every finger of his into her mouth, sucking each digit starting at his pinky and ending at his thumb.

After tasting each of his fingers, she started back at his pinky and touched each of his fingertips to the tip of her tongue, licking them lightly.

She paused with his thumb in her mouth, pursing her lips as she sucked it like a teething toddler, all the while staring at Josh through lidded eyes. Her wet, full lips parted just a bit as she dragged his thumb across her bottom lip.

She guided his saliva-soaked thumb down her neck and over her heaving chest, stopping on her crimson blouse where her hard nipples poked out like daggers. When she let go of Josh's hand, he kept his thumb pressed up against her breast, thumbing her nipples over her shirt.

"Still feel like sleeping?" She whispered to him in a throaty voice.

He shook his head as he pinched her nipples through her top. Jess eased her hand up Josh's inner thigh and slipped her fingers into the fly of his fake-jean pajama pants. She didn't bother checking to see if anyone was looking at them or not.

It's only him and me here...

Just us, and no one else...

Only me and him...

Good God, I'm fucking horny.

Jess's hand easily found Josh's girthy member. He was already still from her earlier oral act. She began stroking his shaft lovingly, making him harder with every touch.

"Mmm." Josh groaned. "Babe, that feels great, but a handy under the table in a café is not going to count towards BINGO."

She rolled her eyes. "Didn't I tell you I had a plan? Just follow my lead and act natural."

Jess pulled her cell phone out of her purse and started snapping selfies of them with her left hand while jerking Josh off with her right.

"Smile for our wedding invitations, future husband." She said in a stiff, plastic voice that was almost as obvious as the lie they were perpetrating.

The fabric of Josh's pajama pants was as thin as it was impossibly soft. The outline of his hard cock was easily visible down one side of his thigh.

"Just put it on video." He said in a hushed tone that only she would hear, despite the many café customers sitting only a few feet behind them. "And you're just dry tugging it now. That hurts."

Jess pushed her coffee cup to the middle of the table. She set her cellphone in front of it, propped up by the cup, then hit record on a video.

It took a bit of adjustment until she found an angle where they were both in frame. Josh gave her his *Oh my God, who fucking cares* look of frustration, but in the end, Jess was very excited that she was about to capture this all on video.

While Jess and Josh had made a few sex tapes of themselves during the course of their relationship, it was always a spontaneous, kinky idea that didn't end well. Their videos always turned out too dark, too blurry, too grainy, or too bad of an angle for her to enjoy later on.

In the end, their passion always took precedent over their videography.

But not this time.

Jess was a firm believer in the philosophy that everyone should make a sex tape in their 20s. it was sage advice handed down to her from multiple middle-aged women independently of one another.

"You will always want to relive the glory days of your sexual prime as you grow old. You will be thankful you did, and by the time you can truly appreciate it, it will be too late. Also, you will want photographic evidence to show your future husbands that you were once hot."

The fact that she always received the same advice from used-up old hags seemed like a very bad omen, but it seemed unwise to ignore their guidance.

With the video running, Jess could not only see her and Josh in the frame, but the other people in the coffee shop sitting behind them as well. This would allow her to easily tell if the couple was drawing unwanted attention without suspiciously looking over her shoulder like a paranoid tweaker.

And now that Jess could clearly see that everyone in the coffee shop was minding their own business, she pulled out Josh's cock and went down on him.

Although no one in the shop could see exactly what the two were doing, anyone who looked in their direction would simply see Jess's head bobbing up and down in Josh's lap.

Jess looked directly into the camera as she sucked his dick in the crowded café. At first, she only went down on him for a few seconds before coming back up. Still, everyone around them was wrapped up in their own little caffeinated world.

"Whoopsie. I dropped something."

Jess's hand groped the café floor as if she were searching for something while she took Josh's dick to the back of her throat. Jess released herself from her anxiety and embraced her primal love for sucking dick.

"Goddamn, woman. What did you lose down there? Your inhibitions?"

She almost gagged when she laughed with Josh's hard cock all the way in the back of her throat.

"Mm-hmm." She managed when she recovered.

Jess had to actively concentrate on not making her typical horny noises while sucking her boyfriend's cock. Before long, she came up for air and wiped the trail of cock sucking saliva from her lips.

Not one person turned their head in their direction.

Well then. Time to ride a dick.

Giving head had left Jess moist between the legs, though she was still nowhere near as naturally lubricated enough to feel comfortable taking Josh's fully erect cock in her tiny hole.

Jess flipped up the front of her skirt, exposing her smooth, tight pussy on the video. She licked her fingers and started pleasuring herself.

This is shaping up to be a pretty good sex tape! But it's only just begun...

If anyone would happen to walk past the window of the coffee shop at that moment, they would see a black-haired beauty with her legs spread wide, playing with her pussy while simultaneously jerking off the gargantuan dick of a tall, muscular behemoth of a man.

It was like a behind the scenes look at a real life porn shoot. Only real, and discreet.

To any of the coffee shop customers sitting behind them, all they saw was a couple sitting closely with her head rested on his shoulders.

And still no one was paying any attention to them.

It was then that Jess decided it was time to stand up and move over into Josh's lap. With her hand still on his cock, she guided him slowly into her tight, wet hole. When she did, Josh exhaled loudly.

"Whew!" Josh breathed.

Jess thought to herself, *Oh, that's nice.*

But what she said was "Omigod, omigod, omigod!" under her breath.

Her bare ass lay flat against Josh's lap, the entire length of his dick deep inside her.

Every time, she thought to herself. *Every time he takes my breath away.*

It took her a moment to recover, but then Jess played it off like she was posing for a selfie.

"*God,* does your dick get bigger every time we have sex?" Jess whispered with her best ventriloquism.

"Funny, I was just wondering how your pussy manages to get smaller each time we fuck." Josh matched her tone.

She shifted her weight, teetering and tottering on one side of her butt cheek, then the other. She settled on sitting with her legs pressed together, hanging off to one side and dangling from Josh's right side.

Jess could see out the window now and into the parking lot as people came and went down the sidewalk, never bothering to look at them through the window. The thought of someone on the other side of the window watching them got her heart racing.

She fidgeted around on Josh's lap. She could see from the video on her phone that everyone in the café was busy either sipping their coffee or playing on their phone. A few people brought their laptops into Intelligista and were absorbed in their work.

Oh, they're making this too easy. She thought. *Time to really test the limits.*

Josh had his legs spread wide. With Jess's legs throw over one side of his legs, her feet couldn't reach the ground.

She tried to bounce up and down on his lap, like an excited child telling Santa what she wants for Christmas, but she couldn't get enough air. Defeated, Jess considered moving into another position when suddenly Josh picked up her entire body.

With one hand cupped underneath her butt cheek and the other under the crook of her knees, Josh slowly lifted her up before bringing her back down on his dick. It was the most nonchalant, inconspicuous way of ridding her boyfriend's dick while still appearing as two innocent love birds to any bystanders who might look there way.

Though none did.

Jess decided that she liked getting fucked this way. It was a concession, though, because she was really looking forward to riding his dick the way she did on the balcony yesterday. She wanted to ride him wildly in front of everyone at the coffee shop.

That was the fantasy, anyway.

But this – this was nice, too. The way he so effortlessly lifted her up and down, pounding her pussy while she did absolutely nothing at all was hotter than she could have imagined.

Jess felt like a tiny, little fuck toy to be played with in his powerful hands. Each time he brought her down on top of him she felt herself getting more and more wet.

Taking all of Josh's hard cock in her again and again at his own pace felt pretty amazing, but she also ached for clitoral stimulation.

She desperately wanted to play with her pussy.

At the same time, she also realized that was impossible. It would attract too much attention. What they were doing was innocuous. Then again – no risk, no reward.

She pressed her legs together tights, feeling her pussy lips wrapped around Josh's throbbing dick. She could feel every inch of him sliding in and out of her. She could feel her pussy contract around the contours of his cock deep inside of her. She could feel his dick getting harder inside of her, penetrating her deeper still.

Finally, when she could resist it no longer, she spread her legs – just a bit – so she could slide one of her tiny hands under her skirt to play with her pussy. She began rubbing her clit in little circles, matching Josh's pace.

Holy cow! I am so wet right now!

But she didn't consider that Josh had a perfectly balanced grip on her. The moment she tried to spread her legs a little bit more, she lost her balance and slipped from Josh's grasp.

Jess made a sort of yelping noise when she realized Josh dropped her.

Luckily, his dick broke her fall.

She fell with her ass flat on his lap, sending his dick penetrating deep inside her. it would have been even deeper if not for Jess bubble butt offering padding between them. Jess's feet just barely hit the floor. She could support herself only on her tippy toes.

She immediately checked the camera. A few heads turned in their direction after she yelled out in the middle of a bustling café.

She froze like a bunny caught in a flashlight, still as a statue. She could feel Josh's throbbing cock inside of her, but she dare not move. Josh did the same.

A few seconds later, most people looked away. Except for the perverts ogling here. She couldn't shake those. Ever.

"What are you doing?" Josh laughed. "That was fucking *hot*."

"I know." She whispered back.

"Just let daddy take care of everything, okay? Don't move."

"Then daddy needs to play with my pussy and fuck me at the same time."

"I'm sure I can manage that." He replied.

She couldn't see his face but was certain he must be beaming right now.

Jess cleared her throat and then leaned forward to take a sip of her coffee. She was forced to rearrange her cellphone when she put her cup back but kept the video running.

Jess leaned forward again, raising her ass up off of Josh's lap just enough to bounce her ass on his dick. Then again. And again. The moves were subtle and virtually undetectable, but the effects were pronounced.

This could work.

"I need you to rub my clit as fast as you can, okay?"

Josh took over with a firm grip on her booty, the other reaching around to her front, between her legs. She turned her head enough to steal a kiss from him. He tasted like coffee. She imagined they both did.

Still better than morning breath.

Josh bit and sucked on her lower lip, then parted Jess soft pink lips with his tongue. For a long moment, they shared a passionate kiss together before Jess finally broke it off.

"Don't stop for anything, okay? And I want you to cum inside of me as soon as you're able."

"I fucking love you."

"Love you, too."

Jess put her hands on her knees and started grinding her ass against his lap in circles. Josh bounced her ass up and down life he was dribbling a basketball on his lap.

She was surprised how quickly her was able to find her clit, flicking it firmly with his fingertips. The pleasant sensation caught Jess off guard, forcing a moan out of her. She stopped herself mid-moan, snapping her mouth tightly shut.

Jess focused inward, no longer paying attention to the people in the café. She just didn't care anymore.

All she wanted to do was cum.

And then leave immediately afterwards.

In fact, the moment Josh began playing with her pussy she felt an orgasm just withing her reach. She could get it if she wanted to. And if she was about to cum, that meant that she needed to get her boyfriend to cum inside her as soon as possible.

She clenched as tightly around his cock as she could manage. Josh made a noise indicating tat he obviously noticed. Jess gripped the end of the table with both hands, using the leverage to bounce her booty as fast as she was able, throwing a little twist into it just for fun.

Josh continued massaging her clit. His touch felt so fucking good that it was distracting her from what she was doing.

What was I doing again?

Oh, yeah. Getting Josh off so that I can get off.

She knew right away that Josh must have realized she was very close to orgasm because of all the little noises she always started making right before she was going to cum. She didn't care enough to stop herself. She didn't care if everyone on the block saw what they were doing.

All that matters is me and him.

And getting this nut.

"Hm, ah, oh, hm, fu, ka." Jess whispered nonsense as Josh bounced her ass up and down even faster.

It wasn't the quickened pace that made her cum, but rather the way that Josh threw caution into the wind so he could take control and fuck her more aggressively. It was the way that he handled her that made her explode. The way he made her feel like his little fuck toy in the middle of a crowded café.

Jess closed her eyes and imagined everyone in the coffee shop and on the street staring at her. That pushed her over the edge.

Jess never understood how many women could simply let an orgasm pass over them without their man knowing. When she would cum, whether it was her doing or someone else's, there was no hiding it. Her orgasms typically involved lots of screaming, choking (ideally), full-body spasms that would sometimes last long afterwards, and sometimes even blacking out

Thankfully, she was never in a situation where she needed to fuck quietly.

Until now.

"Oh, my FUCKING God! Holy FUCK, Josh! Oh, shit! Oh, fuck YES!"

She completely forgot where she was. And for a moment, she didn't care. Her orgasmic moans never failed to turn Josh on in any situation.

And that warm, wet feeling between my legs must be all of my boyfriend's cum inside of me. Yay!

But the moment Jess was able to catch her breath, reality came crashing back down on her.

She was still in the coffee shop.

Oh. Shit.

Jess took a deep breath to help ground her. She ran her hand through her hair, which she was certain must look like a mess by now. Jess cleared her throat, then she grabbed her phone, stood up, and walked out the door without checking to see how many pairs of eyes she had on her.

It was one of the most empowering moments in her life. When she realized that she really didn't care about what other people thought of her.

Still, she thought, *it's safe to assume we won't be welcome back at Intelligista any time soon.*

CHAPTER 14

Day 4 - Office

It was a beautiful sunny day in Los Angeles. An especially nice day to be outside sketching new clothing design ideas.

Jess was on lunch break, sitting outside in the employee break area at her work. She sat at a picnic table with her feet kicked up, sketch pad in hand, relaxing and drawing. She hummed a little tune as she finished shading a design for a new, retro-inspired romper.

Birds chirped away under the blue sky without a single cloud overhead. A warm breeze blew through her long hair as Jess smiled to herself, focused on her work without a care in the world.

In the distance, she thought she could hear someone calling her name.

"Jessss... Jess?" The voice grew louder and louder. "Jess!"

She turned around to see the beaming face of her co-worker, Ashley.

The small-framed woman was wearing the same circular glasses and ponytail that she always saw her with. But today, there was something different about her that Jess couldn't put her finger on.

She was wearing a cute, tan-colored V-neck crop top that showed off way more skin than she typically did. Jess hadn't realized it until that very moment, but Ashley actually had much bigger boobs than she let on. The extra small crop top she wore made her chest look very sexy indeed.

Jess imagined that Ashley had a hard time finding clothes in an extra small size.

No wonder she always wears clothes that are too big for her... She is so tiny, even compared to me.

"Jeee-esss!" Ashley took a seat at the table next to her. "Guess what?"

Jess set down the sketch pad and pencil. Judging by the ecstatic look on Ashley's face, she could think of only one thing.

"Ashley! Did you get your Bingo yet?"

"Yasss!"

Ashley jumped at Jess, embracing her in an unexpected hug.

"I'm sorry, but I had to tell someone."

"Jess did not know Ashley all that well and could only guess as to what her inner circle of friends were like. The impression she always got from her co-worker-turned-friend was that she was very tightly wound. She was only a few years older than Jess, but acted very motherly.

Dare I say, prudish, even.

Despite the fact that they both worked for a clothing company that made, among other things, scantily rave outfits for women, Ashley made a point of always dressing very conservatively.

Until today.

"That's okay. Tell me all about it! Oh, uh, is that a new top? I love it!"

Ashley's cheeks took on a pinkish hue as she looked down at her crop top. She tugged at the bottom hem, as if doing so would somehow make the shirt longer.

"Oh, thank you. It is new. I saw it and it reminded me of you."

Now Jess's cheek's reddened at the thought of Ashley thinking about her boobs while shopping. A smile crept onto her lips as she got a mental image of Ashley trying on tops while picturing Jess.

Jess quickly changed the subject. "So, which ones did you and Freddie end up doing together?"

Ashley flashed a toothy grin as she pulled in a lungful of air. "Well, I'll be honest, it was a hard sell to Freddie at first. That's why I had to start with something small. When Freddie and I were in college, we used to sneak onto the rooftop and, you know, fool around. So, for old times' sake, we went up to the top floor in our apartment complex, laid down a beach towel, and well, let me tell you, Jess, we had such a good time that later that night we went for a swim in our community pool. The pool is right in the middle of four apartment building balconies so I'm absolutely sure that someone must have seen us. But you know what, Jess? I didn't even care! It was such a magical evening. And just between us girls, a little bit kinky if you know what I mean. Oh, but could you imagine? Two times in a single night?"

"Wow. That really is something, Ashley." Jess tried her best to sound impressed.

"I feel so young again." Shley said, placing a hand on Jess's shoulder and giving her a warm smile. "Thank you, Jess. You really did an amazing thing for my sex life."

"Oh, it's nothing, really. I'm happy to hear your relationship is going so well. So, have you given any thought to which ones you want to do next?"

Ashley waved a hand dismissively. "Oh, I don't know. I'll definitely have to work up to some of these, and a few are just plain ridiculous. I mean, come on, a movie theater? Really? What kind of slut has sex in a movie theater?"

Jess chewed her bottom lip. She could feel her traitorous complexion betray her, blushing again. Thankfully, Ashley didn't seem to notice.

"I definitely want to do it on our balcony. And Freddie and I have done it in his car once or twice when we were in college. I'd like to revisit that, I think, but I'm brave enough to do most of them."

Ashley sighed to catch her breath, then started again.

"This is definitely something to keep in my back pocket for spur-of-the-moment occasions, though. I mean, it's not like Freddie and I need to have sex in *all* of the locations in a single week, or anything."

Ashley laughed. Her face was getting redder and redder as she kept talking. Jess couldn't figure out if her co-worker was trolling her or not.

"I also think it would be really hot to do it in a park. Maybe even romantic. Oh, but listen to me babble on and on! I can't believe I'm talking to you about my sex life. What you must think of me!"

"Josh and I had sex in the middle of this park right across the street from our house. It was the most romantic thing ever. He surprised me with a picnic and wine. Then we cuddled naked as we watched the sunset over downtown L.A. it was honestly an experience that I'll remember for the rest of my life."

Ashley's mouth hung open slack.

"Are you serious? Oh, Jess! That's straight out of a romance novel!"

More like an erotic novel, Jess thought to herself.

"I'm so jealous! See, Freddie would never do anything like that for me. Oh, but that reminds me. I have a question for you about the Bingo card."

"What is it, Ashley? You can ask me anything. I like gossiping about our sex lives with you." Jess said, trying to put Ashley's nervousness at ease.

If Ashley's face wasn't red before, her entire body turned a shade of crimson at the mention of their sex lives.

"Well, it's called 'Exhibitionist Bingo', right? But you see, the thing is that I, well, that I..."

"What is it? You can tell me anything, girl."

"That's sweet. You're so sweet, Jess."

"Thanks. So, what is it, Ashley?"

"Oh, well, it's called 'Exhibitionist Bingo', but I prefer anal sex to vagina sex. Do you think that matters?"

The fact that this did not surprise Jess one bit was a bit shocking. If she had to venture a guess, Ashley looked like someone who preferred getting fucked in the ass.

Ashley covered her face in embarrassment while she anxiously awaited an answer. Jess waved her hand dismissively in the air.

"Of course not, Ashley! Sex is sex, right? And if I'm being honest, I do anal with Josh all the time. Including at some public places on the Bingo card."

Ashley sat on the edge of her seat, suddenly very interested. "Really? Like what? I mean, I know you've done the library one already, but which other ones did you and Josh do? Wait. Nevermind. That's personal. I'm sorry, I shouldn't have asked."

"Well..."

Jess told Ashley all about the places on the Bingo card where her and Josh had sex in the last few days. Ashley's timid prudishness seemed to vanish completely as she repeatedly asked Jess for more details about her exploits.

"And you're trying to do all of them in just one week? Seriously? Jess, that's more than three times a day!"

"I know. That's why we're calling it 'The Exhibitionist Bingo Challenge'. But Ashley, I hope you don't think any less of me, or think I'm a slut or whatever because of this."

"Are you kidding me? I think this is the most extraordinary thing I've ever heard! Jess, if you can pull this off, you will forever be my hero."

"Ashley, please don't tell anyone. I'm serious."

"Of course, Jess. And I hope you won't tell anyone about my little... preference."

Jess zipped her lips closed and threw away the key.

"Seriously, Jess, I am so jealous of your life."

"It's nothing, really."

"It is something. It's our little secret."

Jess laughed. "Yes, it is that, isn't it?"

"And Josh... He can... I mean, he's like..."

"My boyfriend." Jess said, hoping that would finish their conversation.

"Yeah, I *know*. But, Jess, three to four times a day? Can any one man *do* that?"

Jess searched Ashley's eyes, trying to figure out if she was asking a serious question or just trolling her.

"Ashley, how long have you and Freddie been together?"

"Married ten years now. But we've been dating for twelve or so. He's a few years older than Josh, though."

"Girl, all men can be seduced. Doesn't matter how old they are."

"You say that, but you don't know Freddie. He's a lot more interested in what's new on Netflix than he is me."

"You should bring some of the Festival Drip outfits home. Tell him it's a work thing and model them for him. He'll go crazy, I promise."

"Is that what you do with Josh."

Jess gave her a look. Ashley looked her up and down.

"No. I guess with your body, you don't need to, do you?"

"You've got a really nice body, too, Ashley. You just need to show it off a little."

Jess picked up her sketchpad and showed it to Ashley.

"Here, I'll make you one. You would look so cute in a romper like this."

Ashley staring longingly at Jess's sketchpad.

"I don't know. Do you think I could pull something like that off?"

Jess laughed. "Trust me, if I make it, it'll look good on you."

"Okay…" That seemed to satisfy Ashley. "Jess, if you ever come across anything like these Bingo cards again, will you share it with me?"

Did we just become best friends?

"Of course, Ashley. Josh and I are always doing fun stuff like this. Oh my God, wait until you hear about the Prank War we just had a few months ago…"

CHAPTER 15

Day 4 – Restaurant

"The fuck you mean, 'not satisfying'?"

"Exactly what I said. It wasn't all that satisfying." Jess said through a mouthful of food.

Jess sat at a table at Chipotle eating a taco salad on her work break. She had Josh on video chat on her phone as she shoveled queso and guac into her mouth by the forkful.

Because she did not have the luxury of a long work break, Jess only had time to either eat lunch or call her boyfriend. So she chose to eat and talk at the same time.

"But I *felt* you cum all over my dick. Your pussy always quivers when you cum."

The family sitting next to Jess got up to leave, food still unfinished.

"You totally made me cum, babe. That's not what I'm saying. I didn't say I was disappointed. I said I wasn't satisfied."

Josh rolled his eyes in the video chat.

"As in, I'm still horny. God, read between the lines. I woke up and asked you for morning sex, then you tricked me into having a clandestine orgasm in the middle of our favorite café."

"Clandestine? I tricked you?"

"Hold on, I'm think there is an echo on your end of the call."

She could tell from the expression on his face that he was vexed. And that made her smile just a bit.

"Alright, alright, you want satisfaction, Mick Jagger? Meet me at our gym after work. I've been fantasizing about this one for a while."

"I pray that calling me Mick Jagger is *not* part of your fantasy."

"Only one way to find out. Fair warning, it'll also be a normal gym day. So I'll bring your gym bag from home."

"This sounds like a very un*satisfying* set up thus far."

"In any case, we were able to put a big X through 'café' today, weren't we? Whether you found it *satisfying* or not. I think this will make it up to you."

"Careful. Don't oversell this to me, babe, because I've got to be honest with you. I've had an *awful lot* of gym sex fantasies, too."

"Jess! You dirty girl, you! What kind of fantasies are we talking about?"

"The kind of sex fantasies that aren't realistically achievable." Jess shoveled more taco salad into the mouth. "Like getting fucked on the weight bench or having a hot trainer stick his dick in my ass while on the elliptical."

"Hot trainer?"

"Oh, relax. You're always the hot trainer in my sex fantasies."

Mostly.

"I'd better be-" his voice cut out for a second. "Hey, I've got a client calling me right now. Got to go, babe. Remember – gym after work!"

"I'm excited! And forming expectations!"

Josh laughed. "Love you, bye."

She blew him a kiss. "Love you."

When Jess ended the video call, she looked around and realized that the entire Chipotle lobby was empty.

"Where did everybody go?"

Jess finished her meal in silence as she fantasized about ways to incorporate different exercise equipment at the gym into sex.

CHAPTER 16

Day 4 – Gym

The gym that Jess and Josh went to was a decent drive out of the city, on the cusp of the suburbs. Because the location lay across a sea of freeway, it was pretty much inaccessible during daily gridlock hours. What would normally be a brisk 15 minute drive became a grueling 90 minutes of traffic in the mornings and late afternoon.

Lucky for Jess, her work was in the next town over from the enormous, plain gray building that housed their gym. It was part of a larger series of buildings that made up one of the largest outdoor shopping centers in the area.

Unfortunately, the multitude of shops all shared a single parking lot. So not only was the commute to the gym an ordeal, finding a parking spot was its own nightmare. Adding to the cacophony of chaos were the abundance of teenage drivers who plagued the shopping center.

It just wouldn't be a trip to the gym without watching a teenager texting as they back into another car in the parking lot.

So, Jess chose to park waaay in the back of the lot, where the only competition for parking were rouge, orphaned shopping carts. It was the gym, after all, and she would count the extra 30 seconds of walking to the front entrance towards her workout.

Sitting on Josh's lap, bouncing on his dick in the middle of the crowded café seemed like an eternity ago now. But the whole experience had seemed like nothing more than a tease to her – a free sample in the food court of exhibitionism. And like all free samples, it left her wanting more.

Whatever the reason, the whole incident in the café that morning left Jess feeling extra horny all day at work. Throughout the day, she snapped a couple nudes out of boredom. She would end up deleting them all before showing the pics to anyone, but it did satiate the exhibitionist inside her enough to get through the work day.

Jess didn't like having to censor her true feelings during sex. It felt like she was living a lie. At least, that's what it felt like in the café that morning.

No matter what Josh caid, sex in public always felt like a clandestine affair. The act of having to stifle herself in front of other people would always detract from her overall experience. Though the thought of other people watching her get off *did* turn her on.

If only there was a way to explore her newfound enjoyment of exhibitionism in a safe, legal way where she didn't have to restrain or censor herself. While other people watched, of course.

But sometimes, the risk of getting caught can be just as erotic.

Whatever Josh had in store for her at the gym, Jess had already made up her mind. She would not restrain herself during sex, no matter how many people might catch them in the act.

Once Jess made it into the gym, she realized that it would be a lot of work just to locate Josh. They belonged to a two-story super-gym complex. It housed several basketball courts, racket ball courts, an Olympic-sized racetrack, swimming pool, sauna, steam room, juice bar, and hundreds of exercise machines.

I'm never going to find him in here!

Jess sighed at the task in front of her, then started off towards the cardio machines.

"Jess! Hey, Jess!"

Josh jumped off the treadmill closest to the front door, where he was waiting for Jess to arrive. He jogged over to her wearing his cobalt blue mesh basketball shorts and a white sweat-soaked tank top that showed off his glistening, muscled arms.

As Josh came running up to her, she could see the outline of his meat stick flopping around in his shorts. Jess blushed as she stared at the outline of his dick.

All of her gym sex fantasies came flooding back to her at once.

He was already covered head to toe in sweat. It made his white tank top cling to every contour of his muscled, beefy chest and sculpted six-pack abs. His biceps bulged as he lifted up Jess's gym bag, proffering it to her.

God, I am one lucky girl.

Seeing her boyfriend like this was a lot for her to take in. And she drank him in thirstily. If she was horny before coming to the gym, she was positively *aching* for him now. His touch. Those powerful arms lifting her up, ravishing her body.

"Jess? Are you okay?"

His voice tore her away from her fantasies and brought her back to reality.

"Okay. Well, here is your gym bag. Hey, your skin looks a little flushed. Are you sunburned?"

If she wasn't embarrassed before, she definitely was now.

"I'm... I'm fine." She took her gym bag from him.

"Look at that, it went away. How weird."

He put the back of his hand up against her forehead. Satisfied she wasn't feverish, he planted a kiss on her cheek.

"Go change. I told you this would be a normal gym day."

"But..."

"You want your *satisfaction?* You've got to earn it."

She scowled at him, pointing the tip of her finger into his stupid sweat, muscly, sexy chest.

"I'm going to be really mad if you lured me here with the promise of sex and then pull the rug out from under my feet."

Josh laughed. "This one *is* on the list, isn't it? Just go and hit your normal workout for now, babe."

Jess pulled the back of his head down to her level so she could get another kiss in. A few drops of his sweat dripped on her cheek.

"I'll be thinking about you." She said in her best seductress voice.

"You'd better be." He kissed her again. He tasted like salty sweat.

"God, you need a shower."

Josh smiled lasciviously. "I'm going to go hit the weights." He slipped from her grasp and patted her on the butt. "Now go." He said before starting for the second floor of the gym.

Jess always kept her gym bag packed and ready for her next workout. That way whenever she got home from the gym she could simply toss her sweaty clothes in the hamper and stick a fresh pair of gym clothes back in her bag.

It was a relatively small bag considering the only items she ever kept in it were a sports bra, yoga pants, a clean towel, a fresh bottle of water, and a dozen new ankle socks.

Jess loved the feeling of brand new socks. The springiness and softness was just something that couldn't be recreated after the first wash. Plus, you could never have enough clean socks.

Preferably new ones.

Jess was never a gym rat like Josh was. He had specific days where he would only work out certain muscle groups. He kept a detailed log of what exercises he did which days and how many sets. He needed to have specific things to drink before, during, and after each workout. He was obsessive about it.

But yeesh. He certainly got results.

For all the work he put in, he definitely reaped the rewards. Josh was not jacked in the way that freakish bodybuilders were. But he did have well-defined muscles everywhere you would expect to find muscles on a man, which were, in Jess's opinion, pretty neat to look at.

Jess often wondered if the sleeve of tattoos that Josh had along his left arm made his muscles look more pronounced or if it was her imagination. But for his height and personality, Josh's colorful tattoos all over his sculpted body suited him perfectly. Jess loved the way they looked on him.

Sometimes, when they lay naked in bed together, Jess would lightly trace the outlines of his tattoos with her fingertips. She always found it amusing that such a big, handsome man would be so incredibly ticklish.

Jess's workout routine, by comparison, was unorganized and chaotic.

She made it to the gym whenever. Typically, that meant whatever days Josh could talk her into going with him and whenever she couldn't come up with a good excuse to get out of going. She liked the treadmill, elliptical, free weights, and when the mood should strike her, the punching bag.

There was no pre-loading or post-loading with Jess. She drank water from a bottle, then refilled it from the water fountain.

Still, whatever she was doing seemed to be working for her. Her workout sessions, though infrequent, coupled with (mostly) healthy eating habits allowed her to keep her figure. Plus, the cardio-focused exercise regimen afforded her enough stamina to keep up with Josh's marathon sex sessions.

Jess stood in front of the full-length mirror in the women's lock room as she changed into her purple sports bra and black stretchy yoga pants and tied her hair up into a pony tail. The outfit did an excellent job of conforming to her every curve, Jess noticed, as she ran the palm of her hand down her breasts and over her hips.

She realized that it felt as though she were wearing nothing at all just as much as it looked like she was wearing nothing.

Alright. Let's go turn some heads.

She stepped back into the gym and hopped on the nearest free treadmill. As she fell into a comfortable jogging pace, Jess picked up her fantasies exactly where they left off.

Jess had always considered herself an imaginative person. To successfully do her job as a fashion designer, she needed to see things that other people did not. Though, sometimes, she thought that she might have an overactive imagination.

As she worked herself into a sweat pumping her legs as fast as they would let her, Jess tried to imagine what Josh had in store for the two of them.

She let her fantasies play out. She saw herself laying on her back, getting fucked on the free weight bench. She pictured a fat cock stuffed in her mouth on the row machine. She envisioned Josh holding her legs up against his shoulders as he pounded her pussy raw on while she lay back at an incline on the upright bench press.

Jess even remembered watching a porn video one time of a women laying flat on her stomach on top of one of those giant medicine balls as one man ripped apart her yoga pants and spread her legs so he could fuck her from behind while another guy pulled down his gym shorts in front of her so she could suck his cock. That one didn't interest her, personally, but it sure was hot to think about.

At their gym, there was this large metal cage with many different hand and foot holds at various heights. While Jess never learned exactly what it was called, she often used it to stretch before and after workouts.

Being a gymnast when she was younger meant that she was already naturally very flexible. She couldn't help but wonder how many different positions someone could have sex in while stretching in the metal cage.

And the more she thought about it, the more she began to *obsess* over it.

When she next looked down at the treadmill, she saw that she had already ran 6 miles. She was positively soaked in sweat. Although she had no idea how much time had passed, she knew that Josh typically only worked out for a little over 60 minutes every time he came to the gym.

Smiling inwardly, she hopped off the treadmill in search of the metal cage. She wanted to see if she was still flexible enough to pull off some of the positions she had been fantasizing about.

Jess ran up the stairs to the second floor where she knew the stretching cage was located. With her white hand towel, she dabbed the sweat from her face and hair. As soon as she located the cage, she turned around and realized that it was parallel to the weight-lifting machines.

Jess entered the cage and kicked one leg up into a hand hold above her head, then leaned into her leg as she stretched. Her eyes darted back and forth from one machine to the next. Then she saw Josh on a back press machine.

She watched as his arm muscled bulged when he pressed outward on the machine. He didn't notice her at first. Jess felt like a voyeur spying on him. Then she switched legs, kicking her other foot high above her head and leaning into the stretch. Something flashed across Josh's face as he did a double take in her direction.

Their eyes met.

Jess was facing away from him with her legs spread wide. She bent down to touch the ground, her ass practically bulging out of her stretchy black yoga pants. She looked at him from between her legs, upside down. Her hair dangled upside down as she bit on her lower lip.

Josh flexed every muscle in his body. His wild eyes locked on her body with testosterone fueled, animalistic need. The lethal look in his eyes made her heart skip a beat.

Jess continued stretching, shifting her legs further apart until her ass touched the ground in full splits. Her pony tail whipped around as she twisted her torso back behind her again as she stared at Josh through lidded eyes.

He was the only one who recognized her bedroom eyes. He was the only object at the receiving end of those lustful green eyes. Josh recognized it instantly.

That was her *I'm horny, what are you going to do about it* look.

Jess sat on the floor, her legs split in either direction when she suddenly saw Josh striding towards here. His raptor-like glare fixed on her, a predator about to claim its prey.

Jess's heart was in her throat. That look on his face scared her, but at the same time excited her to be the object of his prey. She wanted him to devour her, to ravish her.

As he stalked closer and closer, adrenaline flooded her veins. Her panicked breathing quickened.

Without so much as a word, Josh picked her up by the waist and threw her over his shoulder. He was a hunter who had captured his prize. A conqueror claiming his woman.

With her flung over his shoulder, he effortlessly carried her down a flight of stairs. Jess couldn't help but to kick her feet helplessly, fidgeting, squealing and giggling the entire way. She was having the time of her life.

The people they walked past looked seriously concerned. Josh paid them no mind. He carried her past the cardio machines, past the front desk, both of them leaving a trail of sweat dripping in their wake.

Onward, Josh carried her with his arm wrapped around her abdomen as if she weighted no more than a sack of grain. Jess clung to the back of his tank top, smiling, laughing, and kicking her feet playfully the entire way.

Josh strode purposefully into the men's locker room. He carried her past men of all different ages and in various states of dress, turning the heads of one and all. They all stopped what they were doing to stare at the spectacle, but not one tried to stop Josh.

He carried her ass-first through the locker room. She could not see where he was bringing her, only the people who craned their necks as they passed by. She saw him turn a corner in the men's locker room, saw the floor turn into tiles and heard the sound of rushing water.

When he abruptly stopped, he set her down more gently than he had picked her up. She glanced around to see where this Viking raider had taken his woman captive.

She was in the last shower stall in the men's locker room.

Josh hooked his arm around her waist and pulled her up against his sweaty body, smothering her lips with his own. His hands traveled down her backside, finding their way to her ass, squeezing and savoring his juicy prize.

After admiring her from afar, he had taken that which he desired, which was the ultimate fantasy.

Suddenly, Jess understood why Josh had brought her to the gym. This testosterone-driven lust for her was unlike anything she had seen from him lately. It was primal, urgent, and ferocious. Both of their fantasies come true.

Exhibitionist Bingo unlocked something deep within both of them.

Josh backed her up against the wall and accidentally hit the hot water button in the process. The showers in this gym did not have a typical dial that controlled the water temperature, but rather two stainless steel buttons. One hot, one cold. When pressed, they dispensed water for an undisclosed amount of time.

Warm water rained down on the couple. Jess gasped wide, taken by surprise. Josh didn't even seem to notice it; the water did not slow him down one bit.

Jess's back was pressed up against the shower wall, Josh kissing on her neck. She ran her hands up the back of his now completely see-through tank top. Jess squeezed her eyes shut as their tongues explored each other's mouths with a sense of urgency.

When Josh broke off the kiss and took a step back, Jess opened her eyes. She immediately missed the weight of his body up against her. She could still feel the ghost of his firm chest pressing up against her soft breasts, the touch of his hand exploring her curvy bottom. Her body felt forlorn without him.

Josh's raptor gaze still fixed on Jess as water rained down on her body. She reached back and tugged the tie out of her hair, shaking out her wet dark hair as it fell over her shoulders.

Josh's gaze intensified to deadly seriousness. A fiery craving plain on his face. Jess's heart skipped a beat when Josh ripped his tank top off his chest as if he were Superman.

Is this really my boyfriend? The same man who just this morning was too tired to dress himself?

She reached out to brush his chest with her fingertips, painting his abs with her touch. His chest heaved his every breath. She could feel his heart racing, just like her own.

In an instant, his hand was against her cheek. He filled her mouth with his, licking her lips, sucking, biting, teasing her with his tongue.

Josh pinned her against the wall. This time, Jess hit the hot water button on purpose, sending warm water pouring over the couple. Jess felt the powerful muscles in his back, pulling him even closer. She never wanted to let go.

Jess felt his nails clawing down her back, pawing at her flesh needfully. He slipped his hands underneath her tight black pants, pulling them down and exposing the bubbly curves of her ass. Josh cupped her butt cheeks in his hands, giving them a firm squeeze. The sensation elicited a little groan of pleasure from Jess while he nibbled on her neck, planting a series of biting kisses.

He unpinned her from the wall long enough to pull her pants the rest of the way down. Jess eagerly kicked them all the way off and away, unconcerned where they ended up.

Once again, he pressed all of his weight up against her, pinning Jess to the wall in a way that really turned her on. Again, she hit the shower button and they were greeted by a wall of water and wetness. Jess closed her eyes and tilted her head back, letting the water wash over her.

Her sports bra now completely soaked, her hard nipples shown through. Josh's body was slick with sweat and water as he pressed himself tightly against her breasts. Jess raked her fingers over his corded muscles, caressing his exposed chest, bicep, and abs.

His mouth hard on hers, she could taste his sweat and saliva. Water from the shower rained down upon them as Jess squeezed his shoulders. Josh caught her wrists, and with one powerful hand, he pinned them together against the wall, above her head.

He ran his other hand up Jess's side, slipping his fingers underneath her dripping wet top. In an instant, he peeled it up and over her head, and then it was gone.

Jess stood there completely naked in the middle of the men's locker room shower. Josh had her hands pinned up against the wall as water poured over her every curve, washing away the sweat.

They both had the same needful look in their eyes. A look of craving and desire. A look of lust so powerful that nothing and no one could get in their way.

Me and him. Nothing else matters.

Nothing could keep them apart.

Jess slipped from Josh's grip and fell to her knees, tugging down on Josh's gym shorts. He gave no resistance, and the shorts came off easily. Josh kicked them away, behind him.

Now they were both fully nude in the locker room shower.

He was already rock hard. Jess took him into her mouth without hesitation. Josh threw his head back, making sounds of passion. Jess twisted her hands around the base of his cock as her head bobbed up and down, lips wrapped tightly around his shaft.

She felt the tip of his engorged dick slide down the back of her throat as she opened herself up to him. She wrapped her tongue around it, licking his cock as it passed between her soft pink lips. It felt good having his dick in her mouth once again. It felt exciting.

Jess longed for the taste of his white, hot load in her mouth. She longed for the deliciously gooey texture in her mouth, on her tongue, and all over her lips. She craved the salty-sweet taste of his cum. That satisfying feeling when he shot his load into the back of her throat – that was what she worked for.

And he delivered.

Drinking his cum was every bit as satisfying as she imagined. Jess greedily lapped up every drop of Josh's semen as she jerked and twisted his hard cock into her mouth, her lips wrapped around his tip. She made the same gratified moaning noises that she would if she had been eating her favorite chocolates – and savoring it even more.

When she was done, Josh helped her to her feet. He didn't have to tell her what he wanted to do next – the two were already completely in sync.

When Josh went to place Jess's arm around his neck, she understood. She jumped up into his arms, hugging his neck tights, legs wrapped around his waist. She locked her feet around his back.

With Josh's hands supporting Jess under her ass, he lifted her enough to slide his still hard cock, slick with her saliva, deep inside of her. Slowly, bit by bit, he lowered her onto his dick progressively, penetrating her deeper each time so as to not hurt her tiny pussy by giving her his full girth all at once.

Each time she felt his warm dick inside her body she wanted more. Josh fucking her this way was rapture and this locker room shower was her nirvana.

She clutched his body tightly. Her breasts, slick with water, pressed firmly up against him. She squeezed her thighs around his body.

Faster and faster, she felt his dick impale her body.

Faster and faster, her heart raced.

Faster and faster came her raucous moans of ecstasy.

With a throaty, low whisper, she moaned into his ear, "You're going to make me cum!"

Josh knew he had to catch up. That was evident by the way he started fucking her faster still. He wanted to cum at the same time as her. They always came at the same time.

And this time was no exception.

She dug her nails into his back as she felt her pussy tighten around his cock.

Holy shit, he was right. My pussy does *quiver when I cum!*

She could feel her juices sliding down his dick as he thrust up into her. She could feel his warm cum inside of her, dripping out of her pussy and onto the shower floor.

So much cum.

Even when she was done, he continued to fill her up. *God, is he* still *cumming?!*

When they were done and she finally caught her breath, he set her back down gently.

"Careful. The floor is wet." He warned her.

She didn't know if he was referring to the water from the shower or the small pool of their co-mingled bodily juices.

"I fucking love you." She stood on her tippy toes so she could kiss him on the lips.

He smiled, his hands still firmly gripping her hips.

"Wait here for ten seconds." He replied with another kiss.

Then he was gone. Jess was left alone and naked in the back of the men's locker room showers.

CHAPTER 17

Day 4 - Sauna

Not more than a few seconds after Josh had disappeared, an old, balding fat man came waddling into the showers wearing nothing but a white towel wrapped around his waist.

When he saw Jess standing there, wet, naked, and alone, he seemed to get a spring in his step.

"Get the fuck out of here! Get the fuck out! Go!" She screamed at him.

His smirk wilted. Red in the face, he turned around and waddled back to wherever he came from. All the while, Jess continued yelling just to make sure that no one else came into the shower with any funny ideas.

Where is Josh? Why would he just leave me here like this?

She started crying. She felt abandoned and positively vulnerable. This was here nightmare scenario. Josh left her.

Alone and naked with a room full of perverts presumably gathering on the other side of the locker room currently scheming on how they might rape and murder her.

This is it. This is how I die. At the grubby hands of fat old perverts in the men's locker room.

Then she saw Josh charging down the row of showers with a towel wrapped around his waist and another in his hand.

"What happened? Are you alright?"

He wrapped the towel around her. She cinched it around her chest, covering her from breast to thigh. Still, she couldn't stop crying.

"Where were you?" She sobbed.

"Getting us towels. What happened?"

"You didn't see a group of gross old men plotting my demise?"

"Plotting your... Baby, no." He wiped the tears from her face with his towel, then replaced it around his waist. "Aw, I'm sorry. I just thought that going to grab you a towel was better than parading you around naked in the men's locker room. Here, I'll put our wet clothes in my locker for now. Take my hand."

She sniffled and held Josh's hand.

Josh located all of their discarded wet clothes. Together, they walked over to Josh's locker in silence, turning the heads of every man in the locker room in the process.

There was no congregation of old perverts that Jess could see. Just a couple of men younger than Josh who had probably never seen a naked woman in real life before.

"Now where are we going, baby?" she asked after he deposited all of their clothes into his locker.

"Somewhere we can unwind and relax."

Jess giggled, "didn't we just do that?"

"Oh, babe. That was only just the beginning." He said and squeezed her hand.

Jess wasn't sure what he was planning, but the way he said it put a smile on her face.

Still glowing from their passionate, public shower, Josh lead Jess by the hand to the back of the gym. They walked into a large room with an indoor swimming pool. He lead her around the bubbling spa. She followed him as he lead her into the gym's sauna.

Jess paused to take in the mischievous look on her boyfriend's face as he held the door open for her.

The two were greeted by a face full of steam. As they blindly groped their way into the back of the steam room, they at last found the wooden rack of seats. Josh and Jess sat at the very top, where the heat was the most intense.

The couple sat with their backs against the wood paneling and simultaneously breathed out a relaxed sigh.

"I have to admit it, Josh. This steam room was a brilliant idea. It feels amazing." She breathed the steam in deeply.

"Doesn't it? I feel more relaxed already."

He put his arm around her neck. Jess's head fell against his shoulder, a blissful smile on her face.

"Plus, lots of health benefits to saunas, they say." He continued with his eyes closed.

"Yeah? Such as?"

"Well, getting really sweaty, for one. That's always exciting for me."

She laughed and slapped his arm playfully, then rubbed his muscled bicep. "How are you so horny all the time?" She asked.

"Probably because I know that you are just as horny. Because our sex drives are synced up. And because we're naked and *alone.*"

He went to uncinch Jess's towel around her chest, but she slapped his hand away.

"We're not naked and we're not alone."

"You're right. The fact that anyone could walk in at any moment is half the fun."

Jess narrowed her eyes at him with her *are you kidding me?* look. Then she got up and disappeared into the steam. A moment later, Josh heard a loud hiss as more steam flooded into every corner of the room.

Josh could barely see his own hand in front of his face, though he couldn't miss Jess swaggering back up to him, swaying her hips, her towel dangling from the pink of her outstretched hand. She dropped the towel at Josh's feet.

"Now at least one of us is naked." He whispered seductively.

Josh threw off his towel and watched it disappear into the blanket of steam. With her index finger, Jess pushed his erection down and watched it spring back up again when she let go.

"Baby, I still have a stomach full of your cum. Now it's your turn."

She took a seat next to him, her bare ass against the edge of the wooded bench, legs spread wide open.

"Hold on."

Josh disappeared into the steam. He returned a moment later with both their towels. He quickly folded one up and placed it at Jess's feet so he could kneel down on it. The other towel he proffered to Jess.

"You're going to want to sit on this, because I'm not going to stop until I have a stomach full of your cum, too."

Jess laughed, but took the towel from him and placed it under her butt.

"Thanks. This is actually way more comfortable."

"Right? It's like they build these things specifically to be uncomfortable for people who hook up in the sauna."

"We'll show them!" Jess said, then grabbed Josh's head and shoved it between her legs.

Eager to please, Josh hungrily and hornily went straight for her clit. He wasted no time with kisses and foreplay like he usually did when going down on her. He just feverishly flicked his tongue on all the perfect spots.

"Oh my guh- Fuck, Josh!" She heard herself cry out.

As much as Jess loved sucking dick and swallowing cum, Josh loved eating pussy even more. In fact, he loved eating pussy so much that he tried to hide the fact that he enjoyed it as much as he did from Jess. He was worried that she would think his kinky obsession with eating, licking, playing with, and worshiping her pussy was weird. Therefore, Josh did his best not to divulge exactly how much he enjoyed it (very much) or how often he wanted to do it (every chance he got).

She knew that Josh was worried that if she knew all of his kinks that it would change the dynamic of their relationship. But she wanted him to have a kinky little secret that he could keep to himself, and on the grand scale of kinky sex secrets, having a pussy eating fetish hardly even registered.

Besides, the secret was his to keep. If Josh knew exactly how much she enjoyed sucking dick, she worried it would change their dynamic, too.

The couple would often bet on things and the winner of the bet got to choose a movie for them to watch while the loser had to go down on the winner for the entire length of the movie. On more than one occasion, Jess noticed that Josh would throw these bets just to get some alone time with her perfectly smooth and tight pussy.

He dreamed about it. He fantasied about it. He loved the taste of it. He loved the detailed intricacies of how his tongue could always elicit different responses from her. He even loved the occupational hazard of eating her ass.

And Jess loved it, too.

Josh lifted up Jess's thighs, pushing her knees up to her breasts before plunging his tongue deep into Jess's asshole. She jumped in surprise and whimpered.

"Oooh my God, yes! More of that, *please*, daddy!"

Jess leaned back and grabbed the back of her thighs, pulling her legs up even more. It was a move that meant she was giving Josh full access to her pussy, ass, and clit. The Holy Trinity, as he sometimes called it. Jess called it The Devil's Playground.

Josh ran his tongue around the rim of her asshole, tickling it with the tip of his tongue. His entire mouth wrapped around her ass, teasing her.

Jess couldn't sit still. His tongue reduced her to a fidgeting, giggly mess. "Oh, ye-he-hesss! Daddy has come out to play at the Devil's Playground at last! Oh, fuck, daddy, yes! Keep doing that. And stick a finger in me or something."

Josh opted for the "or something" option.

He knew that Jess was a woman who appreciated variety. He knew that since he only a few minutes ago filled Jess's pussy up with cum, she would appreciate getting fucked in the ass this time.

Sometimes she liked having her pussy pounded. Sometimes she like having her ass and pussy licked. And sometimes she like getting fucked in the ass.

She was refined like that.

And like any classy bitch, Jess could appreciate the subtle differences between a clitoral, vagina, and anal orgasm. And Josh loved her for it.

Normally she required a comfortable amount of lube to do the deed. But since Josh had been licking her asshole like a camel at a desert oasis, she was certain no lube would be required.

When Josh told her that he wouldn't stop until he had a stomach full of her cum, he set an expectation. But he knew that the only time she ever had a squirting orgasm was with anal stimulation.

After she told him to stick a finger in her, Josh gave her asshole one final, sloppy lick for good measure before sticking the tip of his engorged cock in her ass.

"Oh. Okay. That's even better, I guess." She said, her lips forming a tight "O" as Josh slowly penetrated deeper into her ass.

He pushed her legs up further until she was pressed together like a folding chair. Arguably the most difficult way of having anal sex.

"Your dick feels so fucking good in my little ass, babe, but why don't I just sit on it."

He shrugged, then pulled out.

"Lay the towel down so I can sit on top of it." He told her.

They switched spots. Jess got up and Josh sat down on top of the towel over the wooden bench of the sauna. His stiff dick shot straight up in the air like a flagpole.

Jess took the other towel and wrapped it around herself from her nips to her hips.

"What are you doing?" Josh laughed at her.

"In case someone comes in. It'll look, you know, inconspicuous."

Josh raised one eyebrow, giving her a look.

"I'm not stopping if anyone comes in, you know!" she said, hands on her hips.

Josh chucked again, "Shut up and take this dick in your ass, already."

"Yes, daddy."

Jess climbed atop him, sitting on his lap in a way that looked innocuous while she lowered herself on his dick. She worked it in slowly, Josh's hands on her hips guiding her as she grinds her ass up against him. Jess, meanwhile, rubbed on her clit as Josh fucked her in the ass.

Already, she was close.

But the moment she bare butt checks were flush against his hips, they felt a gust of cool air in the room from one end to the other.

Someone had entered the room.

True to her word, Jess did not stop bouncing her ass up and down on Josh's cock. She felt annoyed, and admittedly her heart jumped a little, but she was still too horny to stop now.

To anyone who saw the couple, it looked like they were both wearing towels hiked up to their hips. No one would be able to tell Jess was grinding on Josh's dick as she moved her bottom underneath her towel.

Jess saw the silhouette of two people as they entered the steam room. She could just barely see the outline of their bodies as they took a seat on the wooden bench opposite Jess and Josh. It looked like the newcomers were settling in far away from the couple.

As soon as Jess realized that the two people across the room were going to keep their distance, she began wiggling her ass in wide circles, sliding up and down his throbbing dick.

Jess moved her hair off of her shoulders. It was sticking to her skin, so she gathered it to one side while bouncing up and down on Josh's lap.

She looked over her shoulder and saw his face. He was biting his lower lip, face contorted in the warm pleasure of his dick deep in Jess's ass.

She could tell he was struggling to keep quiet. Jess was finding it next to impossible.

Jess looked over to the other side of the steam room to see that the pair of people over there were moving around a lot, but still keeping their distance. Knowing that, Jess spread her legs a bit more.

As she brazenly played with her pussy, she watched the strangers across the room bob their heads up and down.

That's curious.

She worked up the courage to bounce her ass even higher, taking the full length of Josh's thick cock in her ass. Josh, meanwhile, placed his hands underneath her cheeks to soften the sound of flesh slapping against flesh.

Then a high-pitched moan pierced the silence of the sauna.

Jess froze.

I don't think that was no.

Again, she heard a loud, feminine moan of pleasure.

That definitely wasn't me. And it definitely wasn't Josh. That means…

"Oh, fuck yes!"

Jess looked over her shoulder at Josh. They both had the same confused look on their face.

"Oh, yes!"

With no one adding more water to the hot coal, the steam in the room began to die down. Jess could begin to see the outline of the two strangers in the room with them a little bit better.

One was clearly a woman. Jess could see that her hair was dyed pink, blue, and purple and tied up into two buns on the top of her head as her entire body bobbed up and down.

"Ohhh, God, yesss…"

This time there was no mistaking it. Jess and Josh put their anal sex on hold to watch the perfect strangers across the room having sex.

As the steam began to dwindle and thin, Jess saw something that made her heart skip a beat. She felt her eyes bulge out of her head.

Could it be?

"Miko?! Miko, is that you?" Jess cried from across the room.

The woman with the multicolored hair suddenly froze.

"Shit," she cursed under her breath.

"You know here?" Josh asked, but Jess ignored him.

"Miko, it's me! Jess!"

There was a tense pause where no one said anything. No one moved. No one breathed. Josh heard the sound of a single drop of sweat from his balls hit the tiled floor.

Miko had a hard time placing Jess, but Jess remembered the exact moment her and Miko met. How could she forget?

Jess ran into Miko outside a pharmacy the day that Josh swapped out lube for super glue and glued a rainbow-colored unicorn tail butt plug to Jess as a prank. Jess was forced to run around all over town in search of a way to remove the butt plug.

Most people overlooked the rainbow tail sticking out of Jess's skirt, but Miko immediately recognized it for what it was. The two instantly bonded over their shared love for animal themed butt plugs after Miko confessed that her boyfriend sometimes made her walk around for days at a time wearing a cat tail.

"Jess? Oh my God! Jess!" Miko jumped up and ran across the room to give Jess a hug.

It took her a few seconds to realize that Miko was completely naked and covered in glistening sweat.

The tiny Asian woman had her hair tied up into multicolored buns. Her lashes were unnaturally long in a way that was hauntingly beautiful. Miko's breasts were much smaller than Jess', but with soft pink nipples and hard, pointy areolas, they suited her petite body perfectly.

Jess didn't notice any tattoos on Miko when they first met, but she was shocked to see how many her pale white skin could artfully display. Floral tattoos stretched all along one side of Miko's naked body, from her thigh to her chest, including an intricate mandala resting in her cleavage and something that

Jess was too embarrassed to get a closer look at right above her cleanly shaved pussy.

Hm. All of her tattoos are in places that can be covered up in public, Jess realized.

Wait. Is that Hello Kitty? She "accidentally" identified the tattoo on Miko's lower pelvic region.

As petite as Miko was – and she was an unquestionably tiny woman – she was always a little bundle of endlessly talkative energy.

"Jess!" Miko skipped across the wet steam room floor and practically knocked Jess over with her sweaty, naked embrace. It was all she could do to hold her towel in place.

Jess gave her a one-armed hug without getting up off of Josh's lap. After releasing Jess from her affectionate hug, Miko saw that Jess was blushing.

Miko looked down at her naked body and took a step back, laughing nervously. She walked back over to where her naked companion still waited and returned holding a towel.

She didn't cover herself with the towel. Instead, Miko clutched it between her breasts with one hand like a security blanket. It seemed enough for her.

"Jess! It's so nice to see you again!" she grinned happily.

"Funny running into you here of all places, Miko." Jess said, glancing over in the direction of the man she was fucking only moments ago. "Is this your boyfriend you told me about?"

Miko had previously painted a picture of her abusive boyfriend. The man sitting on the other end of the steam room seemed socially awkward, young, and stacked like a body builder. Although was close enough to hear their conversation, he made no indication that he was listening.

"Him?!" Miko coughed the word. "Oh, nooo... He's more like a... Personal trainer?" She didn't sound very sure.

Jess and Josh exchanged a look.

"And this is your boyfriend you told me about, or a friend, or...?"

"Yeah, sorry, Miko. This is my boyfriend, Josh. Josh, this is Miko,"

"Hi, Josh!" Miko leaned in to give Josh a very affectionate hug.

"Uh. Hi, Miko." Josh had a look of utter panic on his face. He looked at Jess and held up both hands in surrender, as if to say *See? I'm not trying to touch your hot, naked friend!*

Still, the way his cock throbbed deep inside her ass told her a different story.

"Miko?" Jess said softly.

"Yes, Jess-Jess?" Miko relinquished her naked hold on Josh.

"Forgive me if I'm being forward, but Josh and I couldn't help but to notice what you and your, er, friend... were up to."

"Oh, shit, really?" She laughed nervously. "Sorry, I thought we were the only ones in here. Honest! We'll leave you two in peace."

She started walking away, but Jess grabbed her by the elbow.

"No, Miko, that's not it. I wanted to ask you a... favor."

Miko turned to eye the couple up and down.

"A favor?"

Jess nodded. "I was hoping that you and your friend could just... you know... like, move a little closer? Next to us?"

"Move... closer to you?"

Miko stared at Jess. Then she stared at Josh. Then, finally, a look of recognition landed on her face at the same time her towel slipped from her hand and landed on the floor.

"Oh, shit. Are you two...? You want us to...?"

Jess gave her elbow a little squeeze. "Please, Miko? For me?"

Jess finally felt confident enough to start wiggling her bottom on Josh's lap once again.

"Of course, Jess! After all, we're butt plug buddies!" Miko said, then energetically skipped over to the other side of the room where she collected her fuck buddy who was sitting there patiently.

Josh looked at Jess and mouthed, "Butt plug buddies?"

"You wouldn't understand. Butt plug buddies is a bond that runs deeper than blood." Jess shrugged, hoping there was still enough steam left in the room to hide her bright red face.

A second later, Miko came over with the man she entered the steam room with trailing behind her.

"So... it's cool if we, like, fuck here right next to you guys?"

"Yes," Jess told here. "And there is actually a very good reason for it that I can't explain right now, but I'm asking you to trust me. As a butt plug buddy."

Jess winked.

Miko winked back.

"Strength in numbers." Jess said and tapped the empty space on the wooden bench right next to where Josh was sitting.

Satisfied with that answer, Miko smiled happily and waved for her friend to sit down next to Josh. Miko set her hands on his shoulders and climbed up onto his lap.

He must be at least four times bigger than she is.

"Jess, are you sure about this?" Miko hesitated once again.

"Miko, sweetie, for this entire conversation my boyfriend has been fucking me in my ass. Just join us." Jess said while she bounced up and down on Josh's dick.

"Maybe this will put here at ease, babe." Josh reached in front of Jess and pulled off her towel.

"Josh!"

Jess could feel the blood return to her face. *It might as well take out a mortgage there.*

"Oh my God, Jess, you have such nice tits!" Miko was frozen, unable to tear her eyes away from Jess's naked body.

Jess went back to fucking Josh.

"I'll let you touch them, if you want." Jess offered. "But it would really make me more comfortable if we weren't the only ones in the room having sex."

Miko blinked, finally pulling herself out of the trance.

"Oh. Right. Okay."

"Show me what you two were doing earlier." Jess said, grinding her ass hard against Josh's hips.

Miko yanked off her friend's towel and, to Jess's surprise, an enormously hard dick sprang to life. Jess was certain that there was no possible way Miko was fucking this guy.

I mean, there's no way. It's just not physically possible.

And yet, Miko climbed atop him as if it would actually fit inside of her. She planted her thighs on either side of his legs and, facing him, mounted his terrifyingly long cock.

Miko spit in the palm of her had and rubbed it between her legs. It took her several attempts, but eventually she was able to fit the tip of his dick inside her outrageously small vagina.

Maybe his dick just looks big by comparison to Miko's teensy, tiny pussy.

Either way, Jess couldn't take her eyes off the spectacle. And neither could Josh. And the way Miko was moaning told them both that it was more pleasure than pain. Though it was any wonder she didn't attract the attention of the gym management.

I wish I could be that inhibited. Jess thought. Though maybe it was a good thing she wasn't.

Jess tried to think of a way to interrupt Miko's unbridled squeals of joy.

"Oh, Miko! I just love those tattoos all over your body! They're so hot!"

"Oh, thank you, Jess! Your boyfriend had a lot of hot tattoos, too!"

The fuck is that *supposed to mean?!*

Jess could tell that Josh enjoyed the compliment but wouldn't comment on it for fear of his girlfriend's wrath. He was kicking back while Jess bounced on his dick as they both watched this tiny Asian girl take a cock that she was definitely not genetically predisposed to take.

Meanwhile, Jess could feel Josh's cock inside of her ass, throbbing as if it wanted to get even harder than it was already. She continued rubbing her little clit, but without additional lube it was starting to hurt.

"I must confess. When we first met, I always knew something like this would happen." Miko said to Jess.

The Jess blurted out, "Miko, let's race to see who can get their man to cum first!"

Without waiting for her to respond, Jess started wiggling her butt on top of Josh even faster.

"Mmm, But I don't want my man to cum just yet." Miko cried between moans of pleasure.

"Then how about you and I race to see who can cum first?" Jess amended.

"You're on!" Miko said with renewed enthusiasm.

With that, the girls started riding their respective men as if they were carnival rides. Miko was sliding up and down in her man's lap with her arms wrapped around his neck, grinding ferociously. Jess leaned forward, bouncing her ass as if she were a jockey riding on horseback, furiously rubbing her pussy.

Their screams and moans echoed off the steam room walls coupled with the sound of flesh slapping against wet flesh. Each woman was aggressively trying to finish first.

The doors to the sauna opened and a middle-aged man wearing gym shorts entered. Blinked. Then immediately backed out without question. Neither woman even seemed to notice.

Through the tangled onslaught of sensual screaming, someone screamed "Oh, oh shit, I'm going to cum!"

It was the man that Miko was fucking.

"No! Not yet! I'm *so* close!" Miko screamed back at him.

She started banging him even faster, driving her pussy down to the base of his massive cock, slapping the bottom of her thighs against the top of his loudly.

In a strangled voice, he cried, "I can't help it! You pussy... it's just so tight!"

"Don't!" Miko slapped him on the shoulder in protest.

He let out a long, anguished cry. Miko yelped and jumped off of his cock, which continued to sputter semen in every direction.

"Ew! I told you not to cum inside of me again! Shit! My boyfriend is going to be so pissed!" Miko slapped him repeatedly in the chest, but he hardly noticed.

In a huff, Miko picked up a towel off of the steam room floor and wrapped it around her lower half, leaving her tits exposed, then stalked out of the steam room fuming.

A moment later, after he finished ejaculating all over the floor of the sauna, Miko's companion grabbed his towel and tucked away his erection.

"Miko, wait! I can suck it out like snake venom!" He said, charging after her.

And then Jess and Josh were alone in the sauna once again.

"Well... I guess you lost?" Josh said plainly.

"Shut up. I need to concentrate." Jess replied.

Admittedly, the entire ordeal with Miko joining them proved more distracting than it did comforting, though she never stopped bouncing on Josh's dick. And now that she had a bit of silence, she could concentrate on getting fucked in the ass and the resulting orgasm.

She focused on her clit and how good it felt. Josh thrust his hips upward while she drove her booty down on him. All it took was a little concentration and silence for Jess to feel her anal orgasm within her grasp.

Ah, here it comes.

As drawn out as it was, her orgasm came and went in seconds. She had hoped to squirt like a fire hydrant, however, it was more like the gushing of a broken water gun.

That's disappointing.

"You came already?" Josh seemed to be distracted still.

"Yeah. Where were you?" She asked, looking back at him.

Jess stopped bouncing her ass on his lap, though his hard cock was still deep inside her.

"Kay. Bend over so I can cum in your ass real quick."

"Sure thing, babe."

She got on her hands and knees on top of the wooden bench. Josh sat up on his knees, fucking her from behind, doggy style. To distract Jess from the pain of hard wood against her knees, she reached between her legs so she could massage her pussy.

With both hands on either ass cheek, Josh got behind her and started pounding her from behind faster than she ever could fuck Josh by herself. She felt him inside her even harder and deeper than ever before.

The clapping of skin against skin echoed in the small steam room along with Jess's uncontrollable moans resulting from her anal pleasures. Each time Josh drove the full length of his hard cock into her ass she made a different sound.

"Oh-fuck-yeah-feels-so-good-should-have-done-this-from-the-start-oh-fuck-my-ass-just-like-that-right-there-babe-I-want-your-cum-in-my-tight-ass-yeah-yeah-yeah-right-there-so-good-fuck-so-good-I'm-gonna-cum-Josh-oh-fuck-I'm-cum-ming-Josh-yes-Josh! Oh, yes! Right there! Oh, fuuuck yesss, babe. Mmm, God I love feeling you cum in my ass. No, don't pull out just yet. Leave it in a minute. Let's just sit here for a little. Mmm… So warm. God, I think I just squirt all over the bench. Is this my cum or yours? I guess it doesn't matter."

Jess was still on her hands and knees, bent over with her ass up in the air casually playing with her pussy. Josh stood behind her, cock still deep inside his girlfriend's ass while he wiped the sweat from his forehead and ran his fingers through his hair.

That was how the woman who entered the steam room found them as they basked in the post-coital afterglow of each other's musky love. She froze, looking from Jess to Josh before adverting her gaze to the floor. The woman quickly backed out the door faster than she came in. She had that *I'm telling on you* look on her face.

"Okay, maybe we should go now." Jess said at last. "Where is my towel?"

Josh pulled out gently, then retrieved both of their towels, now dampened from sitting on the filthy sauna floor. Jess was chagrined to have to take Josh's dick out of her ass so soon – she would have been content to sit there a few minutes longer – but at the risk of being permanently banned from their gym, getting the fuck out was the wise decision.

After all, it was kind of amazing they were able to get away with as much as they already did.

But the jury is still out as to whether we will get away with it or not.

They had one more shower before leaving the gym. Josh returned to the men's locker room to shower by himself, and Jess to the women's shower by her lonesome.

While they individually got clean, their minds were united in thinking about the steamy, dirty things they did in the gym that day.

CHAPTER 18

Day 4 - Home

"So that's ten down already."

"For the last time, Josh, you don't count the free space in Bingo!"

"Okay, so nine, then. There are still a lot of these we haven't done yet." Josh said, studying the Bingo card on the coffee table. "Do you still think we can bang out all of these in such a short amount of time?"

"Only if we step up our game and start banging more each day." Jess said, giving him a lascivious look.

It was Friday morning, and the couple was sitting in the kitchen having coffee. Once more, they stared down the mysterious Exhibitionist Bingo card with determination.

"And how do you propose we do that?" Josh asked "Did you have something in mind for tonight?"

Jess set down her cup of coffee so she could put all of her effort into giving Josh an incredulous glare.

"Aren't we still going to that Kaskade show at Avalon tonight?" She said with one raised eyebrow.

Josh ran his fingers through the back of his hair nervously. "Oh, yeah. I must have forgotten."

"I didn't." Her eyes narrowed at Josh as she took another sip from her coffee cup. "Even if you bought those tickets months ago."

"Okay, so if we find a place to hook up at Avalon, we can check the Nightclub box." He said, tapping the corresponding square on the Bingo card with his index finger.

"Technically, I think Avalon counts as a nightclub, bar, and concert." Jess pointed to the squares she referenced.

"Nope." Josh swatted her hand from the table. "That's cheating. Each square needs to be its own thing."

"Josh…" Jess rolled her eyes. "Who is going to know?"

She stood behind him, wrapping her arms around his chest. Josh took a step back, giving her a look as if she just let loose a lud and long fart.

"I'll know. We'll know. It's a hollow victory, Jess."

She scoffed. "But technically, Avalon is all of those things!"

His attention was back on the Bingo card. "I think it should count as a 'concert' because we can have a drink at the bar across the street."

"And would that be enough of a *fulfilling victory* for Josh Jacobs?" A lightbulb went off in Jess's brain. "Or – we could just have sex in different spots around Avalon. You know, like we did at the gym. Like, once the bar, and then on the dance floor, and then on stage in front of everyone…"

Josh was already shaking his head. "The gym was different and you know it. Besides, I want to fuck you at the bar, then we can figure out how to have sex in Avalon without getting caught."

"But I like getting caught." Jess whined.

"No, you don't." He said taking her into his arms and embracing her in a hug.

"Okay. You can fuck me at the bar. But baby? That's still only two."

"Nothing gets past you."

She pounded a fist on his chest. "Be nice to me!"

Josh chucked but held his gaze on the Bingo card. He stepped up to the kitchen table and slowly moved his hand towards the piece of paper with outstretched finger.

His finger stopped as it hovered over one of the squares on the Bingo card.

"This one here."

A smile spread wide across Jess's face. "I love it." She kissed Josh on the back of the neck. "Now I'm excited for tonight."

"Perfect." Josh reciprocated the smile and kiss. "I'll meet you at the bar in Hollywood after work, then?"

Jess gulped down the rest of her coffee and moved to grab her car keys. "It's a date."

CHAPTER 19

Day 4 - Bar

A typical Friday night in Hollywood is a hotbed of activity.

And Friday night on Hollywood Blvd was always a fucking madhouse. The streets were guaranteed to be packed with a hodgepodge of tourists, locals, and homeless running amok – all in search of their personal preference of sinful delights courtesy of the city of angels.

Parking was a nightmare at best. Non-existent at worst. Even the $40 parking lots filled up to capacity on most weekends.

That's forty American dollars. To park your car for a few hours. In a parking lot where there was a pretty good chance of your car getting broken into, stolen, or pissed on by homeless and drunks.

Or all three, if you were particularly unlucky.

One only needs to stand on the corner of Hollywood and Vine for a few minutes on any Saturday night to watch the antics between the unreasonably drunk and their shepherds quickly unfold.

Merchants selling everything under the sun gather on the streets at night to hawk their wares. From delicious smelling street meat pandering to the inebriated, bodegas swindling tourists, street pharmacists peddling shockingly wide array of goods, sex workers with their wares unapologetically on display, and costumed superheroes shamelessly slinging selfies – anything can be bought and sold in Hollywood regardless of how tangible it might be.

Downtown Hollywood is perhaps most famous for the many nightclubs, bars, and venues all within a few relatively condensed city of blocks – including the world famous Avalon.

The three-story buildings has been the host of many artists recorded live albums over the course of its long history and is a benchmark on the road to success for L.A. musicians. Having a big name like Kaskade perform at Avalon was not uncommon. Neither was the massive crowd of club kids waiting outside in a line that wrapped around the building.

As soon as Jess and Josh saw the line to get into Avalon, they made a B-line for the nearest bar.

"Holy shit. Do we have to wait in that?" Jess asked, disheartened to see the long line of people – but not the end of it.

"Not sober, we don't," answered Josh.

He led her by the hand down the street and into a narrow little dive bar called *The Room.*

That, too, was packed.

All of the booths were full of posh, fancy-dressed Hollywood club-goers. Even the standing room was full of people at the bar, all vying for the attention of the two bartenders to get their drink orders in.

Not my crowd at all, Jess thought.

Still, when Josh mentioned that they go to a bar to hook up before Avalon, Jess was quite insistent that they go to *The Room.* Jess could think of no better place to hook up and go unnoticed than a room full of self-interested Hollywood egomaniacs and narcissists.

The couple elbowed their way through the crowd as they searched for a place they could fuck in comfort.

"Wait a sec," Josh said suddenly. "Isn't that your friend from the gym?"

He nodded in the direction of a tiny Asian woman who looked like she could have been an alternative model. Her pink, purple, and blue hair was pulled into two short pigtails. The tattoos on her chest shone through her pink studded vest and black bra with pink lace trim. Her racy mini skirt – also pink – ended just above her ass cheeks. On her head she wore a pink and black costume cowboy hat.

"Oh, wait." He said, "That girl has clothes on. False alarm."

"Miko wears clothes. Sometimes." Jess insisted, then, "Miko! Miko, over here!"

She pulled Josh's hand as she led him through the crowd towards Miko on the other side of the bar.

"Jess! Oh my God!"

Miko ran up to Jess and the two women screamed and hugged as though they hadn't seen each other for years. Miko's eyes darted to Josh standing behind her, then back to Jess.

"And you brought your boyfriend. Hi, Josh! I almost didn't recognize you."

She is totally picturing my boyfriend naked right now.

Josh stood behind Jess and wrapped his arms possessively around her waist.

"Hi, Miko. Did you figure out that problem of yours since I last saw you?" Josh asked in reference to the last thing Miko screamed as they ran out of the sauna.

Jess discretely elbowed Josh in the gut for even asking. Miko, meanwhile, turned a shade of scarlet.

"Oh. Uh, yeah. It's been, um, resolved." She stared at the floor.

A heavyset, tall man with a messy crop of blonde hair spilling out from his head in every direction stepped up beside Miko. He was nearly two feet taller than she was and more black slacks with a black button up that made him look like either a bouncer or valet.

The large man looked at Josh with his arms draped around Jess's waist, then imitated the move with Miko.

"And is this your boyfriend?" Josh asked, only to receive another elbow to the but courtesy of Jess.

Miko looked up at the man with his meaty arms wrapped around her as if she were just noticing him for the first time.

"What? Him? Oh, no. This is my friend, Fred."

"Frank." Said Fred in a deep, gravelly voice.

"Whatever. These are my friends Jess and her boyfriend Josh."

"Pleased to meetcha," Fred said, sizing Josh up as if the two were about to enter a boxing ring.

Jess wrapped her arms around Josh's as he held her, subtly rocking from side to side. "I told Miko about the Bingo card and she wanted to meet us here."

"So, you want to try your hand at BINGO, do you?" Josh said, exchanging a secret, perverse smile with Miko.

"Jess sent me a picture of the card you guys found. I've already got Sauna and Gym crossed out!"

Josh opened his mouth to say something, but Miko cut him off. "And yes, Josh, they were two separate instances."

Jess burst out laughing.

"This place is crowded, yeah?" Josh said, looking around and trying to change the subject.

"Yeah..." Miko replied, her gaze lost in the distance. An instant later, she snapped back to realize. "Could you go get us some drinks?" She said to Fred. Then, to Jess and Josh, "What are you drinking?"

"Vodka." They replied in unison.

Miko smiled, as if she just read their minds.

"Three vodka doubles, Fred." She told Fred.

"Frank. Four vodka doubles, Frank." Fred said, then trotted off to push his way through the throngs of people standing in line for the bar.

Miko turned to Jess, tenderly touching her elbow. "This is way different than the gym." She observed, looking around the place. "I don't know how we're going to get away with this here."

"I think we can use that to our advantage." Jess said, pointing to one of the corner booths.

Upholstered in shiny black vinyl, each booth looked brand new. The low lighting paired with dark wooden tables deftly matched the seats, creating a darkly elegant atmosphere through the entire bar.

"How would we go about getting ourselves into a booth?" Jess asked.

Josh frowned. "It looks like bottle service only."

"Then let's just join one." Miko said simply with a thumb and forefinger pressed to her cheek, still surveying the room. "There." She waved her hand in the direction of the least populated table. Technically, the three of them could all fit into the booth, but fitting Fred's big ass might be a bit of a stretch.

In the wrap around corner booth sat two surly-looking men and one woman. They were all engaged in conversation but looked bored of it. It was certainly not the booth that Jess would have picked if she were entertaining the idea of stealing someone else's bottle service table.

Regardless, Miko seemed very confident that her plan would work as she walked purposefully over to the trio in the booth.

When she sensed doubt coming from Jess, she whispered in her ear, "Trust me. I'm very good with people."

Now I'm even more nervous.

Jess and Josh followed closely behind Miko as she slid into the booth like she owned it. Now that Jess got a little closer she could clearly see that all three of the people in the booth were just kids.

College students.

The man sitting on the far end of the booth, the one furthest away from Miko, had dark, messy hair, tan skin, and more a blue UCLA hoodie.

Who wears a hoodie to a bar in Hollywood, then orders bottle service?

The guy sitting at next to Miko wore his hair in dreadlocks with a simple pair of jeans and T-shirt. The woman who sat in between the two men was the only one Jess acknowledged as having any fashion sense. She wore a dazzling sequins black top and glittery black skirt that matched her caramel mocha skin as beautifully as it matched her long, curly hair. The curves of her body filled out her top and skirt perfectly without revealing too much.

At least one of them knows how to dress.

Jess also recognized her as having the most intelligent-looking eyes out of the three. Up until Miko sat down in their booth, she looked borderline suicidally bored at whatever the two men she was with tried to pass as conversation.

Jess only heard the tail end of what Miko was telling her as she and Josh stepped up beside her at the end of the booth.

"...and it's called Exhibitionist Bingo."

Jess slapped the palm of her hand against her forehead.

Great...

But immediately after Miko finished talking, two out of the three faces lit up like Christmas. If Jess had to guess, it was the little Mexican kid in the UCLA hoodie who was the third wheel.

Jess didn't hear much more of their conversation, but less than a minute later, everyone in the booth scooted over to make room for Jess and Josh.

She let Josh hop in the space at the very end of the booth so she could sit on his lap. There was just barely enough room for all of them.

Jess's strappy black bodycon dress was just tight enough to hug her every curve. It was an off-the-shoulder cut, so it already exposed a generous amount of cleavage, only leaving about an inch or so in between the fabric and her nipples.

The clingy black dress fell to her upper thigh, so when she climbed into the booth to sit on Josh's lap, she kept tugging at the bottom of her dress as she crossed her legs.

Hopefully, no one drops anything under the table.

"These are my friends, Jess and Josh." Said Miko by way of introduction.

"Hi, I'm Ashley." The woman in the middle said with a dazzling smile.

"Sup wit it. I'm Kels." The man sitting closest to Miko with the dreadlocks dapped Jess and Josh.

"Carl," the guy at the end of the booth wearing the UCLA hoodie grumbled.

"Jess and Josh and playing Exhibitionist Bingo, too! Isn't that fun! Oh, and that idiot walking around lost holding our drinks is Fred." Miko said, pointing to the man she came to the bar with.

Fred was meandering around the bar like a lost puppy – albeit an enormous puppy – as he juggled four drinks in his hands. Jess watched him in amusement as Fred's face went from scared to angry to sad, then back to scared.

Carl, meanwhile, slumped down further in his seat and started picking the label off of the table's champagne bottle.

"Thanks so much for letting us share your booth," Miko said. "Let me get you guys some drinks. What do you guys want?"

Each of them called out the name of a different cocktail simultaneously. Miko smiled. It was a testament to their friendship that Jess realized this meant she was frustrated with their answers.

Miko pointed at Fred. "He only understands very simple commands. Things like 'four vodka doubles' or 'put penis in butt'. He gets confused and forgetful when you give him complicated commands like 'arrive on time' or 'use lots of lube.'"

Miko finally got tired of watching Fred putter around and called him over with their drinks. Then she gave him her *come-hither* stare until Fred leaned in close over the table.

"Fred, baby, we need more drinks."

"But I-"

"Ah!" Miko made a loud noise as if she were trying to get a dog to stop barking. "Four more vodka doubles and three…"

She pointed at Ashley, who spoke very loudly and slowly to Fred. "Three liiiiight beeeers."

Miko snapped her fingers in front of Fred's face to get his attention.

"Fred! Do you got that? Repeat it back to me."

"Uh, three vodkas, four beers? And my name is Fra-"

"Four vodka doubles. Three light beers." Miko repeated.

"Four vodka. Three beer?" He said, staring at Miko as he waited for her approval.

"Good boy. Go fetch our drinks, and then you can sit."

He nodded enthusiastically, and then the big man ran off towards the bar once more.

I love this woman more every time we hang out.

"He's still going to find a way to fuck it up. You watch and see if he doesn't." Miko sighed deeply.

She pulled up the picture of the Exhibitionist Bingo card that Jess had sent her on her phone and showed it to Ashley and Kels. Carl edged even further off on his side of the booth, but Ashley seemed positively captivated by it.

"See? I already did sauna and gym. Not with this idiot, though." Miko slipped her arm around Jess's shoulders. "But these two did like, a *lot* more, right?"

Jess could feel her face burning. She was embarrassed, but at the same time, quick to brag about her deeds.

"Josh and I did nine so far." She said, trying to make it seem like it was no big deal.

Kels whistled low. "Wow, *nine* of these? How long have you guys been at it?"

Jess glanced behind her at Josh. "What has it been, babe? Five days now?"

"Three." Josh corrected. "You found the card three days ago, love."

"Oh my God! Jess, you're my hero." Ashley gushed. "But don't you guys, like, have a Bingo already?"

"We're going to do all of them. Everything on the card. In less than a week." It was the first time Jess announced it out loud to anyone other than her boyfriend.

The booth was silent. Ashley and Kels were stunned.

"You see? Isn't she so fucking epic? That's why we need your help! I'm only going for the Bingo, so I just need this one and then three more. But Jess and Josh are going for the record." Miko had all of them eating out of the palm of her hands. "So you see, that's why we need to use your booth to discretely have sex. And that's why the two of you," she pointed to Ashley and Kels, "should join us."

Kels turned to Ashley, who turned a glowing shade of crimson red. "Come on, girl. Let's play some Bingo."

Ashley looked away, staring off into he distance. "I don't know..."

Kels wrapped his arm around her. "Psh, don't act like you weren't going to fuck me by the end of our first date, anyway."

Jess nearly spit out her drink.

Did he say their first date?

She didn't think it was possible, but Ashley's face got even *more* red. And yet, Jess knew from the falsely incredulous look on Ashley's face that she was totally thinking about fucking Kels right at that moment. She had been there herself more than a few times.

"Wait, this is your *first date*?" Miko said, incredulous.

"Well, technically, it's our third date. But this was supposed to be our first *real* date together." Kels explained.

"What the fuck does that even mean?" Josh asked from underneath Jess.

"The first two don't count!" Ashley insisted. "But, yeah, it's our third date." She admitted shyly.

"Third date?! What are you thinking, girl? You'd better fuck him before I do!" Miko shouted.

She had both Ashley and Kels laughing nervously, but Jess got the impression she wasn't kidding.

"I mean, he is pretty hot..." Miko said, eye-fucking Kels. "Plus, think about what a great story it would make at your wedding!"

Ashley spit out her drink. "W-wedding?!"

More nervous laughter. And then Fred returned with their drinks, and not a moment too soon. Although the man had a hard time remembering drink orders, he had a knack for carrying them all in his massive arms.

He set all seven drinks down on the table at once. Both Ashley and Kels simultaneously reached for their beers and chugged the entire contents in just seconds.

"Whoo! That's the spirit!" Miko stood up in the booth, pumping her arms in the air, cheering them on. "Now, you two have a life-changing decision to make. You can either live a fun, exciting life like Jess and Josh here, or you can basically go be Amish."

Jess and Josh got out of the booth so Fred could scoot in next to Miko. She whispered something in his ear, and Jess saw the smile spread across Fred's face like a toddler trying ice cream for the first time.

He picked Miko up and set her gently on top of his lap as easily as if she were a doll. Then Josh sat down and Jess jumped up on his lap.

Ashley and Kels just kept smiling nervously at Miko.

"Kels, don't look at me! You'd better kiss that beautiful woman sitting next to you. Would it make you comfortable if we all did it at the same time? Here, follow my lead."

Miko swung her legs to the sides of Fred's legs and threw her arms around his shoulders. Jess recognized it as the same moves she put on the guy she had fucked in the sauna yesterday.

She drew his mouth down onto her and the two started making out. Fred was aggressively attacking Miko's lips and she swore she saw the tiny Asian woman bite him at least twice in an effort to slow him down.

Jess took a deep breath. She would really have to go through with this in front of all these people.

I guess this is it. Time to show these kids how it's done, Jess thought, then immediately felt gross for thinking it.

She twisted her torso around so that her lips could meet Josh's. Their kiss was in many was the exact opposite of Miko and Fred's. Theirs was slow, intentional, and intimate. Their tongues met in a passionate tango of masculine and feminine energy. A sensual push and pull, give and take, yin and yang.

Jess had one hand on the back of Josh's head, sensually raking through his hair. Her other hand was buried in his lap.

Jess already had his cock out and was working him up with gentle, delicate strokes. She wanted nothing more in that moment than to have his hard dick in her mouth instead of her hand.

But I'll also settle for having it in my vagina.

Soft little moans of pleasure reached Jess's ears. From the corner of her eye, she could tell they were coming from Ashley as she made out with Kels. Meanwhile, Kels's hands had completely disappeared underneath the table.

When next she heard someone at the booth moan, it took Jess a moment for her to realize that it was her making the noises. Josh's wandering hands found their way underneath Jess's tight little dress.

Since Miko touted Jess and Josh as some sort of risqué, adventurous couple who were authorities on the subject of public sex, she felt like she had to be the first to pull the trigger.

Take the lead. Show initiative. Go!

The thought that everyone might be waiting on them to be the first couple to engage made her a little more than self-conscious. The way that Miko talked them up put her in a position where there was no backing down now.

The sly little slut! This was her plan all along!

No. That was crazy. This was Jess's idea first, after all. She came here with the intention of fucking her boyfriend in front of a bar full of people, after all.

And it's just us, anyway. Just him and me and no one else.

She gave the back of her clingy black dress a little tug so it scrunched up over her bare ass. With Josh's tongue still inside her mouth, she lifted her bottom up and guided his hard cock in between her legs.

As wet as she was, it slid right in without much effort. Just the tip at first, then little by little, more and more, thrust by thrust, until Jess had her back firmly pressed against Josh's chest and was sliding up and down in his lap.

The overall ambiance of the bar, her slinky black dress, and her proximity to the massive crowd of people made Jess feel a little bit like a stripper.

An undercover stripper, maybe.

The way that she moved and gyrated her ass against Josh's lap, brazenly riding his cock in front of a crowd full of people was such a turn on.

People waiting in line at the bar were starting to stare at her. She realized that, to the average bystander, it probably just looked like she was a drunk chick giving her man a lap dance.

Unsurprisingly, next to her she saw that Miko and Fred had taken up a much less discrete approach. Clad in her pink cowgirl outfit, Miko was riding Fred the same way that Jess watched her fuck her personal trainer in the gym yesterday.

She had her arms wrapped around Fred's neck, with his hands gripping all the way around Miko's tiny waist. The two made no attempt to hide the fact that they were fucking right there in the booth, save for the lucky fact that Miko's moans were drowned out by the crowd of people.

Miko and Fred sat face to face, both with very intense looks about them, staring at one another with the type of burning intensity that Jess thought unbecoming of Miko. Still, she was an exemplary exhibitionist, as Miko truly did not give a care that everyone who saw her could tell she was fucking Fred's brains out.

God, look at her ride that dick. That cowgirl outfit is putting in work today.

Much to Jess's surprise, Ashley had also joined in. She sat on Kels' lap as he grabbed a hold of her hips, assisting her in bouncing up and down on his dick. Ashley leaned forward, resting her huge tits on the table in front of her while she twerked on Kels' thick cock.

Congrats to the lucky couple, Jess wanted to say as she admired Kels' girthy member,

Although it wasn't hard for Jess to stifle her little moans of passion, in a bar that was packed full of people, it wasn't long before they had half of the crowd all staring at their booth. Carl, who up until now had only been leering at Ashley, now actively participated in getting the crowd worked up.

And the second one drunken idiot yells "Whoo!" the rest of the lemmings fall like dominos. Before long, Carl had everyone cheering on the six people having sex next to each other in the smallest booth at the bar.

That's okay, Jess thought. She had already been through this once before. This time, she was prepared and knew exactly what to do next.

Without slowing her pace, Jess twisted around to lick the vodka off of Josh's lips and whispered to him, "Finish fast."

Jess knew that a little twist of her hips wouldn't be enough to get her boyfriend off. What she didn't expect in that instant was for Josh to take complete control.

He pushed her legs flat together, then shifted her whole body 45 degrees so that both her legs were dangling off to the side of his lap perpendicularly, like a child sitting on Santa Claus.

With on hand underneath her thighs, one hand pressed against the small of her back, Josh lifted her entire body up and brought her back down on his cock. Again and again and again.

I always forget how strong he is!

Jess could do nothing buy press her dainty hands up against her firm, muscular chest and he dominated her. Soon she was overwhelmed by waves of pleasure rushing through every limb in her body. Jess's moans were caught in her throat as she whispered dirty little words in her boyfriend's ear.

Gazing up at him, she saw only fire in his eyes. He was using her body as his own personal fuck toy. Jess loved being dominated this way. And she loved the way her boyfriend looked when he dominated her.

It made her feel desirable. It made her feel *powerful*.

She flexed her pussy, tightening up her little wet hole as much as she could. She could feel every inch of Josh's cock with every thrust. She felt every contour of his dick as he stuffed her to the hilt.

She marveled at how good he felt inside of her tight pussy, amazed at how perfectly they fit together, always in sync. It felt so good that she could hardly breathe. So good that rapture spread throughout her entire body.

A primal growl escaped Josh's lips. His pace slowed as he came inside of her. She felt his warm, wet cum fill her. She felt her pussy spasm wrapped around his hard cock.

Instantly, Josh's body went slack. Every muscle in his body relaxed as he set Jess down, releasing her from his grip. Jess and Josh let out a simultaneous sigh of satisfied relief.

Suddenly, Jess was aware of her surroundings. Miko still sat on Fred's lap with her arms around his neck as she continued aggressively humping the shit out of him like a little pink bunny rabbit.

Next to Miko, Ashley was still twerking her booty up on Kels' dick while Kels leaned back in his seat, hands behind his head, clearly enjoying himself.

And there at the end of the booth, Carl sat and watched them all, creepily touching himself through his jeans. Most of the people at the bar were watching them. Those who weren't actively watching were whispering to each other about them.

Jess wanted to scurry out the back door. She wanted to be free of all the scrutinizing eyes she felt boring into her. but she knew all of this was essentially her doing, and she didn't want to leave Miko all alone.

So instead of getting the fuck out, like every fiber in her being was screaming, she did her best to relax – and drank everyone else's drinks while she waited for her friends to finish fucking.

Josh put away his cock and Jess pulled her dress back down to a lady-like length. There was not enough room in the booth to sit anywhere other than his lap. So after Jess fidgeted on Josh's leg and finished the remaining alcohol on the table, she decided it was time to urge her friends on.

"Miko, you look so fucking hot right now riding Fred's dick. Like a sexy little pink Asian cowgirl. Fred, you'd better still be hard right now."

She leaned over the table so she could heckle Ashley and Kels. "Holy shit, Josh, Ashley has a big ol' booty! Yeah, girl! Bounce that ass on his dick! Hey, Josh, look at her ass bounce on Kel's huge cock! Wow, Kels has a big dick, too, Josh. Did you see? I said look at Kels' big dick, Josh. LOOK AT IT!"

No one seemed to be paying attention to Jess's commentary, or at least, no one wanted to acknowledge it. She felt like she was narrating the director's cut for a real life porno.

Maybe if I encourage them even more, they'll finish faster.

"Ashley's ass just swallowed up that big dick like it was nothing! So hot. Ashley, your ass is incredible!"

"Fuck yeah, Miko, ride that fucking cock! I bet it feels so fucking good in your tight little pussy. Fred is so lucky to have this bad bitch riding his dick in front of a bar full of people. That's right, Freddie, they're all watching you and they're all jealous that you're fucking this bad ass bitch right now."

While Fred started blushing at the attention, Jess's words of encouragement got Miko worked up. She started humping Fred even faster, grinding against him and gyrating on his lap even harder. Then she stopped and threw her head back in a lioness moan of pleasure that could rival any porn star.

"Fuck yeah," Miko sighed breathily, "Thank you, Jess."

"No problem, babe."

Miko climbed up off of Fred, stood up to stretch, then tugged her skirt back down over her pussy.

"Hey, I didn't finish yet." Fred said angrily, gesturing to his still hard cock.

Miko shrugged. "You had your chance."

"Come on!" Fred was incredulous.

"Go finish in the bathroom. Maybe Carl will help."

"Not fair! You guys keep calling me Fred, but my name is-"

But Miko was already headed towards the door.

"God, whinny little bitches are such a turn off for me." Miko said in Jess and Josh's direction. "Let's get out of here."

Jess jumped out of the booth, followed by Josh.

"Um, good luck on your Bingo, Ashley, Kels. Nice meeting you guys!" Jess waved as she ran to catch up with Miko as fast as her heels would allow.

Every face in the bar followed them on their way out, smiling and grinning like boys watching their first porno.

Is everyone in this city so immature?

CHAPTER 20

Day 4 - Nightclub

The cool night air hit Jess's face like a baseball bat. It felt good being out in the night air. It was a sobering feeling.

She needed sobering.

Once outside and enough paces away from the bar, Miko lit up a cigarette.

"That good, huh?" Josh asked with a smirk.

Miko narrowed her eyes at him and blow smoke in his direction.

"Did you say you were going to see Kaskade at Avalon tonight, Jess?" Miko asked before taking a long drag on her cigarette.

Jess was surprised that Miko remembered something that Jess only mentioned in passing.

"That's right. Josh and I bought tickets months ago."

Miko took another pull from her cigarette. Her eyes darted nervously to the entrance of the bar, and then back to Jess.

"Could I go with you guys?"

"Miko, I would love that, but it's been sold out for weeks."

She waved her hand dismissively. "That won't be an issue." Miko looked back at the front door to The Room. "Do you mind if I come with you guys? Please? I need to get away from Fred before he starts getting clingy."

"Oh, say no more, girl. Let's start walking." Jess said, then grabbed hold of Miko's hand.

The three of them ran across the street in the direction of Avalon. Jess stood in the middle holding both Miko and Josh's hand. Miko quickened her pace, glancing suspiciously behind her every few paces.

As the trio turned the corner of Cahuenga, they heard a familiar voice call out Miko's name.

"Miko! Where are you? Miko? Where did you go?"

It was Fred.

"Oh, shit, you guys." Miko ran a few paces in front of them.

Jess and Josh, meanwhile, couldn't stop laughing.

"It's not funny!" Miko crouched down, trying to make herself even smaller.

"It's alright, Miko. I think we lost him." Jess tried to assure her.

"Are you sure? I could tell that one was going to be clingy, but by then it was too late." She stuck out her bottom lip, pouting.

Josh poked his head back around the corner.

"Yep, looks like we lost him. For now, anyway."

Miko's muscles visibly relaxed.

"Thank *God.*" She sighed in relief.

Jess and Josh continued in the direction of Avalon.

"Um, Miko? You know we're going to the show tonight to fulfill the 'concert' part of BINGO, right?" Jess explained.

"Yeah, I figured as much. But wouldn't Avalon count as 'concert', 'nightclub', and 'bar'?"

"You see?!" Jess elbowed Josh in the ribs.

"But I can see why Josh wants to do each of them separately... I'm excited, you guys!" Miko's entire demeanor seemed to change now that Fred was solidly out of the picture.

"But, um, Miko?

"Yes, Jess-Jess?"

"How are you going to get into the show without a ticket? And, if you don't mind me asking, who would you hook up with if not Fred?"

Jess felt stupid as soon as she heard the words come out of her mouth.

"Oh, Jess. I think you already know the answer to both of those question."

She is going to slut her way inside, Jess thought to herself.

After walking a few more paces in silence, Miko opened up. "My boyfriend owns Avalon. They... know me there." She admitted.

Jess and Josh exchanged a look.

"Your boyfriend owns Avalon?" She said in incredulous unison.

Miko nodded slowly.

"Well. At least I'll finally get to meet your boyfriend at last." Jess said enthusiastically.

"Oh, I doubt that *very* much." Miko said cheerfully. "He's almost never there."

Jess had to stop herself from asking a million more questions. Instead, they walked in peace the rest of the way to the venue.

When they finally reached the massive three-story building, there was still a line out the door that stretched all the way into the adjoined parking lot.

"Are you kidding me? How did it get *bigger?!*" Jess threw up her hands in frustration.

Defeated, Jess and Josh started walking towards the very back of the line.

We'll be lucky if we get inside before the show is over, she silently lamented.

But Miko had other plans. She pulled both Jess and Josh by the hand to the front of the line and the main entrance.

"Where are you guys going? The entrance is this way."

They followed Miko as she completely bypassed the line, getting dirty looks from every club kid and Hollywood douchebag they passed along the way. Together, they followed Miko to the front entrance as she walked right up to the bouncer.

When they reached the front, the bouncer immediately recognized Miko and looked *very* excited to see her.

He was a burly, stout man that was probably an inch or two taller even than Josh. His arms were like hams, or the guys from the Shake Weight commercials.

He looked like he was born to be a bouncer.

"Miko! Miko, my sweet geisha doll, how are you?" He spoke in a gravely voice befitting a man of his stature and girth.

"Hi, Raul!"

Miko got a running start and jumped into Raul's massive arms. He caught her, lifted her into the air, then shoved his tongue as far down her throat as physically possible.

After a few seconds of this public display of affection, he set her down on solid ground and pulled his tongue back into his own mouth.

"Raul, I'm doing something called Exhibitionist Bingo and I need you to meet me in the back room in a bit, okay?"

"Exhibitionist Bingo? What's that?" His voice sounded like rocks falling downhill.

"Can you just meet me inside? In the usual place." Her voice was honey coming out of a helium balloon.

"Yeah, okay." Raul opened the velvet rope that barred the entrance to Avalon and waved Miko inside.

"Oh, and they're with me." Miko said, gesturing to the couple behind her.

Jess and Josh exchanged a stunned look as Miko stepped into the venue. Raul dutifully held the rope open, eyeing the two suspiciously.

Jess ran inside holding Josh's hand before the big man had a sudden change of heart.

So much for buying tickets months in advance.

They could hear the bass from across the street. When they were standing outside the entrance Jess could feel it reverberate in her chest. As soon as they entered Avalon she got hit by a thick bass line that she felt throughout her entire body.

The interior of Avalon somehow looked even bigger than it did on the outside. With an expansive dance floor and balcony seating. Dancers writhed up against one another on the tightly packed dance floor while laser lights of green, red and blue oscillated overhead, creating magnificent designs and patterns.

It was like an endless fireworks display, only instead of explosions in the sky there were a series of thunderous bass drops emanated from the dense wall of speakers and subwoofers.

Up on the main stage, Jess could barely make out the silhouette of Kaskade behind two sturdy-looking turntables. The immense LED wall of visuals behind him was almost blinding up close.

From anywhere in the building, the music was deafening. It was certainly not conductive to conversation.

Once inside, Miko pressed her finger up to Jess's ear and leaned in close to tell her something.

"I'm going upstairs to the lunge."

She could hear Miko's voice clearly after she plugged her ears. Jess marveled over the fact that Miko knew the old trick used by ravers and club kids to communicating on the dance floor. By plugging up Jess's ear, she was able to clearly hear the vibrations of Miko's voice over the loud music.

Jess was very familiar with the raver hack.

I guess it's really not that *surprising that Miko knows it, too.*

Jess nodded to Miko, then leaned in and plugged her ear.

"I want to dance for a while."

Miko smiled and replied, "Come find me when you want to take a break. I have a surprise for you."

Then Miko pointed a finger up, indicating that she was headed to the top floor of Avalon where Jess knew there was a chill little lounge type area with its own DJ. It was only about a quarter of the size of the ground level dance floor and a completely different vibe. Jess had been there many times before. On the last of such occasions, they were playing lo-fi hip-hop beats to an older crowd of hippies.

Jess wasn't sure what surprise Miko had in mind. She wasn't even sure if she wanted to find out. While she was outwardly grateful that Miko had helped them bypass a crowd of people that rivaled most DMVs, she was still a little salty that Josh and her spent over $100 on tickets that were essentially worthless.

I knew I shouldn't feel that way, but I do.

Regardless, they were inside now and she wouldn't let anything ruin what was shaping up to be a fun night out.

Pulling Josh by the hand, Jess led him into the most dense crowd of people she could find on the dance floor. The two wadded into the sea of bodies, then Jess whirled around and pulled Josh up against her. His arms seamlessly slipped around her waist to her lower back as he pulled her tight against his hard body.

Jess laughed. She was still feeling the effects of vodka from the bar, though she could not remember how many drinks she had. Or how many of other people's drinks she ended up stealing.

Are we really going to do this right here on the dance floor?

Everyone in the crowd was doing their own thing. No one seemed to be paying any attention to Jess and Josh. And why would they? They were just another couple on the dance floor. One of many.

It's just us. No one else matters. It's just him and me. Me and him. She repeated her mantra.

She felt good. She felt buzzed. She danced in step with every beat of the music.

She guided Josh's hands against her body. Starting at her hip, sliding up her waist and finally cupping her breast. She held his hands there, smiling lasciviously at him with her tongue sticking out.

She turned around, pressing her back into his solid chest. Josh's big, powerful hands swept along her body as they danced, exploring every curve. He ran his finger up her thighs, playing with the hem of her dress.

Jess pushed her ass back into his hips and felt the heat coming from the stiffness in his pants. She could feel his warm breath on the back of her neck, smelling of vodka and desire.

It was a dance of lust and need. Every move, every caress, each little intimate connection built up an ever-increasing amount of sensual energy between them. The mounting sexual tension bubbled and percolated, making Jess crave each touch more than the last.

Each time she felt his warm skin press up against hers, Jess's heart pounded in her chest. Every intimate caress only served to increase her arousal. Her desire was palpable.

The Dance of Desire only has one inevitable outcome. One way or another, it always ends the same way.

Sweat bristled on Jess's skin as she slid both of her hands through the back of Josh's hair. She pulled his mouth on to hers. She was dying to taste him.

The Dance of Desire had worked up her thirst and left her lips parched. She felt like her entire body was dehydrated and only the wetness of his lips could bring her back to life. Only his kiss could revive her.

Josh had clearly felt the effects from the Dance of Desire as well. He kissed her with the urgent need of an addict trying desperately to get his fix. In each other's arms, they drank in one another's desires.

Jess felt Josh's steel embrace encircling her. he did not want to let go. He would never let go. She was hit with an aching need when she felt his hands on her ass, raising her dress every time she shook her hips to the beat.

She was overrun with desire.

She wanted him so bad that it hurt. It was a painful, aching, lustful desire peaking on ravenous. Jess had never wanted anything more than she wanted him in that moment. And she needed to put an end to the pain.

Jess reached down between Josh's legs and unzipped his pants. In an instant, his hard cock was out and in her hands. It was throbbing for her, and only her, amid a dance floor comprised of hundreds of gorgeous women.

It's only me and him. Him and me.

She turned around and backed her bare ass up against him. His dick was buried vertically between her bubbly butt cheeks. Josh had to crouch down a little in order to the tip of his stiff member home where it belonged.

Jess felt a wave of relief wash over her as he entered her from behind. She arched her back forward a little in order to take all of him into her dripping wet hole.

Okay. He's inside me now. We're actually doing this.

To Jess's right and to her left, people were dancing so close that they bumped up next to her on every other beat. They weren't paying attention to what her and Josh were doing, although part of her *wanted* them to see. Although to anyone who might look their way, it looked like they were dancing together the same as most couples at Avalon.

But they weren't interested in what other couples did. They were fulfilling their own kinky exhibitionist desires by making love in front of hundreds. Now that Josh was fucking her on a dance floor packed with people, Jess was overcome with a new type of kinky, horny energy that drove her into a wild rage.

Why does that turn me on so much? Is there something wrong with me?

She held up the hem on her slinky black dress just above her booty so that Josh could fuck her without it riding up. Josh had a clamp-like grip on her right elbow. He pulled her ass into his hips, thrusting in time with the music.

Jess was in heaven.

Drunk sex on the dance floor at Avalon. I never thought I'd be here.

When she pushed back against him, he planted hot little kisses on the back of her neck. He nibbled on her earlobe, sending shivers down her spine and throughout her entire body.

Oh, God. He knows exactly how to drive me wild.

Josh ran the flat of his hand up her stomach, holding her closer. Occasionally he could chance a caress of her ample breasts over her revealing dress.

Jess fought off the overwhelming urge to get naked then and there. She was enjoying their discrete sex, but she also knew that it couldn't last forever.

Best to wrap this up quickly, I think.

He felt good inside of her. She could feel his throbbing cock pounding her pussy in time with the music. Fucking in front of this many people was such a turn on that before long she could no longer contain herself.

Jess swept her hand around Josh's backside, her fingers clenching a fist full of his butt cheek. Jess's breathing and heart rate practically doubled in a matter of seconds. She could tell that Josh felt the same way.

He slid his hand up the front of her dress, giving her large, supple breast a firm squeeze over her dress. He pinched her hard nipple through her dress, making her jump. She clasped her hand on the back of his so he couldn't take his hand off her tits.

Please don't fucking stop, she thought to herself.

It was the final touch she needed to send her over the edge.

Every muscle in her body clenched at once. Then released a moment later with a sharp exhale, emptying out her lungs.

"Oh, Josh, ah fuck. Yeah, baby. Ohmi-Gawd! Don't-stop-don't-stop-don't-stop-don't-stop!" Her cries were lost in the music.

The rhythm of their dance changed to one of rapid beats, pounding away to half beats and even quarters. In one out of every four beats, Jess would dip down and Josh would drive his hips forward until finally, with one final, long-lasting embrace, their two bodies separated.

Jess spun around, grinning, and planted a kiss of gratitude on Josh's lips.

For the first time in a long time, she looked around the dance floor. Couples of all ages were wiggling and writhing their bodies together just like her and Josh. Everyone in the entire venue seemed to be doing the Dance of Desire in one form or another.

And none of them paid any mind to Jess or Josh at all.

This made her heart happy. Jess giggled. Then she started laughing hysterically. Once she started laughing, she couldn't stop.

She felt like she had just gotten away with something mischievous. And that made her feel powerful.

Jess hugged her boyfriend, laying her head against his chest.

"I love you." He said, and he didn't need to plug her ears in order for her to understand him.

She squeezed him and said into his chest, "I love you, too."

Together they stood in the middle of the dance floor, a couple in a sea of waving bodies. Jess suddenly thought that after making love in the middle of a crowded dance floor, actually dancing seemed a little mundane.

Together, Jess and Josh pushed their way out of the cluster of people. She led him by the hand to explore the rest of whatever Avalon had in store for them.

Hand in hand, they walked away from the dance floor, past the bar, around the VIP section and down a long hallway to a place that was much quieter.

"Where are we going?" Josh asked now that the two could hear each other once again.

"Exploring." She answered simply.

Josh did not protest. Led by Jess's sense of adventure, the two proceeded down a flight of stairs, through another double door, down another flight of stairs, and through another long, curving hallway.

Jess had no clue where they were going, but the increasing lack of elegance between floors indicated that they must have found their way into a service corridor.

Even this far down, they could still hear the booming bass from above.

She was surprised that the venue went this far underground. She was equally surprised that no one tried to stop them thus far. They didn't encounter a single soul down here.

"This place is wild."

"Are we even inside Avalon anymore?"

"Don't know. But isn't it weird that we haven't seen anyone yet? Is this place, like, abandoned?"

"I was just thinking the same thing."

"Do you think this place is, you know, haunted?"

"Stop that, Josh! You know I have a phobia of ghosts!"

"I ain't afraid of no ghosts."

"Well, I *am*!"

They continued walking through the poorly lit underground hallway. It was in a state of poor repair.

"Why did you say that? Now I'm scared! Come on, let's get out of here."

"You remember the way back?"

"I..."

The thought about it, then shook her head fervently.

Josh squeezed her hand to try and comfort her.

"Don't worry, babe. If any ghosts try to attack us while we're down here, I will throw myself in front of you to protect you." Josh said, giving her hand another squeeze.

"You'd better!"

"Remind me, what exactly do ghosts attack with?"

"You know. Like, ectoplasm. And stuff."

"Terrifying."

Josh started leading the way. He had to practically pull Jess by the hand as they attempted to retrace their steps.

"I'm just going to cover my eyes and you tell me when we're back near civilization."

"Don't you think that's, like, a million times worse?"

"If I can't see the ghosts then they can't get me!"

"Babe... I don't think it works like that."

"Well, it worked in Super Mario."

"Super Mario is not an authority on paranormal activity."

"Tell that to Luigi!"

"Seriously, Jess. Open your eyes. You're going to want to see this."

"Josh, if I open my eyes and I see creepy twins at the end of this hallway I will kill you myself."

"If you kill me, I'm going to haunt the shit out of you."

"Stop joking! I'm serious!"

"So am I. Open your eyes, Jess."

Jess took in a big breath and as she exhaled opened her eyes.

Well, he's not wrong.

"This makes the whole trip worth it." She said at last.

"Right? Told you."

"But does it actually work?"

"Only one way to find out."

Side by side, Jess and Josh ran to the end of the hallway where they found a very old-looking service elevator. There was only one button to the right of the elevator. Josh reached over to push the button, but Jess slapped his hand before it reached the button.

"I want to do it." She huffed.

"You are such a child."

"You love my child-like sense of adventure."

He put his arm around her.

"That I do."

They kissed just as the elevator button lit up.

"Yes! It works!"

The dusty doors slid open to reveal an old, unupholstered elevator cart that looked like it had all of the carpet and padding torn out from the walls. In their place, jagged, rusty nails pultruded from the corners where one might expect there to be upholstery.

Gross. But working, Jess thought.

Tentatively, the two stepped inside. Sure enough, the elevator had buttons inside for all of the floors, from "R" to "B3", which, given the number of stairs they descended, Jess presumed they were currently on B3.

Jess wasted no time in smashing the "R" button.

Nothing happened.

She hit "R" fifteen more times. Then "1". Then "B1". Then she hit all of the buttons, not getting a reaction from any of them.

Jess looked at Josh with the sour face of disappointment.

He shrugged. "The Bingo card didn't say the elevator had to be working."

Jess just stared at him with her *are you fucking serious* face.

"It also didn't say it had to be clean." He added.

Jess sighed.

Is this what my life has come to?

"I guess there is a certain... ghetto charm to doing it in a run down service elevator. I mean, it'd be the most action this thing has seen in a hundred years."

The elevator doors slammed shut.

"That's the spirit." Josh pulled her body close to his in the middle of the elevator. "Let's play 'Don't Touch the Walls or You Get Tetanus'."

Jess laughed, but the more she looked around the more she realized that the elevator had probably been used as either a primitive torture chamber or a way of setting straight disgruntled employees at one point in time.

There were carpenter's nails sticking out of every surface. The only part of the elevator that didn't seem like a death trap was the rusted metal doors. Being trapped inside this thing was exactly what Jess imagined when she did her best to picture the total opposite of sexy.

The tiny metal death trap devoid of any sex appeal sucked all arousal out of the air.

"But... do we have to?"

"How about we do a SAW role-play?" Josh said, breaking into his best raspy Jigsaw voice, "You have three minutes to cum inside your girlfriend or I'll cut the elevator cables."

"So what if the elevator cables are cut? We're already at the lowest level."

"Yeah, but then we'd have to walk back through all of those spooky deserted hallways."

"Stop it!"

"You know what this place reminds me of? Silent Hill."

"Josh!"

"What? I happen to think those faceless nurses are sexy."

"Well, I don't!"

"I know what we need."

Josh hit the highest button underneath "R". The "3" button lit up and the elevator started moving.

"Josh, are you crazy?"

He started pawing at her.

"Now anyone can stumble upon us at any moment. Who knows who might use the service elevator next and catch a glimpse of us fooling around?"

For the first time since getting in the elevator, Jess cracked a smile.

"I thought you might like that, you dirty little girl, you." Josh licked her lips. "Hey, how hot was it when we were fucking in front of all those people on the dance floor?"

Josh slipped her dress off her shoulder, exposing her large breasts.

"Josh!"

"What? It's just you and me here, right?"

He pushed her breast into his mouth and started sucking and licking her nipple. Jess involuntarily let out a throaty grunt as she struggled against Josh's firm grasp.

He squeezed both her tits, pressing his tongue down even harder, nibbling on her nipples. Her moans came out in little coughs.

Well... It is on the Bingo card, so...

Then she pulled her dress down the rest of the way. Josh took a step back, admiring her magnificent naked body as she stepped out of her little black dress.

"That's the spirit." He said, then started licking and sucking her other nipple. "God, you make that dress look so fucking sexy. No wonder I can't keep my hands off of you."

He spoke in a low growl dripping with testosterone. "You are so fucking irresistible."

He kissed her in the center of her chest.

"Completely gorgeous."

He kissed her collar bone.

"Drop dead sexy."

He kissed her neck.

"And you're all mine."

He kissed her lips, then whispered, "I want you so fucking bad right now."

Jess stood on her tippy toes as she stuck out the tip of her tongue just enough to lick Josh from his chin to the tip of his nose. Then she whispered three little words that were so faint, he could barely hear them.

"Then take me."

With an explosion of animalistic urgency, Josh picked her up and spun her around. With a grunt, she spread her legs and bent forward at the waist. Josh helped her along, his hands all over her naked body.

Dick in hand, he brushed up against the fleshy wetness between her legs. He could see the see the feminine juices glistening between her legs. He was shocked at how wet she was. *She* was shocked at how wet she was.

To be fair, a lot of that is probably his cum in me from earlier.

Josh did as instructed and took her from behind, sliding the full length of his hard cock into her tight little pussy.

Jess's voice cracked in a scream as soon as he started fucking her. her cries of ecstasy echoed off the walls of the small elevator. Jess held nothing back. They were alone at last.

Adding to the erotic cacophony of moans, Josh started slapping Jess's ass as hard as he could. He pulled on her dark curls, sending her ass smashing back into his hips forcefully, driving his cock even deeper inside of her, causing her to moan louder still.

Josh reached around to grab Jess's perfect tits. She knew the tell tale signs of Josh's finishing moves he liked to do just before he was about to cum. She was almost there, too.

"Oh, yes! Fuck me harder! Harder, damnit! Pull my hair! Spank my ass! For God sakes, fucking *choke me!* Oh, fuck yeah, yeah, yeah. Oh my God, I'm going to cum. Fucking cum inside of me, baby. Please, baby, I love feeling you shoot your cum in my little pussy. So good."

"You know when you cum on my dick, I can feel your pussy contract around it, right?"

"You mean like this?"

"Oh my God! Fucking hell. No wonder your pussy is always so tight every time we fuck."

"Are you finished cumming inside of me yet? Then pull your dick out of me and let's get going. I don't like this place."

"That was so fucking hot. You see? The elevator wasn't such a bad place to have sex after all."

"Well, we certainly earned that Bingo square. That's for sure."

Jess put her slinky black dress back on, being careful not to get any cum on it.

The elevator was still stuck on the 3rd floor. As soon as Josh finished putting his dick away, the elevator doors opened on their own accord.

Jess and Josh both looked up at the same time to see none other than Miko. She was holding a black leather leash with Raul, the bouncer, on the other end wearing a collar and crawling on all fours.

For a few pregnant seconds, no one said anything. Josh double checked to make sure his dick was put away and Jess smoothed out the front of her dress, making sure it covered her in all of the places a dress was supposed to cover a woman.

"I thought I heard you two in there." Miko said simply.

"We didn't think anyone was listening!" Jess felt her face redden.

"Well don't just stand there and hog the elevator all to yourself. It's our turn." Miko said as she shooed Jess and Josh out of the elevator.

"Hey! You're turn for what exactly?" Josh asked while he and Jess stepped out into the third floor hallway.

"What, are you trying to BINGO block me, Josh? For the elevator, of course, silly."

Miko stepped into the small metal death trap, pulling Raul along behind her with the leash.

She went to go push the button, but stopped when Jess blurted out, "Miko, you mentioned you had a surprise for us."

Jess looked from Miko to Raul. "Well, I can say that I'm a little surprised."

Miko pointed down at the elevator floor forcefully. Jess and Josh exchanged a look of confusion.

"Uh, Miko, I like being your friend and all but-"

"Oh, stop that, Jess. It's nothing like that. Just get in here with us real quick."

Neither of them moved.

"I promise you'll like it. I swear."

Jess and Josh simultaneously shrugged, then squeezed back into the tiny elevator with Miko and Raul. It was a tight fit into the service elevator that was made to carry only one or two people at a time. Jess was extra careful not to touch any of the many rusted, jagged nails sticking out of the elevator walls.

When the doors slammed shut Jess was suddenly feeling very claustrophobic.

Miko reached down into her bra and pulled out a little white plastic card. She waved it in front of the elevator console, the hit the button labeled "R".

The button lit up green and the elevator suddenly jumped to life.

Everyone remained still and deadly silent. It took Jess a few seconds to register what just happened.

"Wait, you have an elevator key card?" she asked, incredulous.

"It's mine." Rual spoke in the rough baritone of a lifetime smoker.

Miko immediately swatted his beefy shoulder.

"Shush! I did not say you could speak."

The big man's eyes sank to the floor. "Sorry."

She slapped the back of his head.

"What was that?"

"Sorry, *mistress.*"

Before Miko got another chance to brutalize her men pet, the elevator doors opened to reveal the night sky. The rooftop horizon was lit up by the expansive buildings, lights, and neon chaos that is the Hollywood skyline.

"Wow. What a view." Josh said under his breath.

Jess was thinking the same thing, only the sight of the city all lit up at night took her breath away.

She stepped out of the tiny metal death box and onto the gravely footing that made up Avalon's rooftop. She heard the hard crunch of tiny flame-retardant rocks underneath her feet with every step.

Josh followed closely behind her. Both were transfixed by the beautifully illuminated city sky at night. Jess couldn't take her eyes off of it. The lights just stretched on and on into the horizon, forever.

"Surprise!" Miko, still inside the elevator with a firm grip on Raul's leash, was almost giddy by Jess's reaction. "You two enjoy yourselves, now." She added in a sing-song voice.

Then the elevator doors snapped shut and they were gone.

"Wait! Miko! How do we get back down!" She asked a moment too late.

Jess and Josh were all alone together on the Avalon rooftop. As breathtaking as the view was, Jess couldn't help but notice that the rooftop elevator shaft did not have a call button on their side.

This was a one-way ticket.

CHAPTER 21

Day 4 – Rooftop

"Is she coming back for us, or...?" Josh's voice trailed off.

They both knew the answer to that question. She had only known Miko a short time, but she knew for a fact that the woman was easily distracted and as impulsive as they come.

Jess felt panic rising in her throat. Her heart started racing as she frantically surveyed her surroundings for another way down.

But there was nothing else on the roof. No other way down. Not even a flight of stairs. It was just the one-way elevator shaft and a bunch of tiny rocks.

Who would build something like this?

Probably the same person who built a half-finished service elevator with carpenter's nails sticking out of the walls.

Josh sensed that she was starting to freak out. He stood behind her and wrapped his hands around her waist, pulling her into a backwards hug.

"Miko gave us this gift. Let's just enjoy this moment and let future Jess and Josh worry about how to get down." He whispered into her ear.

He was right. Irresponsible, maybe, but he always knew the right things to say. Josh was an expert in the art of talking her out of panic attacks.

Jess turned to face Josh and pressed her face into his chest, nuzzling against him affectionately.

And to stay warm. It's freezing up here!

Josh encircled her back with his arms, petting her with one hand running up and down the exposed skin on her back. Together, they gazed out into the sea of Hollywood lights.

Even though Avalon was only three stories tall, it sat on the top of one of Hollywood's rolling chaparral hills, allowing them to see buildings both high and low.

"I get why they call it Tinsel Town now." She said softly. "All of these glimmering, sparkly lights. It's like looking at a giant Christmas tree."

Josh squeezed her tight.

"Hey, you can see the Hollywood sign from up here!" Josh pointed to the iconic white lettered sign spelling out the name of the city.

"It sure is beautiful up here." Jess sighed.

"Only because you're here. Right now, I'm holding the single most beautiful sight in all the city. And she shines brighter than all of these lights put together, illuminating my life." He looked down at Jess, staring into her eyes with that fiery look in his eyes that made her shiver.

Or maybe that was the cold night breeze.

"Josh, if I didn't know any better, I'd say you're trying to charm my pants off."

"You're not wearing any pants." He pointed out.

Jess was sure she was blushing. She tried to hide it by burying her face into the rock-solid warmth of his chest. Josh took her chin in his thumb and forefinger, tilting her face up to meet his.

There it is. That raptor stare.

He looked at her with the hungry gaze of a predator and burning eyes of desire. She felt a chill run down her entire body that had nothing to do with the cold.

Then she melted in his arms.

How does he do that?

When he kissed her, she could taste the longing on his lips. He kissed her like she was the only thing that could absolve his forlornness. He squeezed her tight as they made out on the rooftop and she could feel fireworks going off all throughout her body.

Good, she thought, *the fireworks will keep me warm.*

With her eyes closed, his kiss made her feel like she was being lifted up into the night sky. His touch made her feel like she was levitating. His soft caresses from her head to her back made her feel dizzy.

If it weren't for Josh's steel embrace, she would have surely fallen over.

Josh pulled back for a moment, ending their passionate kiss. "I love you, Jess. More than words can say."

"I love you, Josh." She looked up at him and giggled. "I was just thinking how incredible it is that, after all this time, your kiss still makes me dizzy like a little girl." Jess said, then pressed her cheek into his chest.

God, but he is warm!

"I still feel like I'm seeing fireworks when I'm with you."

"You mean like that?" Josh gestured behind Jess.

She spun around and was greeted by an array of colorful explosions in the sky. Burst after burst of dazzling lights sparkly in the night.

See was seeing fireworks. Real fireworks.

"You're seeing this, too, right?" She asked for confirmation.

Josh laughed. "Jess, you always make me see fireworks."

She turned back to Josh and wrapped her arms around him tightly. Together, they watched the distant fireworks display with a shared sense of awe, basking in each other's love.

After a while, Jess said, "This is how you make me feel."

Josh, lost in a world of his own thoughts, looked at her and said, "What?"

Jess clasped her hands over his. "When we're together, I feel like there are millions of little fireworks going on inside my body. But when we're apart? I feel like the quiet night sky."

"You mean calm?"

She shook her head. "Dull and cold. My life is boring without you."

"I've always felt that way about you. It's like I was stumbling around in the dark before. Then you came into my life and illuminated everything. My beautiful, guiding light."

She turned around to look upon handsome face staring back at her. She was still buzzing, only now she felt drunk on his love. She felt it burning inside her, warming her skin.

"I know what you're thinking and the answer is yes, my love." Josh scooped her up towards him and met her lips in a kiss.

Millions of tiny fireworks.

His tongue parted her mouth, and she accepted it eagerly, wanting only more. More of him, physically, emotionally, spiritually. She wanted all of him.

Josh started to undress her, sweeping the straps of her dress off her shoulders. Jess stopped him and pulled back.

"Wait, wait, wait. What is it that you think I'm thinking?"

"You're thinking, 'damn, I wish my boyfriend would fuck me on this roof while we watch fireworks'."

"How did you know?" Jess giggled as she wiggled out of her dress, pulling it down to her waist.

Her perky tits spilled out into the night air, hardening her little pink nipple immediately. Jess was grateful that it was the middle of summer. Night time in winter would be a miserable time to hook up on this rooftop.

She started unbuttoning Josh's shirt from top to bottom, cold fingers fumbling with one button at a time. She pressed her chest into his, her large, soft breasts between them.

Josh's kiss made Jess forget her own name. It was stupefying enough to increase her difficulty with his shirt buttons. Finally, in heated frustration, Josh stepped back and ripped his shirt off, Superman style. Buttons went flying into the darkness and over the rooftop.

Josh shrugged out of his torn shirt, and that, too, the wind carried over the edge of the roof. He didn't seem to either notice or care. Their skin was touching now, chest to chest, and that's all that mattered to both of them.

Jess undid the clasp on his belt and pulled it free with one strong yang. Josh unzipped his pants and kicked them loose, praying that they would not be blown off the roof.

Jess stepped back to admire Josh's nakedness in the moonlight. Even in the dark shadows of light, his muscular, chiseled features made Jess wet just by looking at him.

Staring at his nude silhouette made her incredibly horny, renewing her lust for him. Seeing her boyfriend naked always reminded her of all the dirty, nasty things they did together. *All* of them.

She could resist him no longer. Jess jumped into his arms. Thankfully, he caught her.

Jess wrapped her arms around Josh's neck, smothering him with kisses. Even though she felt safe in his firm grip, she wrapped her legs around his back and locked them together.

As he held her up, she heaved her bare breasts into the solid wall of muscle that is his chest. Josh hoisted her up by the back of her thighs, effortlessly tossing he up into the air and catching her like a child once again.

Each time he broke off their kiss, he tossed her higher into the air. Jess couldn't stop herself from giggling each time she became airborne. He held her up high enough so that her large natural tits jutted out into his face. When he took one of her nipples into her mouth, playfully sucking and giving her breasts a little nibble, Jess's girl-like laughter turned into the sensual moans of a woman.

Josh lifted her ass higher and pulled her warm, naked body closer to his. He could feel the wetness between her legs rubbing up against his abs. He mouthed her tits with the hungry urgency of a newborn baby. Josh cycled his attention from one of Jess's breasts to the other, licking and slobbering over both of them equally.

As she let him play with her tits, Josh listened to the seductive little feminine moans of his girlfriend while building up his arousal. She knew that the sexy noises she made turned him on, but that wasn't why she did it.

God, his mouth feels good right there.

He lifted her up. Squeezing her perfectly round, bubble butt in his hands drove him absolutely wild. Her sexy feminine energy stirred the animalistic lust buried deep inside of him. His mounting arousal continued to snowball until he could resist her no longer.

Josh let out a deep growl as he lowered Jess onto his solid steel shaft. As soon as he did, Jess buried her face in the crook of his neck.

"Oh, yes, take me, Josh. Take me again. Make me your little fuck toy. I want it, baby. Yeah, give it to me. Oooh fuuuck yeeeah!" Jess squealed and squirmed in Josh's arms, whispering her deepest, dirtiest desires into his ear.

And Josh delivered.

Her arms locked around him. Her legs locked across his back. She pushed her big, perky tits firmly up against his chest. Josh bounced her ass up and down in his hands, driving his rock solid cock in between her legs. Penetrating her deeply at a fast, rhythmic pace. The sound of he ass cheek clapping against his hips filled the night air, echoing off the rooftops.

Jess went from whispering dirty little nothings to professing her pleasure at the top of her lungs for all the city to hear. As she screamed her tits off, Jess returned to the Exhibitionists Manta.

It's just me and him. Him and me. No one else is around.

"Oh, FUCK! Yeah, fuck me! Whoo! Yea, yea, yea! Oooh, fuck YES, Josh! Omiga, Omiga, Omiga, Oh my FUCK!" Jess wasn't just screaming. She was projecting in her very best porn star impersonation.

Josh had complete control over her body while she was in his arms. She didn't have to do anything; he pounded her pussy downward while thrusting deep up inside of her. Deeper and faster. Faster and deeper.

Jess gasped a sharp inhale, her breath was caught in her throat. As she was getting fucked silly on the rooftop, she took in a lung full of the cold night air.

She could no longer form words that expressed the waves of heavenly deliverance that filled her each time Josh's cock slid deep inside of her. he was simultaneously flirting with her g-spot and her clitoris, stimulating both. It was almost all too much for one mortal woman to handle all at once.

She could no longer form words. She couldn't think straight. Josh had, for all intents and purposes, fucked her brains out.

All she could do was let her body respond to what he was doing to her. All she could do was make the primitive sounds of a female in the those of the best, hottest, most intense intercourse of her entire life.

Jess had no idea how long her orgasm lasted. But as she came hard, again and again and again, Josh joined her in whooping and hollering, deliberately being as loud as humanly possible. The crescendoing roar of a lion and lioness that echoed throughout the jungle.

As silence fell across the land, the two lovers remained in their tangled embrace. Locked in each others arms, their two bodies wrapped into one, their shared a passionate kiss while their breathing returned to normal.

"That was... wow. I... I think I blacked out." She confessed.

Josh just laughed, not knowing if she was serious or not.

When Jess finally returned to reality, she suddenly realized that something was going on below, at the foot of the building.

"Josh, do you hear that? It sounds like people screaming."

He gently set her down and pulled up his pants.

"Where is that coming from?" He asked.

The two edged to the side of the rooftop to look over. On the streets below, from the entrance to Avalon and all along the line that still stretched around the side of the building, every single person in line was looking up and cheering.

Cheering for them.

It reminded Jess of the rooftop scene from Independence Day. Only they were the visitors from above.

From three floors down, amidst the whooping applause, they heard the faint cry of people shouting things up at them.

"Fuck her right in the pussy!"

"You can do it all night long!"

"Give it to me, baby!"

"Flaunt it if you got it!"

It was all childish nonsense.

Jess looked over at Josh, mortified. Cold and naked, standing on the rooftop in the middle of Hollywood, she felt her entire body blush.

Josh was rolling on the ground laughing, arms wrapped around his stomach.

"Okay, laugh it up." She looked around for her dress. "I'm going to go greet all of my adoring fans. How do we get down?"

Josh tried to compose himself, standing. "I was just wondering the same thing. Elevator is locked and there are no stairs that I can see."

She put her hands on her hips. "I'm going to be pissed if they need to send a helicopter to airlift us out of here."

"Why? Because you're naked?"

"What? No! Because the bill for that would be outrageous!"

Josh shrugged.

Jess recovered her dress and Josh found his shirt, minus half a dozen buttons. Separately, they searched the entire rooftop, illuminated only by the light of the moon. The longer they searched, the more nervous Jess became.

She walked over to the ledge and looked down. Anytime she peeked over the edge of the rooftop, she felt dizzy. And terrified. Mostly just terrified.

"Find anything yet?" She called to Josh from the other side of the roof.

"Uh... Maybe? Definitely! ... Definitely maybe." He replied from the darkness.

"Not reassuring in any way... Josh, I don't like this any more. I want to get down." There was fear and panic in her voice.

"The good news is that I *did* find a way for us to get down."

"Good. Great. Let's do that."

"The bad news is that you're *not* going to like it."

Josh appeared from the darkness on the other side of the roof and took Jess's hand. He led her to the edge of the rooftop opposite the entrance to Avalon on the ground floor, where there were no lights at all. But even in total darkness, Jess could see exactly what he was talking about.

"You're right. I don't like this one bit." Jess whimpered.

She tried to turn around, but Josh pulled her by the hand.

"I'm afraid this is it, baby. But it'll be okay. Just hold my hand."

There was an old fire escape on the side of the building that looked like it went down to a back alley behind the building. It looked like it hadn't been used in over a hundred years. Even in the moonlight Jess could tell that parts of it were rusted through and covered with dust, dirt and spider webs.

Josh jumped out into the third floor fire escape scaffolding. The metal clanged and creaked under his weight. He reached over the ledge of the roof to pickup Jess by the waist and hoist her into the old metal scaffolding.

Then Jess made the mistake of looking down. They were only three floors up, but it might as well have been three hundred to her. As soon as she saw how far down it was, she scurried back onto the rooftop.

"I can't, I can't, I can't do it, I can't" Her voice cracked.

"Jess... It's the *only* way."

"No. I can't. I'll stay up here and you can go around in the service elevator."

"Baby, I don't have a key card to work the elevator. Besides, I have no idea how to find it again."

Jess looked over the edge and tears began to well up in her eyes.

"Why would she do this to us? I swear, when I see her next, I'm going to push her off of a roof, and then we'll see what's what."

"Babe, what you're talking about is called *murder*."

"So? California prisons still have conjugal visits, right?"

Josh sighed in frustration. He had obviously forgotten about how deathly afraid of heights Jess was.

"Okay. It's okay. I have an idea." Josh said calmly.

Jess stood about three feet above him on the roof while the fire escape hung over the side of the building. Josh reached up and tore a strip of fabric off of the bottom of her dress, effectively turning it into a mini skirt.

"Hey! What-"

Josh tied the black fabric around Jess's head like a blindfold.

"I like this idea even less." She grumbled.

Josh took hold of both her hands, squeezing them to comfort her.

"Sh, sh, sh. Baby, listen to me. I'm right here. I'm going to carry you down the fire escape in my arms. This way, you'll never have to look down."

Without waiting for her to reply, Josh picked her up and threw her over his shoulder like he was carrying a pack of potatoes. She squirmed in his arms, whining like a scared puppy.

"I've got you, okay? I'll never let anything bad happen to you. You know that."

The very first step he took caused the fire escape to warble and shift. Jess heard a loud metal clang and she pictured the whole thing coming apart as they fell to their deaths. On his second step, the sounds were even more pronounced.

Jess screamed.

"Sh, sh, sh, it's okay. It's just old."

"Wine is old! My grandma is old! This thing is so ancient that it's probably on Indiana Jones's most wanted list! It's so old that if Giorgio Tsoukalos was here, he'd tell you it was built by aliens!"

"Who? Look, I need one of my arms to climb down the ladder, okay?"

"No."

"... What?"

"Don't tell me! I don't want to know!"

"Um, okay. But I'm taking my hand away so I can climb down the ladder."

Jess had her arms around his neck so tight that she was practically strangling him. As soon as he started making his way down the ladder, Jess started screaming in his ear again.

"No! Don't drop me! Please don't drop me!"

"Baby, I'm *not* going to drop you. Don't you trust me?"

"Yes. It's gravity I don't trust."

Jess jumped at every creak in the rusted fire escape. Every inch of twisted metal bent under their combined weight. Josh couldn't tell whether the fire escape had never been used before or had seen heavy traffic for an extended period of time.

There was no doubt that the fire escape was unsafe. But it was also their only hope.

When they made it to the lowest level on the fire escape, Josh had to release the lock on the ladder so it would slide down to street level. He pulled and kicked the ladder release lever, but it wouldn't budge. It was rusted shut.

And without the ladder dropping down to street level, that meant a *very* long jump.

"What is going on?" Jess asked when she heard Josh repeatedly kicking the ladder release lever.

Josh had an idea as to how he could get both of them off the fire escape and back on solid ground, but he was positive that Jess wouldn't like it and would certainly never agree to it.

But if he could pull this off, then she would be safe.

Scared shitless? Yes.

Mad as hell? Definitely.

Physically unharmed? Well... Hopefully.

CHAPTER 22

Day 4 – Back Alley

She was practically choking him out with her iron-clad grip around his neck. He had one arm on the final rung of the ladder and the other on Jess's back, supporting her weight.

Josh could see the cement ground of the back alley about 15 feet below them.

"Baby, I can't breathe. Could you loosen your grip?"

"Not a chance."

"I can't breathe. Don't you trust me?"

She loosened her grip around Josh *just* enough.

Then he whispered in her ear, "Whatever happens, remember, I love you. I've always loved you."

He ducked under her arms, shaking free of her grip. With only one arm, he threw her up into the air as hard as he possibly could.

Josh let go of the ladder and fell to the alleyway below.

Jess flew up, her repeated screams of horror pierced the night sky as Josh landed hard on the city street. He staggard on the balls of his feet, teeth clamping down.

He recovered just in time to hold his arms straight out. Jess tumbled from the sky and fell right into his arms, just barely catching her, blindfolded and shrieking bloody murder.

If he had been a fraction of a second late... Well, the fall probably wouldn't have *killed* her, but their trust definitely would not have survived.

Josh held her close and pulled off her blindfold with his teeth.

Jess opened her eyes and looked around. Only when she could see that she was safely down from the rooftop did she stop screaming.

She immediately wiggled free from his arms and started swatting his bare chest.

"What are you thinking! I thought I was going to die! I'm going to kill you! I'm afraid of heights! You know that, Josh, how could-"

He grabbed her arms and pushed his lips onto hers to shut her up.

Little did he know that all of the adrenaline coursing through her veins was an aphrodisiac. The little fact that he was standing in front of her shirtless was also a bit of a turn on.

I suppose near death experiences will do that.

Jess alternated between kissing his passionately and smacking the shit out of him. Feeling his muscled body, then kissing him again.

Josh pulled her close until he was safely out of arm's reach, hoping to take the part where she hit him out of the equation. Instead, Jess started clawing and groping wildly at his body.

After a lengthy and painful make out session, Josh finally pulled away, holding Jess at arm's length by her waist. She looked up at him with big, doe eyes.

"Josh, that was crazy. What were you thinking?" She asked with tears in her eyes.

"You're safe, aren't you? We're on solid ground, aren't we?"

A tear ran down her cheek.

"I thought I was going to die."

"Aw, babe. You know I would never let that happen. If you die, that means that I'm already dead."

"I thought you *were* dead." She sobbed.

Josh opened and closed his mouth, realizing his words were not helping the situation.

"I'm right here." He said at last., softly.

Jess wiped the tears from her eyes, clearing her throat so her voice didn't crack.

"At least we got off the roof." Josh proffered.

Jess spun around, suddenly aware of her surroundings.

"Josh... Where are we? This looks like some kind of..."

A look of recognition lit up both of their eyes simultaneously.

"Back alley." They said in unison.

Jess cursed Miko under her breath. Was this the woman's plan all along? Did she purposely lock them on the roof to get them to come down into the back alley, serving up yet another location on the Bingo card?

"I'm going to kill that woman." Jess whispered to herself.

"What?" Josh asked.

"I said I'll give you a chance to make it up to me, Josh. One, and only one."

Jess stabbed one finger into his chest. A wry smile appeared on his face. Of course he was thinking the same thing that she was thinking. Why wouldn't he be?

"You're going to fuck me and make me cum in this back alley. If you can do that, all will be forgiven."

Josh coughed a laugh. "Are you worried that Miko will get ahead of us in BINGO?"

"*No one* gets ahead of us in BINGO, Josh." She took his face in her hands and offered up a gentle kiss. "And I intend to keep it that way."

Josh returned the kiss. "How does she have, like, and endless number of guys everywhere she goes?"

"I know. It's annoying."

Josh had his back up against the wall of the building. Jess stepped up beside him facing the wall. She planted both hands firmly against the wall, bending forward slightly at the waist, and spread her feet shoulder's width apart.

Josh's smirk seemed to fade.

"Baby, my dick really hurts. Can't we take a break?"

Jess had already assumed the position. She wouldn't take no for an answer.

"Breaks over, babe. Come on. If you don't come and get this, I'll find someone who will."

Josh looked around the deserted back alley.

"From this pool of likely candidates? Should I be jealous"

"Shut up and fuck me already." She kept her hands planted against the wall as if she were getting frisked.

Josh sighed. "How about a blow job, then? Help me get things started?"

Jess's gaze swept over her shirtless boyfriend leaning against the brick wall in the dark back alley, eyeing him up and down while he begged her for a blow job.

Jess sighed. "Find something for me to put under my knees and I'll see what I can do for you. I guess."

Before she even finished talking, Josh fished out part of a pizza box from the top of a nearby dumpster and tossed it on the ground in front of Jess. She eyes it as if he had just thrown a pile of human excrement at her feet.

Josh pulled down his pants to his ankles. She made a sort of whining noise as she just stared at his flaccid dick with a look of disgust.

"Having second thoughts?" He asked.

"No. I was just thinking about... pizza." She lied.

"Tell you what, after I give you the best orgasm of your life in this disease-ridden cesspool, I'll take you out for pizza and beer."

Jess raised one eyebrow, giving him a look of disbelief. "Best orgasm ever, huh?"

It took Josh a while to figure out that she was fishing for words of encouragement. For motivation.

"Uh, hey, babe. Wouldn't it be fun if we role-played like we were on the set of a porno, or something?"

The look of disgust on her face softened. He knew how much she enjoyed role-playing.

"What am I, then? Your fluffer?"

"What? No! You're the leading lady who is trying to put herself through nursing school and your friend in one of your classes did some light modeling work and heard that you were having trouble paying tuition this year so she referred you to a modeling gig to earn a little extra cash to help pay for school but when you get there you realize that it's really a porn set and not modeling but you say fuck it because you need the money for school and deep down you always fantasized about doing something like this and it turns out that the money is way better than being a nurse anyway plus everyone on the set is like super nice to you because you're so pretty so after making a couple of movies you find out you kind of really like doing the work plus you're really good at it and you go out partying with some of your co-workers and they get you high on cocaine but you like it so much that you start doing coke before every movie you do and then you start doing it every day and you can't get out of bed without a little bump so you fall into a drug addiction and you stay out all night partying but soon the drugs stop working and you become so numb that you don't even know why you're doing it anymore so you leave the adult industry and return to nursing school years later after you're all burnt out and used up but this time you have lots of money so everything is going great up until one of your teachers recognizes you from one of your movies and he threatens to get you expelled so instead you blow him and then blackmail him into giving you passing grades and then right as you're about to graduate nursing school you find out that your grandmother is diagnosed with leukemia and the only way to save her is a really expensive operation that she can't afford so in order to save your grandmother you have to pay for the life-saving operation but you already spent all of the money you made from your adult movies on nursing school so you make a triumphant return to porn and this is your highly-anticipated comeback movie your fans have been waiting for but no one knows that you're really doing it so you can pay for your sick grandmother's operation.

And I'm, like, the pizza guy. Or whatever."

Jess stood there for a moment, contemplating the premise of Josh's role-playing scenario.

"Come on, Josh. That's completely unrealistic. My grandmother is most likely on Medicaid, and they cover most leukemia-related surgeries."

"It's, like, *super* advanced leukemia," Josh said while idly playing with his dick.

Tears welled up in Jess's eyes. "Advanced leukemia? Poor old Gram. That sounds bad."

Josh nodded slowly. "It is. It's *very* bad. It's also a *very* expensive procedure. Highly experimental." He took a big step forward, closing the distance between the two of them. "And the only way you can save your dear, old gram is by making this the biggest, best, hottest comeback special of your career."

"Okay. I'm ready." Jess flipped her hair back, then knelt on the cardboard pizza box in front of Josh. She took his cock in her hands and brough her lips to the tip of his dick. "Wait, wait, wait. What's my porn name?"

"What? Who care?"

"My fans care!"

Josh said the first thing to pop into his head. "Uh, Backalley Bertha."

"No! That is *not* sexy! I can't save gram with a name like that."

"Fine. What do you want it to be?"

"Nurse Sex-a-Lot." She said with a sense of finality.

Josh snickered. "That's the worst porn name I've ever heard. It's not even a name. It sounds like a bad Doja Cat song."

Jess looked down at the ground, crestfallen.

"What about Pearl Cummings?" He tried to say with a straight face.

"Ew, no! Pearl is an old lady's name. What about Platinum Pussy?"

"Again, not a name."

"What about Pussy Rain?"

"Even worse. How about Rain Cummings?"

"Oh, I like that.... *Platinum* Rain Cummings."

Josh rolled his eyes. "Yeah. Sure. Whatever. You gonna suck this dick or not, *Miss Cummings?*"

"Call me…" She whipped her hair back dramatically. "P.R.C."

"Never in a million years will I call you P.R.C. while we're having sex." Josh started to windmill his dick out of boredom. You know what? We'll just cross that bridge when we come to it, *Miss Cummings.*"

"But I-"

"And… Action!"

"Hold on! I need to get into character. This is Miss Cummings big comeback special we're talking about here."

Jess suddenly snapped into her new identity.

"It's a porno shot in a back alley. How hard could it be?"

"Apparently not very hard at all." She said, staring down at his dick. "For you, at least. I've seen a lot of porn that took place in crusty back alleys just like this."

"Have you, now?"

"It was kind of my thing for, like, a few weeks in high school. Now if you'll excuse me, I'm trying to draw inspiration."

"Am I speaking to Jess or Miss Cummings?"

She ignored him, taking her place on her knees in front of him.

"I'm ready. But can we have the graphics department do something like the words 'Presenting Platinum Rain Cummings Big Comeback Special' but the word 'Comeback' spelt with a 'U'.

Ooh, and then do a star-wipe to a picture of me with a bunch of cum on my back."

"Are you kidding? Do you know what the budget for this film is?"

"But it's for Gram, though." She pouted.

"Alright, alright. I'll talk to the graphics department and see what we can do."

"Yay! Thank you, mister pizza delivery director!"

And with that, Jess happily took Josh's dick into her mouth and started sucking. It was a very exaggerated and dramatic blowjob.

"Mmm... Mmm... Mmm..."

Just as Josh was getting hard, she abruptly stopped. There was a loud popping sound when she pulled his cock out of her mouth.

"Pst. Hey, pizza guy. That's your cue."

"It is?"

Jess rolled her eyes as she continued stroking Josh's saliva-soaked cock.

"Haven't you ever seen gutter punk porn? Like, did you even read the script?"

"Script?"

From her perch on the pizza box, Jess looked up at Josh and sighed, blinking her vibrant green eyes.

"You're supposed to face fuck me. Duh." She whispered while jerking his dick just enough to keep him hard.

"Oh. Uh, sorry."

"Look, I know this is probably your first day on set, or whatevs, and I know I'm kind of, like, a big deal but try not to get star struck or we'll find another pizza guy who knows his cues. I will *not* jeopardize *my* comeback special because of some peon like you. Try and get that through your thick skull.

"The overall premise for the movie is that Platinum Rain Cummings wanders down a shady back alley and gets fucked like a whore by the pizza guy – that's you. And this is the scene where I get face fucked. If I have to tell you again how to do your job we'll find a hobo to do it for you and he'll still remember his cues better than you do."

"Wow. Platinum Rain Cummings is kind of a diva, huh?"

"I'm going to pretend like I didn't hear that." Jess said.

Jess crouched down and spread her knees apart so her torn dress rode up, exposing her bare ass. She started rubbing her wet pussy with one hand while stroking Josh's cock with the other.

"Now shut up and fuck me like a whore, pizza asshole."

Josh grabbed a fist full of Jess's hair by the back of her head and pulled her mouth over his dick, shoving her hard cock all the way down her throat until she choked.

Jess opened her mouth as wide as possible, extending her tongue all the way out while Josh fucked her face. She relaxed her throat so Josh could force his dick in and out of her mouth as he pleased. She felt the tip of his cock slide all the way down the back of her throat.

Trails of saliva dripped down Jess's lips and off her tongue. She angled her hips so that all her spit rained down onto her pussy, rubbing it all in and using it as lubricant.

Josh, however, found his motivation with great difficulty. He loved Jess, and no mater how many times she told him that she like being fucked like a whore, he had great difficulty thinking of her that way.

But this was role play. Just because he couldn't think of her as a whore didn't mean that he couldn't fuck her like one.

"Yeah, take that cock in the back of your throat, you filthy fucking slut. Choke on that fucking dick."

She let him face fuck her until her face turned purple. Josh ripped the top of her dress so her tits came spilling out. Jess drooled all over her chest, making her breasts glisten with saliva. Then Josh slapped the shit out of her tits as if he were spanking her ass until they were both bright red. All the while, Jess never stopped furiously rubbing her pussy.

At last, Josh unsheathed his cock from the back of her throat, dripping with trails of her spit. When he pulled his cock out of her mouth, Jess was surprised at her ability to take the entire thing in her throat. She always marveled at how big it was, fully erect, and how such a petite young woman was able to fit all of that inside of her orifices.

All of her orifices.

But Josh wasn't done with this one just yet.

"Suck my fucking cock and swallow all my jizz, you fucking whore."

She smiled at him as she drooled all over the front of her exposed body. Jess leaned forward on the pizza box, grasping the base of Josh's mighty cock and licking her saliva off of it.

"I said suck my dick, bitch." Josh winced when he said it. She knew it hurt him to play this role, but he played along anyway because it was what she wanted.

Jess eagerly sucked his cock while she stroked him, twisting his shaft into her mouth until he quickly climaxed in her mouth.

"Oh, fuck yeah. Swallow my fucking cum, you little slut."

But after busting for the fifth time that night, he didn't have much left to give.

"Did you cum? That was pathetic. I want to feel you shoot ropes into the back of my throat." She begged him.

"Shut up and get up against the wall." Josh was tired and wanted to finish the scene while he was still hard enough to do so.

But Jess wasn't going to make it easy for him.

"Make me." She said defiantly.

Looking up and him, Jess pursed her lips to the tip of his cock while she continued stroking him. She sucked on the end of his dick like it were a straw she was trying to suck boba out of, playing with it on her lips.

Josh caught a hold of her wrists and pulled her to her feet, then with his pants still pulled down around his ankles, he bent down and picked Jess up. All the way up.

He threw Jess over his shoulder just like he did when he carried her down the fire escape, then he gave her ass a brutal spanking. He trotted over to the wall with her slung over his shoulder, cum and spit dripping from her lips.

With every step, he slapped her bottom hard. With every spanking, Jess let out a little yelp.

"You" *SLAP* "will" *SLAP* "not" *SLAP* "dis" *SLAP* "oh" *SLAP* "bay" *SLAP* "me" *SLAP* "now" *SLAP* "be" *SLAP* "a" *SLAP* "good" *SLAP* "fuck" *SLAP* "ing" SLAP "whore" *SLAP* "and" *SLAP* "stand" *SLAP* "up" *SLAP* "against" *SLAP* "the" *SLAP* "wall." *SLAP*.

When he did finally set her down, Jess immediately set her hands against the wall obediently, facing away from Josh. She looked back at him through lidded eyes, dress torn at both top and bottom, biting her bottom lip.

Now that Josh was fully in character, he wanted to rip her dress completely off of her body. But as hot as that would be, he couldn't have her walking home completely naked. It was bad enough that he was missing her shirt and her dress was torn. If they lost even another scrap of clothing, it would make the trek home very awkward indeed.

Instead, he pulled her slinky black dress down, scrunching it together at her waist like a little black tutu. Her ass was glowing a shade of pink red. Josh admired the outlines of his handprints all over her booty.

She looked back at him lustfully but dared not speak. Josh gave her bubble butt one last hard smack for good measure, then reached in front of her to pinch her nipples. Jess took his rough foreplay and was grateful for it, cooing as she bit her bottom lip.

Josh kicked her feet apart until she widened her stance. As Josh rested his hand on the side of Jess's waist, she made soft, lustful noises in anticipation.

He stood close behind her, teasing her with expectancy. Just before he slid his long, hard cock into her tight wet hole, he whispered to her, "I can't believe I'm about to fuck the shit out of the talented Platinum Rain Cummings."

She giggled, breaking character for just a moment. "Make sure you sell it."

He nodded. "For Gram."

"For Gra-OH MY GOD!"

With little warning or warm up, he shoved the entirety of his thick cock to the back of Jess's pussy, penetrating her until he could penetrate no more. It was something that Jess was neither accustomed to nor enjoyed. It was unexpected and painful. Josh knew that Jess's tight pussy needed to be stretched a bit before he could enter her fully.

But he wasn't fucking his girlfriend. He was fucking Platinum Rain Cummings, and though they shared a vagina, PRC liked the sudden and unexpected pain, Jess decided.

As soon as he sheathed his sword in her all the way to the hilt, all of the air was forced from Jess's lungs. She threw her head back, gasping for air. Jess pushed her head against the dirty concrete wall, white-knuckling her hands as she got her bearings.

"ouch, ouch, ouchy!" she whispered under her breath, not wanting Josh to hear her.

Jess balanced her hands one the wall with one hand stuck between her legs, rubbing her clit in a desperate attempt to derive some pleasure from the pain. Josh soon picked up on this and switched to half-thrusts instead of breathing the full depths of her vagina.

"Omigod, omigod, omigod, oh FUCK!"

While Jess had planned on making wild, unrealistic porn star noises as soon as Josh started fucking her, but the tenacity with which he ravaged her body was so utterly complete that it shut off the part of her brain that she used for things like reasoning and planning. Only the most primal part of her brain was functioning, allowing her to do nothing but react to external stimuli.

Which, in this case, was Jess's response to being fucked like a whore on the set of a back alley porn.

Her mouth fell open as she tried to widen her stance, but her thighs were already shaking. Josh continued drilling her at a steady pace, but felt like her wobbly legs would soon collapse at any moment. She tried to communicate this face to Josh, but had a hard time articulating words.

"Oh, guh, uh fuh, Joss... oh mi... fuh mi puzzi... ah, yea... uh, fuh, fuh, fuh, yea, yea, yea, Joss. Gah!"

Sensing her trembling thighs, Josh lunged forward and scooped up her right ankle, holding one of her legs extended up as he fucked her. Jess balanced herself with on hand on the wall, one hand on her pussy, one legs on the ground and the other leg being manipulated by Josh.

"Up... Up... Hold it up... Here." Jess managed to get the words out between lungs full of air as she tapped her collar bone above her bouncing bare breasts with her free hand before returning it to its rightful home on her clit.

Josh got the message and hooked the bottom of her heel on the top of his shoulder.

Thank goodness for a childhood in gymnastics.

"Oh my God, fuck yeah, that's so fucking good. Fucking me just like that. Right there."

Her entire demeanor changed the moment Josh had her doing the standing splits with one leg above his head. Like all good role-playing, Jess forgot where Jess ended and Miss Cummings began. By all outward appearances, she dropped the entire role-playing pretense and gave into was becoming really good, hot sex.

Jess grabbed her boobs and squeezed tight. Then she slapped her ass and pulled on her butt cheeks. Josh was hitting her clit and g-spot with every thrust, driving her crazy.

"Oh yeah, right there, baby. Just like that, just like that. Oh, you make my pussy feel so fucking good, baby."

Josh recognized Jess's porn star moans as authentically hers. That was how Jess liked to talk dirty, no Platinum Rain Cumings, or whoever the fuck she was pretending to be. She was taking his dick the way that Jess like to take his dick. She orgasmed the way that Jess orgasmed.

The façade of role-play slowly melted away.

Josh continued to pound her pussy with her foot hooked over his shoulder, next to his face, allowing for the best angle of penetration. Again and again and again, getting a very Jess-like reaction from her each time.

She began to beg him in a low, husky, sultry voice, "Please, baby. Please cum in my pussy. Please? Cum inside of me just one more time? Oh, please, baby. Oh, fuck, I want it so fucking bad right now. Please, baby. I want to feel you shoot your hot cum into the back of my pussy. I want to feel that shit inside of me. Oh, God, you feel so fucking good. Ah! Yeah, baby, just like that! Fill me up. I can feel that! So good. So fucking good. Oh, yeah... Holy shit, baby, are you still cumming? So warm and wet... What the fuck, *still?* Are you done? I didn't know you had that much left."

"Neither did I" Josh said as he continued to thrust his cock into her cum-soaked pussy.

"What was that, like, fifteen ropes?"

"At least."

Josh at last pulled out and unhooked Jess's leg from around his neck. She stumbled, bracing herself against the wall.

"Oh my *God*! Look at all of it!"

Jess laughed and spread her pussy with her fingers as thick droplets of gooey white jizz trickled down her thighs. She scooped up one particularly voluminous glob of cum with two fingers and dipped it into her mouth as if it were melting cheese.

"Mm! Seriously, babe, you cum enough to feed all of China."

"Is that what happens when you donate sperm?" Josh said as he pulled up his pants and, to Jess chagrin, put his cock away.

"I don't know, but can I be your exclusive sperm donation concierge?" She asked while fixing her dress up as best she could.

"What does that entail?"

"Being open for twenty-four seven around the clock sperm donations. But it's an exclusive contract. I don't want you taking your business elsewhere."

"In that case, we've already been in business for quite some time."

She took him by the hand and pulled him close.

"Look at that. I guess we have, haven't we?" She said with a kiss on the cheek.

"You could probably wring out that dress and get a few more donations out of it, after tonight."

"And why would I do that? Business is consistent enough. And I could always just wait for tomorrow's donation."

"I would say that you can safely rely on a steady supply of donations coming in on a regular basis for the foreseeable future." He squeezed her hand.

"It's a fairly stable and long-term contract, then?" She squeezed his hand back.

"Oh, I'd say it's very long-term."

Hand in hand, the two walked down the dark back alley towards the main street.

Jess let the cum run down her legs as they walked, ignoring the temptation to wipe it on her shredded black dress. The dress was already torn, but she didn't want to ruin it further with white jizz stains all over it.

Besides, part of her really like the idea of walking around in public with hey boyfriend's fresh cum still inside of her – and some of it outside of her, trickling down her inner thighs for all to see.

That's one way to keep my legs warm, she thought.

When they reached the mouth of the back alley that opened up to Hollywood Boulevard, an eight-foot-tall chain-link fence barred their path.

Josh looked up at the fence and frowned. When he looked over at Jess, she was already halfway up the fence. She easily crested the top of the fence and flipped her body up and over to the other side. Only then did she pause to smile at Josh.

"Well? What are you waiting for?" She asked from a top the fence.

"Just admiring the view." He smirked.

"Perv!" Jess pulled down her dress with one hand, clinging to the fence with the other.

Josh was preparing his witty comeback when they heard a police siren from the street beyond the fence. Red and blue flashing lights splashed across the back alley walls. Then a police spotlight appeared on Jess, blasting her with bright light.

"Oh, shit!" Jess panicked. She dropped from the fence, falling at least six feet and breaking one of her heels in the process.

Then she took off running.

"Stop!" A man yelled from a police loudspeaker.

The police squad car door opened and slammed shut.

"Hey! Stop!" someone yelled behind her.

Jess did not wait to find out whom the voice belonged to. She heard footsteps close behind her and started running in the other direction.

When Jess glanced over her shoulder, she saw Josh running a few paces behind her followed by two LAPD cops pursuing closely at his heels.

Hindered by her broken heels, Jess kicked off both of the $500 Louis V stilettoes and ran barefoot down Hollywood Boulevard. All manner of filth lay in the streets like landmines for a woman running from the police with no shoes. She desperately hurdled over broken glass bottles, used syringes, human excrement, and worse as she pumped her tiny fists as fast as she could.

"L.A.P.D. freeze!" the cop behind them yelled.

"Go! Go! Go!" Josh cried, urging her onward.

She heard voices chattering on the police radio that she couldn't quite make out.

This is it. I'm going to jail. They'll make me register as a sex offender. I'll be a pariah and a harlot. My life is over.

Her heart was pounding in her chest, tears running down her cheeks. She felt adrenaline propelling her poor little bare feet as she padded down the busy street.

When she reached the Hollywood and Cahuenga intersection, the traffic light turned red. The sidewalk with flooded with drunk pedestrians in every direction and cars going both ways in the street.

Jess pivoted left, cutting downhill on Cahuenga, past all the inebriated club goers and night walkers.

"L.A.P.D. freeze!" she heard a cop yell in the distance behind her. She had no idea where Josh was, but at least it seemed like she was gaining distance from the police.

Jess continued down to Cahuenga and Sunset Boulevard, tired, out of breath, and sweating. Her lungs burned and her feet hurt but she kept running, turning right on Sunset only because the light was green.

She wasn't entirely sure why the cops were waiting for them at the mouth of the alleyway, but she was certain that it couldn't be anything good. At any rate, now that she was running away from the police, she was committed. She couldn't stop, no matter what the police or her feet told her.

In her head, she repeated to herself, *Just keep swimming, just keep swimming…*

She spotted another parked police car at the next intersection, but she wasn't sure if they had noticed her or not.

Just keep swimming, just keep swimming…

In the distance, she saw the entrance to the Hollywood Metro station. When she looked behind her, she couldn't see the police anymore.

But neither could she see Josh.

Tears welled up in her eyes. Did he get arrested? Would she have to go bail him out? Would they arrest her if she went to go bail him out?

Just keep swimming, just keep swimming…

As she neared the entrance to the Metro station, Jess slowed down. Then she stopped to catch her breath. Whatever happened to Josh, she couldn't just leave him.

She stood outside the entrance to the subway, hunched over and desperately trying to catch her breathe. Her mind started reeling with all sorts of possibilities that might have befallen Josh.

None of them were good.

"Jess! Hey, Jess!"

She jumped when she heard someone calling her name. when she looked up, Jess had to squint to see someone coming up the stairs of the Hollywood Metro station.

It was Josh.

Her heart burst with joy once more. All of her fears sunk to the bottom of her mind. Jess pushed her feet to move onward.

"Josh!"

Her lungs were punishing her. Her body was drained. She was tired. Exhausted. Dead. The only thing that drove her forward was Josh's smiling face.

And the imminent fear of being arrested.

Jess was so relieved to see him. He looked equally relieved to see her. She jumped into his arms and he spun her around once, twice, three times. Enough to make her a little dizzy.

Josh carried her down the stairs to the Metro subway station. He lifted her up and over the turnstile. Jess could only laugh and squeal with happiness that they were safe – for now.

"Let's get out of here, my love." He hopped over the turnstile with debonair grace.

"Baby! Oh, I'm so glad to see you! Wait, how did you get ahead of me?"

He smiled a handsome smile in reply.

"I saw you turn down Cahuenga, so I led the cops straight down Hollywood Boulevard. Then I cut down another back alley and lost them." He said simply.

"You led them away from me?"

"Of course." He shrugged.

"My hero!"

She jumped into his arms again. This time he wasn't ready for it and dropped her clumsily. Jess quickly recovered.

"Don't look now, but there are two cops behind us and they look like they're searching for someone – Babe! I said don't look!"

"They're coming this way."

"Quickly, on the train. Let's go."

They descended a final flight of stairs just as the train pulled into the Hollywood station. The couple kept their heads down, which only made them look even more suspicious. Without buying tickets, they slipped into the train just as the doors closed behind them, finding two unoccupied seats close to the door.

As the train started moving, Jess spotted the two officers standing on the ramp, looking around like a couple of bumbling idiots.

Jess started pounding on the train window. As soon as the two cops saw Jess and Josh waving at them from inside the moving train, they lost their shit. One cop elbowed the other, pointing angrily at the couple and jumping up and down like a madman.

Then the other cop started talking into his radio while he locked eyes with Jess.

Shit. Maybe that was not smart.

Jess turned to Josh with a grim expression on her face.

"I guess these *were* the droids they were look for..."

They sat in silence for the rest of the train ride home.

CHAPTER 23

Day 5 - Train

The L.A. Metro train trekked along noisily, bumping and jostling all of its passengers as it went.

Unlike most major cities, the L.A. Metro system of underground subway trains is an entirely underutilized and often overlooked form of public transit. Building an underground subway system in the middle of a fault line was neither easy nor cheap. The city of Los Angeles paid a fortune to create the Metrolink and Amtrak, which were neither well-publicized nor well-maintained forms of transportation.

In recent years, more homeless rode the trains than paying commuters. Still, riding on the Metro in L.A. was a world apart from riding the subway in New York or even the BART in San Francisco.

The one thing that never changes no matter which form of public transit people take is that they first thing people do is try to find a nice, quiet spot where they can be left alone.

Although this is almost never a possibility, it didn't stop Jess and Josh from occupying a seat in the very back of the train, wedged in the corner right next to a bum carrying four full garbage bags of empty soda cans.

Jess sat on Josh's lap, covertly riding his dick. Though the train was littered with homeless and commuters, plenty of recent practice at having sex in public made her confident enough to ride his dick freely.

Until the next stop.

Bing. "Now approaching Santa Monica." Came the feminine robotic voice over the loudspeaker.

A dozen riders walked into the caboose where they sat.

"Shit." Jess cursed under her breath, drawing the attention of several strangers.

She was only still for a moment on Josh's lap before she began grinding up against Josh's hard cock once more. Each time the train took a left turn or right, every time it abruptly stopped and started up again, Jess exaggerated her movements so she could adjust herself, bouncing every which way on her boyfriend's dick.

But after 45 minutes of this, what started as a kinky, clandestine fuck soon become frustrating and drawn out. At which point, Jess's patience began to wear thin.

"Hmm, fuck, baby, I can feel you so hard inside of me. God, this dick is so good. Ah, fuck, I love riding your cock."

"Baby, there is someone sitting right here next to me." Josh whispered to her back.

"Oh, God, I don't even care anymore." Jess began brazenly bouncing up and down in his lap, oblivious to everyone around her.

The two girls sitting beside Josh, only a few years younger than Jess, began giggling and whispering to one another. All of a sudden, they both had their phones in their hands. They were recording Jess as she slid up and down Josh's shaft, impaling herself on his horse cock like a pogo stick.

Jess grabbed a hold of the seat in front of her and began twerking on Josh's dick loudly.

"Ah, ah, ah, yeah, baby. Fuck me back. I want to cum already."

"Jess! There are people watching!"

"I told you I don't care! If you want me to stop, you'll have to get me to cum first."

Most people who shared their train politely ignored the two. They had seen weirder things than a couple having sex on the Metro before. Some were actively starring. Several were filming them.

"Just fuck me back. Please, baby? I'm close." She whined.

Josh sighed. He lifted he butt up off of his lap and began thrusting hard upward. Everyone in the train was silent as they listened to the sound of Josh's hips smacking up against Jess's bare ass. Her mouth fell open, framed in a smile.

"oh-oh-oh-fu-fu-uck-ye-ye-yeah-ah-ah-ah-go-na-ah-cum-mm-mm-mm."

He kept pounding her pussy until he felt her clench around his hard cock. Shortly after Josh felt Jess cum all over his dick, he began to cum inside of her.

"Whoo! Bay-bee! I can feel you cum-ming!" Jess teased in a sing-song voice.

Jess slowly ran her tight little pussy up and down the length of his steel erection, watching the cum trickle out of her pussy and down the sides of his cock.

Watching his semen spill out of her vagina and drip down his dick only turned him on more. His dick throbbed hard still inside of her.

"Ooh, it tickles." Jess giggled uncontrollably.

Josh wanted nothing more than to grab her ass in both hands and continue fucking the shit out of her using his own cum as lubricant. He wanted pound her pussy hard from his seat on the train. He wanted to grab hold of both her titties and throw her down on the floor and fuck her brains out in front of everyone on the Metro while they all clapped and cheered for them.

And he probably would have done all of those things, too, if he didn't hear their stop being called on the loudspeaker.

"Venice. Baby, this is us. Let's go."

Jess continued to wiggle her bottom on his lap until he let go of her, at which point she stood up to re-tie her bikini bottoms so that they covered her drippy wet pussy in front of everyone watching.

Once her bikini was back in place, Jess scooted out from their seat on the train with Josh right behind her. He had his fully erect dick stuffed into the waistband of his swim trunks.

It was not at all discreet.

"How much vodka is left?" Jess asked as they stepped off the train.

"Not much. I told you to slow down when we were pre-gaming for the beach."

"I'm still horn-ny. And dru-unk."

"I've seen you drunk and horny and you're barely either of those right now."

"Tipsy and turned on?" She compromised. "Tipsy and in need of tip!" She amended.

Josh put his face in his palm and sighed.

"What? That was funny. I'm funny."

"Didn't you *just* cum, like, a minute ago?"

"So? It just so happens that I *like* cum, Jo-osh!"

"I can literally still see my cum on your ass."

"You don't know that it belongs to you! What if it's *my* cum, Jo-osh!" she stopped to wipe the cum off her ass with two fingers. Then she popped those two fingers in her mouth.

"So?"

"Hmm... Okay, I think it is yours."

"See?"

"Not fair! Why do guys get to cum so much and us girls so little? It's a cruel world."

"Not true. I can feel you cum all over my dick every time we have sex."

"But I don't *see it*."

"I've seen you squirt lots of cum."

"That's different."

"Is it?"

"I don't squirt every time we have sex. Only when you put it in my butt. Why is that?"

"You're asking me? Besides, I can cum enough for both of us."

They walked by someone who was on the train with them earlier.

"Hey, thanks for the free show, guys. Do you have an OnlyFans."

Josh and Jess shared a look in silence. After a few seconds, the train guys just kept on walking, embarrassed.

"Did that just happen?" Josh asked.

"Another day on the L.A. Metro." She shrugged.

CHAPTER 24

Day 5 – Beach

It was a short but busy walk to Venice beach. On a Saturday afternoon, the place was crowded with tourists. After seeing traffic jams and full parking lots, the couple was happy to take the Metro down to the beach for the day.

And after sharing an orgasm on the way there, it was more eventful than most train rides.

"Where do you want to set up?" Josh asked as they walked through the warm beach dunes.

"I mean, anywhere there is room would be good."

It was the right answer. The beach was so crowded that there was scarcely room for them to roll out their beach blanket and the folding chairs they brought with them.

Josh and Jess lucked out. The only reason they were able to find a spot so close to the water was because they caught an obscenely obnoxious family leaving after their mother had forgotten to apply sunblock and ended up looking like an oversized basketball.

No sooner after they left did they have their blanket, chairs, and cooler set up. And because they weren't tourists or bumpkins, they both applied an ample layer of sunblock prior to leaving the house.

Jess brought a large sun hat, which she removed as soon as they laid down their beach stuff. She wore a sheer white coverup and triangle bikini top and bottom set with little Super Mario characters on it and a small cum stain on her bikini bottoms. She wore a matching fanny pack, also covered in Super Mario characters, full of sunblock and her designer sunglasses.

Josh wore his blue Cookie Monster swim trunks and a cotton tank top that he popped off the minute they hit Venice beach. He already had a perfect golden tan, a stark contrast to Jess's pale creamy skin.

It was perfect sunny Los Angeles beach day weather. Josh sighed a lighthearted sigh of relief as all of his stress melted away.

"This is nice. Why don't we 'beach' more often?"

In response, Jess waved a hand in the direction of the multitudes of people occupying every inch of the beach in every direction.

"Oh. Yeah. Well, do you want to go in the water, babe?"

Jess glanced over at the ebb and flow of the tides. Out in the ocean horizon, surfers sat on their boards, all waiting on their boards for the next big wave to arrive. Closer to shore, body boarders paddled along, swimming in the shallow water.

On the shore, just where the water met the sand, the entire coastline was teeming with families, tourists, and children as far as the eye could see, all running around and screaming like wild animals. It looked like everyone was having a great time.

Only "everyone" was a *lot* of people.

"Maybe later." Jess answered.

The couple lay out on their beach blanket side by side in silence. But what was silence between the two of them was an cacophony of noises coming from every inch of the beach.

It was seagulls screeching overhead. It was children screaming. It was Chinese families chattering away with no concept of personal space. It was teenagers blasting "Angel of Death" on their phones. It was people arguing over parking spot in the lot behind them. It was volleyball players yelling at each other over who missed which shots. It was all of this and more.

While Jess lay on her back with sunglasses on, tanning her pale skin, Josh leaned over and tapped her on the shoulder. "This is why people have private beaches, isn't it?"

That put a smile on her face. "You know, I've always thought that owning a private beach was crazy up until this very moment." She kissed him on the lips. "Now I get it."

The two passed back and forth a large bottle of vodka. When it was empty, Jess asked, "Will you put more sunblock on me? I want to get drunk enough to pass out in the sun."

Josh obliged, slathering Jess's body with enough sunblock for a brief visit to Mercury. When he was done, she reciprocated the favor.

Josh's complexion was perfectly suited to the beach. He looked like he fit right in at Venice's famous Muscle Beach. With his tan skin, lean, muscular body, and big frame, he resembled a linebacker combined with a surfer.

Josh had colorful tattoos covering half of his body, going all the way up his left arm covering half his chest, going down his side and going down to his pelvis. As much as Jess loved Josh's tattoos, as much as they turned her on and as fucking hot as she thought he looked all tatted up, he had unsuccessfully tried to convince Jess to get blasted with ink for years.

He always told her how hot she would look with a few choice tattoos, but in the end she was always too scared of needles to commit.

Then, one day after plenty of alcohol and sex, he finally convinced her to get her first and only tattoo. Jess had a heavy metal unicorn on her right forearm. And Josh fucking loved it.

Josh always warned her about the addictive properties of getting tattoos. But as much as Jess loved her punk rock unicorn, she did not feel compelled to get any more. Ever.

Jess tied her dark hair off to one side. Her skin was not typically very tan. She enjoyed the contrast of her pale skin to her jet black hair and naturally hot pink lips. It was a look very much suited to her complexion.

But adding a little sun kissed tint to my skin wouldn't hurt, she reasoned.

Or at least, that was the argument that Josh used in order to coax her into going to Venice beach. That and the promise of sex on the beach.

Abruptly, Jess rolled over to her side and sighed longingly. "When are we going to fuck?"

Josh just shrugged.

Then, a minute later.

"Will you take off my swimsuit so don't get tan lines?" she asked Josh after flipping around face down, as to not expose herself.

He knew it for the seductive ploy it was. But he obliged her anyway.

"You know," Josh said as he untied her bikini top and bottom, pulling them away. "I was just thinking how hot you would look with a few more tattoos on your arm to complete your sleeve."

She scoffed. "Not this again, Josh. I will *never* get a sleeve."

He ran his fingertips down her arm. "Well, a guy can dream, right?"

"Yeah. Keep fucking dreaming."

Josh removed her bikini bottoms and sat on her bare butt as he traced his fingers up and down her forearms. Jess lay with her hands folded under her head, her bare breasts propping her up on the towel below her.

"You could be one of those Suicide Girl models if you had a few more tattoos, babe." He began massaging her back.

"You really like those Suicide Girls, don't you, babe?"

"Why? Have you been going through my phone?"

Jess laughed. "I don't want to be a model. I like designing clothes."

Jess liked the feeling of his weight on top of her. and she liked his touch on her back and forearms.

"Mmm, that feels good."

"Yeah?"

He continued massaging her back, moving up to her shoulders.

"Mm-hmmmm... Ooh, right there. You know, you could be a masseuse with a little more practice."

Josh laughed. "I don't want to be a masseuse. I like being a graphic designer. Besides, do you really want me touching naked women all day long?"

"Mmm, as long as I'm one of those women I really don't care."

"Really?"

"Mm-hmm... Maybe you can find one of those Suicide Girls to bring into our bed."

"Reeeally?"

Jess giggled. "Yes! Are you thinking about it right now?"

"What makes you ask that?"

"Because I can feel your huge boner in between my cheeks right now."

"Oh shit! I'm sorry babe!" He sat right back up.

"I didn't say I didn't like it."

"Yeah? Well, I have an idea how we can earn that 'beach' BINGO square…"

"Oh, Josh, my love, I think you just read my dirty little mind."

Out of her beach bag, Jess tossed Josh a travel-sized bottle of coconut oil. He caught it and smiled devilishly.

"Babe, sometimes I swear to God you must by clairvoyant." He said, opening the bottle and squirting a generous amount into his hands.

"If that's Greek for 'in love with a handsome, brilliant man,' then yes, I'm extremely clairvoyant."

Josh laughed. "I fucking love you. You know that?" he reached into his swim trunks and rubbed a generous amount of coconut oil all up and down his shaft. Then he applied even more to Jess's bare ass cheeks until they glistened in the sun.

"Whoop!"

"What? Is it cold?"

"No, it feels good." She sat up on her stomach, arms folded underneath her head as if she were tanning.

"Well, brace yourself because it's about to feel a whole lot better." Josh surveyed the beach to see if anyone was watching them, then he leaned forward across Jess's back to whisper in her ear, "and if you don't attract any undue attention, I think we can get away with this for as long as we please."

Jess snorted. "Baby, when you look like this, it's impossible for you *not* to attract undue attention."

"Fair point." He kissed the back of her head. "Hold your breath."

"What? Why?"

In one fluid notion, Josh undid the Velcro fly of his swim trunks, pulled his oiled up cock out and slid it effortlessly into Jess's ass. She made a little noise when he did, though it was not nearly as loud as he thought it was going to be.

Josh was worried that she would give them away as soon as he penetrated her tight little asshole, but to her credit, she remained as silent as a mouse. A mouse getting fucked in it's ass by a big horse cock.

"Mmm. Ooh. Baby, you know I don't care where you put it, but out of curiosity, why my ass?"

"It looked good." He said honestly.

Josh sat on her thighs, on the lower part of her big bubble butt as he slowly rocked back and forth, fucking her in the ass. He applied more coconut oil to Jess's back and began massaging her, moving his entire body as to not arouse suspicion.

Jess swept her long, onyx hair out of his way and off to one side. With his legs firmly planted on either side of Jess's hips, Josh leaned forward to massage his girlfriend's back, each time plunging his dick deeper inside of her tight ass.

"Oh, God, I love anal when I'm drunk."

"I know." Josh said. "Me, too."

"Don't stop."

"I won't."

But as the day wore on and beachgoers all came and went, some became suspicious as to why Josh was massaging his girlfriend for so long. Still, Josh was surprised at how incredibly quiet Jess was being as he continued fucking her in the ass for well over an hour. Every five to ten minutes, Josh generously applied more coconut oil until the entire travel-sized bottle was gone.

But none of these things were the real danger they faced while having anal sex on a public and very crowded beach.

"Uh-oh. Babe, you're starting to get a little red."

"Well, shit. Hurry up and cum in my ass, then. And squirt some more coconut oil down there, while you're at it."

"We're out. And what about you?"

She made an uncomfortable whining noise.

"Ugh, there is no chance I'm going to cum right now. Baby, please just make it quick."

Josh sighed. He was really enjoying covertly sliding his oiled up cock in and out of her ass over the last hour. Yet, he suddenly wished that he had cum in her ass during the many times he was close but pulled back so he could keep going longer. He had plenty of opportunities that he passed up on every time.

"I can do that, but it's going to be obvious as fuck."

"Good." She said, kicking her feet idly up and down. "It's about time you learn what it feels like."

Josh laughed. "I love you."

He started pumping faster and faster, using what residual oil was left as lubricant. He was turning more heads with every thrust of his hips. But in order to get enough friction to get the job done, he had to go even faster.

Throwing caution into the wind, he braced his hands on Jess's lower back and started pounding her ass into the sand. Neither of them could hold back their loud grunts and moans at that point.

"God, your tiny asshole feels so fucking good wrapped around my co-ooo-ock!"

She felt his warm cum shoot deep inside her ass when Josh orgasmed with his throbbing dick inside of her. unfortunately for her, the lube on her ass was wearing thing. What started as exciting, kinky anal sex ended as something painful for her.

"My butt is all numb." She said when Josh pulled out and tucked his dick back into his swim trunks.

"Well, I came inside of you." He announced.

She laughed. "I know! I can feel your cum in my ass. I'm not *that* numb."

Josh stood up and she felt his weight lifted off her bottom half.

"Tie my bikini back on, jerk! Don't just cum in my ass and leave me!"

"Sorry, my legs are numb, too. And I really have to take a piss."

"Tie my bikini back on and we'll go pee in the ocean together. Thanks, now help me up."

It wasn't until Jess stood up that she realized that a lot of people on the beach were staring at them That was when she pulled out her exhibitionist's mantra.

"It's just him and me. No one else matters."

"What was that?"

"Oh, nothing. Hold my hand. I want to pee in the ocean next to you. It'll be fucking romantic."

Josh laughed. "You're such a wierdo."

Together, they walked hand in hand into the cold Pacific ocean until the water was up to their stomachs.

"Is that warm spot you?" Josh asked her wit one raised eyebrow.

"Probably. I *am* peeing right now. Have been for a while. Couples who swim in each other's pee stay together. Everyone knows that."

"Remind me why I love you again?"

Jess pulled down her bikini top, flashing Josh her perfect tits.

"Those are two very good reasons."

"Right? Don't forget about them, because they won't forget about you. And speaking of the girls, what are we going to do to even out my front tan?"

Before Josh could answer, a huge wave came by and dunked them both underwater. Josh never let go of her hand as they were submerged. Josh pulled her close to him, but only their heads were visible above water now.

"You okay?" He asked.

"It's gone!"

"What's gone? Your inhibitions? Because it seems like you left those at home today."

"My top, you jerk!"

As Josh pulled her close, even underwater he could feel her bare breasts and hard nipples brushing up against him. Sure enough, the wave had carried away her top.

"Where did it go?"

The two of them swam around for a bit in search of Jess's top, but it was nowhere to be seen.

"Did it sink?" Josh asked, still holding her hand.

"I don't know!" she cried. "That was part of a matching set! My Super Mario bikini!"

"I'm sorry, babe, but it's in a better place now. Looks like King Koopa won this round."

"It's not funny!"

Josh hummed the game over music in Super Mario when Mario dies.

"Josh! What am I going to do?!"

"Finish working on your tan?"

She started crying.

"Alright, I'm sorry, baby. Listen, just stay right here. I'm going to go grab you my tank."

Josh swam to the shore, grabbed his tank top from their beach camp, then swam back into the ocean out to where Jess was neck deep in water, all the while holding his shirt above his head to keep it dry.

"Here. It's not Super Mario, but it'll have to do for now."

Josh and Jess waded to short until the water was only waist deep so Jess didn't get his tank top wet. For about 30 seconds before she put on his tank top when she was swimming out of the water topless, Jess was turning the head of every single man in her proximity.

CHAPTER 25

Day 5 – Fitting Room

After their misadventure peeing together in the ocean, the couple had decided that they'd angered Poseidon enough for one day and decided to pack it in.

Even after putting on Josh's tank, the top revealed an ample amount of side boob. She was still turning heads, but on the Venice beach boardwalk, there is always something even more strange lurking around the next corner waiting to turn your head until it snaps.

They stopped briefly to watch someone juggling chainsaws in front of the Venice skate park before continuing down the boardwalk.

"Come on, let's find a place where I can buy a new swimsuit." Jess tugged on her boyfriend's hand, pulling him along to the row of stores set up all along Venice beach.

"Only if you can find a place to get a new bikini that has fitting rooms."

Jess put her hands on her hips. "What is that supposed to mean? Are you calling me fat?"

"What? No, babe. *Fitting rooms.*"

"Oh. *Oh.* Ohhh"

"You have no idea what I'm talking about do you?"

She blinked, staring at him on the sidewalk, holding his hand. "Fitting rooms for... trying things on."

"Bingo."

Her face lit up.

"Yes! Yes and more yes! Although I'm not even sure I want to get a new bikini. I need my boyfriend to help me try out some new styles. Like, you know, something that doesn't get swept off at the very first fucking wave that hits?"

Jess led them into a boutique swimwear shop right on the boardwalk.

"On the plus side, at least the ocean washed all of your pee off of me."

"It also washed all of your cum out of my ass."

Her comment turned the heads of several women in the store, including one who dropped her shopping bag upon hearing this. Jess and Josh giggled amongst themselves upon seeing everyone else's reaction.

Jess browsed the swimwear isle, eying all of the different styles and colors. Josh followed closely behind her as he nonchalantly whistled a tune.

Josh soon got tired and sat in the chairs by the fitting room with the other boyfriend's while Jess piled up a cart full of different style swimsuits and marched into the fitting room, winking at Josh as she walked by.

Josh counted at least two employees working the front of the store and half a dozen customers walking around, browsing aimlessly. He was waiting for the perfect opportunity to join Jess in the fitting room so they could enjoy themselves at their leisure.

Josh especially felt bad after cumming in her ass on the beach without giving her an orgasm, leaving her high and dry. He wanted enough tie to make this one count. And he wanted her to be able to enjoy it.

She did him a solid on the beach. It was time he paid her back. Beyond buying her a new swimsuit. Or twenty new swimsuits, based on what he saw her bring into the fitting room.

Jess emerged wearing the first swimsuit. It was a god-awful floral pattern tube top style two piece with a small skirt surrounding the bottom.

"No" he said before she even made it out of the fitting room area, pointing back to the fitting rooms.

"What?"

"Try harder."

"You don't like it?"

"You're joking, right? For Christs sake, Jess, you design clothing for a living. You should know better than this."

She laughed her way back into the fitting rooms.

A few moments later she came out in another two piece just as bad as the first. The bottom looked like granny panties while the top awas a keyhole strap supported by the neck. While Jess's tits made the two-piece look good, it was overall not a good-looking swimsuit.

"Well?"

"Babe. Do better."

She walked back to the fitting room with her tail between her legs.

Josh watched other shoppers come and go. Jess soon emerged again, this time wearing a metallic gray one piece swimsuit. It stretched around her crotch like a bodysuit and scooped down her chest. Not only did it reveal ample cleavage, Josh relished the fact that he could see her hard nipples penetrating through the fabric.

He liked it. He liked it so much that when he tried to stand up, he had to sit back down immediately because he was pitching a tent in his swim trunks.

"Oh my, yes! This is the one."

Jess smiled, happy that her boyfriend seemed so enthusiastic about this swimsuit. She noticed exactly how enthusiastic he was.

Jess did a little spin for him. The swimsuit covered her ass entirely. Although Jess was fond of thong style swimsuits, this one really suited her. it was everything that Baywatch wanted to be. What Baywatch should have been.

"Babe, there are no words to convey just how much I love the way this swimsuit looks on your body." Josh said, grinning.

Jess bit her bottom lip, "Actions speak louder than words." She had that lustful look in her eye when she winked at him, then scampered back quickly to the fitting rooms.

Josh glanced over at the clerk, who was currently helping out another customer, then ran into the women's fitting rooms when no one was watching, his huge erection leading the way.

As soon as Josh closed the fitting room door behind them, the two giggled mischievously. Then Josh pushed her hard against the wall. His lips were on hers. His hand ran up the side of her body. Jess watched the two of them in the mirror while the two made out in the privacy of the women's fitting room.

Finally, when she was able to pry her lips from Josh's long enough to get a breath in, she said, "Well, this must be the right one if it has this sort of effect on you."

Josh slid his hand down the length of her body, from her crotch to her tits and back again. His hands felt amazing over the material of the swimsuit.

"Let me put it this way," he began softly, "I'm not sure if I want you wearing anything else ever again. I even want you to sleep wearing this. And you're only allowed to take it off for sex. Actually, you know what? You can keep it on during sex, too."

Josh took a step back so he could drink all of her in at once. He was trying to figure out how they were going to have sex while you was wearing the one-piece.

The entirety of her swimsuit was made up of a very thin fabric that just barely covered her vagina. As soon as Jess sat down on the fitting room bench, she spread her legs wide and pulled the fabric covering her pussy off to the side.

"Nevermind." Josh mumbled to himself.

He already had his dick out. It was as hard as Jess had ever seen it. The only issue was that swimming in the ocean had dried her out considerably.

With no time to lubricate, Jess licked two of her fingers and began rubbing her saliva all over her pussy, teasing herself to wetness. But when Josh went to eagerly stick his dick inside of her, she stopped him with a firm hand to his chest.

"Wait, babe." She whispered softly and seductively.

"What? What is it? Fuck, I want you so bad right now."

There was a certain yearning in his voice that really turned Jess on. But even that was not enough to overcome a vagina full of sea salt. Embarrassingly, Jess knew that if they were to fuck at that moment it would only bring her pain.

"Could you, like... I need you to..."

"What is it? I'll do anything."

"Spit on it." She lowered her eyes to the floor, blushing.

"Did you just ask me to... spit... on your pussy?"

She nodded slightly, unable to look him in the eye. "Just, like... lick it, maybe?"

Josh frowned. He had in his hand a mega-erection that went above and beyond how hard his dick normally got. He was inches away from penetrating her. Now she was asking him to pull back.

She saw the ultra horny look on his face and felt bad that she even had to ask. But at that moment, there was no way she could take all of that dick all at once, given the current dryness of her vagina.

"It would be kinky. You know, eating my pussy in a fitting room? Please? You owe me." The crimson in her face spread.

I can't believe I have to beg my boyfriend to eat my pussy.

She was mortified.

Josh nodded and forced a smile as he got on his knees. He delicately pushed her knees apart until she was spread eagle sitting on the changing room bench. He looked up at her with puppy dog eyes, sad that she wouldn't just let him fuck.

But how do I explain that the ocean dried me out like sandpaper? Now I feel bad...

But that bad feeling passed the moment he started licking. Josh wasted no time on foreplay. He dove face first into her pussy, going immediately for her clit.

The initial shock of Josh wrapping his lips tightly around her little clit almost knocked Jess backwards off of the bench. She lifted her feet up, kicking the air wildly trying to regain her balance.

Jess supported herself on her elbows, sitting upright and trying *very* hard not to make any noises. Yet try though she might, she could not stop the little moaning sounds that started deep in her throat.

"This is *good*. I *like* this. We *need* to see how it *reacts* to getting *wet*. As *so far* I think it's *pretty* goo-AH-good." She said, her voice raising in volume on every other work as she tried to cover up the noises she made while her boyfriend ate her pussy.

Josh's tongue darted in and out of his mouth like a snake on meth. Jess grabbed a fist full of hair on the back of his head, pulling him towards her.

"Good... Good... Good... Ah! Oh my go... Gooood. Ngh, okay, okay, let's get that dick of yours wet, too."

Jess knew that if she let him continue, she wouldn't be able to contain herself. And she didn't want to be the reason they got caught up.

Besides, if she got thrown out of the store now, she wouldn't be able to buy the swimsuit.

Josh jumped up, dick harder than she had ever seen it before. She straightened up on the bench, realizing that she was at perfect dick-sucking-level. His big, juicy cock throbbed and twitched in front of her, making her mouth water as much as her pussy.

Jess wrapped her soft pink lips around the tip of his cock and relaxed her throat in preparation for the task in front of her. She looked up at Josh, locking eyes with him as she leaned her head forward until her nose touched his stomach, forcing her lips to the base of his shaft.

Josh threw his head back as Jess engulfed his erection in her throat.

"Ach! Babe! Be careful with that!"

She knew what he meant. He was so fucking horny in that moment, so fucking hard from watching her try on swimsuits that he was ready to bust at any moment.

That's okay, Jess thought, *worst case scenario, I get a throat full of cum... Best case scenario, I get a throat full of cum.*

She licked his hard cock while bobbing her head up and down, feeling him deep in her throat. Jess moved the swath of fabric covering her pussy to the side so she could play with herself as she sucked his dick.

I feel like I'm about ready to bust at any second, too.

She tried to communicate this to Josh while his dick was halfway down her throat. "Mmm, mm… Mmm, mm-mm."

"What? Babe, I can't understand you. But you're going to make me cum if you don't stop."

"Hmm! Mm-hmm, mm-hmm."

She kept going, bracing herself to take his hot load down the back of her throat as she flicked her clit as fast as she could.

Fuck, this is so hot. I'm about ready to-

"I'm cumming!"

Josh shot rope after rope of salty sweet semen into Jess's mouth, and she swallowed one as quick as he could provide them. The moment she felt him cum in her mouth, it pushed her over the edge, triggering her own orgasm.

She made herself cum as she swallowed all of his.

"Ahh… Oh my God, babe, did you just swallow all of that?"

In response, she pulled his cock out of the back of her throat and opened her mouth triumphantly, showing her boyfriend that she had indeed swallowed all of his semen.

"That was a lot of cum you swallowed. I'm impressed. Wait, what were you trying to tell me earlier?"

"I said it tastes like ass." She said as she stroked him with one hand.

"My jizz tastes like ass?"

She giggled. "No! Your jizz tastes like cum, silly. Your dick tastes like ass."

"Well, it was inside your ass for the better part of the afternoon."

Jess licked the residual cum and saliva off the tip of his dick. "I'm not complaining. I like ass."

"Me too."

Jess laid back on the fitting room bench and guided Josh's obscenely hard cock into her soaking wet pussy.

"Ho-my-fuck, your dick feels so big!"

Just as they were starting to really get into swimsuit sex, there came a knock on the fitting room door.

"Is everything okay in there?" It was the female attendant's voice.

"Ahh-umm, y-yes! Just, ah, seeing if this one is – Ahh! – a good fit!" Josh took mischievous pleasure in fucking her even harder when Jess tried to answer.

"Umm, okay. Well, hurry up, I guess." They listened to the footsteps of the attendant as she walked away.

The same thing went through both Jess and Josh's head at the same time. If they didn't hurry up and finish soon, they would be caught.

It was a rule of having sex in public, Jess was learning, that you should always try and finish as fast as was reasonable. A rule that didn't mesh well with their tantric lifestyle.

It would be another six minutes before Jess could get her rocks off. And, holy fuck, it was a big, *messy* orgasm.

When it happened, Jess started cumming HARD.

"Yieee!" Jess squealed as she grabbed hold tightly onto Josh's bare butt cheeks, savagely pulling him towards her.

The moment Josh realized that Jess was in the middle of an orgasm, he started pumping hard and faster. A little *too* hard, and a little *too* fast.

When he came, Josh, who rarely loses control of his faculties, screamed out, "HO-LY FUUUCK!"

It was loud enough for the entire store to hear him.

Jess could feel him cum HARD. Then, as he pulled back for another thrust, he accidentally pulled out. Instead of shooting all of his cum inside her pussy, like a gentleman, he shot rope after rope after rope of viscous, voluminous amounts of semen all over Jess's brand new swimsuit.

Like, *all* over it.

From her tits to her hips and all down her stomach, the sticky white bodily fluid shown prominently against the gun metal gray fabric of Jess's one-piece swimsuit.

Jess lay on her back, laughing hysterically as she continued watching Josh cover the entire front side of her body with his cum.

"Now *that* is a *lot* of cum!"

"Shit! I can't believe I did that! Why are you laughing?"

"Because it's *hilarious*."

There was another knock on the fitting room door.

"Excuse me!" the attendant sounded much more insistent this time.

Jess swung the door open. When the attendant saw Jess wearing one of their most expensive swimsuits that was *literally* dripping with cum, she nearly fainted.

"Hi! We had to run a few tests to make sure this swimsuit holds up. I'm going to wear it out."

Both the attendant and the store owner looked at Jess as if she were covered in raw sewage, though they were all too happy to take their money.

They were even happier when the couple left their store.

"Come one, I'm going to jump in the ocean again before this all dries and stains." Jess pulled Josh's hand towards the ocean.

"I think it's quite becoming. It's like semen tie-dye. You always wanted to start a new fashion trend."

"That's not the trend I want to be known for!"

"Maybe we'll find the other half of your bikini in the ocean."

"I've already mourned for the loss of my bikini top. It's in a better place now."

"At the bottom of the ocean, at the mermaid Goodwill."

Jess and Josh went for one last, very brief swim before catching the train back home.

CHAPTER 26

Day 5 – Bodega

They didn't get back until very late due to trains breaking down and maintenance on the Metro. It wasn't until they were forced to board a bus to get to the next Metro station that they suddenly realized that taking the train was a terrible idea in the first place.

At least we completed the 'train' BINGO square, Jess thought.

As they sat outside the bus station in their swimsuits, trying desperately to avoid the leers of bystanders, Jess held Josh close to her.

"Baby, I'm hungry. Can we go grab some snacks while we wait?"

"I don't see why not."

Jess started to drag her boyfriend over to the bodega behind the bus stop. As they walked through the parking lot, Jess squeezed Josh's hand.

"I just wanted to get away from all of those weirdos staring at us." She whispered to him.

"I know. Me too."

"What's their problem, anyway?"

"They've never seen a beautiful woman before."

"Oh, stop it."

"Are you kidding me? You look like a Sports Illustrated swimsuit model in that thing."

Jess pulled him close, wrapping her arms around him and pulling him into a kiss. She wasn't sure if he was just joking or not.

They walked into the bodega had in hand. Josh nodded to the clerk in a way that said, *Sup? I'm not going to rob you.*

The clerk nodded back in a way that said *I wouldn't care if you did because I get paid less than minimum wage to work at a place that gets robbed fairly regularly and in any case you'd be doing me a favor if you did because every day after working 9 hours in their little slice of hell on earth I go home craving the sweet release of death.*

"Ooh, look! They have Milky Way!" Jess waved the candy bar in the air.

They walked around each aisle, browsing. Jess knew that they had about an hour to kill before the arrival of their bus, so she took her time, luxuriating in the nuances of every single item for sale.

The store was particularly large as far as neighborhood bodegas go. Jess lingered in the Mexican candy section, trying to decide between mango chili candies and watermelon chili candies.

"Grab both." Josh advised.

Jess smiled, then stood on her tippy toes trying to reach the mango chili treats sitting on the very top shelf. Josh chuckled to himself, watching her struggle to reach the candy that remained just out of her grasp.

When Jess jumped, her fingertips just barely grazed the bag of chili mangos. Josh stood back, watching her full, firm ass bounce and jiggle as it poked out from her swimsuit. She raised up on her calves trying to reach the item of her desire, leaning forward so that her tits danged in front of her, barely contained by her one-piece swimsuit.

She turned to Josh, who was staring at her with a smug look on his face. Jess followed his gaze, looking down at her chest before she realized he was staring at her hard nipples poking out through the thin fabric of her swimsuit.

But he wasn't the only one. The store clerk was leaning so far over the countertop trying to get a better look at Jess that he nearly fell over.

"Ack! I've almost got it! Josh, don't just stand there! Help this damsel in distress." She said, pointing to the chili mango candies like a child.

"Keep at it, babe, I think you're almost there." Josh folded his arms, leaning against the wall as he and the store clerk both enjoyed the show.

Jess reached for the candies and jumped several more times, her tits and ass jiggling hypnotically with every movement. After a few more failed attempts, Jess slipped and fell down on her butt, legs folded under her.

"Owie, owie, owie..."

Josh snorted, stifling his laughter as he stepped in and easily plucked the object of her desire from the very top shelf.

Stupid freakishly tall boyfriend. Why don't bodegas ever cater to the vertically challenged?

As he handed Jess the mag of chili mango, she saw something sparkle in his eye – and it wasn't dust from the items that had been sitting on the bodega's top shelf for years and years.

Josh extended his hand, helping her up. She stood up, then fake fell into his arms so that he would catch her and she could push her boobs into his chest.

"Why don't you leave the snacks out here for a minute while we go into the cooler and pick out some drinks." She said while painting his muscled chest with her fingertips.

"What are you talking about? I saw you struggle for these candies. No snacks left behind."

She gave him an incredulous look. "Josh..." Jess's eyes narrowed.

He snatched the food from her hands and marched up to the front of the store.

"Hey! Jerk."

Josh set all of the snacks they had picked out on the store clerk's front countertop.

"Could you please hang onto these for a few while we browse your brews? We'll definitely be back to buy it but, uh, it might take us a while to, like, *find the right drinks.*"

Jess could have sworn she saw Josh wink at the man. The Hispanic bodega clerk smiled and nodded. Jess was uncertain if he fully grasped what was happening, though he seemed happy to oblige.

Josh purposely marched back over to where Jess was standing and grabbed her wrist. His other hand was stuffed awkwardly in the pocket of his swim trunks. With Jess in tow, they both marched over to the refrigerated section of the store and through the door to a cooler with a sign above it that read Beer Cave.

The moment they were inside the cooler, Josh let go of Jess and started looking around the room manically as if he were trying to find some sort of secret passageway.

"Josh, what's going on? It's cold in here." Jess crossed her arms over her chest, rubbing her shoulders to warm herself up.

Once the two were alone, Josh pulled his hand out of his pocket. His erection sprang forth, creating a massive tent in his swim trunks.

How long was he been walking around like that, Jess wondered.

Then he said something that put everything into perspective.

"This place counts as 'grocery store', right?"

Jess didn't know what to say. He wanted to have sex. In the beer refrigerator. In a bodega. While they waited for the bus.

What surprised Jess the most was that she didn't see this coming. Though she wished he had given her a heads up, this entire thing seemed improvised.

She didn't *feel* horny the way she did every other time they had sex in public. She wasn't even turned on. Plus, the way Josh was acting made her feel rushed and panicked.

The train ride to the beach this morning was undeniably hot. The few people on the train whom she knew were all watching them only added to the kinky thrill. Plus, she was able to hide Josh's dick at her leisure. *That* was fun.

Sex in the fitting room was exhilarating. It was entertaining to see how incredibly turned on Josh was – plus his dick got *so* hard! Jess would never forget the look on the fitting room attendant's face when she stepped out of the changing room *covered* in cum. *That* was almost certainly fun.

Even Josh fucking her in the ass for hours in the middle of a beach that was packed to the gills with tourists had its own kinky appeal. Even if she didn't orgasm at the time, when she thought back to that moment it turned her on. The thought of him cumming in her ass in front of hundreds of people – *that* was fun.

But fucking in a room that people referred to as "The Beer Cave"? She just wasn't feeling it.

"Babe…" She started.

But he either ignored her or did hear her. Josh continued darting around the cooler, looking behind all of the shelves, led by his erection.

"I think that if you stand right here, I can bend you over like this." He showed her the position he wanted her in, bending over one of the refrigerated shelves next to the Coors Lights.

"Baby…"

"Or maybe if you hook your foot up on this shelf here I can take you from the side."

"Unless, of course, you just want me to lift you up as we can do it standing up. That's a tried and tested method. Right? Jess?"

"Josh… I don't know if I'm even wet enough. I mean, I…" She looked away.

Josh looked at her and, for the first time since entering the refrigerator, he actually saw her. His expression changed. The entire vibe in the Beer Cave shifted. Josh had a sorrowful look on his face, remorseful.

"Oh my God, Jess. I'm so sorry… you're not even feeling it, are you?"

She shook her head from side to side, slowly.

Josh took her face into his hands.

"I'm sorry, babe. It's just… that swimsuit *does* things to do. I got swept up in the BINGO craze."

She smiled, squeezed his hand, and stood up on her tippy toes so she could give him a kiss on the cheek.

"It's okay, Josh. I'm lucky to have such an understanding boyfriend. I just want to go home, baby. I'm feeling all sexed out today."

"That's fine by me."

Josh spun around in a circle and when he was facing Jess again, he was holding two tall boys in his hands. "Fancy a drink for the ride home?"

"Yes! But not Steel Reserve." She pointed to the beers in Josh's hands. "I'll sip a Natty Ice, though."

He spun around once again and this time held two 40oz Natural Ice Lite beers in his hands.

"For the lady." He said, proffering one to her.

She took the beer out of his hands, giggling. "Thank you, babe!" she gave him another kiss. "Come on, let's go grab my chili mangos."

At some point, Josh had lost his erection. Jess knew she shouldn't, but she felt bad for denying her boyfriend sex. Especially for letting a precious BINGO opportunity slip through her fingers. She knew he wasn't trying to make her feel bad on purpose. If anything, it was Josh who felt bad for pressuring her.

But forty ounces of beer made that better. It made *everything* better.

I'll make it up to him.

After that, they were not the only ones drinking forties at the bus stop. Only after realizing that more than half of the people waiting at the bus stop were either actively drinking or already drunk did Jess realize that they were deep in the ghetto.

She laughed out loud to herself upon realizing this. Jess had ghetto friends. She met them under similar circumstances.

And she reckoned it was time to make more ghetto friends.

"Is you a movie star?"

Jess nearly spit out a mouth full of Natty Ice at the question asked by an older man with thick, long dreadlocks and a little gold in his mouth.

But before she could answer, Josh seized the opportunity.

"Yes! This is the famous actress Louis L'amour. You probably recognize her from that western movie that just came out. I'm her manager. My name is Sidney. Sidney Sheldon."

Josh stuck out his hand to shake with the golden toothed gentleman who happened to be sipping on a Steel Reserve.

"Eh, I think I remember her! That the one with the horses?"

"Yes. It was the one with the horses." Josh replied. "So, you've seen it?"

"I seen it. Maaan, you look much more beautiful in person, miss L'amour."

"Oh, why thank you." Jess said in her best fake British accent.

"So, yous a real movie star? Wacha doin' waiting for tha bus wearin that?"

"Miss L'Amour is doing a new film where she's a... lifeguard who... drives a bus. So we're here today doing research for her upcoming role."

"Aw, yeah, yeah. I read bout that. How yous like to research your roles before a new movie. So what's the name of this new movie, miss L'Amour?"

"Baywatch Bus Driver." She said grandly.

"Have you seen the movie trailer that just came out? It's all over the internet right now." Josh pressed on.

"You know what, Sidney? I think I have!"

"Hey, that's great! Whoops, here comes the bus. So, can we count on your to see Baywatch Bus Driver when it comes out in theaters?"

"Oh, I most definitely will. Yeah, I see all of miss L'amour's movies. I can't wait to sees it."

"Tis always a true pleasure to meet a fan. Fare thee well."

"I can't wait ta tell my kids all about how I met Louis L'amour at tha bus stop today. They won't believe it!"

When they boarded the bus, the couple was sure to sit as far away as possible from the golden toothed gentleman they were talking to. From their vantage point in the back of the bus they could see him engage strangers in animated conversation while pointing to Jess.

The two were grateful when they reached their stop and they could get off the bus, having done enough research for one day.

Having long since finished her forty of Natural Ice, Jess was feel pretty good, a little buzzed, and in dire need of a place to go pee. The sun was starting to hang low in the sky, but they still had a lot of walking to do until they got home.

"Baby, I have to pee so bad." She was jumping up and down doing the pee-pee dance.

"And? You're wearing a swimsuit. Just go."

"You did *not* just say that, Josh. It's not a diaper and I'm not a crazy astronaut. Plus, ask yourself, do you really want to walk the rest of the way home with your girlfriend who smells like she pee'd on herself?"

"I guess not. Just pop a squat."

"I could, but I'm a classy ass bitch. Besides..." She pointed to a large building with bright red lights surrounding the front entrance.

It was their neighborhood grocery store.

"Well, what exactly were you thinking?"

"I'm thinking I want to go there to use their bathroom and I want you to follow me."

"Follow you too..."

She smiled a mischievous smile.

"To watch me pee."

"And after that?"

"And maybe to fuck me in a grocery store bathroom." Jess was still feeling a little bad about the Beer Cave incident, but after forty ounces she was feeling a bit more frisky.

Josh returned the smile. "We don't have to, you know. Because if you're not into it, I'm not into it."

She reached between his legs and squeezed the outline of his cock in his swim trunks.

"Oh, I'm not into it. But you know who is? Famous movie star, Louis L'amour." She winked at him.

"You mean, the star of the upcoming film Baywatch Bus Driver, Louis L'amour?"

She nodded. "The very same."

"You know, I always aspired to be a starfucker."

"Is that why you became my agent, Mr. Sheldon?" she slipped into her terrible British accent.

"Yes. Yes, it is. I've based my entire professional career on this chance encounter right here, so that I might be able to screw young starlet Louis L'amour in a grocery store bathroom." He deadpanned.

"Well, Mr. Sheldon, now is your chance. Let's go."

They started waling towards the building with renewed purpose and vigor. Jess had to pee so bad that she thought she was going to explode. Popping a squat right there on the streets of downtown L.A. was looking like a more and more appealing decision.

Besides, if she did go pee in the middle of the street, she almost certainly wouldn't be the first. Practically every inch of downtown L.A. had been pissed on at some point in time.

But now she was looking forward to banging her sleazy talent agent, as well. So she held it.

By the time they entered the large grocery store, Jess let go of Josh's hand and broke into a dead sprint for the women's restroom. She seated herself in the large handicapped stall, practically jumping on the toilet to let loose a long and powerful stream.

"Ahhh…" She sighed deeply in relief as she listened to the *tinkle, tinkle, tinkle,* of her pee splashing in the toilet.

And a moment later.

"Excuse me? I'm looking for a client of mine, Miss Louis L'amour?" She heard a familiar voice from outside her restroom stall

"Sir, this is the women's restroom." Replied a woman with a deep voice.

"Of course. I'll just be a second."

"Pervert."

Jess heard a loud *slap* and then footsteps in the distance.

The door to Jess's restroom stall swung open and Josh stepped inside.

"Why, miss L'amour! It appears you left the door to the bathroom stall wide open. What if TMZ were to find you on the toilet like this?"

"I wasn't waiting for TMZ. I was waiting for you, Sidney." It was not easy for Jess to try to be both British and seductive at the same time, but she tried. "Now you close that door behind you and come over here. I want to give you something to show you how much I appreciate you believing in a bird from across the pond, like myself. That's right, be quick about it, now."

Jess was still peeing when Josh locked the restroom stall door and walked over in front of her. She tugged down his swim trunks to his ankles and took his dick in her mouth.

She felt him harden as she jerked his shaft and sucked on his balls, working him up to a full erection. Once he was hard enough, she wrapped her lips around his cock and began deepthroating him vigorously.

The moment Jess stopped peeing, she brough her hand down between her legs and began rubbing her pussy.

"You have no idea how long I've waiting for this, miss L'amour." He said in a soft growl. "I've wanted you ever since I first laid eyes on you coming out of the tent you used to live in on Skid Row."

Jess laughed with Josh dick in her mouth, choking and coughing. She stroked him until her giggle fit passed.

Two can play at this game.

"I always knew you were the one for me, Sidney. Ever since that day I saw you on Skid Row paying those eighteen homeless clowns to jerk off on you. I knew then it was true love."

Josh snickered. She knew that he loved the way she was always able to come up with outrageous role-play backstories on the spot.

She leaned in to whisper intimately in his ear, "I want you to fuck me like a bus driver."

Josh got a kick out of that. He helped her to her feet turned her around and bent her over the toilet. Although Jess didn't know how bus driver's fucked, she imagined that doggy style was probably pretty close.

Seeing Jess prance around wearing her sparkly silver one-piece made Josh instantly hard. He peeled the fabric from around her ass and rubbed the tip of his cock up and down her pussy, surprised that she was as wet as she was.

"I want you, Josh. I mean, Sidney."

He slid his throbbing cock into her tight little hole. Jess moaned a long, low and breathy moan as he did. She let loose a series of sharp inhales and exhales as he fucked her from behind.

Josh grabbed a fistful of her hair, pulling her backwards. The sound of her firm and fit ass cheeks slapping against Josh's bare thighs echoed in the bathroom along with the sound of toilets flushing from the other restroom patrons.

The other women in the restroom stalls completely ignored the very obvious sounds the two of them made while banging in the handicapped stall. Jess started making little squeaking noises, which made Josh feel a little more brazen in his delivery.

"Yeah? Do you like that, Louis? I'm going to make you a star the second I'm done fucking you in this grocery store bathroom, you little fucking slut. Now bend over and take daddy's dick."

The dirty talk always helped. Jess could not remember a single instance where Josh talking dirty to her didn't turn her on or make her cum even faster. And he was very good at it – at least when he wanted to be.

She had the misfortune of knowing men in the past who were not so good at talking dirty to her. Men who were either very quiet during sex or had a hard time coming up with sexy things to say on the spot.

But Jess and Josh knew how to feed off of each other's libido. They also shared the incredible super power of being able to cum at the same time – most of the time.

When Josh talked dirty, his voice was deep gruff, and masculine. Jess's dirty talk was much more light and breathy. It was authentic and, more often than naught, silly.

"Ah, oh yes, fuck me, mister Sheldon. Yeah, earn that commission. Oh, fuck yes. Do you like fucking your little starlet slut? Make this famous pussy cum, daddy, make me cum."

Josh pulled back on her hair hard as the two came at exactly the same time. Jess arched her back and Josh grabbed a fistful of her tits while he came inside of her.

It was a wonderful thing for both of them.

"Oh, shit! Oh my *God!* Oh FUCK! Mmm..."

Jess was panting, trying desperately to catch her breathe even after Josh pulled out and the two were adjusting their clothes.

"Whew. That was good, mister Sheldon." Jess spun around and gave him a kiss, lingering on his lips.

"It was everything I imagined it would be, and more, my love." He returned the kiss.

After cleaning up, the two of them looked around the store. Even with their clothes on, everywhere they went they turned heads.

"Do we actually need anything while we're at this store?" Josh asked.

"Yeah," she replied, "And Uber home."

CHAPTER 27

Day 6 – Church

"I don't know about this..." Jess said hesitantly.

"You made a commitment. You need to honor that commitment." Josh said as the two walked up the sidewalk steps holding hands. "We should go to church more often, anyway."

"Yeah... But, like, maybe for different reasons?"

Josh was looking dapper in his deep midnight blue suit with a white button up shirt underneath and magenta tie. His hair was neatly combed and gelled to one side to make it look like he had just gotten out of the shower.

He looked very business casual in his Sunday church clothes. It was a very sharp and smart look. Jess almost felt bad that it turned her on as much as it did.

Almost.

Jess wore her lacey magenta dress with white trim. The hem went down to her knee and had this soft white fabric underneath. Although Jess wasn't used to wearing such long, conservative dresses, the two looked very fetching indeed when they stood side by side.

They looked like a couple on their way to church.

If they only knew...

As people began pouring into the church, the two took their seats at the very back of the pews and settled in to listen to a sermon on the subject of love.

During the sermon, Jess and Josh held hands while they listened to the preacher. They gave each other's hands a squeeze during certain parts throughout the sermon on professing love that pertained to them specifically.

It wasn't long before Jess started getting bored. She did what she did best whenever she got bored and started looking for ways to make mischief.

First, she held her pew bible up in front of her, blocking out the view of other church goers as she began unlacing the top of her dress. She pulled the front of her dress down, exposing a choice nipple. Then she elbowed Josh, making sure that only he could see her tits hanging out of her fancy church dress.

"Put. It. Away... Put it away." He whispered at her angrily.

Jess pretended that she was going to tuck her nipple back into her dress, then "accidentally" slipped and pulled down the top of her dress. Both of her voluptuous breasts completely spilled out. Jess covered her mouth and gasped, feigning shock and surprise before tucking her tits back into her dress where they belong.

A few minutes later, Jess covered Josh's hand with her own. He looked over and gave her an innocent, loving smile. Jess smiled back, then slipped her boyfriend's hand up the bottom of her dress. Unfortunately, her garment was far too long to move his hand anywhere exciting without someone noticing their debaucherous behavior.

But it did seem to vex him. And vexing her boyfriend brought Jess endless amounts of joy and entertainment.

Josh pulled his hand away from her and folded them into his lap. His eyes narrowed, giving her a very disapproving glare. She smiled back innocently.

That was when she noticed his erection.

She pretended not to notice and continued to hold his hand like all good church-going couples were doing. Jess edged closer and closer to Josh. Every time she inched her hand between his legs, he would move it back to his thigh and away from his boner. Again and again, Josh continued resist her.

Until he didn't.

She settled both of their hands right on top of the enormous tent in his blue slacks. Josh pretended not to notice, keeping his eyes forward.

Jess gave him a little *squeeze*. Try though she might, Jess was not brazen enough to unzip his pants and whip out his cock right there in the middle of a crowded church. So she did the next best thing.

An over the pants hand-job.

She knew this wouldn't count towards the Bingo card, but it was the only thing she could think of in that moment. For the next ten minutes, Jess yanked his hard dick through his pants. It went on much longer than Jess thought he would let it go on.

Then he moved her hand off of his cock.

"It's starting to chaff." He whispered to her. "Let's get out of here before you grind all of the skin off of my dick."

Jess giggled and followed his lead.

As Josh stood up, Jess was impressed with the stealth at which he fluidly tucked his massive erection into the belt of his pants, concealing it completely. She couldn't even tell he was still hard.

As Josh led Jess out the back of the church, she couldn't help but wonder how often he walked around with a huge boner without her even realizing it.

Once they made it through the corridor toward the front of the church, she asked Josh as such, to which he smiled a toothy grin and replied simply, "Often."

Jess wasn't sure why, but the thought of Josh walking around on his day to day with a massive erection tucked into his waistband tickled Jess in a way that made her smile.

Josh was cautiously walking down the church hallway, trying each door they passed as they went. Every one of them was locked.

"They really don't trust these church-goers nowadays, I guess." Jess shrugged.

"It's probably to keep those punk kids out who sneak off during service to try and find a place to hook up." She snickered.

"I blame teenagers. They're everything wrong with this generation today." He said facetiously.

"Which generation?" asked Jess.

"I don't know. All of them."

"Darn teenagers." She shook a fist into the air.

The next doorknob turned under Josh's hand. He and Jess shared a look. Cautiously, he opened the door and peaked inside.

"It's empty. Come on." He whispered.

With the door open just a crack, Josh slipped inside with Jess closely in tow. Jess closed the door behind them quietly.

Inside, the room was dark. There were no windows. Jess caught an eerie vibe from the place and held onto Josh closely. The minute Josh flicked on a light switch Jess let out a lungful of air in relief.

It looked like a small breakroom. The kind you would find at any business. There was a small folding table with three chairs around it, a mini-fridge, and a flat countertop with the only item on it being an old school coffee-maker that looked like it hadn't been used in a very long time.

"Well, as much as I wanted to bend you over the alter and fuck you silly under the big stained glass windows, I guess this will have to do." Josh said as he casually strolled around the break room, assessing his options.

Jess strolled over to the folding table. She checked to make sure that it was locked upright, the moved the chairs out of the way. She once had a folding table collapse under her when she and Josh were having sex, and one time was more than enough.

"Baby... "She said sweetly, rubbing his stomach. "You've got a great imagination." She rubbed the top of the folding table. "This *is* the church alter." She gestured to the cabinets that lined the break room over the countertop. "And these are the big stained glass windows."

A devious smiled crept into the corners of his mouth. "I see that now."

He swept his hands around her waist and kissed her on the neck as he pulled her close.

"Just remember what I said." Jess said as she found the zipper on her pants. "No G word in this house. It calls his attention and I don't want him to see all of the terrible..."

She reached into his pants and pulled out his long, hard shaft.

"Awful..."

She licked her hand and then slid it up and down the length of his cock.

"*Filthy...*"

Jess parted his lips as she locked eyes with Josh, lowering herself to her knees. She had her tiny hands wrapped around his monster dick.

"... And sinfully sensual things I pray you're about to do to me."

She licked the full length of his genitals, from his balls to the tip of his thick cock, stopping at the end of his shaft to playfully tease it. She placed his tip on her lips and licked it like a lollipop. Then she slid the entire length of his member down the back of her throat taking his dick as far as she could take his dick into her mouth.

As she deepthroated his dick, sitting on her knees in the breakroom of the church, Jess started making these sexy little moaning noises that she knew really turned Josh on.

They also helped cover up the sounds of her gagging on his chocking hazard sized cock, which did the opposite of turn him on.

"Fuck, babe, that feels so good. But we're kind of on a time deadline here. Let's save some of daddy's cum for later in the day, shall we?"

As she ran her mouth up and down the length of his cock, she looked up at him and gave him a look that said *don't rush me, dude!*

Josh changed tactics. "Baby, you look so sexy in that dress. I want to fuck you on the church alter so badly."

She looked up at him and gave him her best seductive smile with his dick still in her mouth. Finally, after a particularly deep, deep, deepthroat, she pulled it out and took a big sharp inhale of air and said, "and I want to swallow all of daddy's cum in the house of g- uh, in church. You're not the only one with an overactive sexual imagination. This is *my* fantasy, Josh."

She plunged his dick deep into her mouth yet again. "And after you make a mess in my mouth, you're going to bend me over this church alter and cum in my pussy. And I want to feel it. Like, immaculate conception type shit. Kay?"

She started sucking his dick again. And that was that.

With that settled, the only thing that could stop them now was someone walking in on them. Which, Jess realized, could literally happen at any moment.

She spread her legs, hiking her dress up to her hips and dipping her fingertips between her legs to feel how wet she was at the prospect that they might get caught fooling around in a church.

She figured that the sermon would last at least another twenty minutes, probably much longer. She would have to try and get it all done by then.

Yet as much as she kept sucking, kept licking, kept deepthroating and kept doing all of the things that she knew her boyfriend liked, he just would not cum in her mouth.

"Baby, you close?" she asked, then wiped the drool from her lips.

"Don't think so."

"What's the matter?" she asked in a sympathetic tone, like how a mother would ask her sick child what was wrong.

She had been sucking his dick for more than ten minutes at that point. And this wasn't the casual, leisurely dick sucking that Jess enjoyed when her and Josh were at home, chilling on the couch watching a movie together. This wasn't the type of dick sucking that she purposely wanted to last for hours at a time.

This was cocksucking with a purpose. This was Jess's A-game. She was disheartened to say the least that it wasn't working.

"I... I *don't* know." He answered honestly.

In any other situation, Jess would have made him cum a dozen times over. That fact that he was withholding only made her want it that much more.

Well, you can't win them all.

Jess got up off of her knees and, with much effort, forced a smile. "It's okay, babe." She bent over the plastic folding table in the middle of the room and looked back at Josh. "So, are you going to fuck me on this alter, or what?"

Josh didn't wait for her to ask twice. He picked her up at the waist with his powerful arms. Jess giggled as he lifted her into the air, then set her down on the table, facing away from him.

It was totally unnecessary, but still very fun.

He pressed her back down until her boobs were smushed flat against the table and her ass poked out in front of him. He lifted the back of her skirts, eager to have his way with her.

It was time for Josh to live out *his* fantasy.

"Nice granny panties." He laughed.

Jess frowned, though he couldn't see her face. "They go with the dress, jerk! Besides, I had to wear underwear in church."

He wiggled her panties free until they dropped to her ankles. Josh threw the bottom of her dress and all of the excess fabric over her back until he could give her bare ass a squeeze and a spanking.

"Ohh!" Jess squealed.

Josh wedged his big dick in between his girlfriend's legs. She exhaled sharply, muttering something Josh couldn't hear under her breath in between soft, quiet moans.

"Are you... praying?"

"If you want me to, daddy."

In response, he thrust his cock deep inside her. Each time his hips slapped against her bare bottom, Jess moaned, grunted, and squealed as quietly as she could manage.

Wow, his dick feels so good, Jess thought, *but can he finish in time before the service lets out?*

"Why did you have to wear your granny panties to church? You didn't wear a bra." He pointed out as he lunged forward, pulling down the front of her dress and exposing her perfectly round tits to make his point.

Her boobs bounced against her chest as he fucked her from behind.

"This. Dress. Has. A. Built. In. Wire. Bra. Ah! Josh! Pull. My. Hair! Ooh! Yes. Just Like That!" she was only able to get one a single syllable in a full breathe every time Josh thrust his hard dick deep inside of her.

He pulled her hair as requested, creating more force that sent her ass flying back into contact with him. Harder and harder with every tug of her jet black hair, fucking hard harder, penetrating deeper.

Each thrust brought her closer to heaven.

He leaned forward and cupped an armful of Jess's soft, full tits as he reigned he back with her hair as if her were riding a wild stallion. She pushed back against her and he tightened his grip of her, hips smacking her ass with more impact.

"Oh my guh. Oh goldslager. Yes, yes, oh my gargoyle, yes. Hmm, oh fuck, oh fuck, oh Godiva, yes! Oh my fucking goodness, yes! Oh, baby, fuck me right on the alter, Please, daddy?"

But it was too later. Jess felt her pussy clench around Josh's meaty cock as he throbbed and jumped inside of her. She felt a flowing wave of pleasure wash over her, surging through her entire body while his warm fluids exploded inside of her.

"Oh, goodness, yes! Immaculate conception, baby!" Jess cried.

Josh pulled his dick out. He had stopped cumming.

"Don't say that." He whispered harshly.

"What? Why? Why did you pull out so fast?"

"Jess, you're still on birth control, right? Remember that conversation we had were we both agreed that we weren't ready to be parents just yet?"

Jess giggled as she tucked her tits back into her church dress. "Oh course I remember. I was only joking. Geez, don't be so serious all the time."

"Baby, we are having sex in what appears to be the staff break room of a church. Pretending that it's an altar. Because a Bingo card told us to. What part of this is serious?"

She laughed harder. "I guess you're right." But now she felt like she had to ask. "But what if I did get pregnant. What would you do?"

He gave her a very serious look. "Babe, you know I would go along with whatever you choose. And if you decide you want to have a child with me, well, I can think of no one better I'd rather start a family with."

"Well, good. That was the right answer. But for the record, I am most certainly *not* ready to have a baby for at least a few more years, I fucking love it when you cum inside of me, and I fucking *hate* condoms."

"Oh, they're *so* bad."

"Right? Well, I'm glad we're on the same page. Wait, did you hear that? Shh…"

She held up one finger to his lips. Josh looked around, panicking as he stuffed his cock back into his pants while it was still dripping with cum.

"I don't hear anything." He whispered.

"Shh!"

Silence filled the room for an anxious moment.

And then Jess farted.

"Jess!"

She started rolling on the floor, grabbing her stomach, doubled over in laughter.

"Wait, Jess, I think I really hear something."

"You're not about to get me with my own joke, Josh."

"Be quiet."

She was about to say something until she heard footsteps in the hallway. Then she heard voices coming from outside. A *lot* of voices.

Shit, service just got out.

"Josh! Where are my panties?" She whispered.

He pointed to the white cotton panties across the room. How they got all the way over there, she had no idea. Quietly, she tiptoed across the room over to where her underwear sat on the ground. One hand balancing on the countertop, she stepped into her panties as they listened to the voices on the other side of the door.

It sounded like the entire church was passing through the hallway all at once. Jess considered just swinging the door open and jumping into the crowd, trying to blend, but that option seemed just as bad as getting caught red handed.

No, they would have to remain in their hidey hole until the crowd of people passed by.

She could hear people's conversations in perfect accuracy as they waked by. So she could only assume that, if they were to listen, the people on the other side of the door could also perfectly hear every little noise that they made from inside the break room.

The individual muffled voices got louder as they approached the break room and fainter as they walked away. Jess ushered Josh into joining her squatting underneath the church altar, AKA, the break room folding table. It was as decent a hiding spot as they would find in the tiny room. Together, they huddled under the table in case someone happened to walk in on them.

When they were crawling underneath the table to hide, Jess's hand accidently brushed up against Josh's belt.

Did he just tuck his erection into his belt? Well, there's only one way to find out.

"Jess, what are you-"

"Shh!"

She unzipped his pants and, sure enough, his hard cock instantly sprang right out of his pants. And it was still glistening with cum and pussy juice.

Oh, let me get that for you, Jess thought.

Before she knew what was going on, she found her lips wrapped tightly around the tip of his dick. He did not resist her sucking his dick as they both listened to the conversations of the people passing by.

"...such a lovely sermon today. And so topical to..."

Slurp. Slurp.

"...Told you we should have left early. Look at this crowd. Do you know what parking..."

Slurp. Slurp. Mm...

"...can get the kids ice cream on the way home and then when we get back to the house you and I can go upstairs and..."

Slurp. Gulp. Slurp. Slurp.

"...see what she was wearing? I swear, that entire sermon, all I could think about was her..."

Slurp. Slurp. Gulp. Mm... Oh...

"...we'll have to make arrangements with the pastor. You know how these things go. The fruits of forbidden love and all..."

Slurp. Slurp. Slurp. Slurp.

"...was an excellent sermon, father. And I do say, it certainly put me in the mood for..."

Jess was at peace. At long last, she was content to leisurely suck Josh's dick without feeling rushed. She also felt a lot better about herself knowing that pretty much everyone in attendance at church was just as sex-crazed as she was, even if they didn't openly admit it.

Then the footsteps winding down and trickling out. Every now and again they would hear another person go by, but Jess was content to be sitting on the floor, idly playing with her boyfriend's dick in her mouth without the pressure of having to make him cum. Although the possibility of getting caught still hung above their head, that was also part of the kinky appeal that made it fun.

Jess could feel that Josh was also very relieved to be in this position. There was no more stress, no pressure; only pleasure. The pleasure of him and his girlfriend being alone in the back room of some church and her being able to just casually play with his dick while they waited.

But the moment all of his stress melted away, something amazing happened.

"Oh shit!" Josh cursed under his breath.

He clutched Jess's hand hard, pulling her head down on top of his dick, forcing it into the back of her mouth. She relaxed her throat and let it happen.

Then he started to cum in her mouth, Jess was pleasantly surprised to feel him suddenly and unexpectedly fill her mouth up with semen. Judging by Josh's reaction, he was just as surprised as she was when it happened.

If Josh didn't push Jess's head down when he did, he would have gotten his cum all over her nice church dress instead of all down the back of her throat.

Then something even more unexpected happened.

As Jess put all of her concentration into swallowing Josh's cum as quickly as he could give it to her, the door to the break room burst open. In walked two pairs of feet.

"Oh, father! Oh, father!"

"You can call me Daddy."

They couldn't see much from their vantage point underneath the plastic folding table, but Jess knew right away from their voices that it was the pastor giving the sermon and one of the women that they heard pass through the hallway earlier.

Plus, Jess recognized the woman's shoes. She was the only one wearing red Prada heels to church. And she never forgot a pair of stilettoes.

Jess put a face to the heels. She was a middle aged woman with short cropped blond hair wearing a pencil skirt and low cut dress that showed off her huge, ambiguously fake tits.

Even by Jess's standards, it was a scandalous thing to wear to church. She specifically recalled thinking how slutty this woman looked coming to church. During the sermon, she sat next to her dorky-looking husband and two blond hair twin boys. But the woman spent the entire sermon making bedroom eyes at the pastor.

Jess thought nothing of it while she was giving her boyfriend an over-the-pants hand job during the sermon. But now here they were, slutty old Prada heels and the priest hooking up in the church break room.

And just after the pastor finished speaking for well over an hour about love and the virtue of honoring commitment.

The two were so wrapped up in the throes of passion that they didn't even see Josh and Jess under the table, even as her boyfriend continued to shoot his cum down Jess's throat. She stroked his cock as quietly as she could, sucking out the last few drops of his deliciously salty sweet jizz.

Even though she got her prize, she was mad at Prada heels for ruining the one and only time Jess would have the opportunity swallow a mouth full of cum inside of a church. It was a unique fantasy of hers that she had long before the Bingo card fell into her possession, and she had certain expectations as to how it would go.

Sure, she was able to take her time sucking his dick, but in her fantasies, it was always a big, long cum shot that she luxuriated in. And the cum always tasted much sweeter in her fantasies, too.

Close enough, I guess.

Caught up in the excitement, the pastor pushed the slutty, Prada heeled housewife into the break room table that they were hiding under. She tripped on Josh's long legs, flipping over the table in the process.

Both the pastor and the housewife locked eyes with Jess while Josh's dick as still in her mouth.

Jess froze like a deer in headlights. She could feel Josh pull his dick out of her mouth and away from her hands. He tucked himself back into his pants, then quickly and calmly helped Jess to her feet.

"Father, that was such a great service today." Josh said, then took Jess by the hand and ran out of the room.

Jess could still feel Josh's warm cum all over her lips and thick clumps of it dripping down her chin. She licked it off of her lips and wiped the viscous white fluid from her chin using two fingers, then licked that off her fingers, too.

"Father." Jess nodded.

The housewife and pastor stood in front of them, aghast, unblinking.

Together, Jess and Josh ran out of the church hand in hand, laughing all the way to hell, and then the parking lot.

They still had to get ready for the church's annual harvest festival carnival later that evening.

CHAPTER 28

Day 6 – Carnival

"I feel like a teenager again." Jess said taking a swing from the bottle of vodka before passing it back to Josh.

"Not going to lie, it's been years since I got drunk on a bottle of cheap liquor behind a grocery store."

They sat on the ledge of the loading ramp out behind the Albertsons grocery store. Jess dangled and kicked her feet off of the edge of the ramp. She rested her head on the side of Josh's shoulder.

They were both still wearing their church clothes.

"Thank you for not making me feel too old to do this. Or too young. I feel like I'm the perfect age when I'm with you. "she said gently.

"What do you mean?" Josh asked, taking another big gulp from the vodka bottle and offering it to back to Jess.

She help up her hand.

"I'm good. I think I'm just drunk."

Josh downed the last bit of liquor in the bottle, then tossed it into a nearby dumpster.

"You ought to be, as much as we drank."

He jumped down from the loading dock, a six foot drop onto solid concrete. Then he extended his hands out to Jess.

"Come on. I don't want you falling and getting hurt."

Jess looked down at the drop to the ground. It seemed much larger from her perspective.

"I'm scared."

"Just jump. I'll catch you."

"But... Gravity..."

"Have I ever let anything bad happen to you while I am around? Like, ever?"

She gave this serious consideration, then looked down at him and smiled a drunken, girlish smile.

"No!" she answered, then closed her eyes and kicked off the loading dock.

Josh caught her, then spun her around in his arms a few times.

"Weeee!

"See? What did I tell you?"

Jess giggled as she wrapped her arms and legs around him, forcing him to carry her.

"You're like my personal security detail. No, wait, you're like my guardian angel. A big, sexy guardian angel."

Josh continued walking in the direction of the carnival across the street while carrying Jess in his arms like a toddler.

"You take such good care of me." She cooed, nuzzling his neck.

"That's because I love you."

"I love you, too, Josh. So much. Geez, sometimes I think about how much I love you and it's crazy."

"How so?"

"Well, like how you're about to carry me across the street like you're fucking Frogger or something because you think that I'm so drunk I can't walk and you're trying to protect me from myself or some shit like that."

"Some shit like that." He answered. "Or maybe I just like carrying you. Ever think of that?"

"You only like to carry me when your dick is in me."

"I can't deny that."

"God, you're so fucking *chivalrous*. And you try to be lowkey and super chill about it, and I think that's why I love you so much."

"I forgot how fucking cute you are when you're drunk."

"I *am* drunk!" She laughed. "And you are, too!"

"Am I?"

"Fuck! I can never tell... what were we talking about?"

"How much you love me and what an awesome boyfriend I am."

She laughed and kissed him sleepily on the neck.

"You *are* an awesome boyfriend. Look at you, carrying your drunk girlfriend around town. But, oh my God, can I tell you this? Okay, I love your dick, like *so* much. And I think it loves me, too. But today it, like, threw up in my mouth, or whatever."

"My dick threw up in your mouth?"

"Oh my God, *yes!* But... I kind of like it when that happens." Jess gasped suddenly. "Oh! And did you see the priest's face when he saw me with your dick in my mouth? He was, like, so embarrassed because we caught him with that bimbo with the Prada shoes! We all froze up, but then you pull it together and rescued me. And that is why I love you."

They reached the entrance to the carnival.

"One ticket please." Josh said.

The ticket taker nodded to Jess in his arms.

"Oh, this is just my backpack."

"HI! I'm a backpack! Nice to meet you!" Jess yelled gleefully.

"Uhh, your backpack is going to need to buy a ticket, too." The ticket taker told them.

"That's okay." Josh slapped down some money on the table and continued walking into the carnival. "Keep the change."

"Josh, that was a lot of money." Jess whispered into his ear.

Josh shrugged. "It's for charity. I think."

He continued walking through the carnival with Jess in his arms.

"So, where to first?" He asked.

"I have to pee."

"Of course you do."

Josh walked over to the closest port-o-potties. Jess jumped down out of his arms and scurried over to the bathroom. As soon as she opened the door he could smell the mess inside. Jess retched and slammed the door shut, then proceeded to the next port-o-potty in line.

"Nope." She said after glancing inside. Then she went over to the next one. "No wammy! No wammy! No wammy!" she chanted as she edged closer to the next bathroom.

Jess pulled the port-o-potty door wide open. "Oh my God! Who would do such a thing! This is a crime against humanity!" she let the door swing shut. "Ugh! I want to unsee that!"

"So... Whammy?" Josh asked from the sidelines.

She nodded. "Definitely. Is this seriously all there is? Three port-o-potties at a carnival that sells deep fried twinkies and giant legs of turkey bigger than my head? This is how port-o-potties like that last one get Chernobyl'd. You know what? Fuck it."

Jess stumbled over behind the three stinking port-o-potties. Josh followed at a distance only to witness what hijinks his girlfriend was about to get into this time.

"Babe, I don't think that's such a good- Oh. Okay. Whatever, then."

He watched as Jess pulled off her panties and tossed them in the direction of the port-o-potties, landing in something Josh desperately wanted to believe was mud. Then she hiked up her nice dress to her waist and popped a squat there in the dirt behind the blue portable bathrooms.

There was a long line of people who were all waiting to use the port-o-potties. Every single one of them turned to watch Jess pissing in the dirt behind the bathrooms, aghast.

Josh, being the lowkey chivalrous gentleman he was, swiftly ran into the Chernobyl'd port-o-potty and grabbed a wad of toilet paper for Jess to wipe with.

"That was a quick piss for you." He said, handing her the wadded up toilet paper.

"My hero!"

She pulled her dress up further and wiped her vagina with Josh's toilet paper in front of everyone, then tossed the toilet paper in the same patch of "mud" that her discarded panties were sitting in.

"And how many times do I have to tell you, Josh. Guys *piss*. Girls *pee*."

He chuckled, then walked around to her other side so he could hold the hand that she didn't just wipe her pussy with.

"What now, my love?" He asked.

"I chose the first activity. Now it's your turn." she said generously.

Josh wasn't sure if he would consider peeing in the dirt as a carnival activity, but he decided to roll with it.

"Is it weird that watching you pee in the dirt makes me a little bit horny."

"You're always horny."

Josh shrugged. "I'm a visual person. You flash your pussy at me, and I want what I see."

"I did *not* just flash my pussy at you!"

"Babe, you flashed half the carnival."

"Stop exaggerating."

"Did you or did you not just wipe your vagina in front of a line full of people waiting to use the bathroom?"

"Yes! Ladies wipe. You saw me wipe. And in any case, we're here to fuck, right? So, let's fuck."

"Can we 'carnival' while we try and find a place to fuck?"

"You're in charge. We can do whatever you want."

They continued walking through the carnival for a few minutes in silence. The Jess started laughing uncontrollably.

"What is it?"

"Want to know a secret? I'm always horny, too."

"You have no secrets from me. I know you're always horny, babe. Why else would we be doing this stupid BINGO expedition in the first place?"

"Okay. As long as we can be horny together. And it's not stupid, it's romantic... Hey, what do you think is the best ride to do it on?"

Josh had ideas, but admittedly the "Carnival / Amusement Park" BINGO square was perhaps the one he gave the least amount of thought and planning to.

"Actually, I've always wanted to fuck on the Gravitron, but that's mostly because I think it would be challenging. You know, just to see if we can do it. But there are always so many people and the ride is so short that it's not even a viable option."

"You wouldn't mention it if it weren't a viable option." Jess pointed out as they continued meandering through the carnival at a leisurely pace, periodically stopping to look at things.

"I think those big, flying swings would be cool. But we would have to get them to strap both of us into the same seat. I've only ever seen them do that where it was a parent holding their small child."

"I want to ride the swing on daddy's lap!" Jess jumped up and down, excited. "Think they'll buy it?"

"It would be awesome to fuck on a roller coaster, but they have those bars that click into place."

"Too scary."

"Bumper cars."

"Whiplash."

"Teacups?"

"Motion sickness."

"What else have they got here?"

"Not much."

"Tunnel of Love?"

"Pretty sure they discontinued that ride because people kept getting pregnant."

"We could bang inside the Fun House. It has the word 'fun' in it."

"Babe! Kids run around inside the fun house. And I'm too young to start teaching sex ed."

They continued their stroll around the carnival, spirits crushed. Until...

"Babe, I have an idea! Wait right here." Jess said, then took off running.

"Are you sure you'll be alright?" He called out to her.

"It's a surprise!" she replied as she ran out of sight.

Josh found a nearby bench to sit down on. The longer Josh sat by himself, the more nervous he became. He decided to buy them some funnel cakes while he waited. Then he decided to eat both of their funnel cakes because Jess still hadn't returned.

The minutes dragged on, but Josh had faith in his girlfriend and sat on the bench, licking the powdered sugar from his fingers while he awaited her return.

Soon, Jess came running back to Josh wearing the biggest grin on her face that he had ever seen since she found out that they were making a Mean Girls reboot.

"Come on, I have a surprise for y- Hey! Did you eat a funnel cake just now? Josh! I was only gone a minute!"

"How did you know?"

"That's either powdered sugar or cocaine on your shirt and either way you didn't share with me. Now I'm not even sure you deserve my surprise."

Jess dabbed her fingers on the white powder on Josh's shirt and popped them into her mouth.

"And I'm honestly a little disappointed you're not on coke because you're going to need the energy for this."

She dragged Josh by the hand, practically sprinting through the fair grounds. When they finally stopped, after catching his breath, Josh gasped in astonishment at the her surprise. He couldn't believe it.

"But, babe, we-"

"Come on! Let's go inside!" brimming with excitement, Jess dragged him into the Gravitron.

Josh was confused but followed suit. He thought he already explained that having sex on the spaceship-themed ride, while a personal fantasy of his, was all but an impossibility, but he didn't want to burst her bubble.

The ramp leading to the entrance of the Gravitron clanged as the two charged up it.

"This is Pedro." Jess introduced the ride operator, and young man with a thin mustache.

The short, Hispanic adolescence stood next to the Gravitron control console located in the middle of the starship – the only area on the ride that didn't move outrageously fast.

"Sup?" Pedro said to Josh.

"Hey." Josh nodded back.

"Pedro here has agreed to let us use the Gravitron for as long as we want – just you and me. Pedro just wants to watch. He's... into that." Jess explained.

Josh took another look at Pedro. He looked like the type of carnie who would install hidden cameras in port-o-potties when he got older.

"Um. Cool?" Josh said. Then he realized something. "Babe, you're *pretty* drunk right now. Are you sure you're not going to, like, throw up one me or anything, are you?"

"What? No! I'm a lady and I'm not that drunk. Anyway, I'm more horny than I am drunk. Hey, help me get this dress off. No! Not you, Pedro! I was talking to my boyfriend."

It was really dark inside the Gravitron. Josh supposed that was a good thing.

"Uh, hey, Pedro. Could you close the entrance?" Josh waved to the door that lead out into the carnival.

"It closes automatically when the ride starts, *senior*."

"Come on, Josh. If a priest already saw your dick today, then Pedro deserves to see it, too."

"It's not my dick that I'm worried about." He said.

Jess was already out of her dress and butt naked inside the carnival ride. She folded it and draped it neatly over the railing.

"Pedro, can we leave our clothes here, in the center of the Gravitron with you so we can do the ride naked?" She asked after the fact.

"Si." Pedro's beady eyes ran up and down Jess's curves.

"See? Come on, Josh. Take your clothes off and let's get this party started." She tugged on his pants so hard that she nearly fell over.

"It's alright, I can do it." Josh quickly undressed and placed his clothes next to Jess'.

He wanted to limit the amount of time that they were both nude in front of Pedro. He couldn't help but feel a creepy vibe coming from the man. The sooner they got this over with, the better.

Josh just hoped there weren't any cameras inside the ride.

The only clothing Jess kept on were her magenta heels, which under the blacklights inside the Gravitron were the same color as her nipples and lips. Pedro could not take his eyes off her. Josh couldn't blame him. Inside the dark lighting of the ride, she had an eerie glow about her.

By the time Josh got complete naked and was ready to start the ride, he was already fifty percent hard.

"Okay, so how does it work? I just have to stand over here?" Jess said as she laid back and pressed her bare buns against the sliding black walls.

As she did, she slid up a little bit.

"Whoo! These walls slide up and down!" she giggled.

"Jess, have you never ridden the Gravitron before?"

"No. It just goes around in circles, though, right? I'm excited!"

"Is her first time?!" Pedro asked, incredulous.

Josh shared his outrage and Jess's excitement. The one thing that both Pedro and Josh had in common were that they were both shocked that someone could have lived to Jess's age without having been on the Gravitron once.

"Oh, this *will* be fun." Josh said, taking his place against the outer sliding black walls.

Then he flipped upside down, doing a handstand right next to Jess. The befuddled look on her face was priceless.

"Hit it, Pedro!" Josh cried.

Jess was cracking up. "Josh! Why on earth are you upside down- Whoa, my God!"

The Gravitron spun to life. Jess's back slammed hard against the outer wall.

"I can't move! I can't move!" she started screaming.

With great effort, Josh reached over and pulled on Jess's thigh further away from him. As centrifugal force stuck them flat against the walls, Josh pulled Jess's hips toward his face, then she twisted her body so that she was laying completely on top of him into a sixty-nine position.

The entire time, she never stopped screaming.

While Jess's pussy naturally flew into Josh's mouth just the way he planned it, she had to struggle to get her head up and get her mouth around Josh's dick.

Meanwhile, Josh being on the bottom, upside down, and being crushed by Jess's weight, had the more difficult job. Yet he was doing an above average job of going down on her, of eating her pussy and licking her clit, given the circumstances.

Jess's body felt weird. She had never done anything like this before. It was difficult for her to focus on giving Josh a blowjob in zero-G while she kept sliding up and down on the moving walls.

She finally understood exactly what Josh meant when he said that this would be a challenge. It was without a doubt the most difficult blowjob of her life, and earlier that day she was sucking his dick in front of a priest.

When Josh said it would be a challenge, she was thinking more along the lines of a TikTok challenge, or how Exhibitionist Bingo was a challenge – not a physically demanding and excruciating experience.

But here she was, naked and drunk, laying on top of her boyfriend and suspended vertically by her great nemesis – gravity.

She did her best to help him maintain an erection. She gave him the best blowjob she could, considering the situation. And yet, she had no fucking clue how they were going to have sex inside the Gravitron.

Just as Jess started to get the hang of sucking cock while centrifugal force pressed her naked body up against the wall, Josh reached up and tapped her on the back. It surely must have strained him to do as such, considering she could barely lift her head up and down on his dick.

He tapped her again, as if she was supposed to know what it meant. She was just about to spit out his dick and yell at him, then, at the next spin, he flipped her body around so that he was on top of her.

Oh, so that's what it meant.

Josh was at least twice as big as Jess. As if the force of gravity pressing her up against the wall wasn't enough – Josh's amplified weight on top of her was immediately crushing her.

He pushed himself up against the wall as it slid up again, doing a push up, and flipped himself upright so that Jess and Josh now both faced the same vertical direction.

Then he started laughing hysterically.

"I knew it! Look at your tits!"

She hadn't realized it with everything going on, but the force of the ride had inverted her boobs. With no bra to contain them, her breasts were pushed into her body and sloping upwards, towards her shoulders.

As she looked down at her tits, Josh took her nipple into his mouth, grabbing her other breast and giving it a squeeze that made her tingle. It was a weird feeling, but felt good nonetheless.

Jess could feel his dick poking into her stomach as centrifugal force stuck them to the walls.

"Fuck me in zero gravity!" she yelled over the din of the ride.

"It's not zero-g! It's.. oh, well, nevermind."

Josh pushed her knees apart, centering himself between them. With the ride moving them every which way, it was difficult for Josh to get his dick inside of her, but he somehow made it work.

It wasn't the most romantic thing they had ever done. It wasn't the sexiest thing they had ever done. It wasn't even all that pleasurable. But they were doing it, and it seemed to give Josh an endless amount of entertainment.

"Fuck yeah! We're fucking on the Gravitron, motherfucker!"

It took Josh a lot of effort to fuck her and with every thrust he looked more tired.

"Touch yourself." He yelled at her as they hit another turn and the walls moved again.

He kissed her neck, bit her earlobe, sucked her tits, anything and everything he could think of that might turn her on. It might have been working to keep him hard inside of her, but Jess was feeling more queasy with every passing second.

"Cum in me." She yelled. "Hurry up and cum in me."

He understood and redoubled his efforts. He pumped hard and faster. Although it felt good, Jess's stomach felt sick. The only think that really kept her going was the zero-g kissing. And the feeling of her boobs flying up and down.

The Gravitron, as it turns out, was not a very sensual ride.

We should have found the Tunnel of Love.

"Kiss me." She cried. "At least kiss me when you cum inside of me."

He put his mouth on her and pumped harder still. She knew that Josh was about to cum inside of her when he started moaning into her mouth.

Good. I've had just about all I can take of this.

She could feel Josh cum inside of her as the Gravitron took a hard right turn, sending them up the walls yet again. Then to the other side. And then back to the other side. Up and down. Side to side.

Is Pedro fucking with us? And after all I did for him...

"Blegh!" Jess felt it coming up but could do nothing to stop it.

At least she was able to move her mouth off of Josh's in the last second before she barfed all over the Gravitron. Jess spewed up something dark green on the black paneled wall next to her. interestingly enough, it stuck to the middle of the wall.

The ride spun to an abrupt stop. Jess and Josh both sank back down to the ground.

And then her barf slumped to the floor.

"Oh, no, *senorita!*"

Pedro screamed when he saw Jess throw up. He was evidently watching very closely because the moment she puked all over the ride stopped.

"Uh, sorry." Jess burped.

"Senorita, no!"

Her and Josh dizzily found their clothes were they left them and dressed in a hurry.

"You got he hundred bucks for me, senorita?" Pedro asked with his hand held out.

"Jess, did you promise him a hundred dollars?!" Josh demanded.

"Pedro! I've given you something much more valuable. The experience of knowing you should always collect your money upfront. Also, you saw my tits, so we're even."

Pedro looked pissed. He cursed them in Spanish as he went to go grab something hidden underneath the ride control console.

Josh dug through his pants and held up his wallet. He did not want to find out what the carnie was hiding.

"Hold on, Pedro. I'll pay you. Jess, go wait outside the spaceship and to NOT piss off any more carnies while you're out there waiting."

"Yeah, yeah." Jess waved a dismissive hand in the air as she walked outside the ride.

Whatever. This place smells like vomit anyway.

Once she was outside and got some fresh air in her lungs she felt much better. The cool night air felt great on her face and was sobering on her skin.

She combed her fingers through her hair to make sure there was no puke hiding there when Josh came walking down the ramp of the Gravitron, shaking his head disapprovingly.

"What?"

"He is NOT happy."

"That can't be right. No one has ever seen me naked and been unhappy."

"Babe, you just don't mess with carnies. That is a valuable life lesson that Pedro back there was about o teach you with his poison tipped blowdarts and nunchucks he keeps underneath the ride's control console back there."

"He does *not*."

"Oh, yes he does. Dude showed me. Darts tipped with toad venom and motherfucking nunchucks. He is quite proud of them. Pedro is a regular Bruce Lee."

"Baby... can we get the fuck out of here?"

Josh held out his arm. "Let's go find you a toothbrush. Then you can finish what you started."

She giggled. "That sounds like an *excellent* idea."

She took his arm and together they walked towards the carnival parking lot.

CHAPTER 29

Day 6 – Home

Later that night, back at home, the couple cuddled up on the couch and shared a big bowl of ice cream while they binge watched TV.

"I think you still owe me an orgasm, mister."

Josh laughed. "I do. Would you like to redeem said orgasm now or later?"

Jess luxuriated in the idea as she took another big bite of ice cream, thinking of how she should answer.

"What about half now and half later?"

Josh laughed, "I don't think that's how it works."

Jess ran her fingertips lightly across Josh's arm as she moved his hand over her breast.

"Then how does it work?"

"I'll tell you what, just because I like you, I'll give you one for free right now and one at a later date of your choosing."

"Ooh, lucky me." Jess said as she assumed the position in which she wanted to be fucked.

She threw off her nightgown and laid down on her side on the couch. Jess never really gave it much thought, but the spooning position was probably her favorite way of making love.

She liked the closeness of their bodies. She liked to feel the heat of his body up against hers. She liked the feeling of his firm yet gentle caress while they were making love. And she most definitely loved being the little spoon.

But when it comes to fucking for the sheer fun and pleasure of fucking, well, she was up for anything, really.

As Jess pulled her nightgown up and over her head, stripping herself completely naked, she made her devious intentions clear.

She said in a voice that was as soft and seductive as she could manage, "Technically, you owe me two. One for the carnival. One for the beach."

She pulled Josh's arm over her like a blanket as she wiggled bubble butt back into his concave hips.

"Oh, I know." He said in a low, gravely voice that Jess found irresistibly sexy. "Why do you think I offered you two?"

"So, I don't get four orgasms off the strength, then?"

Josh laughed a deep, throaty, manly laugh. "Don't push your luck. My dick hardly works as it is after the crazy week we've had."

He eased himself between Jess's legs. No matter how many times they had sex, he never got sick of the feel of pushing his hard cock into his girlfriend's tight little pussy. And she felt the same way.

Jess sighed a long, deep sigh of pleasure and relief when he entered her. Josh and Jess seemed to always know what the other was thinking, and right in that moment, they both knew that the other was thinking *Holy fuck, that feels* so *fucking good.*

Josh loved her warm wetness. He indulged in it. Just as Jess adored the feeling of his stiff member penetrating her again and again while they lay on their sides, from the back.

They both loved the slow, rhythmic pace of making love to one another.

"Mmmm..." Jess moaned sleepily.

It was almost hard to believe given the copious amount of sex that the young couple were constantly having, but Jess had an above average vagina when it came to the subject of sensitivity. She was very sensitive and *very* receptive. She blamed her nymphomanic desires and high sex drive on the fact that she felt everything in such great detail, although Josh was also partly to blame.

"Tomorrow is the final day, you know." He whispered low, cupping her breast and driving his hips into her from behind.

"Already? Has it already been a week?" she cooed, moving her body in rhythm with his.

He pulled her chest so her back was flush with his chest. He moved his hips up and down slowly, intimately grinding his body against her ass, going deeper into her feminine warmth with every thrust.

When they made love like this, it was as if they were moving together as one organic entity. They were of one being. One mind. One soul. One love.

"Yes." He answered.

"Yes." She responded to the sensual pleasures he offered up to her. "Mmmm... I wish all of these Exhibitionist Bingo locations were as free and easy as this."

She wrapped her arm around his arm. She tangled her legs together with his legs. She pulled tightly against him, never wanting to let go.

"That's why 'Home' is the free space on the card." Josh said between planting little kisses on her neck and shoulders.

"Today was a lot of work." She whined. "And you know what? After all of that craziness at the church and carnival, this is *by far* my favorite moment of the entire day."

"Yeah?"

"Mm-hmmm... Yes." Josh wasn't sure if she was answering his question or responding to something else of his.

"What about getting drunk behind the grocery store?"

"That was in my top five favorite moments of the day, but you carrying me on your back was probably my second favorite."

"And the other top five?"

She giggled a little.

"Peeing in front of strangers. And the look on the priest's face when he watched me swallow a mouth full of your cum."

Josh chuckled. "I did enjoy listening to church gossip while you treated my dick like an unmeltable Orangecicle. But there is nothing in this world that compares to winding down at the end of the day by making love to the woman I love most in the world while binge watching TV and eating a bowl of ice cream."

"Mm-hmmm... God, I love your dick. So, so much." She pushed her head back into the solid muscle of his chest, breathing hard.

"Yes. My dick seems very fond of you, too. And my heart."

"Hey, you know what would make this moment even more romantic?" Jess reached across the couch and grabbed the TV remote, fiddling with it.

"Yule Log? Damn, woman. That *is* romantic as fuck."

"I can think of no better way to end the day than making love to my man in front of a fake ass roaring fire."

"A real fire, maybe?"

"Too much work."

"Then I'm glad I got the seventy inch."

"I'm glad I got your eight inch." She said, pushing her ass back into his for emphasis. "Time to collect what you owe me."

"I'm more than happy to settle up."

Josh and Jess made love all night in front of the fake TV fire and fell asleep in each other's arms.

CHAPTER 30

Day 7 - Home

When Jess awoke the following afternoon, Josh was still pressed up behind her with his arm draped over her body, cupping her bare breasts and hugging her tight.

His morning wood was just as hard as the Yule Log wedged in between Jess's thighs. Jess felt like she fell asleep with a water bottle wedged between her legs.

She turned off the Yule Log which had been running all night and lulled them to sleep in the late hours of the evening. Jess stretched out on the couch with a big yawn like a cat awakening from a long nap.

Then she looked at the clock.

Shit. It's Monday. I'm late for work!

She threw off Josh's hand and jumped up off the couch, waking him in the process.

"Good morning, my darling beauty queen."

He yawned sleepily from the couch as he watched Jess stomp around the living room naked and frantic. She didn't know what to do first.

"Come back and lay with me a bit longer." He beckoned.

"I'm late for work!" she cried, fanning herself with her hand. "Shower. I need to shower. No, I don't have time to shower. I need to go!"

Jess grabbed her car keys from the countertop and ran into the garage.

"Clothes! You need to wear clothes when you leave the house, babe! Remember?" Josh called out to her.

A moment later she came running back inside and started pacing like a maniac. Josh hopped up off of the couch and steadied her shoulders in place so she would stop running around like a lunatic.

"That's it. You're calling off work today. Call and tell them that you're taking a personal day for your mental health."

Jess looked at the clock again and her eyes went wide with panic.

"I can't call in sick. The day is already half over!"

"Then what's the point in going into work?" Josh asked in between yawns.

"I can't. I... I..." she was looking around, desperately searching for something like a wild animal.

Josh shook her by the shoulders. "Jess. Jess! You're already, like, four hours late. And I'm not letting you roll into work without taking a shower. You reek of sex. Besides, Esteban would want you to take amental health day."

Josh reached for her phone sitting on the coffee table and pushed it into her hands.

"Call him. Or I will."

Jess looked at the phone. Then she looked at Josh. Then the phone.

"I... I..."

"Jess, this is *exactly* why you have mental health days in the first place. And it'll look a lot better if you call your boss than if I call him. Even if the workday is half over already."

She stared at the phone in her hands.

"I..."

"Call. Him."

"You're... not giving me a choice here, are you?"

He raised one eyebrow and gave her a look.

"You just tried to get in your car and drive off without any clothes on if I hadn't stopped you."

"I would have realized I needed clothes... at some point."

"I'm going to take the day off to be with you."

"But-"

"And don't say it's different just because I work from home, because it's not."

She started dialing. Josh could hear the phone ring on the other side.

"Uh, hello? Esteban? Yes, this is Jess. I know I'm late... What's that? Yes, I am safe. What? Nooo, I *don't* think we should do a video call right now. Uh, listen, I need to take a..."

Josh silently mouthed the words "mental health day" while she was on the phone.

"A, uh, mental health day. What's that? Why are you glad I'm taking a personal day off? Aw, thank you for your concern. I guess I have been a little distracted lately. Yes, everything will be fine tomorrow, I promise. Thank you, Esteban. Okay. I will. See you tomorrow. Bye."

Jess hung up the phone and looked at Josh. "Esteban says 'hi'."

"See? He wants you to be well-rested and focused. Plus, you've been doing so much for the clothing company lately. Now, march that cute little booty of yours into the bedroom so we can cuddle while we plan our day."

Jess hesitated but ultimately complied with Josh's demands. They both fell into bed together and began cuddling naked over the sheets.

As he lay on his back, Jess rested her head on top of his chest, closely nuzzling him as she ran her hand up and down his chiseled abs.

"You're so good for me." She said absently.

Josh pet her head, brushing her shiny black hair all the way down her back with his fingers.

"I know. I wouldn't want it any other way."

"I was scared at first, but I'm glad you forced me into doing this today, baby."

"I know."

"Because there is no way I would have done this myself. I would never use my mental health day unless forced to."

"I know. Which is why I used them for you. This is precisely why you have paid mental health days in the first place."

"Well, right now, my mental health thanks you."

"I love you, too." He said, gently petting her as she lay there wrapped in his strong arms. "Moments like these are the reason I get up in the morning. And for the that, my emotional well-being thanks you."

He kissed the top of her head. She kissed his chest back.

"Aw. Well, if we could complete this Bingo card today, my physical and sexual well-being would thank you. Actually, my entire being would thank you *very* much."

"I thought you said it was more trouble than it's worth."

"That was before my schedule suddenly cleared up today."

Jess tried to grab her phone on the nightstand, but it was out of reach. Josh took it and handed it to her.

"Thank you, my love." She said, kissing him again on the chest as she unlocked her phone and pulled up an image of the Bingo card.

"Wow, the only ones we haven't done yet are 'Drive-Thru', 'Museum', and 'Pool-slash-Hot Tub'."

"Really? That's it?"

"You realize it's been a *very* busy week for my vagina, right?"

"Care to give it a break, then? Anal sex Mondays?"

Jess busted up laughing. "I'm open to the possibility. Though I'm not certain my ass could handle all of that in one day, either."

"I'll refill the coconut oil bottle." Josh offered.

"Oh my God, could you? How clutch was that?"

"You need to start carrying that with you everywhere."

"Yeah, right up until it breaks open inside my purse and destroys literally everything I own."

"That still sounds better than getting fucked in the ass with no lube, though, doesn't it?"

"Josh, do you have any idea how much my handbag costs?"

"So, which hot tub are we going to use?" Josh asked, changing subjects.

"I don't know, but it would be pretty funny to go to the same gym we already hooked up in and use their spa. I would love to see the faces of the people who work at the gym when they see us return."

"Well..." He gave her a look.

"Oh no, I already told you, I don't want a UTI, and there is no quicker way to get one than to hook up in a gym spa."

"How do you treat a UTI?"

"Like, cranberry juice and..."

"What? You *love* cranberry juice!"

"I don't love them! I drink them when I'm on my period... and yeah, I kind of enjoy them."

"If you let me fuck you in the gym hot tub and you end up getting a UTI, I will personally serve you up vodka cranberries for a week."

"Josh, I... Sometimes it takes up to a month."

"Two weeks. Don't push it."

"All day, every day. Vodka cranberries, as many as I want?"

"As many as you can drink over the course of two weeks, and no longer."

Jess hesitated.

"Grey Goose, or Popov?"

"Is that even a question?"

"We literally drank a handle of Popov vodka behind the grocery store just yesterday!"

"Yeah, but we did it, like, ironically."

Jess laughed. "Okay, deal. But if we get there and I decide that after we're in the hot tub that I want anal instead, you still have to serve me vodka cranberries."

She extended her hand to Josh and they shook on it.

"Actually, anal in the hot tub might be better anyway."

"I was thinking the same thing. But we already shook on it, so no taksies-backsies."

"You think I want to take this back? You realize that over the next two weeks, I'm going one-for-one with you on the vodka-crans, right? Hell, maybe two-for-one since you're such a lightweight."

"Oh my God, I weigh all of, like, ninety pounds. And half of that is my enormous tits, and they don't have a liver of their own."

She batted at Josh's arm like a playful kitten for a while before she decided it was time to get up and start the day.

"Come on, lazy bones. I feel like shit when I stay in bed after noon."

"It's your mental health day. You can stay in bed for as long as you want."

Josh made no attempt to move. His gaze swept up and down Jess's nubile naked body as she did a few light yoga stretched in the bedroom.

"You're right. It is. And my mental health is telling me to get this show on the road." Jess said, grunting once as she dropped into Warrior pose.

"Hmm, my mental health is telling me to lay in bed and watch you do naked yoga all day."

"Get your lazy butt up. We're going to the gym so we can do anal in the hot tub."

Josh groaned. "I guess that's worth getting up for."

CHAPTER 31

Day 7 – Drive Thru

"It's about time," Jess complained as Josh climbed into the driver's seat of the Audi.

"Shush. You know I'm a slow starter." He buckled his seatbelt before starting the car.

"Well, thank goodness you're not a fast finisher," Jess said, laughing at her own joke.

"Seat belt." He reminded her.

"Okay, dad. Geez."

Jess rolled her eyes, then pulled the seat belt over her purple sports bra and clicked it into place.

She was wearing her gym outfit, which was essentially the same thing she wore every time Josh dragged her to the gym. A form-fitting sports bra and stretchy black yoga pants. The spandex top and bottom clung to her every curve, letting her feel like she was wearing nothing at all while working up a sweat at the gym.

After the way that Josh peeled her wet gym clothes off of her while they were in hooking up in the shower on their last visit, it was hard for Jess to think of anything else when she put on her sports bra and yoga pants. Even as she pulled her sports bra over her head just a few minutes ago, the memories came flooding back to her.

She smiled her own private smile from the passenger seat of the car. Jess could feel herself getting wet right now just thinking about the last time she wore these clothes.

She was so lost in thought that she completely missed whatever Josh was talking about.

"Huh? What did you say?"

"I said you can call me daddy."

"Yes, daddy."

He chuckled. "Good girl."

He put on his sunglasses as he turned onto the highway. It was another wonderfully sunny (read: hot) afternoon in Los Angeles. The sun was shining bright without a cloud in the sky.

Josh was wearing a different set of matching turquoise tank top and gym shorts. His cotton tank top clung to his muscled chest much in the same way that Jess's sports bra clung to her. And just as Jess knew that her gym clothes turned on Josh, seeing him clad in his gym clothes was an arousing experience for her.

After a long night of making love and cuddling naked in bed all morning, Jess was ready to embrace the last few locations left on the Bingo card.

But as fun and kinky as a week packed with public sex was, a part of her was also relieved that it was about to be over. Jess enjoyed exploring her inner exhibitionist, but she could not deny how stressed out she had become in the last week.

I really do need this mental health day. I feel like my anxiety is at an all time high.

As Josh hit a bit of traffic on the freeway, a mischievous idea popped into Jess's devious brain. She decided that it was time to play one of her all-time favorite games while Josh was driving and she was bored.

The game was called "Let's See How Horny We Could Make Josh While He Drives."

And although Josh was never aware that she was playing the game with her, she was almost always the winner. The only rule, Jess decided, was that there was to be no physical contact. Other than that, everything was fair game.

Jess derived an endless amount of entertainment from seeing how wild she could drive her boyfriend while he was driving and unable to do anything about it. It was torture for him, and hence, extremely entertaining for Jess.

So, let's start the game slow.

"You know, I'll always remember the hot sex we had in the shower every time I put on these gym clothes from now on."

He kept his eyes on the road, "It was pretty hot, wasn't it?"

"Are there any items like that of yours that you associate with me?"

"Are you kidding me? At first I thought that it was just something that guys do, you know, associating certain items with particular... events. But if I'm being honest with you, virtually every single outfit of mine I can trace back to a time we had sex the day I was wearing it."

"Such as?"

"Well, I'll never forget what I wore the first night we were together. Remember my dalmatian boxers?"

"Oh my God! Your dalmatian underwear! Of course, I could never forget those. I love them so much!"

"I know they're your favorite. And I never told you this, but I've always thought of those as my lucky boxers because I was wearing them the night I met you."

"Aw, that's so sweet... Hey, what was that move you did to me on our first night that made me fall in love with you?"

Josh started laughing.

"I wouldn't call it a 'move'. You just had no idea what good sex was like until I came along."

"I didn't."

"And falling in love works both ways, by the way."

Damnit. Score, Josh: 1, Jess: 0.

"Josh?"

"Yes, my love?"

"I'm horny."

"I know, sweetie. We'll be at the gym soon. I brought the coconut oil."

"How are you going to fuck me in the ass underwater? The lube will wash away."

"We'll cross that bridge when we get there."

Time to step it up.

"Baby?"

"Yes, love?"

"I'm, like, *really* horny."

When Josh casually glanced over in her direction just for a second, his eyes nearly popped out of his head.

Jess had her sports bra pulled up over her boobs and was staring at Josh like a dog in heat, biting down on her lower lip. She looked down at her tits, then back up at Josh through lidded eyes.

Josh did a double, then a triple take.

"Oh my God, Jess put those away! What if someone sees?"

"The only person I want to see them isn't even looking." Jess pouted.

"Babe, I'm driving."

"Okay, okay, I'll put my enormous knockers away."

Josh laughed, keeping one eye on the traffic ahead. "Knockers? Really?"

"There. Are you happy now?"

"Yes, but I – Jess!"

She pulled her bra back down to cover her breasts. Then she pulled her stretchy black yoga pants down to her knees and was playing with her pussy.

"What? I told you, I'm horny. And you said you're driving. Plus, this way no one can see what I'm doing."

"Are you going to really sit in the passenger seat and masturbate the entire drive to the gym."

"No! Not for the *entire* drive… Just the rest of it."

"You're just teasing me, aren't you?"

"I don't know what you're talking about, Josh. I *have* to do this. Because my boyfriend won't help me."

"I'm driving!"

Focused on the road, Josh heard the passenger seatbelt unclick. He heard Jess shuffling around in the seat next to him, but because he was changing lanes, he couldn't spare a passing glance.

Once Josh was safely in the slow lane, she looked over at the passenger seat.

"Jess!"

She giggled mischievously as she waved her bare ass at Josh. With her yoga pants now pulled all the way down to her ankles, Jess was on her knees facing the passenger side window. As she mooned Josh from the passenger seat, she spready her cheeks with both hands.

"I wanted to show you how wet I am. See?"

"Why are you doing this?"

"Well, it sounded like you didn't believe me when I told you I was *really* horny. So I wanted to show you."

Jess reached between her legs and slid three fingers into her pussy, fingering herself until she was wet enough for it to make sloshing sounds.

"God, I am *so* wet. Look. Look at how wet I am."

"I'm driving, baby, I can't look. I know you're horny. We'll be there soon., I promise."

"Listen, my pussy wants to talk to you. Can you hear how wet I am? Josh? Listen, Josh."

She was fingering herself with one hand and rubbing her clit with the other, all the while inching her bare bottom closer and closer to Josh's face.

"Babe... Please..."

"Oh... Ooh... It feels so good. God, I am *so* fucking *wet*. I wish someone would *fuck* me." She moaned softly while masturbating right next to Josh's face.

"Alright. I get it. I'm pulling over."

As Josh pulled the car onto the next freeway exit, Jess was starting to think that she might end the game with a come from behind win.

Hopefully in more ways than one.

"Don't move. Don't you fucking move a muscle." He said as the car pulled up to a red light.

Josh unclicked his seatbelt, leaned over, and took Jess ass in both his hands. He pushed back her big round butt cheeks and started feasting on her ass and pussy. While the car was stopped, he licked, sucked, slobbered, and pushed the tip of his tongue as far down into his girlfriend's ass as possible.

"Oh my goodness, Josh! What's gotten into you!" Jess feigned surprise as she squealed and wiggled with delight under his tongue.

I guess this means I win, Jess thought.

Josh continued to savage Jess's ass all the way up until she started yelling. "Green light! Green light!"

Impatient L.A. drivers behind him were already honking. Josh sat back down in the driver's seat, threw the car into Drive and peeled out.

"See what you made me do, you vile temptress! No, don't put that thing away. I'm not done with you yet. Keep it up. Don't sit down. Don't fucking move a muscle."

"Yes, daddy."

Josh pulled into a gas station on the next corner. Even with Jess's limited visibility and her face stuck out the window like a dog, she understood what was about to happen.

When it all clicked, she said, "See? This is why I love you so much, baby. You're so smart."

To which Josh replied, "I am about to fuck the ever-loving shit out of you for doing this to me, woman."

Josh pulled the Audi forward into the automated drive-thru car wash. As soon as the tires of their car hit the guiding tracks at the entrance to the car wash, Josh had his pants off.

"You asked for this." He warned her.

Jess faked a scream of terror, but kept her ass help high next to Josh's face just as he demanded.

The car was automatically pulled into the drive-thru car wash. With both hands free, Josh grabbed her ass once again and buried his face in it. He ran his tongue from her clit to her asshole and back again many times.

Then he flung his feet over the center console to the passenger side, then pulled her entire body ass-first over to the driver's side onto his lap.

Jess was forthcoming about how wet her pussy was, and Josh's hard cock slipped inside right away. Jess sat awkwardly in the front of the car, half in the passenger seat and half in the driver's seat while Josh bounced her booty up and down on his dick.

The car wasn't even inside the car wash yet. Several people at the gas station pumping gas were staring at them. But there was nothing anyone could do now. She was his.

"Oh my God, yes, yes, yes! Ooh, oh, yeah, fuck me, Josh! Oh yes, fuck he harder. Harder! Yeah, fuck the shit out of me. Just like thaaahhh!"

Josh was in a blind rage, furiously fucking her by pulling her ass roughly down on top of him. Her ass slapped against Josh's thigh's loudly as Jess cried out.

This is going to leave a bruise for sure…

Josh slipped one hand underneath Jess's sports bra, manhandling her big, natural breasts under the stretchy fabric. The move cost him leverage bouncing her booty on his dick, so Jess started doing it for him.

Finally, Josh pulled her top up and over her head violently. She was sure he was going to rip the thing off of her, but luckily the fabric held together. Josh discarded her sports bra into one of the corners of the car and it was gone.

He slapped and squeezed her bouncing tits while Jess kept grinding up and down on his cock. He let her fuck him for a brief period of high energy rough sex while he played with her magnificent tits.

Then Josh took control from her. He listed her ass up and held it firmly a few inches above his waist. Then he started jackhammering her pussy from below, powerfully driving his cock deep inside her.

The impact of every deep and fast thrust made her yelp.

"Joooosh! Ah mi gah oh shi ah fuh JASS!"

He was doing things to her that rendered her speechless. Jess was so contorted in the front seat of the car that she didn't even know how she ended up into any number of positions that Josh moved her into.

The car wash was short – relatively speaking. She saw the light at the end of the tunnel. Josh still had Jess sitting in his lap with her yoga pants pulled all the way down to her ankles. He had slapped her as so many times that her entire bottom was red.

Her tits bounced up and down fervently as Josh hammered her pussy from below with no intention of stopping anytime soon even as the car departed from the car wash.

Jess had barely enough room to fit one hand between her legs so she could diddle her skittle. Pleasure came in sudden waves. Jess could hardly believe it as she was struck again and again by multiple orgasms.

Josh ravaged her pussy in the middle of the drive-thru car wash – and he continued to do so even as the was ended. He was fucking her as hard as fast as he ever had as the car idled out into the gas station parking lot.

"Ja-ja-ja-ja-Josh!" Jess screamed cries of passion.

They were now out in the open. The newly cleaned Audi was front and center out in the middle of the gas station, creeping along slowly with no one at the wheel.

People coming and going into the gas station could easily see through their windows. Jess made passing eye contact with a few strangers as they watched her tits bouncing while she sat on Josh's lap.

She fought him off as she made her way back to the passenger seat. Jess found her sports bra wedged between the seats and went to go put it back on. Josh was still groping at her while she pulled her pants back up.

"Josh! Stop!"

"Fuck!" He punched the steering wheel.

"You didn't cum, did you?"

He shook his head. Josh took hold of the steering wheel just in time to avoid running into a gas pump, pulling the car safely to a stop in one of the parking stalls.

"I came a bunch. Multiple orgasms. Not to rub it in your face or nothin."

"You had multiple orgasms in a fucking drive through car was and I didn't cum once?"

"Babe, first of all, put your fucking dick away. People are starring."

He zipped up his pants, but his massive erection created a very obvious tent.

"Second, I told you I was horny. I told you I was *really* horny. Those were self-actualizing orgasms."

Josh was white-knuckling the steering wheel with a befuddled look on his face.

"... What?"

She laughed. "Babe, relax."

She caressed his arms. He was grabbing the steering wheel so tightly that all of his muscles were flexing. She cuddled up to him softly.

"You fucking ravaged my pussy. And we're still going to the gym, right? I still want you to fuck me in my ass. You're going to bust in my booty, right?" She cooed to him.

"Yeah... I guess."

"Don't pout. I'm still excited for that, and you should be, too."

"I am excited. I'm very excited, as you can see." He gestured to the canopy in his pants. "Because this thing isn't going anywhere anytime soon."

"Okay, well, pull out of this fucking gas station so I can kiss it and make it better. Everyone here has seen my tits."

"Fine." He spat grumpily.

Josh still seemed angry about not being able to cum at the same time as her. He pulled the Audi out onto the street and got back on the freeway, where more traffic was waiting for them.

"Also... Ha-ha! How does it feel to be the one who doesn't cum this time!" She teased relentlessly.

"Aw, that's cold blooded."

"But seriously, you really did fucking ravage my pussy, babe. And in a short amount of time, too. I'm glad you're going to fuck me in the ass at the gym. My vagina needs a break."

"You brought that on yourself."

"I did, but I had no idea it would be like that."

"I wish I had self-actualizing multiple orgasms."

"I think those are called 'wet dreams' for guys."

"Girls don't have wet dreams?"

"Oh, trust me, when I was going through puberty, all of my dreams were wet dreams. Shit, I still wake up really wet sometimes."

"Yeah. I know."

"But that's nothing compared to my best friend, Alison. When she has wet dreams, she wakes up like Bigfoot Rapids. She has Disneyland Log Ride wet dreams. Then she can't go back to sleep unless she has an orgasm."

"That's not what I was talking about, but still, it sounds unpleasant."

"Yeah. The girl sleeps in bed with a vibrator and hand towel nearby. Poor thing."

"Are you sure whatever she has isn't contagious?"

"Oh, shut up." She playfully slapped him on the arm. Then she rubbed the muscles in his shoulder. "Hmm."

Jess reached over the center console and unzipped Josh's pants. He was still just as hard as he was when they left the gas station. She tested it first, licking the head of his cock a few times before she started going down on him.

"Mm... Mm... Mm..."

"Ah, fuck, babe. That feels good."

Josh's dick made a popping sound when Jess pulled it out of her mouth. She sat up straight I the passenger seat while still jerking and twisting his saliva-soaked cock.

"Oh, wow." She said, then wiped the drool from her lips with the back of her other hand.

"Oh, wow, what? Why did you stop?" Josh asked, concentrating on the staying in the lines on the freeway. It was a task that he sometimes found difficult while she was giving him road head.

"Huh? I was just thinking how weird it is that your cum tastes so much different than my cum."

"What do you mean? I didn't cum. At least, I don't think I did."

She laughed. "You didn't. I came all over your dick and now I can taste it. I'm used to just tasting your cum, not my own."

"And?"

"Would you think I'm weird if I said I like the taste of my own cum better?"

She shrugged, the leaned over again so she could continue giving him road head, this time luxuriating in the taste. She did far more licking that sucking as she played with his dick just for the fun of it. Josh courteously brushed her hair from her face with one hand while he drive with the other.

"I've only ever tasted your cum and I have to say that I am a big fan."

Jess laughed with his dick halfway down her throat, nearly choking.

"You only think you've 'only tasted my cum.' How many times have you gone down on me *after* we've had sex?"

"I'm sorry. I don't swallow nearly enough of the stuff to tell the difference. You should host your own TV cooking show. I could see it now. 'Cooking with Cum', guest starring Jess."

His dick *popped* out of her mouth as he face hovered over it.

"Don't make fun of the girl who has your dick in her mouth. Especially not while driving, dick." She said before she went back to deepthroating her boyfriend.

"Hey, I wasn't- Oh, FUCK that feels so goddamn good."

Jess *slurped* and *slurped* and *slurped* on his dick. The *popped* it out of her mouth.

"You still haven't cum yet."

"Shit, babe, I'm turning into the gym now." He announced.

Jess sat up in the passenger seat, wiping the trails of spit connecting her lips to his cock with her forearm. Then she checked to make sure all of her clothes were still on.

They were.

"Okay, but here is my concern. You didn't cum at the car wash-"

"That was, like, three minutes!"

"You didn't cum while I was sucking your dick on the drive over here-"

"You kept stopping in the middle!"

"What makes you think you'll be able to cum in my ass when we start fucking in the hot tub?"

Josh looked like he was deep in though as he parked the car, though he did not have an answer for her. Just like every time his girlfriend asked him a question that he didn't know the answer to, he deferred to his old standby answer.

"Because you're beautiful, and I love you, and I'm lucky to have you in my life."

"Aww..."

Damnit. That works on me every time!

They got out of the car and, side by side, they walked into the gym.

"Josh?"

"Yes, love of my life?"

"I..."

Ugh! Stupid romantic boyfriend.

"Just... get your head in the game!"

He nodded solemnly.

"Do you think they'll recognize us?" Jess asked while they stride past the receptionist.

"Oh, no! Not you two again!" a voice came from behind them.

"Does that answer your question." Josh said under his breath.

"Here to ruin the steam room again, are we?"

They turned around to face a young man who was dressed in the same clothes that all of the gym employees wore.

"Excuse me, you must have us confused with someone else." Josh said, though he was red in the face with embarrassment.

Jess took Josh by the hand and they started walking away.

"Well, that was one way of dealing with it." She said when they were far enough away from the disgruntled gym employee.

"Yeah, but you realize if we get caught in the spa, we're going to have to move gyms, right?"

"Are you kidding me? If we get caught in the spa, we'll be legends here!"

He did not share her enthusiasm.

"Being a legend for having sex on every surface in the gym is not something you can put on a job resume. And neither is going to jail."

"Yeah, yeah, whatever. Grab your boner and meet me in the spa."

"I'm going to do a workout first. You know, get that testosterone flowing."

"You realize you just gave me, like, eight back to back orgasms on the drive down here, right? You know what? Whatever. I'm going swimming. Come find me when you're ready to put your dick in my butt."

"I'll bring the coconut oil."

"You'd better."

They kissed and parted ways. Each of them walked towards their gender's respective locker rooms, gym bag in hand.

"Really? Eight?!" Josh called out to her from across the gym.

"What? No! I'm trying to boost your self-confidence!" She yelled back.

Everyone was looking at them after that. Screaming about her orgasms in the middle of the gym lobby was probably not the smartest thing to do for a couple who were trying to be lowkey about having sex in their hot tub, but neither Josh nor Jess could care less.

The Exhibitionist Bingo Challenge had emboldened them, priming them to do and say things in public that they would have considered downright embarrassing just weeks ago. And after crossing off 23 squares on the Bingo card, the couple was nearly all out of fucks to give.

CHAPTER 32

Day 7 – Hot Tub

Jess changed into her new platinum silver one-piece swimsuit. She knew that as soon as Josh saw it, he would go all boner city on her. In fact, she was counting on it.

Having sex underwater was not Jess's favorite thing in the whole wide world. Even less so at a public gym, in a spa that was undoubtedly crawling with diseases. The fact that is was sparsely populated on a Monday afternoon was all but a bonus.

Jess could not remember a time in her life when she did anal underwater. She did not have very high expectations, but who knows? Maybe it'll be nice? And after all, she liked trying new things.

I'll try anything twice, Jess thought to herself.

She spent the next 45 minutes swimming laps in an overly chlorinated gym pool. She didn't realize just how much she enjoyed having the entire pool all to herself until a creepy middle-aged dude wearing bright orange swim trunks jumped into the pool and started swimming obnoxiously close to her.

"Well, hello, beautiful." He said in a voice that was so much like Sean Connery that she thought he was doing an impression.

He swam so close to her that it would have been rude for her not to smile back and say 'hi'. But the second she did, she suddenly wished that she had been rude instead.

Now she opened the door to conversation and instantly regretted it.

"I like your swimsuit." He started literally swimming circles around her.

"Thanks. Can you, like, not get in my way?"

"Oh, ha-ha, sorry."

"Thanks. So do you come here often?"

"This is my gym." He said with a serious face.

"Oh, you own this gym?"

"No, I mean I have a membership here."

He thought he was being very clever. Jess sighed inwardly.

"Me and my boyfriend do as well."

"You have a boyfriend?"

"Yes. I'm waiting for him to finish working out so we can have sex in the spa. It's for BINGO."

He started busting up laughing. Jess dived underwater to try and get away from him, but when she emerged he was right there waiting for her.

"So, does your boyfriend love you?"

"Of course he does. He just doesn't love it when creepy old men talk to me at the gym. A creepy old guy tried talking to me at the last gym we belonged to and my boyfriend caved his skull in with a kettlebell. It was not pretty."

"W-what?!"

"Yeah, we've had to switch gyms, skip town, and assume new identities more times than I can count. I don't even remember my real name, do you know that?"

"My name is Tony."

"The FBI is still after him. I think it's all the steroids he takes that makes him such an insanely jealous and violent man. Oh, wait, here he comes now. Hey, baby, over here!"

Jess started waving to Josh as he entered the pool area wearing his swim trunks.

"Hey, Jess. Who's your new friend? Hi, I'm Josh." He said warmly, walking down to where Jess and Tony were swimming.

Tony started immediately paddling as fast as he could in the opposite direction. "I'm no one! I wasn't talking to her! Please don't cave in my skull!"

Josh watched in confusion as Tony sped off into the showers without sparing passing glance behind him. Jess was doing her best to choke back her laughter.

"What was that about?" Josh asked.

"Oh, I think he had the runs."

Jess casually paddled up to the edge of the pool where Josh was standing.

"Oh. Gross."

He extended his hand to Jess. She grabbed it with both arms and Josh effortlessly lifted her out of the pool. Water was cascading off of her every curve on the platinum swimsuit that clung tightly to her body. When the one-piece got wet, it looked like parts of her naked body were painted silver. From far away, it looked like someone dipped her in liquid quicksilver.

Josh pulled her up and out of the pool as if her had just caught a prize-winning fish, lifting her body up into the air for a moment before hugging her close.

Jess squealed with delight as he tossed her around.

"How was your workout, baby?"

"Great." He wrapped his arm around her back and squeezed up against him. "Did I ever tell you how much I love the way that swimsuit looks on you? I feel like I just caught a silver mermaid."

Jess giggled her throaty little chuckle.

"I'll grant you just one wish for catching this cute little fish."

Josh flashed her a handsome smile, the one that Jess found absolutely irresistible.

Then, to her complete and utter surprise, Josh started singing.

"To catch a mermaid as nice as this, all I could hope for is a single kiss." He held her tight and pressed his lips to hers. "But now that I've tasted this mermaids lips, my wish would be bliss if I could get some of this."

He swept his hand down her back and pinched her booty, giving it a little pat. Jess jumped in surprise, then a wicked grin grew across her face.

She leaned into his chest and whispered in his ear. "Wish granted, my fisherman."

Jess took him by the hand. Together, their feet pitter pattered across the wet pool deck and over to the spa. The heat and jets were set of a timer on a dial, one which Jess had already pre-heated for them while she waited.

Jess couldn't help but giggle a little when she saw the tent in Josh's swim trunks. She rolled her eyes.

He's all worked up already... Perfect.

Jess sighed in relief as she eased her body into the bubbling hot water of the spa. Josh attempted to do the same, but stopped at only the top step inside the water.

"Shit! That's hot!" He yelped.

"Heehee, it's a hot tub, silly." Jess said sitting on the concrete with her feet dangling inside the water.

Josh let out a long lungful of air, "Ahhh... you know, it's actually pretty soothing once you get used to the initial shock of sitting in a pot of boiling fucking stew." He said as he treaded water over to the spot where Jess sat.

"I'm sure that's what all of the lobsters say to themselves up until they get boiled alive. Look! You're sweating, and you skin is all red like a lobster!"

"What? That's from working out. I never stopped sweating. Remember the steam rooms?"

After a good workout, his chiseled features became even more prominent. Jess painted his body with her gaze, taking in every building, rock solid muscle group as he moved around in the hot tub. Or, at least the ones that were still above water.

His skin was a shade more red than normal, and she did notice all of the sweat glistening on his chest, biceps, and his the corded muscles of his abs.

She remembered a lot from the steam room, but until he pointed out that his skin was equally pink and sweaty, that was one detail that eluded her.

"I think I may have overdid it. Mermaids don't like to boil." She said, then leaned over to fiddle with the temperature control dials.

Josh seized the opportunity while she was distracted. He picked Jess up by the waist and pulled her into the water. She screamed as if she was being eaten by sharks.

"Hot! Hot! Hot!" Jess shrieked, much to the delight of Josh.

"That's why they call it a hot tub, silly." He said in his best Jess impersonation.

"Ugh! I do *not* sound like that!" She started climbing out of the spa.

But Josh had other plans.

"Let's see what boiled mermaid tastes like."

In one fluid motion, Josh lifted he to the edge of the spa, turned her to face him, spread her legs wide apart, then peeled her swimsuit to the side to expose her smooth pink pussy.

Using one hand to keep her legs apart and the other to pull her swimsuit to the side, Josh attached her cunt with his mouth as if it were going to be his last meal on earth.

Jess was taken by surprise. It all happened so suddenly. She arched her back and wobbled a bit on the deck of the spa, but after a moment regained her balance by clinging onto Josh's head between her legs.

"Ja-Josh! Ahh! Stop it." She protested but made no attempt to get him to stop. She wasn't sure she wanted him to stop.

"Mm... Mm, God, you taste so good."

She wasn't sure if she was getting wet or if it was just Josh slobbering all over her pussy.

Probably a combination of the two.

Then Josh bit her right on the clit.

"Ow! Watch it, jerk! That hurt!" she said and splashed him in the face.

"I told you I wanted to see what boiled mermaid tastes like." He playfully bit her inner thigh then splashed her back.

"Taste this!"

Jess jumped into the water next to him, splashing all over in the process. As soon as Jess emerged from the water, Josh let out a flurry of splashes in Jess's face.

Before Jess knew what was going on, the two were engaged in a splash fight in the gym hot tub. The two were laughing, splashing, and playing like children as they sent warm water outside of the spa wetting all of the surrounding concrete.

Their water war only ended when Josh got tired of having chlorinated water shot directly into his red eyes, so he grabbed hold of both Jess arms and pinned her to one side of the hot tub so that she couldn't move. It didn't stop her from thrashing around like a fish.

Or in her case, like a silver mermaid.

Josh pulled her hair back and forced his mouth onto hers, parting her lips with his wet and hungry tongue. She could feel his hardness between his legs pressing up against her.

Josh let go of one of her hands pushed the wet strips of black hair out of her face. He held his hand against her neck as their foreheads touched. They were so close that their noses touched as they stared deeply into each other's eyes

It's just him and me. Josh and Jess forever and always.

As she stared into his eyes, Jess bit her bottom lip with yearning. Underwater, she wrapped her legs around his waist.

"I love you." The words barely squeaked out of her perfectly pink lips.

Josh held her with hands just underneath her breasts, his fierce, animalistic eyes wild with desire. He nodded to her.

"I want you." He growled.

After being teased and tempted all day, after an hour of throwing heavy shit around the gym, after thinking and fantasizing about his girlfriend doing dirty, nasty things to him all day long, and after seeing her in that *irresistible* bathing suit, Josh's testosterone was at an all time high.

Jess hated to admit it, but he *scared* her when he got like this. When he got that look in his eye. Like her would burning a city down just to get to her.

Jess knew his sex drive was at its apex. His steel erection unbudging flat against Jess's belly, teasing her with it. It felt so big pressed against her stomach like that. It was moments like that that she felt crazy for wanting it inside of her so badly.

He stood there, holding her, staring at her fiercely, eyes burning, cock twitching.

What is he waiting for?

"Yeah." It was barely a whisper.

She gave a small nod, then spun around and bent over the edge of the spa. She poked her butt out into Josh's hips and his thick cock slid between her big, round ass cheeks.

Josh raked his fingertips down Jess's back until he got to her booty, giving it a hard *smack*. Her ass was half above and half below water, buoyant like a buoy. Without hand, he pulled the fabric covering her booty out of the way while unclasping the front of his swim trunks with the other.

Josh's massively hard erection sprung free out of the from of his swim trunks immediately. His steel shaft sat vertically between Jess's cheeks.

Then Jess's swimsuit had fallen back into place, covering her ass entirely.

Oh, God, stop teasing me.

Josh pulled on the backside of her swimsuit again, but as soon as he let go it immediately fell right back into place, covering her cheeks.

As nice as her designer one-piece swimsuit was, it was not a thong back bottom swimsuit. The fabric in the back covered her entire ass, save for showing off a little of each cheek on the sides. While it made her ass look very nice and firm and possibly even sexier, if that were somehow possible, the thin silver sheen still covered a majority of her butt.

"Jess, I don't want to ruin your beautiful, expensive swimsuit." Josh said as soon as he realized that the fabric in the back would be the only real barrier between them and possibly the best anal sex of her life.

Jess was torn. She very much liked the swimsuit, but part of her wasted to tell him to rip it off of her already and be done with it. More than anything, she liked the way that her boyfriend reacted whenever he saw her wearing it, and for that reason, she would do her best to preserve the things.

Jess quickly ran through all of her options and made an instant judgement call.

"Alright." She said calmly.

Jess looked around the vacant swimming pool area. Their voices echoed in the indoor pool area of the gym. They were the only ones there.

"Alright, baby. Hang tight."

Jess took a big breath, then disappeared underwater. Josh had no idea what to expect as he stood there in the scalding hot water of the gym spa, hard dick in hand, watching the bubbles rise above Jess's head.

When Jess finally emerged, she took a big gasping breath of air. In her hand, she held her silver swimsuit. It was dripping with chlorinated water but neatly folded. She set her swimsuit on the deck of the spa next to the temperature dial.

Josh knew she was naked, but Jess would only come neck-high out of the water. She did not seem prepared to expose more skin than necessary. Getting fully naked in the public gym spa was a bold move, but it solved their swimsuit conundrum.

"As much as I know you like that swimsuit, I'll preserve it's integrity for the time being." She said and gave him a little wink.

Josh chucked, wrapping his arms around her shoulders as he slinked down to be at eye level with her. He pulled her close for a kiss, but as she drew near, Jess disappeared underwater.

He suddenly felt her tiny hands wrapped around his dick. The her lips, tongue, and mouth performing an underwater blowjob.

While Jess had him distracted, her untied his swim trunked and tugged them down. They came off smoothly and without a fight. He readily stepped out of his swim trunks, surrendering to his girlfriend's wishes.

If she had to be naked, they would both be naked in the hot tub at the same time.

Josh was again surprised that she had his swim trunks neatly folded by the time she came back above water.

"I like this even better." He said, smiling a smug smirk.

Jess had a lustful look in her vibrant green eyes as she returned a lascivious smile. Even if neither of them knew what would happen next, they both looked like they had everything planned out.

Jess sprang out of the water to where her swimsuit was laying and placed Josh's folded up trunks next to her own bathing suit. Water dripped from her naked body to the gray concrete floor. She pushed her hands to the edge of the spa, her boobs dangling and dripping, like a penguin jumping out of the arctic sea.

Josh seized the opportunity. He came up behind her and slapped a hand on either side of her ass, parting her cheeks while his tongue darted in and out of her hole. Jess started giggling at the new sensation at first. As Josh began to eat her ass more intensely, her laughs turned to louder and louder moans.

It was the game of "Let's See How Horny We Can Make Josh" from the car all over again.

Only this time, Josh was in on it.

Jess felt very exposed. She was laying out naked in the middle of the gym with her boyfriend eating her ass in the spa. Who was also naked.

As much as she was enjoying the kinky thrill of being out in the open where literally anyone could walk in and see her naked at any moment, her heart jumped with joy when Josh stood up and wedged the tip of his hard cock into the tiny asshole, made slick with his tongue kisses.

It took some effort on Josh's side to get it all the way in, but he was determined.

"Ah, fuck! Yes, put it in my ass. Oh fuck yes, your dick feels so. Fucking. Good! God, I've been waiting for this all fucking day."

Her cries of unadulterated anal pleasure echoed loudly off the walls of the indoor pool area. Jess was content to lay flat on her stomach, pushing up out of the spa with the bottom of her legs still in the water, half in, half out.

Her tits bounced up and down rhythmically as Josh ran the length of his cock in and out of her ass. Josh leaned against her back and from behind grabbed her boobs in both his hands, then let himself fall backwards into the hot tub, taking Jess along with him.

Jess let out a scream of unexpected surprise and delight. Now the two were floating on their backs with Jess on top and Josh fucking her in the ass from below.

She kept trying to grab hold of the edge of the spa to pull herself out, but Josh thought it would be more fun for them to float together in the center of the water. He grappled with her in the water, fucking her while preventing any attempts of hers to get ashore.

Weightless and horizontal with nothing to support them than the water beneath them, Josh clung to her body while Jess splashed around helplessly. After a few minutes of having her ass pounded in the middle of the spa, Jess realized that Josh was right – this was more fun.

Josh was surprised that he was able to achieve more leverage underwater than he was halfway submerged. While he couldn't pull off the fast jackhammer thrusts that he sometimes utilized when fucking his girlfriend silly, he was able to find a perfectly consistent pace that allowed him to give her the full length of his cock from tip to hips.

Once Jess stopped fighting against him, she found that she could truly give in to the pleasure. Boundless anal pleasure that only kept increasing each time he penetrated her juicy ass.

Josh loved the fact that he was able to float there weightlessly while fucking Jess in the ass and at the same time playing with her buoyant tits. He occasionally kicked off of the shallow end of the spa to keep them above water, but it did not impede their ass fucking one bit.

With every thrust, he pulled back on her chest to give himself more power as he drive his hard cock between her firm cheeks. Jess enjoyed the feeling of Josh playing with her nipples at the same time, pinching, caressing, and brushing them between his fingers above water as they floated.

Jess was surprised that she was enjoying getting fucked in the ass in the hot tub as much as she was, considering that the only lube they were using was the residuals of Josh's saliva around her ass and the bacteria-ridden spa water.

Her hands were free to play with herself as she pleased. Jess kicked her feet, trying to float perfectly horizontal as she rubbed her clit.

But all of that changed with a single chance encounter from one of the hot tub jets.

"Whoa-mi-gawd!" Jess cried out as one of the strongest jets in the spa scored a direct hit on her clitoris. "Baby, come over here, in front of this Jet."

She guided him as he continued to relentlessly pound her behind. Jess had to stand up a bit to position her clit just so. Josh still had a firm grasp on both of her tits as she stood so that only her waist and below were submerged in water.

Now, with every thrust, Josh sent a splash of water onto the concrete deck, wetting their swimsuits anew. But that didn't matter to either of them.

"Holy fuck, babe, how are you doing that?"

"It's this jet." Jess said as she tried to edge even closer to the source of pleasure.

I guess he can feel it, too, Jess thought.

Jess got close enough to the side of the spa where she could effectively hump the strong stream of water shooting out from one of the jets. Josh maintained his grip, fucking her ass rhythmically.

"OH fu-huh-huck!" she moaned.

"Oh my God, keep doing that shit." Josh screamed as he fucked her more ravenously than before.

In a very uncharacteristic move, Josh started moaning louder than she was. And Jess knew exactly what that meant.

"Oh yeah, fuck my little ass, baby. Oh, baby, oh fuck that feels so good. So good. Oh, fuuuuck yessss, hooooyeeeeah! Hooyeah! Hooyeah! Umiguh!"

With the jet now on full blast hitting Jess directly on her clit, she felt like she was going to explode. It was *too much* pleasure for her all at once. It felt *too* good. She wiggled and writhed and spasmed around in the spa as she approached rapture.

Meanwhile, Josh was experiencing something that he had never experienced before during anal sex with his girlfriend. The pressure of the water against Jess's clit caused her asshole to rapidly clench and unclench around Josh's cock in time with his thrusts.

Each time he slid his dick into her tight little ass, she clench. Then when he withdrew, she unclenched. Each time Josh penetrated her ass he brushed up against her G-spot.

They were in perfect sync with one another – and neither Jess nor Josh realized what she was doing.

In, clench, out, unclench, in, clench, out, unclench.

The combined sensation felt so amazingly wonderous that Josh and Jess came at the exact same moment in an explosion of ecstasy.

Josh let go of her tits so her could rake his hands all up and down Jess's naked body, from her chest to her thighs, stopping only to squeeze her ass cheeks as he continued to cum inside her.

Jess's entire body was spasming. She flailed about the spa, splashing water every which way as she did whatever she could to maintain contact with her pussy on the powerful jet.

If anyone would happen to walk into the gym's indoor pool at that very second, it would have looked like the two of them were both having a seizure in the spa instead of what it really was – the best anal orgasm the two of them have ever had together.

Fortunately, it was Monday afternoon and the gym was sparsely populated. There were so few people at the gym that the couple didn't even notice the several people who entered the pool area, saw them fucking in the spa, then immediately back out the way they came.

Once Jess involuntarily clenching her ass around Josh's dick, he pulled out. Jess held all of his cum inside her ass as a courtesy to the gym's custodian.

When they were done, Josh dressed quickly. He couldn't seem to get his erection to go away, though. His mind was still on how hot it was fucking in the gym and how fucking good Jess's ass felt.

It also didn't help that his extremely hot girlfriend was still naked right in front of him. He practically had to pry Jess off of the jet and dress her to get her back in her swimsuit.

"We need to get a hot tub." Jess said as Josh pulled the straps of her swimsuit up over her shoulders.

"I was thinking exactly the same thing."

The two dried using a single towel. While Jess was wringing the water out of her hair, she spotted the erection in Josh's swim trunks and smirked.

"You're still horny?"

Josh nodded cooly. "I'm still very horny. I mean, that was hot and all, but I want more."

The way he was looking at her, he might as well have been caressing her voluptuous curves.

"I can still feel your war, cum in my ass, and you're telling me you're still horny? Is it the swimsuit?" She asked, striking a pose.

"Fuck the swimsuit, it's you I want. And I'm not leaving until I get a second helping."

Jess stared at the tent in his swim shorts. He made no effort to conceal it, even as more people entered the swimming pool area.

"I can see that." She said as she finished drying off. "Well, I need a shower to wash off all this chlorine water. I wouldn't mind visiting a certain shower stall in the men's locker room one more time."

Before she even finished talking, Josh swept her off her feet. He carried her in his arms like a newlywed would carry his wife over the threshold of the bedroom on their honeymoon.

He carried her directly into the men's locker room and straight into the showers without stopping to see if anyone was looking at them.

At this point in their exhibitionist expedition, Josh's strategy had evolved into something he called "Ignore and Explore", where he ignored everyone else around them and explored his girlfriend's body. And so far, this new tactic was working swimmingly for both of them.

With the one exception where they had to run from the police.

Josh didn't set her down until they reached the very back shower stall, the one that Jess was already intimately familiar with. As soon as her toes hit the ground, she hit the hot water button sending a wave a slightly less chlorinated water that the spa pouring over both of them.

Josh put his mouth on her neck as he began peeling Jess's silver swimsuit off of her.

Jess laughed. "What was even the point of me putting this on?" she asked once Josh had already pulled it over her boobs and had her nipple in his mouth.

"So I could take it off of you." He answered in between flicking the tip of his tongue against her hard nipples.

She laughed a ticklish laugh.

"I'm happy to do it." Jess hit the hot water button again, drenching them while she undressed the rest of the way.

Josh unleashed the steel lance between his legs. She tried to bend over so she could taste it, but he beat her to it.

No sooner had he peeled off the rest of her one-piece from her body, dropping it between her ankles, was he on his knees in the shower between her legs.

Josh lifted up one of Jess's legs and set it on his shoulder. Her other foot lay flat on the shower floor. And Josh's face wedged deep between her legs. His tongue caressed her vagina, inside and out, before moving back to her ass.

"Ew, I think I taste my cum in your ass."

Jess giggled with delight. "Well, don't eat it all up! Save some for me!"

Josh chucked. "I love it when you act like a little slut."

Who's acting?

Josh, instead, moved his nomadic tongue to her clitoris, where he started lapping up her pussy like a thirsty dog.

"Mmm... You've got nothing on that hot tub jet, but it ain't bad."

"You want me to stop?" Josh looked up at her, one leg still perched over his shoulder.

"Fuck no. I didn't say stop licking." She pushed his head back between her legs, guiding his tongue with one hand on the back of his head.

"Ahh... oh, Josh... I would like to redeem my one free orgasm, please."

Josh came up for air.

"What? Right now? But my dick-"

She forced his face back onto her pussy.

"Yes, right now. Fuck your dick."

Josh mumbled something with a mouth full of pussy.

"Mphm mph hmmhm."

But Jess had a firm grip on the back of his head and would not let go. She pulled him deeper in between her legs and Josh attached his mouth around her little clit like a sucker fish.

Jess's back was against the wall. With her other hand she was playing with her wet breasts, squeezing them and rubbing on her nipples, one and then the other.

"Fuck, Josh, can't you lick any faster? Maybe I'll make that hot tub my new boyfriend – ah, fuck, right there! Just like that! Hmm, oh my god, yes. Stick a fucking finger in my ass like a gentleman, Josh. Oh, fuck, yes. Make it two fingers. Ooh, just like that. Now finger my fucking asshole so I can cum on your face. Ahh! Yes! Right there! Don't stop, don't you fucking stop! I can feel it. Oh God, here it comes... I'm gonna cum!"

With Josh eating her pussy and playing with her ass, using his own cum from before as lube, he was able to get Jess to squirt when she came. Jess sprinkled Josh's mouth and chin with her cum as she started squirting, but after numerous and repeated orgasms that day she felt depleted.

"I must admit, I was expecting a little more. But I always enjoy watching you take a face full of my cum."

Jess swung her leg back over Josh's shoulder so that she had both feet firmly planted on the shower floor, leaving Josh to lick Jess's pussy juice from his face.

"I must admit, I enjoy taking a face full of your squirt as much as you love giving it."

Jess laughed. "I love it when you act like a little slut."

"To be honest, I think we both left a lot of our combined cum in the spa. We really did a number on that jacuzzi. They'll need to drain that shit for sure because of us."

Jess's eyes rolled to the back of her head. "God, I came so hard in the spa! I feel like my pussy was its own jet for minute because of how much I was probably squirting underwater."

"Shall we try for three? The hat trick?"

Jess hesitated. "As much as I want to, and trust me, I *really* want to, I don't think it's a good idea without any lube."

Jess looked crestfallen that the idea that she would not be getting fucked in the ass for the remainder of the day.

"Oh, is that all?" Josh said as he reached for his swim trunks.

He reached unto a zipper pocket in his swim shorts and pulled out a tiny travel-sized bottle of coconut oil, holding it up triumphantly. Jess's mouth hit the floor the moment she saw it.

"Have you had that in there the entire time?"

"Well, you didn't want to carry it in your purse, so..."

"And it never occurred to you once to pull it out until right now?"

"You never asked. Not specifically."

"That's not... You should have... You know what? Just shut the fuck up and lube up my asshole, kay?"

Josh popped off the top of the bottle and squirt a fair amount of oil on his hands. Jess turned around to face the wall. She laid her hands flat against the tile wall as she bent forward at the waist, spreading her legs so that Josh could do as instructed.

She combed her wet hair to one side as she looked back at him over her shoulder, biting her lower lip and waiting patiently. Josh ran a few lubed up fingers between her legs and up her ass crack.

"Ooh! It's nice and warm! Mm, I like that."

As Josh slathered a palm full of coconut oil all along his shaft, Jess hit the hot water button on the shower again. She laughed playfully as Josh got hit with a face full of warm water.

Josh was not expecting it. The surprise from a face full of water caused the bottle of coconut oil to slip from his grasp. When it hit the shower floor, it exploded all over their legs, soaking them both with coconut oil from the waist down.

Jess froze as if someone had just throw a drink in her face. Only she froze with her ass popped out and legs spread shoulder width apart. As she stared, frozen with surprise, looking at josh with her mouth wide open, it gave him the perfect opportunity to slide his cock dripping with lube into Jess's ass.

This, too, caught her off guard. Because now, after fucking in the dingy hot tub, she forgot just how amazing it felt to get fucking in the ass when she was properly lubed up.

Aquatic clitoral stimulation aside, this felt so much better than when he was fucking her ass in the hot tub earlier.

She was not very confident that she could do that thing with her ass that Josh seemed to enjoy so much. The rapid clenching and unclenching of her ass around his cock was more of an uncontrollable spasm brought on by humping the hot tub jet than anything else, although it felt just as good for her as it did for him.

But that didn't mean that she couldn't clench her lubed up ass around his monstrous cock at will, of course.

"Holy fuck, babe, how are you doing that?"

"Yeah? You like that?" she said, tightening her booty around her boyfriend's dick.

"Oh my God, it feels incredible."

He leaned forward to grab a handful of her perky, bouncing tits. It was a move that he typically liked doing, Jess knew, when he was just about ready to cum.

"Nooo, baby, are you going to cum already? I want you to fuck my ass for a little bit."

"I just can't help it. It feels so good."

"Then no special treat for you." She stopped clenching around his slick cock and batted his hands away from her breasts.

"Oh? You want to get fucked in the ass for a bit, huh? You like feeling this big dick in your ass?" He said in a low growl.

Josh slapped her glistening ass cheek, pushing it forward and prying her cheeks further apart for he could drive his slippery cock deeper in her ass. He leaned forward, pressing his muscled chest up against her back.

Josh grabbed the back of Jess's hands and held them above her head, then started to thrust his hips twice as fast. Jess had to look back over her shoulder to watch. She loved watching him fuck her from behind

Josh had both her hands pinned together held above her head. He slid his shaft in and out between her legs, hips slapping against her cheeks with every thrust. Her large natural tits bounced as he pound her from behind, sending droplets of water flying off of both their bodies.

"Yeah? You like that? How does this big dick feel sliding in and out of that little ass?"

"Aw, fuck, babe it feels so good. Fuck, fuck, fuck, oh, just like that. Yeah, yeah, yeah."

"God, I love watching your fucking tits bounce while I fuck you from behind. Fuck, my cock feels so good in your ass."

"Oh, I love it. Don't stop, don't stop, I'm going to *cum!*"

The faster thrusts helped Jess climax faster, but then again, so did rubbing her pussy the entire time he was fucking her. Jess lifted a leg awkwardly, bending over as she desperately tried to get his dick to rub up against her G-spot like he did in the hot tub.

After a minute of contorting and writhing her body against his hard, grinding thrusts, at long last he came into contact with Jess's G-spot. Or at least she thought he did, but at that point, the floodgates were already open.

The force with which Jess squirted downward made it seem like her water broke if she were pregnant. It was as if someone hit *her* hot water button and sent cum shooting down her legs. Even amid the water of the shower pouring over them it was noticeable.

As Jess started to cum all over the locker room shower floor, she clenched her asshole tightly around Josh's cock until she could feel him start to cum in her ass.

Then, something Jess didn't expect happened.

"Whoa! Oh my God, ho-mi-gah, omiguh!"

She felt compelled to slap her clit with unexpected urgency. Every muscle in her face bunched up as she came a second time. Then a third.

After that, things got a little blurry.

Her heart danced at the wonderous and delightful feeling of Josh shotgunning load after load of hot cum deep in her ass. She felt all of it, and each juicy thrust brought an increasing wave of ecstasy. Each wet, gushing orgasm was triggered by the last.

Jess wasn't sure if the warm globs of fluid trickling down her thighs were Josh's cum, or her own cum or coconut oil, or something else entirely.

So many sensations. So much stimulation. She was sweating. Fuck. She was *sweating*.

Josh pulled out and her legs collapsed from underneath her.

"Jess!"

Josh caught her. With his head underneath her shoulder, he helped her to her stand, but her legs still couldn't support her weight.

His erection was instantly gone when he saw she was in distress. Josh's flaccid cock still dripped thick with semen and lube.

"What's wrong?" He asked with worry in his voice.

In response, she just smiled dopily.

"I think it's time to get out of here before-"

"But you haven't even washed my back yet." She said softly, exhausted.

Josh cracked a smile. "I didn't bring any soap."

"Alright. Alright. Just let me... Just..."

Jess collapsed in his arms and everything went black.

CHAPTER 33

Day 7 – Museum

"If we just came from the gym, why do I feel like I'm getting another workout." Jess wheezed and whined during the steep uphill walk to Griffith Observatory.

"It's not that bad. Besides, this is the only way up with the parking lot overflowing. You used to like going for walks in Griffith Park."

"That was when we first started dating and I would follow you to the ends of the earth back then."

"We're still dating and you'd still follow me to the ends of the earth."

"I would. But only if it's downhill."

"The how would we get back, miss smarty-pants?"

"Uber." Jess offered, drawing jagged breaths of air. Then, after a few more steps, a smile speared on her face. "Do you remember the time we were trying to find the Hollywood sign and got lost in the park?"

Josh erupted into laughter. "And then we accidently broke into that person's back yard and starting having sex on their trampoline?"

"We were so lost! I wouldn't be able to find out way back there if I tried."

"Base, If I'm being honest, I was hard the entire drive down here thinking about that."

Jess giggled, her mood suddenly taking a full 180.

"Babe, you've been hard, like, all day long!"

"What can I say? I'm excited to finally be able to complete the Bingo card."

"The final square in seven days!" She pumped her fist.

"The final square in seven days." He nodded. "Though, I'm not sure if the observatory counts as a museum. Maybe we should go bang at LACMA after this. Just to be safe."

"Oh, don't you even start. The Griffith Observatory is at least 51% museum. Remember that cool tesla coil they have?"

"The one that makes my hair stand on end. How could I forget."

"And the asteroid simulator where you get to create a meteor that dense enough to destroy the earth. That one is my favorite."

"I know. You spent almost an hour there last time we were here. Maybe you can just stand there making meteors while I fuck you."

"Honestly, I probably wouldn't even notice if you did. But if it gets us out of here and back home, I'm down for that."

"Well, I'm sure someone would notice."

They both laughed as the two huffed and puffed walking up the hill.

"Hey. Can we talk about what happened at the gym?"

"Can we not?"

"You passed out on me. I was scared shitless."

"Oh, relax. I pass out all the time."

"You do? When?"

"Every night when I go to bed, silly."

"Jess…"

"I said I don't want to talk about it."

They continued walking in awkward silence as they crested the Griffith hilltop. The golden domed building holding the world's largest telescopes sat across a field of green grass like a majestic palace towering over Los Angeles.

The observatory was shockingly populated for a Monday evening. And it wasn't long before they found out why.

"What does that banner say?" Jess asked, squinting.

"It says it's time to update your contact lens prescription." Jess punched Josh in the shoulder. "It says tonight there is a full moon party at the observatory." He amended.

Jess jumped and gave Josh a startled look.

"No, babe, I'm sure it has nothing to do with werewolves." Josh rolled his eyes.

She tugged on his arm in the direction of the car. "But who else would celebrate a full moon other than werewolves?" there was a tinge of fear in her voice.

Josh gave her a pacifying look, then waved at the building in front of them.

"An observatory."

Jess looked around nervously. "What were you saying about this not being a real museum? Let's go to LACMA."

There were people standing all over the observatory lawn. Some looking through little telescopes, others just standing around chatting.

Josh practically had to drag Jess towards the big domed building, drawing the attention of everyone.

"I changed my mind. I don't care about Bingo anymore!" She cried, trying to fight him off.

"Jess..." he pulled her along, giving her a no-nonsense look. "Alright, if there are any werewolves, I will protect you, alright?"

Her eyes darted around suspiciously. "Promise?"

"Promise." He nodded.

That gave her little relief, but she went along with him all the same.

Together, they proceeded into the main entrance of the Griffith Observatory and into the actual museum area. They meandered around a bit, enjoying all of the magical sights that the observatory had to offer. Soon they got so caught up in the beauty of the night and all of the different displays and attractions depicting the planets in our galaxy that they nearly forgot about their main purpose coming there.

After grabbing a quick bite at the observatory restaurant, the two wandered around a bit more, enjoying the many sights of the distant city skyline, the famous Hollywood sign – which no longer looked far off – and other iconic Los Angeles landmarks.

It was a very romantic evening, but Jess grew weary as the sun hung low in the sky.

And the full moon rose, lighting up the night sky.

"Hey, Josh?"

"Yes, my love?"

"Whatever happened to that big telescope?"

"What do you mean? It's in one of the domes."

"I was referring to the telescope between your legs."

"Oh, it's put away for now. I've been waiting for the right time to pull it out. But there are a lot more people out here than I expected."

"I know, babe. But this evening has been really romantic and I want to have sex on the terrace overlooking the city." She said sweetly.

"Outside? Under the full moon? What if a werewolf shows up?" he teased.

"Then I have my man to protect me." she slid her arms around his waist, pulling him into a hug. As she held her head against his chest, she could hear his heart beating in his slowly. She could feel the rise and fall of his breath.

"Kiss me." She whispered to him.

Josh put his hand under her chin, lifting her face as he lowered his until their lips met. Jess moaned softly into his mouth. It seemed like an eternity since he last kissed her. Or at least, since he last kissed her the way that he was kissing her right now.

She tightened the cinch of her arms around his back, pulling him closer. She wanted to savor his kiss under the full moon.

It could be our last, if a werewolf does show up.

Jess lowered herself off of her tippy toes and opened her eyes. Josh's chiseled, handsome face was staring back at her. He had a fierce look in his eyes. Primal, even.

"I love you." He said as he cupped the side of her face.

"Love you, more." She said, kissing the stubble on his chin.

Their kiss was instantly seductive, intrinsically sensual, and intimately sexual. With their lips pressed together, their tongues danced outside one another's mouths while a cool breeze passed by.

Suddenly, a feeling of warmth flooded Jess's head. It started in her brain, then moved down her body with tendrils of heat pulsing within. As she felt the glowing heat move to her endogenous zones, she became more and more turned on.

Her lips warmed, then her nipples hardened and pressed through Jess's shirt into Josh's chest where he could surely feel them. Down into the pit of her stomach, the warm sensation traveled until finally it reached her loins.

Her mouth opened wider. Her tongue moved faster, more eager. She moaned loudly into Josh's mouth as the kiss went on. Josh slid his hands down her backside, one hand on the small of her back, the other cupping her bottom.

He gave her ass the littlest squeeze and she gasped a moan in response.

It's just us. Only me and him. Him and me.

Jess repeated her mantra again and again in her head. It helped her block out the many faces she knew were watching them. She repeated this in her head until it felt like her body was on fire and she could stand it no more.

Jess leapt up into his arms, wrapping her legs around Josh's waist. This took Josh by surprise, but they didn't break their kiss for even a second.

Josh looked as though he was experiencing the same full-body warming sensation that Jess was going through. He swept both hands underneath her bottom to support her weight.

Jess was almost certain that she heard one of the bystanders say, "Aww, look at them. So cute."

But that was before she started humping her boyfriend as he held her in his arms.

She couldn't help it. She started grinding her hips against his rock hard stomach as they continued making out. She hugged him with one arm while she played ran her fingers through the back of his head with the other.

And then a middle-aged woman wearing a three-piece suit appeared next to them and started making a coughing sound that wasn't actually a cough.

They ignored her at first until she did it several more times, each louder than the last. And then reality started crashing down around Jess.

She was suddenly aware of all the footsteps of other people scattered around the terrace. She was aware of the dozens of pairs of eyes traced on her and Josh. She was aware of the security guard closing in on them.

Jess hopped off of her boyfriend and back on solid ground. She pulled on the clothes, straightening them out nervously. The security guard gave them a look that said *Seriously? At the Griffith?*

Jess shrugged and gave her a look that said *What? Astronomy turns me on.*

Satisfied that the couple were behaving themselves for now, the female security guard left it at that and wordlessly walked away.

Jess looked up at Josh and frowned.

Josh returned a smile a said simply, "Idea."

"Good one?" Jess asked.

"No." he replied. "Not at all."

"I'm in."

He gave her a peck on the lips. "Follow my lead."

Jess gave him an optimistic smile and little nod, falling in behind him as Josh moved swiftly to the terrace entrance. He weaved in between tourists tall strangers to get to the upper level that lead to a room containing one of the observatories enormous telescopes.

Jess watched as Josh picked up a sign that read "Open" and flipped it over so that it said "Closed".

This is his big idea?

Josh cupped his hands to his mouth and yelled out, "Ladies and gentleman, thank you for coming to the Griffith Observatory. Unfortunately, the telescope room will be closed for maintenance for the rest of the evening. I need everyone out immediately. Thank you, have a nice day." He said in his loudest projection voice.

Then, incredibly enough, it actually *worked*.

Everyone in the telescope room started leaving all at once. Jess made herself useful by corralling people off of the terrace, repeating the phrase, "Thank you for coming. Goodbye. Thank you for coming. Be safe. Thank you for coming..."

A few seconds later, it was only Jess and Josh in the room. They had single handedly evacuated Griffith Observatory. Or, at least, part of it.

And probably only for a short period of time before that security guard figures out what is going on and comes for us, so...

"Holy shit. Did... that just work?" Josh was in disbelief.

Jess shrugged. "It was your idea."

"Yeah, but I didn't expect it to actually work."

"I am so fucking attracted to you right now. Don't ruin it."

She ran at him as fast as she could, like a linebacker ready to make a tackle. Josh just stood there with arms extended.

Jess leapt through the air. When Josh caught her, she immediately pulled off his shirt and smothered him with kisses.

"Josh, baby, I don't know how much time we have but I want you to take me right now." She said between a flurry of kisses.

Josh carried her to the window in the telescope room so that they could overlook the city skyline. The sky just started to tinge an orange-yellow hue.

This would be the second time we make love watching the sunset over the downtown L.A. skyline... this week.

Though the sun was still up, the full moon shone brightly behind the skyscrapers of downtown, illuminating everything with its eerie moonlight glow. The colors in the sky were rapidly shifting as the sun sank to the east, on the other side of the observatory.

Josh pried her off of his body and set her down on the ledge of the window. Josh wasted to time by violently yanking Jess's stretchy black yoga pants down over her bubble butt and down to her ankles. She let out a little whimper of surprise as he did.

Seeing his aggression and passion really turned her on. Jess turned around to look out the window, bending forward slightly at the waist and spreading her legs. She reached back and spread her cheeks to show her boyfriend just how turned on she really was.

Josh gave her booty one hard *smack*, leaving a big pink handprint in its wake. At the same time, her dropped his own shorts to his ankles, freeing his massive erect cock.

Josh slapped her hands away, then squeezed her ass cheeks open himself so he could see the tight little holes that his underneath. He bent down and stuck his face right in her ass, licking her from clit to asshole, then back.

We don't have time for this... Oh, but it feels so good!

Jess was not lying when she said that she was so fucking attracted to Josh right now. When he lapped up her juices, he found her pussy was dripping with eager wetness. Then, as a parting gift, he rimmed her asshole, seeing just how far he could wiggle his deft tongue inside of her. Jess's entire body shuddered at the pleasant feeling.

At last, Josh finally let go and her ass cheeks fell back into place. He big, bubbly butt completely concealed her wet holes, but Josh knew exactly where to push his dick in to penetrate Jess's moist pussy lips.

She felt wet, warm, and tight around his cock as he entered her. It felt heavenly, as Josh would surely agree.

"Yeah, fuck the shit out of my pussy, baby. Oh, God, I need this. Oh, fuck me, fuck me, fuck me."

"Shh!"

"Did... Did you just shush me?"

"We don't know when they'll be back, right? Be quiet and let me fuck you."

Josh slid his hands over her flat stomach and under her shirt so he could feel her perfect tits and play with her little nipples as he fucked her.

"Ooh, do more of that." Jess cooed.

He pinched and squeezed her nipples while fucking her from behind, hips pounding into her juicy ass.

Then Jess made a pivotal decision that would change their dynamic.

"I want to look at your face while you fuck me."

"... What?"

"I want to turn around and look you in the face while you fuck me. And I want you to suck on my titties. Girls like that, you know."

"Uh... Okay?"

He pulled out and Jess turned around, reluctantly sitting her bare ass of the dusty, grimey window seal of the observatory telescope tower.

Ew, gross, gross, gross...

"Actually... Just pick me up."

"Wait, what's that now?"

"Pick me up and fuck me. Like, when you're holding me? Josh, we've done this before."

"I know. It's just... are you sure?"

"Yes. No. I don't know. Just hurry."

"Babe, what's gotten into you?"

Maybe it had something to do with the romantic evening, maybe it had something to do with the full moon, maybe it had something to do with the fact that she had three anal orgasms earlier and this was the first time they had the chance to have really good sex.

Jess had already cum twice back to back and was riding a wave of pleasure on the way to another orgasm. She reached back to pull her ass cheeks apart, allowing Josh to fuck her deeper and harder.

As soon as she did, she felt Josh start to cum inside of her.

"Oh my God, yes. Oh, fuck yes, I love the way that feels. Don't stop, baby, don't stop fucking me."

As Josh filled her pussy full of cum, it backed up and started trickling down his shaft and balls. Each thrust after that spread his creamy white semen all over her ass and pussy. And still, Josh kept firing away, pumping his hot load into her.

If she could have multiple orgasms, so could he. Jess felt his cu dripping out of her pussy and wished she could see it. She wished she could watch Josh's hard cock covered in their combined cum pounding her drippy cunt. She could feel its warmth sliding down her legs in thick globs.

Good God, I fucking love that feeling.

As she imaged what it would look like, him fucking her from behind and his cum oozing out of her, dripping down her thighs, Jess experienced another profound, knee-shaking orgasm.

She pulled her ass cheeks apart so that Josh could give her the full length of his cock, and as she did she realized that her fingers were covered in their joined cum. She left one hand on her ass, prying her bubbly butt cheek open for her man, while she licked the cum off of the fingers on her other hand.

As she licked the salty sweet cream off her fingers, she realized that she could no longer tell if it belonged to her or Josh.

"I'm cumming" he screamed from behind her.

What the fuck, again?!

Sure enough, she felt another blast of hot, wet fluid deep inside of her. Jess moaned in pleasure as she once again felt him spray his cum deep inside her cunt.

But her pussy was already overflowing with it, so the viscous cream instantly dribbled out of her pussy as fast as he could shoot it inside of her.

Jess looked up just for a moment and saw the full moon's white glow bathing the city in moonlight.

"More! I want more!" she said herself demand. "Let's see how much you can cum inside of me."

Josh laughed. "Babe, you pussy is already overflowing as it is."

Jess felt like she was possessed by something. A wave of warm pleasure flooded her body.

"I said I want more! Don't stop! Grab my tits! Put a finger in my ass! Just don't fucking stop!" her voice took on a low growl unlike anything Josh had ever heard from his girlfriend before.

Jess could feel her pussy rapidly contracting like never before as the wave of pleasure she was riding peaked. And peaked. And peaked.

Just when she thought she could climax no more, the pleasure grew greater for her still. It was all she could do just to breath, and then she couldn't even do that.

She stood there, frozen, bent over but not breathing. Simply feeling Josh's cock inside of her, somehow harder and longer than ever before, stabbing in and out of her. Each thrust brought a brand new batch of semen oozing out of her, dripping down to her ankles.

Then, at last, with one final thrust, Josh pushed his dick all the way deep inside of her and froze, grunting.

She felt even more cum shoot inside of her as Josh continued to squeeze her nipples. His index finger was all the way up her ass, moving in time with his hips. Only then did Jess realize that his other had had been tickling her clit this entire time.

Jess suddenly snapped back to reality. She took one giant step forward so that Josh's cock fell out of her. As it did, more of their combined fluids came gushing out of her pussy.

She turned around to face him with wobbly knees, barely able to stand. Both of them were absolutely covered in each other's cum from the waist down.

Josh's mouth hung slack, a horrified look on his face.

"What... The fuck. *Was* that?"

Jess was able to grasp one massive lungful of air before everything went dark.

CHAPTER 34

Day 7 - Home

Jess still didn't feel comfortable talking about what had happened at the Griffith Observatory. Josh left it alone for a long time, thinking that she would open up to him about it when she was ready.

But that didn't make him any less worried about her.

It wasn't until they had both showered, eaten, and were winding down in bed that he felt comfortable enough to broach the subject one more time.

"You look comfy," Jess said offhandedly as she came out of the bathroom wearing a silky sheer nightgown.

Josh was wearing his softest pajama bottoms, snuggled underneath the comforter with several pillows propped up behind his head.

"Looks can be deceiving." He said elusively.

"Are you trying to cultivate a masculine mystique or are you trying to tell me something?"

"Babe, I'm not going to be able to sleep tonight until we talk about what happened today."

"We finished the Bingo card. The whole thing! We should be celebrating. Do we have any champagne?"

"No. And that's not what I'm referring to."

"You mean all of the awesome sex we had in public?"

"Yes, all of the awesome sex we had today that you say *you can't remember*."

"I remember the important parts... Okay, that's a lie. All I remember is waking up covered in bodily fluids."

"And that doesn't worry you? Don't you want to know why you blacked out?"

Jess heaved a long sigh as she crawled into bed and curled up next to Josh, laying her head on his chest. Josh held her in his arms, petting her head the way she liked and running his fingers through her hair.

"I mean... I have theories... But you're going to think that they're dumb... You're going to think that *I'm* dumb."

He kissed the top of her head and gave her a little squeeze.

"Baby, talk to me... I'm worried."

Jess started, hesitantly.

"Okay, so... I *do* remember what happened. But I had no control over my own body. It was like I watching myself on TV, from outside of my own body."

"How is that possible?"

"If I tell you, will you promise not to laugh?"

"Of course, my love."

"I... I feel like I was possessed."

"Well, it was a full moon, so it's not outside of the realm of possibility."

"You're making fun of me. I'm being serious!"

"So am I. Why don't we go to the doctor's tomorrow, just to be safe."

"No. No doctors."

"Baby..."

"*No doctors.*"

"Fine. Fine. So, what do you want to do?"

"It's not like I tried to kill anyone. Sometimes spirits just want to remember what it feels like to have sex. Think about it. It's probably really lonely as a ghost."

"You're telling me I had sex with a ghost? Was that one on the Bingo card?"

"*No.* Stop being silly."

"You want *me* to stop being silly?"

"Please don't turn this into a whole thing. It was a full moon. I got possessed. End of story."

"End of... Has this happened to you before?"

"I don't want to talk about it!"

"Fine, fine. I'll let it be." Then, a moment later. "But you know what this means, right?"

Jess just closed her eyes and sighed, wishing this conversation was over.

"It means that I'll have to tie you up during the next full moon." He said, smiling at her.

Jess coughed a laugh. "I like the sound of that."

"I wonder if this has anything to do with us having sex in a church-"

Jess pressed her mouth hard against his.

"Shh, no more talking. It's just you and me now. Just you and me to the end.

Epilogue – The Gentleman's Wager

Josh pulled up to Jon's sprawling hillside house in his Audio, the engine purring like a satisfied lover as he parked in the circular driveway. The house loomed impressively, all modern lines and glass walls that screamed success—and maybe a few secrets hidden behind those reflective panes.

Josh had always wondered how his friend and Jon could afford such luxuries when they both freelanced for the same graphic design talent agency. It didn't make sense, but he was happy for Jon's success, however he got it.

Josh stepped out of the Audi, adjusting his sunglasses with a smug grin, ready to savor his victory.

The front door swung open before he could even knock, and there she was: Isabel, Jon's stunning wife, greeting him with a warm, unsuspecting smile and an apron that left little to the imagination.

Oh, what a vision she was—a petite Filipina goddess, barely five feet tall, with flawless olive skin that glowed like sun-kissed silk under the afternoon light. The apron clung to her body, pushing her perfectly sculpted breasts up to the point where Josh was certain they would spill out had she waved to him. Jon loved to brag about his wife's big fake breasts and often invented ways to force them into their conversations.

Isabel stood in the doorway, smiling warmly at Josh, breasts straining against the thin fabric of her apron, drawing the eye inevitably downward to her impossibly tiny waist, cinched like an hourglass begging to be grasped.

As Josh approached, she moved with a graceful sway, her dark hair cascading in waves that framed her exotic features, full lips painted a teasing red.

For years, she'd been blissfully ignorant of Jon's wandering ways, playing the devoted homemaker while he chased thrills elsewhere.

Lucky bastard, Josh thought, *though today, luck was decidedly on his side.*

"Josh! So good to see you," Isabel purred, her voice a melodic lilt with just a hint of that irresistible accent.

She leaned in for a quick hug, her curves brushing against him in a way that sent a playful spark through the air.

"Come in, come in. Jon's been expecting you—he's buried in work, poor thing."

Josh followed her inside, his eyes lingering a second too long on the hypnotic swing of her hips as she led him through the lavish foyer. The house smelled of fresh flowers and faint perfume, a far cry from the wild escapades that had defined their bingo challenge.

They entered Jon's home office, a sleek space filled with multiple screens and design tablets, where Jon sat hunched over, fingers flying across the keyboard. He was tackling Josh's entire graphic design workload—the loser's penalty, as per their bet.

Jon had raced through every Exhibitionist Bingo sex spot on that damn bingo card, thinking he'd claim victory, but Josh had clinched it first, leaving his old college roommate to eat humble pie.

"Well, well," Josh drawled, leaning against the doorframe with a flirtatious wink at Jon. "Look at you, slaving away like a good boy. How's it feel to be my personal design bitch for the week?"

Jon glanced up, his face a mix of irritation and reluctant amusement. He pushed back from the desk, rubbing his temples.

"Hilarious, man. You're loving this, aren't you? Come to gloat, have you?"

Josh savored the torturous look on Jon's face. His friend, normally so confident and care-free, was in a hell of his own making.

It was fucking beautiful.

"I think we both know that's not why I'm here," Josh said slowly, memorizing the way Jon crinkled his brow as he stared at his laptop.

"You didn't forget the other part of our bet, now did you? You wouldn't desecrate the sanctity of a gentleman's wage, would you?" Josh said mockingly.

Jon visibly swallowed his rage. "Yeah, bro. I bought the tickets to the music festival. The wristbands came in the mail today, actually."

Jon stood from his desk so suddenly that it sent the rolling chair across the room. After a few seconds of rummaging through the stacks of papers scattered in unorganized piles around his desk, Jon straightened with a sigh.

"Babe! What happened to that thing!"

Isabel appeared in the doorway without a sound, like a gorgeous apparition with fake tits.

"Jon, sweetie, I don't know what..." She trailed off as her eyes met Josh's.

Shit, was I staring at her chest just now? I don't even remember, but... how could I not? Josh wondered silently as he turned his body to hide the start of an erection, redirecting his daze to a particularly non-erotic section of the ceiling.

"The thing that came in the mail today, Izzy. The thing for Josh and Jess," Jon explained. The stress from taking Josh's extra workload was starting to show.

"Oh, that thing. Don't you remember, baby? I brought them to you this afternoon," Isabel said.

Then Josh felt her soft body press up against his as Isabel reached in front of Josh, grabbing a teal-colored bubble mailer on the opposite side of Jon's desk.

Christ, she really doesn't make a sound when she moves, does she?

This time, Josh couldn't look away. He couldn't help but notice the way she poked out her ass as she reached across Jon's desk. Was that for his benefit, or does she just do that for no reason?

"Here," Isabel said softly as she held up the piece of mail. "It's yours." She pushed the package containing Josh and Jess's wristbands into the center of his chest and held it there.

The moment he made eye contact with Jon's wife, she licked her lips and whispered something like, "Take it."

Or it might have been, "Tickets". Who's to say?

Josh was brought back to reality when he realized Jon had been talking this entire time.

"What?"

"I said, take your fucking tickets. Just know that I don't like losing. You got lucky this time, that's all."

Josh chuckled, sauntering away from Isabel so he could clap Jon on the shoulder.

"Luck? Please, it was skill, pure and simple. And hey, speaking of the festival, Jess's best friend, Ally, might be tagging along. I guess she just got out of a nasty breakup, so Jess thinks this will be good for her."

Jon's eyes lit up instantly, a mischievous glint sparking behind his feigned sympathy. Even without meeting her, his mind was already spinning webs of seduction—imagining whispered conversations under neon lights, stolen touches in the crowd, turning Ally's rebound into his next conquest. Old habits die hard, especially for an exhibitionist like him.

"Ally, huh? That fiery redhead? Sounds like she could use a shoulder to cry on... or more," Jon mused, fantasies already spinning in his glassed-over eyes.

"Uh, no, dude. Ally is the little blonde one."

"The little blonde... Wait... No... You mean THAT trainwreck is coming with us?" Jon's gaze focused, now tinged with fear.

Before Josh could say anything, Isabel appeared beside the two men soundlessly. She tilted her head curiously, those full lips curving into a playful smile.

"So, Josh, what goes on at these music festivals, anyway?"

Josh exchanged a knowing glance with Jon, his voice dropping to a husky, teasing tone that hinted at untold adventures.

"Oh, Isabel, darling... They can get pretty crazy. You never know what kind of wild connections you'll make under the neon lights."

Jess and Josh's spicy adventures continue in *A Very Polyamory Music Festival* – OUT NOW!!!

Exhibitionist Bingo Card

Exhibitionist BINGO

BALCONY	RESTAURANT	PARKING LOT	BEACH	MOVIE THEATER
LIBRARY (SHHH…)	ELEVATOR	GYM	NIGHT-CLUB	BUS / TRAIN
SAUNA	CHURCH	FREE	FITTING ROOM	PARK
BAR	CARNIVAL	POOL / HOT TUB	MUSEUM	ROOFTOP
CONCERT	DRIVE-THRU	GROCERY STORE	CAFE / COFFEE SHOP	STREET CORNER / ALLEY WAY

About the Author

Amateur content creator, polyamorous serial dater, and spicy romance author Allison Eden was diagnosed as a hypersexual at age 19. Using her photographic memory to replay her favorite positions and partners, she channels her nymphomaniac desires into writing both fiction and non-fiction books on all things sex, leveraging her hypersexuality in a way that serves other people.

Allison Eden's bestselling non-fiction for adults, *Sexy Games & More* and *Love Forever Sex Position a Day Calendar* are a sex-positive, all-inclusive approach to modern relationships and dating. While spreading her message of sex positivity through consensual exploration, Alison helps couples re-discover their passion and embrace love's infinite abundance.

Allison Eden's erotic romance fiction series, "A Very Polyamory..." is based entirely on her own life experiences exploring the world of kink. Each book deals with the real life struggles and sensual encounters for one or more specific kinks or fetishes while exploring ethical non-monogamy.

She identifies as a bisexual submissive before a writer. Allison lives in Los Angeles with her poly family and is active in the rave, kink, and LGBTQIA+ communities. When she's not at home with her boyfriend, girlfriend, and bunny named Cum-Puddles, Allison is either at a music festival or a play party.

Follow all her spicy adventures everywhere @YesDaddyAlly

else, then quickly realized the move was inconsequent. She was about to get the shit fucked out of her in a Taco Bell bathroom, after all.

As soon as Jess sat down on the toilet seat, she spread her legs as wide as the tiny space would allow, then hooked her feet around Josh, drawing him closer.

For a moment, Jess wondered how someone could be so fucking horny after having sex not more than an hour ago. But the thought dissipated the moment Josh pulled down his pants.

She put her hand on the base of Josh's already hard dick and greedily stuffed him into her wet mouth, taking as much of him into her oral cavity as she could manage. The little noises she made while stuffing her face full of cock were no different than the satisfied sounds she made while eating her favorite Taco Bell foods.

Unconsciously, Jess pulled up the bottom of her sundress and started playing with her pussy, rubbing, fingering, and teasing herself as she sucked Josh's dick.

Jess could tell that Josh was quickly on the cusp, being the one that didn't cum earlier in the library, and was already very much turned on, although he tried to hide it.

She stopped him before he could cum in her mouth. Jess stood up and turned around, placing her elbows on the top of the porcelain toilet.

Thank God this isn't one of those toilets with just the pipes on the top part, like most commercial restrooms, Jess thought to herself.

Growing more and more eager with each passing moment, Jess lustfully gave herself up to his every whim to do